Also by Susan Isaacs

Novels

As Husbands Go

Past Perfect

Any Place I Hang My Hat

Long Time No See

Red, White and Blue

Lily White

After All These Years

Magic Hour

Shining Through

Almost Paradise

Close Relations

Compromising Positions

Screenplays

Hello Again

Compromising Positions

Nonfiction

Brave Dames and Wimpettes:
What Women Are Really Doing on Page and Screen

Goldberg Variations

A Novel

SUSAN ISAACS

DOUBLEDAY LARGE PRINT HOME LIBRARY EDITION

Scribner

New York London Toronto Sydney New Delhi

This Large Print Edition, prepared especially for Doubleday Large Print Home Library, contains the complete, unabridged text of the original Publisher's Edition.

SCRIBNER
A Division of Simon & Schuster, Inc.
1230 Avenue of the Americas
New York, NY 10020

ISBN 978-1-62090-520-3

Manufactured in the United States of America

To my wonderful son-in-law,
Vincent Picciuto,
with love

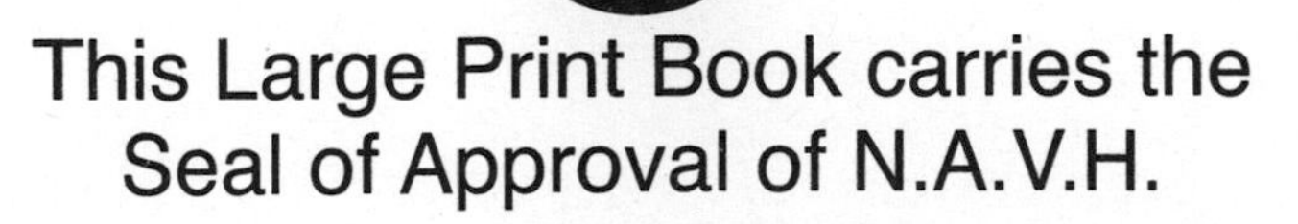

To my wonderful son-in-law
Vincent Piccolo
with love

This Large Print Book carries the
Seal of Approval of N.A.V.H.

One

Gloria

I am not one of those tedious people who feel compelled to speak in smiley faces. Like: *Whenever a door closes, a window opens.* Of course they can never leave it at a lone, bubbly sentence. No, gush must follow: *Gloria, truthfully, deep down, aren't you thrilled it turned out this way? You know, it's always darkest before dawn. But this . . . Oh, God, this is your moment! You get to choose which of these three darling young people is worthiest to inherit your kingdom! Isn't it like some fairy tale come to life?*

Don't ask.

Okay, ask. Here I am, pacing from room to room to room—and I am a woman of many rooms—trying to prepare myself for the onslaught. A limo will be here any minute bringing three virtual strangers to invade my house. All right, they are my grandchildren, but I barely know them. Goldberg, Goldberg, and Goldberg. Sounds like some shtick in a Marx Brothers movie.

Except what I'm living through is no damn comedy. More like a tragedy. Not tragedy with a capital *T,* I admit. The fate of a company like Glory, Inc., which trucks around the South and West demonstrating how to apply false eyelashes, isn't exactly in the same league as Oedipus, that king who put out his eyes because he slept with his mother. Talk about a classic, though I personally found the play creepy. Also, to be honest, a bit boring. Maybe if I'd gone to college I'd appreciate it on a more profound level because I'd have studied it, not just read it. Maybe not. No, definitely not. By the way, do not get the impression from the above that Glory is in the eyelash biz. That's only a minuscule part of what we do.

But getting back to tragedy: I understand it, intellectually and personally. I know the definition: the fall of a great person because of a character flaw he or she possesses. Right? For a long time I lied, said I went to college. When I lived in the East, I said Stanford, though at the beginning I was saying Sanford until I read in the *Times* that John Steinbeck was a Stanford dropout which, needless to say, was humiliating. To make it worse, I couldn't stop recalling all the times people asked me, "Where did you go to school?" I'd say, simply and slowly, "Sanford." They must have known. When I moved west, I switched to University of Pennsylvania. No one ever came back with, *Yeah, sure.* Because I'm so self-educated, I can pass as practically erudite. Well, if I get the name of the college right.

So, no capital *T* tragedy. Not that I'm claiming greatness for myself, but don't I qualify as a sort of tragic heroine anyway? Wasn't it a flaw in my character that caused the corporate cataclysm that led me here, pacing, then eying my watch, followed by a glance up at the TV's closed-circuit channel with its shot of the secured entrance to Los Ranchos Verdes Estates? The only vehicle that's come through during the twenty minutes I've been watching was a tan van, its windows obscured by road dust. DESERT FLOWER AIR-CONDITIONING painted along the van's side panel was so faded the entire van almost blended into the air, all shimmery at the edges, like a mirage.

What if one of them is utterly dreadful? Forget something blatant, like rank body odor or an uncontrollable need to detail a friend's transgender surgery in a loud voice in a restaurant. What if one of them is disgusting in a small way? Half-moons of that blackish-green dirt under fingernails. I've never been able to bear thinking about it long enough to figure out how the green gets there. Or instead of holding flatware properly, they clench knife and fork in fists and saw away at a piece of meat until you hear the scream of bone china getting cut by the knife. The boy could leave urine sprinkles on the underside of the toilet seat for the help to clean. One of the girls might have inch-long fake nails painted with tiger stripes.

I detest waiting. I act. I do not get acted upon. Instead of being five miles down the road at my office at Glory, Inc. doing what I always do on Thursday afternoons (checking inventory spreadsheets and confirming with the L.A. stylists what is and is not selling, accessorieswise), I am stuck at home waiting for the arrival of the three lamebrains I barely know. My three grandchildren. Fine, they're all theoretically smart. I mean good colleges. All gainfully employed, no mean feat nowadays, in respectable starter jobs.

The boy is with the New York Mets. Public relations. The Puerto Rican is a lawyer at Legal Aid in Manhattan. The other girl is number two at the New York office of Paramount which, for all I know, only has two people. But at least they've got respectable CVs.

Still, such a profound dread has been pressing down on my skull that I had to gag down two Excedrin. I hate pills. I exercise daily and I'm not on any serious medication except an asthma inhaler, and that's only once in a blue moon. But who wouldn't have a headache under these circumstances? I fear that once I exchange about four or five sentences with any of the three, I'll discover he or she naïve in a unique and hopeless way—and therefore incapable of running a business like Glory that netted eleven million last year. Eleven.

I'll know soon enough. But though my headache has eased, I feel a little nauseated. The way one does after Belgian waffles. Except all I had for breakfast was two forkfuls of an egg-white frittata. Well, who wouldn't feel queasy? I'm going to have to choose one of those Goldbergs. But as I wait, I keep returning to the moment when not-Oedipus-but-nonetheless-an-important figure, i.e., me, plummeted from a great height due to her Tragic Flaw.

Five months ago, I was in my office, a huge square room with French doors at the far end that provided a panorama of the Sangre de Cristo Mountains southeast of Santa Fe. Visitors would gasp, *Oh, my God!* Whether in sunshine, or in the gray of clouds, made blurry by sand on a windy day, they were always wondrous. When I sat at my desk, however, that heart-bursting sight was behind me. The mountains and the vast sky. Herewith: Gloria Garrison's Law of Commerce 437: Do not get besotted by nature during business hours. Still, beauty is my business. I needed to look at something nonugly. So my office must not only please clients and colleagues, but it also must rise to the Gloria Garrison taste level. If that makes me sound like an egomaniac, I'm not. I simply know that if something is visually jarring or inadequate, it reflects badly on Glory.

Anyhow, because beauty that's too familiar loses its punch, the room itself had rotated through the color wheel each time I redecorated. Naturally, I'd had my all-white period, which made everything flawless until one day I walked in and it hit me: *This is what evangelicals expect God's office to look like. Pure and boring.* Soon after Goodwill removed the white flokati rug and the rest of God's furniture, a mostly blue Persian rug moved in, though for the life of me I can't remember what came with it. Next was the predictable Southwest routine (sage and beige with pops of paled-out orange), then Mexican with stuccoed walls and blue-tiled gas fireplace, followed by Bauhausy, in which the loudest color was tan.

Currently, my office walls are a sky blue I still haven't tired of: such a clean color. Whenever I more than glance at those Venetian plastered walls, when I really take in the luminosity of their hue, my soul feels cleansed—that sensation of inner peace you get when you're just out of a shower with a quality Castile soap. The latest redo had been primarily the blue paint job and reupholstery. I kept most of the furniture from my Bauhaus period. Why get new? You come to a certain age and you comprehend the adage "You can't take it with you" on the deepest level, which is somewhere between annoying and gut-wrenching. Well, someone—I think Jack

Benny—was quoted as saying, “If I can’t take it with me, I won’t go.” Amusing, gutsy . . . except he went. You ask yourself, *Why buy an eighteenth-century Russian tole tray table even if I madly covet it?* I wish, like the ancient Egyptians, I could believe that the furniture I brought into my pyramid would be with me for eternity. Swedish farmhouse-style would wear well. But no pyramid for me. Because there is only nothing to look forward to.

Anyway, my most recent office renovation: As an antidote to the simplicity of the Bauhaus, I did throw in a lot of yellow accessories. Keith remarked that with all that yellow along with the blue walls, I could open my own Swedish consulate.

All right, let me deal with it. With him. Keith Thompson. Until that time five months ago, he was my heir apparent as well as my dearest friend. True, not my heir according to my will, but who knew? Minds change. It could have happened. What was definite, or so I thought, was that one day he would be the owner of Glory, Inc. I was happy,

happy to let him buy me out at a non-gouging, below-market price. And he wouldn't have had to wait until I kicked the bucket to take over. It would have been his just two years after the earn-out period.

Keith had been working for me for seventeen years, and still, whenever I pictured him, my mind's eye saw him at our first interview. In those days, he'd been so stunning you could almost hear people warning themselves, *Don't stare! Just act natural.* Not that he'd completely lost his handsomeness over the years. His dark gold hair, now streaked with silver, remained thick and so silky you had to fight the urge to touch it. He'd never developed that middle-aged cordy neck or a jaw compromised by a second or third chin. His azure eyes (very much like the blue color on my walls) shone with such a clear light they mellowed his iron-jawed cowboy looks with a touch of poet.

But nowadays, up close, Keith came across far older than he actually was. He looked more Medicare Man than his real age, forty-eight. Shocking, the change in him. The sharp angles of his cheeks had flattened out about five years earlier, around the time he'd switched from tequila shots to frozen margaritas, as if the overload of glucose was dissolving the calcium in his bones. Overnight, his once-bronzed, supple skin had aged. If I'd touched it, it would have felt like leather from a dried-out riding boot. However, in the seconds before my Tragic Moment, his cracked, brownish visage took on a glow again. Unfortunately, his face was afire with rage.

"Don't you have one single ounce of decency?" he was roaring at me, though I wasn't paying as much attention to his words. Maybe I should have. I was too transfixed by his nearness, and it had nothing to do with his being a beautiful man. What good would that have done me? No, it was because tiny explosions of saliva were erupting from his dry lips. I could see every droplet of his spit lit up by the noontime Santa Fe glare. That's how close he was leaning in to me. His hands were braced on the edge of my desk. His chin was directly above my cup of paper clips. If he tilted in even one half inch more, his next spritz could wind up in my iced tea.

"Did anyone ever have the guts to tell you, Gloria, that you're an evil person and a complete piece of shit?"

"Of course. Though never in a single sentence." I admit it: I was overly fond of the sound of my own words, especially when listening to myself saying something cruelly clever. I wasn't born with a captivating voice. It was still a work in progress. I often listened to myself, which was helpful, but it sometimes made me miss parts of other people's conversation.

A thousand years earlier, when I was modeling in New York, one of the other girls, Ramona, had advised me, "You could use a little work in the elocution department, Gloria. You've got that—I don't know—Midwest accent and it sort of makes you sound a little like Tilly the Toiler on the Ford assembly line. I'm saying this as a friend. Between you and I, if you want to hook a rich guy, they want to believe you're the refined type, like you're a deb modeling for the fun of it. So . . . here's a quick trick. Make believe you're Princess Elizabeth when you talk. But also, pitch your voice as low as it will go. Remember: Low is lovely. Except, listen: Don't try for the British accent. Not to worry. If you're doing a good princess impersonation, whatever you say will come out classy." (Another girl came over to me later and murmured, "Gloria, darling, listen to me. The word 'classy' is déclassé, just like Ramona. *Never* use it.") Over the years, I'd dropped the princess bit. Anyway, soon after Elizabeth became queen she turned dumpy. So I'd created my own personal ideal, which was a kind of female heterosexual Noël Coward. Okay, admittedly I wasn't such great shakes in the wit department.

"'Evil person.'" I repeated what Keith had said. "'Piece of shit.' How piquant."

I waited for his customary unwilling smile—*You're a bitch and I'm furious beyond belief but hell you are amusing.* Whenever he did that, one side of his upper lip, with its lush brush of a mustache, would rise despite his cheek muscle's valiant attempt to suppress it. Except it didn't happen this time.

"Look at you," Keith kept going, "sitting there like that! An egomaniacal, infantile . . ." He gulped. Using two big words, so close together, wore him out. He stopped to take a deep breath. He'd been playing monosyllabic Western macho man for so many years that despite his intelligence, his vocabulary was shot to hell. Then he swallowed once, twice, and bellowed, "You're a dribbling old lady who's got to wear a bib. An XXL bib."

"It's not a bib, you ass. And you know it!" I shot back, though making sure to maintain my mellifluous voice. His "old lady" was an attempt to thrust a knife in my heart. I certainly wasn't going to cooperate and, metaphorically, drop dead.

"Not a bib?" No drip, drip of sarcasm: a torrent of mockery. "Then what *is* that thing around your neck?"

It's a goddamn insurance policy, I wanted to scream at him—the "old lady" bit had been a surprise, a smack in the face. As for the so-called bib, I was founder and CEO of a beauty and fashion business. So? Could a CEO of such an enterprise go to her next appointment, a meeting with her banker, with a blob of encrusted chicken salad on her white silk blouse? Could she jeopardize the next meeting on her calendar—an interview with a reporter from the *Northwest Arkansas Times*—with Coke Zero dribble stains on the teeny knots between her eighteen-millimeter pearls?

Absurd. Which was why I always wore protection when I ate at my desk. Not a bib, not some plastic monstrosity stamped with SPIT HAPPENS. No, the high-priced expanse of white linen tucked into my neckline was a genuine antique, a nineteenth-century damask napkin. The New Orleans linen dealer had told me he believed the dozen "serviettes" I was considering came from a French château that had belonged to a distinguished Huguenot family. The guy made a point of enunciating Huguenot as "oo-gay-no," practically panting with anticipation for me to show some sign I wasn't comprehending what he'd just said, but of course I was.

"Can I ask you something?" Keith stepped back and crossed his arms over his extravagantly toned pecs. If he truly believed that working out for an hour and a half every day to maintain a thirty-five-year-old physique was going to make all cute young guys decide, *With a body like that, who cares if his face looks like it's made from hundred-year-old crocodile skin?* he was delusional.

Not that Keith was currently in the market for cute young things, I had to admit. His lover/partner of almost twenty years was stretched out on a bed in the ICU at St. Vincent's Hospital with only a ventilator holding off Death. That's what was making Keith scream at me.

Not the fact that Billy was dying in a room that, without a doubt, stank from disinfectant and Keith was ultrasensitive to smells. And not that Billy was probably hooked up to beeping monitors with ever-changing green numbers. Even if a miracle occurred and he survived, the from-out-of-nowhere stroke that had hit him had done such damage that his brain would be about as useful as last week's scrambled eggs—and all this had happened three and a half weeks before Billy's fortieth. Keith and I had been planning the celebration for months. Not a surprise party. Except it would be. Billy would think it was a small birthday dinner chez Glo, as he called my house, and that the big occasion would come the following week. Except he'd walk in to a thousand candles lighting up a hundred fifty of his nearest and dearest. *Surprise!* Except the surprise came a month too soon, and it was no party.

But what had turned Keith crimson with fury at me was not random rage at the unfairness of life. It was me: I have to acknowledge that. What got him was that I had not gone to the hospital. And this was after Keith told me for probably the tenth time, "Gloria, you're like family to Billy and me." Plus there had been at least five repetitions of "Billy always said, 'Gloria is my big sister.'" At one point he asked, "Let me be blunt. Do you have some major issue about—I don't know—hospitals or strokes?" And just in case I didn't get the hint, not ten minutes earlier Keith had come right out and said, "You know, I put you on the list for the ICU. You can go whenever. Every hour on the half hour, day or night. They only let you stay ten minutes, but . . ."

And then, Tragic Flaw time. Instead of sucking it up and telling myself that sometimes, for the sake of business and/or friendship, you've got to make sacrifices, or pretend to be a caring human being, I was honest. Not at first, though. I dropped my voice as low as it could go, which wasn't so hard when you haven't manufactured a drop of estrogen in over thirty years. It could barely be heard: "I have to tell you the truth, Keith. I know you'll think I'm an awful person. But the truth is, I don't think I can bear to see Billy that way."

"That's such bullshit! Come on, Ms. Profile in Courage, you goddamn hypocrite. Say what you mean."

So you don't have to waste time reading between the lines, let me be up front about what my Tragic Flaw is. It is losing control and saying what I truly think. And the worst part of it is, I know how dangerous and potentially destructive honesty can be for me. I thought I'd learned not to let anyone goad me into candor. Except the double whammy of seeing Keith with tears of grief in his eyes, as if Billy were already dead, along with the rise of his upper lip, like he was so repulsed by my selfishness that he was going to vomit, was too great a goad.

I reached into my desk drawer and grabbed my pen. Despite what Keith insisted later, I wasn't brushing him off and going back to work on the spreadsheets. The pen was just a handy object, and I needed something to squeeze in my clenched fist because I was in a pitched battle fighting myself to keep the truth from erupting. I tried with everything I had to subdue my worst self. I couldn't do it.

"He asked for you, for Christ's sake!" Keith said.

"He didn't ask for me," I told him quite calmly. "You know that and I know that. You were the one who told me: He's lost his power of speech."

"Not totally. I'm telling you! He looked

at me and said . . ." Keith made a repulsive sound, a mix of gulp and hard *g*. "It was him asking, 'Where is Gloria? Why isn't she here?' "

I said, "Keith, you're projecting what you want to hear. 'Guh' could mean, 'Get me out of here!' or 'God help me!' Most likely it's an involuntary sound. I don't know and neither do you. In any case, the bottom line is this: There's no way I can be in the same room with someone who is on the verge of dying. Okay? I wish I were a better person, but I'm not. I don't want to risk seeing anyone who's actually dead. I don't go to funerals. And it's not because I'm in the older range, agewise. I've always been this way." Then I kept babbling on, which I shouldn't have: "God knows why. Most of the time, I pretend I have food poisoning. Except that excuse doesn't work when someone has a second death in the family. Then I make believe I have a death in my own family and have to fly out to that funeral. And you know what else gets to me? I'm all for interfaith blah-blah-blah, but the *worst* thing the Christians ever did to the Jews was to get friendly with them. Now you have to go to their funerals and see their embalmed mothers or husbands with freakish makeup jobs in an open casket. So okay? I hate death. Comas are almost as bad. I can't look at Billy on a ventilator."

"Goddamn it! He asked for you! I know what I heard."

"If you think he really can comprehend, then explain to him, 'Gloria just can't handle this, Billy. But she sends you all her love. You're in her heart.' "

Two

Matt

Something about my grandmother, Gloria Garrison, was unnatural, besides her obvious distaste for her grandchildren. It wasn't like she had ten or twenty of us. Just three, and I was the only guy. Okay, she hadn't seen me, my sister, or my cousin in years, since Raquel was a kid and Daisy and I were in our teens, and I hadn't expected her to surprise us at the airport with a Welcome to New Mexico, Goldbergs!!! sign and hugs. But a couple of degrees more warmth wouldn't have hurt. Her assistant's e-mail said, "A town car will meet you outside baggage claim and bring you directly to Ms. Garrison's home."

So we drove for about an hour from the airport in Albuquerque past a lot of desert. Not all sand, like the Sahara: lots of brown covered in areas by thin blankets of pale green. The dry, stunted trees made me feel thirsty. At one point Raquel said, "Look! Horses!" There they were, grazing on the pale green stuff, grown horses and baby ones, too. Even I went "Aaaah" at their cuteness. The driver told us they were wild herds descended from the conquistadors. I sensed my sister on the verge of saying, *You mean from the conquistadors' horses,* but thank God she had the sense to keep her mouth shut.

Finally the driver said, "This is it." Actually it wasn't, because we still had to get past the electronic barrier of Gloria Garrison's gated community. "Gated" may conjure up a bunch of look-alike town houses. This seemed more of a really rich neighborhood with over-the-top security. The couple of places we could see from out behind the barrier were more like mansions than houses.

The driver opened his window and punched in a code, and the double metal bar rose to let the car through.

"Does everyone who comes here have the code?" I asked the driver.

"You get a new code each time," he said as he drove in, his eyes fixed on the raised bar as if he was scared it might crash down onto the car's roof.

We kept bearing right for so long I figured the road must be a spiral. Each property we went by had so much land that the huge houses were hardly visible from the road.

"Do you know how much land these houses have?" I asked the driver.

"Here? I think a minimum of ten acres."

"I bet if you lived here, you'd probably want to drive to your next-door neighbor's for a barbecue."

"There's the distance," he said. "Also to avoid rattlesnakes."

I was sitting up front. When I looked behind me, I could see from the weird look in my sister's eyes—staring back into herself—that it was brought on by more than snake talk. Going up on a spiral road was making her carsick. As a kid, Daisy could always be counted on to moan, "Daddy, stop the car! Now!"

Fortunately, a second later, the driver pulled in front of a pair of ironwork gates decorated with a sun design and *63 Calle del Halcón* in script. The gates were set into a seven- or eight-foot-high wall built from brownish-pink stuff. It seemed to surround the entire property. Trust me: That's a lot of wall.

And a lot of house, made from the same stuff as the wall. Daisy, our cousin Raquel, and I began with the *Wow*s and *OMG*s but stopped almost instantly because—Bing! Bing! Bing!—it hit each of us how uncool we were sounding in front of the driver.

He lowered his window and pressed a button on a metal box like you see in movies and TV shows but not in life. A woman's voice came back, "Yes?"

"It's . . ." He paused too long, like he was worried the box would be pissed to learn who it was. "Buena Vista Limo."

"Like she needs an announcement of who's coming to see her," my sister whispered to my cousin, loud enough for me and no doubt the driver to hear.

Raquel's eyes were fixed on the gates, its sun with wavy rays and *63 Calle del Halcón* all in the kind of iron that isn't rusty but looks like it's been around since the 1600s. She leaned forward. "Do you know what *halcón* means?" she asked me. Raquel was probably born to be the lawyer she became. Not only did she enjoy arguing, which she called debating, but she'd also been born with a great courtroom voice—the richest tone imaginable. If she were a piano, she'd be one of those two-hundred-thousand-dollar jobs in Carnegie Hall. Add to that resonance a touch of huskiness that was mostly sexy but also hinted at a secret life or dark past, which I doubted she had.

However, her voice was spellbinding. When I was fifteen and she was thirteen, I heard only the husky part of it, and I wound up with a two-year crush on her. Just the thought of our family Passover, when I knew I'd definitely see her, made my heart play a driving drumbeat in my chest. *"Halcón."* She repeated it with exaggerated slowness and precision, like a teacher giving a *dictado* in Spanish class. That was Raquel: a voice like a goddess, a pain in the ass personality like Lucy in *Peanuts.*

I'm told, by everyone except Raquel, that I speak fairly decent Spanish. But my cousin had a habit of asking me if I knew some obscure word—*alcachofa* or *secadora*—as if to show me I don't really know the language. "I don't have a clue," I told her.

"It means falcon," Raquel said. The gates unlocked electronically and opened inward, the sun splitting in half.

I said "uh-huh," which felt better than *Oh, I didn't know that.* Daisy didn't have to say anything because she took French.

Raquel's arms were crossed and the side of her mouth was curled into what looked like a smirk. *What's the deal with "falcon" that makes it smirkworthy?* I hated not being in on any joke. Finally I realized a falcon was a predator: It flies off with a bird or small animal in its claws. So that made our grandmother the winged killer and . . . what? We were the prey in her claws? By the time I figured it out, we had driven up a long dirt road. The town car circled a stone driveway around a fountain that was plunked in front of an enormous house with a flat but slightly uneven surface. My mother, an interior designer, would have a better name than pinkish-brown to describe the color: more like *bisque* or *rosado de sud*. She would mock its size and say "sooo excessive," but part of her would be awed just thinking of how much the house could sell for, even in a depressed market. Another part would be tormented by its gargantuan perfection. She hates my grandmother and it would kill her to see her living like the empress of the Southwest.

The house was megahuge. It made me feel like I'd been sucked into one of the movies Daisy used to make me watch when she babysat me, *Honey, I Shrunk the Kids.* Most people's jaws would drop, and then they'd say "beautiful." I found the place stupidly oversized—like triple the square footage of a baseball diamond. Not the land it was on: the house itself.

I assumed because the house was in New Mexico, it wasn't made of stucco; at least it didn't have any of those stucco bumps that look like a dermatological problem. Or maybe adobe is bumpless stucco. Anyway, the word "adobe" always bothered me. It sounded not at all like what you'd use for construction and more like a sauce for a burrito at Taco Bell. So the roof was flat, with round projections of dark logs just underneath that stuck out from the tops of the walls. Cool. The whole huge thing was beautifully designed, with soft corners instead of hard right angles: a Native American pueblo house for Anglo one-percenters. But all this as a residence for one person? Insane. Inappropriate. In fact, I wouldn't have been surprised to see a discreet sign in front: HACIENDA EL TORAH A REFORM CONGREGATION.

The tall wood front door opened, and suddenly there she was, Gloria Garrison, stepping out onto her . . . I think it's called a portico, the outside area with an overhang above. She stood shaded by the portico while the driver lifted our carry-ons out of the trunk. As he did, I glanced over at Daisy, who was already eying me with a desperate and disbelieving What-the-fuck?-She's-not-putting-us-up-at-a-hotel?! expression. Then we looked up at our grandmother. She was immobile, like someone had rolled out a department store mannequin—the Elder Chic model—from the designer clothes floor.

So she was old. I didn't expect her to race down the steps crying, *Let me take those suitcases!* Considering her past behavior toward my parents and Raquel's mother and her indifference to all three of her grandchildren, she definitely wasn't going to gather us into a hug. But did she have to stand there, totally motionless and without expression, like she had stepped out of *The Art of Taxidermy*?

What made this weird reunion doubly uncomfortable was that none of us three had a clue as to why she had wanted to meet us, had paid for tickets, and had summoned us to Santa Fe. For sure, fourteen years earlier, the last time

I remembered that she'd seen any of us, she hadn't exactly glowed with delight at being in our company. And now? Did she realize that Daisy was scared of her? That Raquel detested her and probably had shown up only in the hope that—what?—she could observe such heinous behavior she'd never again have to feel a second's guilt about despising her? Even Jesus would say, *Feh, this woman is hateful!* And that I was uneasy—not about hanging with Granny but that I feared disappointing my father by having his mother find me as mediocre as she found him. He'd called the night before and told me, "There's nothing to be nervous about, Matty. Even she won't be able to resist liking you. Everybody does, kiddo." His pep talk sounded less like reassurance and more like a prayer.

So far—and it had been at least half a harrowing minute—my grandmother's eyes remained on the driver. She hadn't even glanced our way. Wasn't she dying of curiosity?

Meanwhile, as if we'd rehearsed a routine, the three of us waited for the driver to put all our carry-ons on the stone driveway. Then, in unison, we lifted them. Right foot first, we climbed onto the first step. The step itself was so deep it formed a miniterrace. You could hold a cocktail party on it for twenty-five people. We weren't sure whether to move up to the next step where our grandmother was standing. If we hadn't been within hearing distance, Daisy would have been muttering to me, *What are we supposed to do? Stand here till one of us drops dead from dehydration?*

Finally, my grandmother descended the one step to greet us. She managed three quick air kisses, her cheek not quite coming into contact with any of ours. Then she said our names: "Daisy," "Raquel," which she trilled with an entirely unnecessary Spanish *r,* just in case Raquel Goldberg forgot she was half Latina. When she got to me, all she could come up with was something like "Muh," like she couldn't remember if it was Michael or Mark or . . . Then she got it. "Matthew."

Gloria Garrison looked like what she

was, an elderly, successful businesswoman. Her hair pinned up on her head wasn't gray but silver with streaks of other metal colors. Expensive hair. And the way it was twisted into a big knot thing seemed too expertly casual to be a do-it-yourself job. As for her clothes: obviously no Century Village mint-green walking shorts and flowered shirt. She wore loose pants that were silvery like her hair and a white sweater with one of those big necks that are droopy on purpose. The fashionably baggy clothes thin women wear. So not the conventional grandma. No cookies would come out of her oven.

For someone her age, she was tall; I'm six feet, so she must have been five seven or so. While most of her contemporaries were morphing into wrinkly Munchkins, she stood the kind of straight that made you suspect she'd been spending all her free time balancing a book on her head. Her face was whatever the equivalent of "pretty" would be if applied to an old lady. (In Politically Correct World, I'd be forced to say, "She's pretty." But the truth is, no one pushing eighty is truly pretty. The best you can muster is that she used to be. In fact, most people that age are starting to bear a resemblance to those hundred-year-old tortoises you see in pictures of Galápagos. Not her.)

But anyway, my grandmother, who'd once been a model for a fashion house in the Garment Center, Solange de Paris, was as pretty as seventy-nine gets. Besides the good posture business, she was still model slender. Also, even up close, her ivory, pinkish, and peachy skin was weirdly flawless. Her complexion looked as if it had been applied by a genius paint sprayer—the guy who would put the final finish on a Lamborghini right before it left the factory in Sant'Agata. The four of us stood there on the second step under the portico, the three of us arrayed before our grandmother like we were about to start some line dance—the Goldberg. Except we remained frozen. Finally, Gloria Garrison spoke: "Welcome to my home."

Raquel waited longer than Daisy and I did for the smile that would ordinarily follow that sort of line, except my grandmother didn't offer it. So my cousin's "Thank you" to the welcome followed ours by a full second.

"Come in," my grandmother said as she turned and walked inside. My sister and cousin were lucky that the front door was wide because they were both clearly dying to get a look at the place. They raced in at the same instant. It's not that either of them was big. My sister's old-fashioned curvy, like one of those 1950s actresses who looked like they lived a life devoted to not exercising. Raquel had a great body except in miniature. A little over five feet and everything was correspondingly small. Still, two women with overstuffed carry-ons can cut a wide swath. There could have been a major collision, so I held back. As far as I was concerned, Gloria Garrison's "Come in" was about as enticing as the witch's invitation to Hansel and Gretel. Only when my grandmother's body language signaled that she was preparing to close the door, Matt or no Matt, did I go inside.

I stood between Daisy and Raquel in

the entrance hall. My sister was trying to be subtle about memorizing details of the house for our interior-designer mother, so she casually checked out the ceiling—all wood with heavy wood beams. Everything in the house was oversized, like it had been built for the Knicks. The mile-high ceiling of repeating chevrons of dark wood strips held up by giant log beams: cool. Huge spaces. Raquel was looking past our grandmother to a massive table in the rear of the room that held a humongous clay vase filled with an entire Garden of Eden of white flowers. Raquel's expression might have come off as cool to a stranger, but having known her all her life, I knew she was suppressing something between shock and awe.

To make it totally clear, none of us wanted to be in Santa Fe. Daisy had conferenced Raquel and me twice, and the conversation was like, "If you think I'm going to New Mexico to see that bitch . . ." to "I will not be manipulated . . ." with all of us saying the same lines in different ways. But in the end, none of us could tell dear Granny to fuck off. Call it courtesy. Call it fear. Call it rampant curiosity. Call it pleasing our parents.

Hold on a second.

I need to apologize about what I said before, about old people and tortoises and comparing my grandmother's welcome to that cannibalistic Hansel and Gretel witch. I was harsh. But understand: Each thought of her came in the context of a five-volume set titled *A Complete History of the Goldbergs.* Gloria Garrison, of course, was once Gloria Goldberg. In fact, she's a double G—Gloria Goldberg Goldberg Garrison. Born Gloria Goldberg in Cincinnati. Then she moved to New York where she met and married my grandfather, Joe Goldberg. She met him when she was modeling. He owned a Garment Center trucking business. She became Garrison only years later, after she stole his last two trucks and ran out on him.

Three

Daisy

I should have hit the ladies' room when the plane landed in Albuquerque, but I got preoccupied thinking about the visit to Gloria Garrison's, and also whether I'd actually packed my T-shirts or left them on my bed in a Ziploc. So I didn't realize I had an insane need to pee until the town car sped out the airport exit.

"Is there a bathroom I could use?" I asked, a mere hundred minutes later. I was desperate—like those drecky *Gotta go! Gotta go!* incontinence commercials.

"Yes," my grandmother said. A clipped

yes. British aristocrat. Not in terms of accent but in condescension to the lower classes, in this case, her grandchildren. Very Maggie Smith in *Downton Abbey*. My grandmother's "yes" implied she was slightly repulsed, though not surprised, that I didn't have better bladder control.

The entrance foyer was vast. I could only pray she wouldn't press some panel in the wall to reveal a sink and toilet. They'd all be standing there, unwilling eavesdroppers, listening to me pee. I could tell that my brother, despite an attempt at nonchalance—a little slouching, a little putting his hands in his pockets—wasn't exactly relaxed about the visit. I was afraid he'd revert to his ten-year-old self and go *Psssss* for the next three days.

"Down that hallway, Daisy." She pointed. "First door on the left."

"Thanks," I said brightly. I actually say most things brightly. And except for my brother Matty and my best friend since fourth grade, Karen Bonheim, just about everyone thinks I am bright—in the sense of lively. A few would put their money on brash, since I look more like the zaftig, lovable best friend than adorable ingénue. But my job as Paramount's East Coast story editor requires excessive enthusiasm. First I have to charm New York editors into giving me the earliest possible version of a novel, or even a magazine article with a strong narrative. Then I need to decide whether it is material one of the producers affiliated with the studio can use. Since it's easier for them to say no than yes, I naturally have to charm them, too, on behalf of the book—sometimes just to get them to read it or at least have one of their interns skim my coverage.

If I wasn't bringing in good material, I wouldn't be much use to Paramount. So it was sparkle, sparkle eighteen hours a day, which permanently turns my seventy-five-watt personality into a klieg light. That's not to say I am so vibrant I could have my own half hour on NPR, *Garrulous Goldberg and Company.* And no quality I possessed could make me so delightful that gatekeepers at clubs in the meatpacking district would say, *Daisy, it's so dead tonight.*

You gotta javanate it. But at work, if I'm not enchanting, I'm at least energetic and pleasant. No one in the film business would think of me as beige.

Speaking of beige, the hallway she sent me down was just that color. Tasteful. You think beige is always beige, but some luxe magic happens when it's on the walls of rich people's houses that doesn't happen in the post office. Also, the entire length of the corridor glowed from a lighting system discreetly hidden from view. A softly pungent but sweet smell suffused the space; it was like some dried flower, maybe eucalyptus or its desert equivalent, though for all I knew eucalyptus could have been the state flower of New Mexico. Anyway, as I walked into the hallway, I heard my grandmother telling Matty and Raquel, "We can wait for Daisy in the blah-blah-blah." Probably some unnecessary room with a real estate name.

The walls were painted with so many coats they looked like the hide of a very expensive animal. There was no art hanging, certainly no family photographs. My mother would have snorted,

You cannot call a failure of imagination "stark simplicity" and get away with it.

I kept going. Ten feet—or yards—down the hall, I still hadn't found the bathroom. But I did spot decoration. It was set into a recess, the sort of concavity in which you'd find a Russian Orthodox icon: a framed photo.

It must have been from the '70s or early '80s. The huge truck seemed to be from that era, one of those built on a slant to denote forward movement and modernity—more rhombus than rectangle. The logo was different from the red-lettered one my dad had described to me. GLORY, INC. was painted in ombré rainbow letters, one color leading into the next in the spectrum against a pale blue background. A rainbow arced from the *O* in *Glory* down to beneath the period after *Inc.* Instead of a pot of gold at the end, there was the silhouetted profile of a woman in a deep blue. It felt just right; if I were a shadow, I'd rather be the color of midnight than of ink. The truck stood in an Edward Hopper–ish gas station . . . assuming Hopper had gotten Zoloft and good talk therapy. The contrast between the late-twentieth-century truck and old-fashioned background hit the right note: aesthetically aware and modern but with solid all-American values.

Gloria stood right on the step to the driver's seat, looking the way every woman would want to look in middle age. Slim, fit, and fabulous. One foot (in those tight, nearly knee-high boots they wore then) was stuck out in the air, as if the photographer was hoping to convey a sense of action: *She'll open the door and swing up her leg.* Except it came across as posed.

But she looked really comfortable in her body—and chic in a then-fashionable just-above-the-knee skirt. A Venetian gondolier striped T, tucked in tight, showed off her model's long torso and small waist. Her shoulder-length light brown hair was blown prettily to one side by either a gentle breeze or wind machine. She was waving joyously, as in, *Bye! I'm off on my long-haul route!*

I really had to pee. If I sneezed before I found the bathroom . . . I rushed on.

The bathroom had the same type of soft illumination as the hallway. I guessed the idea was just enough light to be flattering to all who looked at themselves, an act you couldn't really avoid since the walls and ceiling were made of those golden, smoky mirrors you see in the bars of hotels. Except who really wants to be flattered by her dim mirror image perched on the pot? Being faced with my murky likenesses from many different angles, none of which was a boon to my thighs, I felt compelled to sit up taller and rest my hands in some nonawkward position above my knees. An instant of paranoia—*one of these walls is actually a two-way mirror*—whipped through my head.

Worse, the second I turned the lock on the bathroom door, some muffled fan started up. That sounds like a good idea for a windowless room with a toilet, except this system drew in cold air. Within seconds I was freezing.

Back to my personality. At age fifteen, while people were already thinking, *pleasant, seventy-five-watt Daisy,* I was actually experiencing a certain awkwardness. (Note: That awkward stage began when I was eleven. Now that I'm twenty-nine, it continues, though blessedly it's no longer accompanied by the two zits that migrated around my face for almost a decade and a half.) Anyway, fifteen and awkward was the last time I saw Gloria Garrison.

My main memory of that encounter is one of the billion varieties of agony everyone invariably experiences during adolescence. That day, it was, *What should I call my grandmother?* She'd come to Long Island for Matty's bar mitzvah. There she was, in the lobby of Temple Beth Israel. Her suit was white. She was wearing pearls the size of pterodactyl eggs. She looked flawless and pure, a vestal virgin emeritus. Or emerita.

Taking my hand between hers, she'd said, "Daisy, you're a young lady now." Her skin was so silken that even with the manicure my mother had treated me to I was positive she must be thinking, *Blech, disgustingly dry hands!*

Naturally I was tongue-tied. Not that she was waiting for a response. Her eyes locked onto mine for just an instant, but then she dropped my hand and began scoping the lobby. No doubt, besides the repulsion, she found me profoundly uninteresting. No doubt, too, that she was probably grossed out by Pimple #1. (On that day, it was located between my eyebrows, directly above my nose, an outsized pale pink pustule that had compacted to rock hardness after two days of witch hazel and Murad. My friend Karen had warned me, "If you make a pimple the center of your universe, it's going to be, like, a supernova," and it was. My mom had it airbrushed out of the photo album.)

I mumbled, "Thank you," before I realized that Gloria Garrison's calling me "a young lady" was not necessarily a compliment. How could I have been so gauche as to have thanked her for what was probably a neutral observation? But by that time her attention was elsewhere, her dark eyes busy scanning the other two hundred guests.

I figured I had to say something to her in order not to be written off as a total loser, but the gem I came up with,

How was your trip to New York? never emerged because I didn't know whether to add on *Grandma, Grandma Gloria, Gloria,* or *Ms. Garrison.* Later, way too late, at the moment her ex, Grandpa Joe, stood before the mike and made the blessing over a challah the size of Tel Aviv, I realized that I could simply have asked *How was your trip?* and not have called her anything.

So . . . after the above diatribe about my dermatological, urinary, social, and self-image issues, it would be hypocritical for me to pick on my grandmother for being egocentric. But I will. From everything I know and have ever heard, she believed that humanity was created merely to be the audience for her one-woman extravaganza, i.e., her life and work.

Admittedly, it had been quite a life. Not that I knew all the details, because my grandmother was not a favored subject chez Goldberg. Except that's not actually true. Even when Matty and I were kids, we sensed that when such strenuous effort was made to avoid the subject of Gloria Goldberg Garrison, she was definitely attentionworthy. So, like good little archaeologists, we dug. Occasionally, we were rewarded with a shard that helped us reconstruct the Life and Times of a Rogue Grandma.

Like when Matty unearthed a cloth-covered box in the bottom drawer of the filing cabinet in the basement while he was searching for a Wu-Tang Clan tape our mother had confiscated. I opened the box and, besides pictures of my parents' engagement party and my dad's tenth college reunion, I found photos of my dad's family from when he was a boy.

These were a major discovery, the Goldberg equivalent of the Dead Sea Scrolls. Examining the evidence closely made ancient life become more and more clear. The physical evidence proved to me that my grandmother loved her other son more than my dad. By a lot. In all the photos, she was standing beside Uncle Travis. Grandpa Joe got stuck on the other side beside my father, Bradley. Grandpa Joe, too, seemed to favor Travis. Even when my grandfather was positioned next to my dad, his smile—at least three-quarters of the time—was beaming away from Bradley, right at Travis.

God, it was bitter cold in that damn bathroom! My fingers ached, to say nothing of my urethra, which had frozen in the off position. I tried to make an analogy between a woman who would permit such a cold bathroom and one who could withdraw all the warmth from one of her kids, but my mind was as unresponsive as my urinary tract. Maybe it was jet lag. Maybe my neurons were slowing down, like atoms do when temperatures approach absolute zero. I couldn't sit there forever; it would be embarrassing to emerge frostbitten, nose, toes, and fingertips chalky white, too numb to realize I was leaving a trail of pee along beige corridors.

Returning to the shards of family history. The evidence gleaned from both life and photos was clear on one point: Gloria and Joe had been a gorgeous couple. Okay, Grandpa Joe wasn't insanely Warnercolor handsome like a Rock Hudson or a James Dean. Still, he had been fantastic looking in that tough guy, broken-nose way of actors in 1940s noir films. Six feet tall—taller than either of his sons would ever get—with broad shoulders tapering into a muscular body. Maybe Michelangelo wouldn't have signed him up to pose for David, but Joe Goldberg could have been the prototype for the Oscar statuette.

But my grandmother was in a different league: a classic beauty. She had actually been a model. She left Ohio in the late '40s or early '50s right after high school to be discovered, which always struck me as both brave and naïve. Once in Manhattan, unfortunately, all the modeling agencies gave her the same turndown: too short and five pounds too heavy, but not to bother losing the weight because her height disqualified her—she would never make the cover of *Vogue.* She lost ten pounds anyway, not only because she wouldn't give up but also because she could afford only one meal a day. Eventually, she found a job as a showroom model for a midlevel designer.

As my mother would add, gleefully, every time she got to that part of the family saga: "A showroom model is *the* lowest rung on the fashion totem pole." My mother detested my grandmother because of Gloria's disdain for my father." I told my brother, "If you had such a bitch for a mother . . . Oh, come on, Matty. Mom may not be June Cleaver, but she's nowhere near in the same league as Gloria GGG."

Mothers are usually easier on sons than daughters, but in the case of Matty and me, our mother was an equal opportunity mom: fond of us to the same degree, which she believed to be love. Well, it was as close an approximation as she could get. I'd decided early on that she wasn't capable of big-time emotion, though she did get a little more animated by our dad having a good year, or by a bolt of vintage Fortuny fabric, than by us. Matty knew this too. It just bothered him a lot more that the supposedly prime person in his life was the only one on earth he couldn't delight.

I was freezing. I sneezed three times in a row, which seemed to be the charm that got me going. Afterward, washing my hands, I noticed a collection of teeny compacts, the kind women in '40s and '50s movies took out with great ceremony to powder their noses. Clearly, I was a break with the past. My grandmother and mother were collectors of the precious. My mother must have had a thousand New York–themed snow globes (the Rockettes, Statue of Liberty, Saks Fifth Avenue, the NYPD with a badge and a police car) on the bookshelves in the den. And on her vanity, she'd stuck a bunch of creepy porcelain hands; you were supposed to stick rings on the upturned fingers so as not to get makeup on your diamonds. Oh, my mother also had another collection going in our guest bathroom, a giant basket of snail shells, the symbolism of which escaped me.

Talking about diamond rings . . . Other than having coffee or a drink with Match.com semiliterates who never called me back and getting the kind of guys on JDate whom your friends tell you to go out with because you need practice with your dating skill set, I hadn't been with a guy in one year and two months.

Sometimes I didn't care. Rarely. Mostly I felt so despairing that I was afraid I'd marry a five-foot-two, three hundred-pound Tajikistani with a unibrow, desperate for citizenship. That was the only type that ever sidled up to me in bars. I wanted to be back in New York. None of us—Matty, Raquel, or I—had thought coming to Santa Fe was a good idea. Why should we? The old lady had shown approaching-zero interest in us during our growing-up years. She'd been contemptuous of my father and downright despicable to Raquel's mother in the time after my uncle Travis died.

It wasn't greed that had propelled us cross-country, because when we turned twenty-one, she'd sent each of us a registered letter saying, basically, *Happy Birthday and Drop Dead because there's not even two cents for any of you in my will.*

What had gotten us on the plane was a parent: Raquel's mom, Adriana; Matty's and my dad. Both of them, we all knew, were yearning for the same resolution: We three would fly to Santa Fe. Together, we'd create just the right chemistry to soften Gloria's heart. Together, we would bring about a change that would make her say, *I was so wrong all these years, so harsh in my treatment of you. Please, I want to make it up by giving you all the love I never knew was in me until I remet these three beautiful young people.*

How could we tell such decent human beings as my dad and Aunt Adriana that their hopes were futile? We had to take the hit and make the trip.

Who else but the coldest bitch west of the Mississippi would keep the bathroom for her guests so freezing as to make peeing a torment?

Getting back to the photo box, one of the family pictures, an old-fashioned Polaroid that had turned a yellowish green, showed Gloria, Joe, and the boys on their final family vacation, on the cliff overlooking the beach at the El Conquistador in Puerto Rico. Less than a year after that last vacation at the El Conquistador, the Goldberg family fell apart fast. Grandpa Joe was by no means superaffluent. But though he hadn't made it into the one percent, he'd still given his family a privileged life. That meant a Tudor in Great Neck, a live-in maid, and a new Cadillac every other year. He had a solid business, trucking for companies in the Garment Center. That was in the days before so much of the manufacturing took off for China. But then the Mob moved in on him.

The way I heard it, Grandpa Joe got a visit from an agreeable, only slightly slimy, low-key associate of the Cassaro family. The man suggested, with great courtesy, he should become a partner in my grandfather's trucking business. Grandpa Joe said he'd think about it, but he knew the world he worked in. Apparently, he went home to Great Neck that evening with a cloud of doom hovering above his head: He *had* to partner with Mr. Agreeable because (as he explained to his beloved wife Gloria) the alternative was unthinkable. Like grave bodily harm, though death was also an option.

For my grandmother, her husband's surrender was not just the beginning of the end. It was the end.

When I questioned my dad about this, he said that even as a teenager he knew something huge had happened between them. Not like a terrible fight. Like the whole marriage had been permanently moved from the temperate zone to the Arctic. It froze and died there.

My dad said he didn't witness much of what went on after the Night of the Freeze. His parents had long conversations and longer fights, but always behind the closed door of their bedroom. Looking back, my dad wondered if the fights had been sincere on my grandmother's part or if she'd simply been buying time in order to plan her getaway.

Years later, he did hear that somehow, within days of the Cassaro ultimatum, Gloria came up with legal papers to prove she owned two of his eleven trucks. Her claim was that Grandpa Joe had signed the trucks over to her for tax purposes. His comeback was that she'd forged his signature and slept with the lawyer she'd pushed him to go to. Before my dad and Travis were old enough to get the bigger picture of what was going on, much less understand the claims and counterclaims, Gloria pulled them out of Great Neck North High School and took them (and the two trucks) to Santa Fe to start another life.

It sounds almost like a dumb riddle: What does an ex-model do with two giant trucks?

" 'The idea for Glory came to me in a flash,' Gloria Garrison declared." That quote came from a 1972 article in *Business Week* my brother came up with. Though Matty was in PR, he'd minored in finance at Duke and was the world's greatest practitioner of due diligence, Googler in chief. Give him any subject and he'd produce enough citations for a master's thesis. Right after he, Raquel, and I received the invitation to Santa Fe, he got busy researching Gloria. He pointed out that consistency didn't seem to be one of our grandmother's virtues—assuming she had any virtues. In a 1987 piece in the *Wall Street Journal,* she'd contradicted her *Business Week* quote. There had been no flash:

" 'Even back in my modeling days, I saw that ninety percent of women weren't doing right by themselves. Their life was one long bad hair day—and every day was no makeup day or wrong makeup day. They hadn't a clue what to wear to make the most of their gifts. And I always thought, if only I could reach them, show them how easy it was to look wonderful.' Ms. Garrison stretched out the first syllable of 'wonderful' as if she were in love with the word."

The article said she'd picked Santa Fe because, after looking at a map of the U.S., it turned out that New Mexico made sense if you wanted to travel both to the South and the West, on the crossroads of two major interstate highways. She said, "I also loved that Santa Fe was a haven for artists . . . for beauty."

When the three of us conferenced about all the articles, Raquel repeated that line and said, "Can you believe she was shameless enough to offer up that shit to a reporter?"

" 'She walks in beauty, like the night—' " I began.

My brother interrupted, "That's a

quote from something, right?" at the same moment Raquel asked, "What poem is that from?"

"It's by Lord Byron. But he didn't have a truck."

My dad once told some dinner guests the story of how my grandmother started her business and ended by saying, "and the rest is history," which my mother contradicted with, "Please, Bradley! It's not even a footnote." Then they did their big ha-ha-ha duet because my dad was always charmed by my mom, especially when she denigrated his mother. And she laughed with delight because she loved being delightful.

But the rest could at least have been microhistory, if such a thing existed. Like if you were interested in a case study of, say, the foment of the feminist movement in the 1960s or the psychology of a housewife who, when her big, tough husband suddenly behaved like a weenie—was transformed into a woman with a mission to make the lives of other women better. Or maybe beauty was the only way my grandmother could think of to make a buck.

In any case, she decided her job was to bring a shot at loveliness into the lives of ordinary women who lived in small cities not generally visited by style mavens. Not loveliness in any serious aesthetic sense: Gloria GGG wasn't trucking fine art to Yuma, Arizona, and Enid, Oklahoma. She was transporting a more conventional kind of artistry: a hairdresser/makeup artist and a fashion consultant, along with a truck full of the tools of their trades.

Her business plan was makeovers. For starters, she sold one truck to get the money to make over the other. She knew it would take a lot to renovate a road-weary, twenty-six-foot bright blue Garment Center behemoth that had JG TRANSPORT on its side panels along with a lightning bolt and a sadly predictable motto, FASTER THAN LIGHTNING.

My dad claimed to have no memory of his first couple of months in New Mexico with her and Travis. He probably was in shock, having been part of a happy East Coast two-parent family and then, practically overnight, sharing a sofa bed with his brother in a motel room. His newly single mother was too busy getting a truck refurbished to bother enrolling them in school.

Still, he had a clear memory of her taking them to what he called "a garage as big as an airplane hangar." My dad and Travis stood before a truck that was being painted "inside-of-a-seashell kind of pink. A very light color. It had . . . I guess you'd call it opalescence," my dad told me. Subtle. One thing he learned from his mother: Don't condescend to your customers. Like the truck was not a Pepto-Bismol pink, the way someone from New York might think the hicks would go for. Across the sides, GLORY INC. and her motto, WHY NOT BE BEAUTIFUL? were in red. Then she took my dad and Travis up the ramp into the truck. It was a complete transformation. Before, my dad said, it had just been a Garment Center truck with pipe racks and big floor clamps for the portable racks they'd wheel on.

My dad said it was such an amazing conversion. There was a beauty parlor sink and plumbing connections, so they could hook up to water and waste, the way RVs can. And there were two fancy hairdresser chairs and a big mirror with the latest in lights. Cabinets for everything, all the products. That was in the back of the truck. Toward the front were racks of clothes and shoes and stuff—samples in all the sizes—and a table and chairs, so the clients could sit down and order stuff from the consultant and have tea or something. So they wouldn't feel like they were doing business, like at a desk. More like two women having a coffee klatch. Friends. And there were a million drawers for accessories so they could pull out a bunch of scarves or bracelets or whatever. "Smart, right?" my dad asked.

Actually, brilliant, as it turned out.

"She told us she wouldn't be able to afford a fashion consultant for the first couple of years, so she'd be on the road most of the time and she'd have to put us in boarding school. She said she picked a great place, near Albuquerque, and she wouldn't have chosen it if she hadn't been one hundred percent sure we'd love it." He shrugged and added, "I think she was embarrassed, too, that she was Garrison and we wanted to keep the name Goldberg. Changing our name would have been such a slap in the face to Dad, especially after losing the business, his wife, day-to-day access to his kids. Two kids named Goldberg at Saint Dominic's School. I told Travis she put us there just for spite, because we wouldn't change our name. He didn't think it was so bad."

"How was it for you?" I asked him.

He waved his hand like he was swatting a fly: *It's not even worth talking about.* But he swallowed so hard I thought, *Oh, my God, he's going to cry.* Instead he went into the kitchen and, when he came back with one of my mother's upscale whole-grain pretzels, he said calmly, "Anyway, my mother was some piece of work."

Four

Raquel

My grandmother said to us, "Raquel, Matthew, I thought we'd have a light bite in the—" She paused, but it was for effect, the way a prosecutor pauses when he's about to ask the one question that will drive a stake into your client's heart. "—conservatory." That word did everything except flash *Money!!* in green neon. It said, *I'm rich enough to have a mansion with a room whose name is so esoteric you haven't a clue as to what it's really for.* What was she conserving? Or was it a conservatory as in a music school, where we'd sit down and someone would play us Bach's *Italian Concerto*? Then she said, "Leave your bags here. Carlos, my houseman, will bring them upstairs."

I swear I wasn't allowing any of my admitted hostility, loathing, and contempt for her to affect my imagination when I say that as she pronounced the name "Carlos," she looked right at me. Who, you might ask, was Carlos? Well, a minute before, a man in khakis, a white shirt, clean-as-new white sneakers, and polished brown skin had come into the hallway and asked, with the slightest Mexican accent, "Is there anything I can do to assist, Ms. Garrison?" Not that she bothered introducing him to us.

But once she said, "Carlos will bring them upstairs," it was reasonable to assume that the shiny guy of sixty seconds earlier was Carlos the houseman. But this is what I wanted to know: How come, when she enunciated those two syllables, "Car-los," she felt it necessary to look simultaneously at a Latino? Me. Did she expect me to tweet *Latinos, listen up! Gloria Garrison deserves* crédito adicional *for her hiring practices and all-around greatness?*

Okay, I'm being mean-spirited, which makes me less like my mother and more like Grandma Goldberg. In fact, if my mother were here and could get into my head to take the measure of my hostility, her face would lose its customary warm-eyed sweetness and her mouth would go slack. She'd manage to control the hand rising to her chest, but I'd know anyway the heartache she was feeling for me because I was so burdened by malice. Actually, that's not a fair picture of my mom. It makes her sound like she's on the fast track for beatification. She's not.

Adriana Calderon Goldberg, my mother, is simply the most balanced human being alive. She is head of social work at Montefiore Hospital in the Bronx, a position that suits her perfectly because it lets her combine her three greatest qualities: rationality, caring, and belief in her own abilities. She supervises a staff whose job is to help families figure out how to care for patients when the hospital runs out of solutions or money.

In her dealings with the caregivers for the physically and mentally challenged and the dying, my mom gets to view humanity at its most noble as well as at its most revolting. She sees people's better angels yet is not at all blind to their illusions, self-delusions, and demons. Her goal is to guide her clients—gently, patiently—toward dealing with reality, as well as with each other, in a decent and effective manner.

Knowing this about her, I shouldn't have been surprised when she pressed me to accept my grandmother's invitation to Santa Fe. "No way in hell I'm going," I told her. "A, I detest her, and B, I'm preparing for trial."

To tell the truth, I was more than a little exasperated that my mom had called me at the office that morning and asked, "Are you free for dinner tonight?" Her usually melodious voice definitely wasn't singing. I asked if anything was wrong, and she said no, she just wanted see me. So even though my boyfriend, Hayden, with whom I live, had made a huge deal before he left for work about how he'd come home by nine for dinner, and a huger deal about something he was braising in the slow cooker, osso bucco or farsumagru, I couldn't refuse her.

Naturally, I didn't assent gracefully. Instead, I did what would infuriate me if anyone else did it, which was ask if it was really important. She'd answered, "To me it is." And no, it wasn't anything she'd care to discuss over the phone. So naturally, the entire day, I had that pulled-tight knot in my upper intestines as I pondered *cancer* alternating with *serious budget cuts at Montefiore/I've lost my job/I may need some financial backup/I can't tell you how it grieves me to have to ask this of you.*

Instead of meeting where we usually did, at an Upper West Side restaurant equitably located between the Bronx and where I live, in Hayden's condo in TriBeCa, I called her back in the late afternoon and said, "Hey, I'd love to have a home-cooked meal. Is that doable?" I wound up taking an hour's ride up to her apartment. I had to.

Except it turned out there was no life-altering disclosure. Instead, my mom said she'd been thinking about the invitation Grandma Goldberg had sent me two days earlier and had been praying I would accept. Not that there was any pressure. She offered me a social worker's smile and told me straight out that despite her MSW and thirty years in the field, she realized she was as capable of passive-aggression as any other mother.

Then she stopped unpacking the Chinese food that had just been delivered. This was as home-cooked as it got on a weeknight. She set her hands on her hips. Not a great distance, because she was tiny. Not so much short—although five feet doesn't shop in the tall department—as built on a teensy scale. Delicate, doll-like, whatever. I'm petite. She's more along the lines of a Puerto Rican Barbie, naturally minus the ridiculous boobs and hoop earrings.

"Raquel," my mother said, "you say you're preparing for a trial. All right. But is that a good enough reason not to go to Santa Fe?" She went back to pulling out the cartons and containers at whiplash speed, setting everything onto plates and bowls. She'd always believed that even if you can't cook a good meal, you should serve one so it looks as though you spent hours in the kitchen: not to make you, the noncook, look good, but to honor your family.

I'm told my dad was awed at the pace at which she did everything. He used to tell her she was half human, half hummingbird and that her energy came from the hummingbird side of the family. He said her heart probably beat over a thousand times a minute. That was years before the Katy Perry song. Besides, my father's life was photographing animals, so he had the credentials to talk about hummingbirds. My mom added, "Truthfully, when are you *not* either preparing or on trial?"

This is true. I was a staff attorney with the Legal Aid Society in Manhattan. I mostly dealt with cases brought by the DA's Public Assistance Fraud Unit. I defended my fellow citizens who were alleged to have defrauded programs like welfare, Medicaid, and food stamps.

Sometimes not the classiest clients, but everybody has a right to counsel. Right? Like the society's motto says, we're all about "making the case for humanity."

It was tough enough from the get-go trying to persuade juries that even though my many, many clients might look and sometimes even behave like scumbags, they were not necessarily guilty of the crimes of which they were accused. But eighteen months after I started my legal career, the economy tanked. Shamming and scamming grew to new heights. My caseload grew from huge to qualifying as cruel and unusual punishment.

"Maybe," my mother said, "your grandmother wants a rapprochement. And please, Raquel, don't give me your help-me-Jesus look." My mother obviously thought she'd caught me rolling my eyes heavenward. I was ninety-nine percent sure I hadn't. But since all I did, day and night, was argue, I let it go. My mom went on: "In her invitation, did your grandmother hint at any reason why she wants to see you?" She held up a plastic container of wonton soup to the light, like a scientist eyeing a suspicious specimen. Then, apparently satisfied, she dumped it into a large bowl so she could then serve it properly at the table.

"*She* didn't send the invitation," I said. "The e-mail came from 'Assistant to Ms. Garrison.' It was so terse it bordered on insulting: 'From midday Thursday to Sunday afternoon.' It said they would arrange for round-trip, business-class air travel. That kind of thing. For all I know, it could have been a computer-generated notification and 'Assistant to Ms. Garrison' is actually a Dell."

"All right. I admit no one has ever used 'gracious' and 'Gloria Garrison—' "

"Gloria Goldberg Goldberg."

"Raquel," my mom said, "I don't like being cut off." She spoke matter-of-factly; someone listening who didn't speak English would think she was communicating a neutral fact, like *I need to buy coffee,* instead of a rebuke. That's her single weird character trait. She never acts angry, even though from what she's saying—and very directly, too—it's clear she is. It's not like she's suppressing anything or into denial about what she's feeling. Believe me, my mom knows when she's pissed. When that happens, she gives whomever she is pissed at forty-seven reasons why she's displeased. Yet she will enumerate them without getting emotional.

Another thing about my mother: She projected honesty. So in the case of her attitude about my personal life, even though she never told me she didn't like my boyfriend, I knew she didn't. The most she'd ever said was she thought the name Hayden Ramos-Cruz was ridiculous, and if his parents wanted an Anglo name, what was wrong with John? Personally, I thought "Hayden" was cool. I realized if I were to ask her directly, she would tell me why she didn't like him, too, not just his name. She'd probably say, *It's not that I don't like him, it's that I have questions about his behavior, his choices. I suppose it all comes down to certain doubts about his character.* But I really had no desire to hear it. I assumed it was because Hayden wouldn't commit. He is thirty-one, six years older than I am. In her mind he is way too old to still have that kind of issue.

"As I was saying," she went on calmly, "the words 'gracious' and 'Gloria Garrison' have never been found in the same sentence. Still, she was a good mother to your father." She did her Big Gulp, the hard swallow she did every single time she said "your father" or "my husband," or "Travis." One year after his death or more than twenty years after—it made no difference. The pain of his loss seems to have remained at a constant level. She switched to Spanish, which for her is the language of personal disclosure. I could say the language of the heart, but that makes it sound sappy. Whatever. "He loved Gloria, he honestly did. Found all her posturing and . . . what would you call it? Her grandiosity. He thought it was endearing."

"Do you think she loved Dad for himself or because he was part of her? Like was loving him just an extension of her narcissism?"

Back to English. "No. Definitely not.

Because your uncle Bradley was part of her, and—I'm not telling you anything you don't know already—her indifference to Bradley, her disrespect . . . She froze him out."

"Well, she was able to freeze out her husband," I said. "Why not her son?"

"In fairness to her . . . ," my mother began. Then she hesitated.

"You want to be fair to her?"

"Why not?" she said. "What does it cost to be fair? Maybe it was some form of self-protection, after having lost your father. Rather than risk that pain again, she cut her ties—"

I shook my head and told her, "If something happened to Uncle Bradley, it would not cause her . . . shall we say excessive pain?"

"Then how do you explain her coldness, her ability to shed relationships?"

"Mom, you're the social worker."

"I'm at a loss."

So was I. Then and now. I followed my grandmother as she led me and Matthew through her house. It wasn't what you'd call a trek, but it was a longer walk than I'd ever taken in any person's residence. At last, the walls on the left side of the hallway changed to glass. You suddenly realized it was a house in the Spanish style, with the atrium at the center.

She didn't slow down at all. It was like, *No big deal, everybody has an atrium, so let's just keep going.* Pretty, but as Daisy and Matt's mother, Cynthia the Decorator, would say, *Something about it . . . self-conscious to the point of lifelessness.* Of course, Aunt Cynthia is infinitely finicky and extremely long-winded when it comes to discussing other people's lack of taste. She invariably finds fault with anything she herself didn't design. But in the case of the atrium, she'd be right.

Lots of desert plants—cactuses and the kinds with the fat leaves, like aloe, except it was something else—and rocks, including a low boulder that was flat on top. Presumably it was meant as a bench. I wondered, despite our brisk pace, if conservatory was what people in Santa Fe called atrium, and we were just heading over to get to the other side of it.

Would the three of us (four, when Daisy got off the pot) wind up sitting on the boulder facing outward? Yoga-style, facing inward? Maybe Carlos the houseman would bring in cushions to sit on and we'd use the boulder as a table. Then some white-aproned maid named something like Purificación would serve us tea. I was wondering whether it was considered elegant to put a tablecloth on a boulder when, suddenly, the glass wall stopped.

We kept walking . . . I guessed toward the back of the house. Outside was so nice, with that perfect blue sky and cotton-ball clouds. Also, by now I was disoriented. Knowing Daisy, she'd need a compass and two sherpas to find us. We finally got to a living room large enough to seat both houses of Congress, but we weren't there yet. Then my grandmother opened a glass door into still another major space, an expansive glassed-in hexagon. It had more couches and big, cushiony chairs and potted plants than a hotel lobby, plus a long bamboo bar. She said, "Here we are. The conservatory."

Five

Gloria

When I was twenty, I actually rejected a guy named Alexander Miller for someone with my own last name, the name I'd hated all my life. But how could you say no to Joe Goldberg?

Well, it was also how could you say yes to Alex, even with the size of his wallet?—He talked too much about the weather, not because he felt socially inept but because he found weather interesting. Also he had an unappealing body shape. No, make that repulsive. He always reminded me of a pickle with arms and legs. Not a stand-up, manly pickle. A limp, froggy kind of pickle. And he took forever to pronounce the first syllable of my name. *Gloooo-ria.* The private high school he went to, Fieldston, probably required a speech course—Introduction to WASPdom: How Not to Sound Like a Jew. But instead of his deliberate pronunciation highlighting how well-bred he was, it just gave me time to get irritated by his airs.

So even though his father owned Coat Craft, one of the Garment Center's giants, I wasn't interested. Or interested only in the sense of *This is what I should want.* Plus I'd already met Joe. God, even now . . . you took his arm and it was so muscular it was like holding on to a bronze statue of Adonis. Admittedly, Alex had graduated from Columbia and Joe had dropped out after his first semester at CCNY. But big deal. Alex was a daddy's boy—you'd see him and Daddy Miller strolling down Seventh Avenue together in three-piece pin-striped suits and rep ties, and even though the old man was about the size of a ventriloquist's dummy, Alex seemed diminished by him.

But Joe was his own man, with his own up-and-coming business. He looked tough. A narrow scar started at the side of his mouth and ran across his chin. When asked about it, he'd say, "It was an accident. I ran into a knife," though after we were married he admitted that he'd been cut by a piece of glass from an exploding seltzer bottle when he was eleven. But he had been in an actual bar brawl once; his nose was a little smashed in, and what was most surprising about that was that someone actually picked a fight with Joe. He had enormous shoulders and a five o'clock shadow at ten a.m. His talk was tough too, with a New York accent with a gravelly sound. Yet when he stepped into an office or a restaurant—anyplace, really—people somehow knew: *He's a class act.* I was a goner the first time he walked through the Solange de Paris showroom. Someone introduced us: "Gloria Goldberg, this is Joe Goldberg." And Joe smiled and said, "Cousin Gloria," and made it sound like a love song.

Oh, I was going on about my grandchildren. Though God knows I have all my marbles, I admit that on occasion my mind wanders. At least they're all good-looking, though oddly, the boy is the only one who appears to have my kind of flair. Elegant, unfussy, though being in his midtwenties, he's pointlessly dressed down. His sister is major makeover material; she does nothing with herself. Yet nothing she's wearing is wrong: It would have been charming when she was sixteen. Now it's simply too young for her. I want to tell women, *Eschew sunflowers, for the love of God! Why are you dressing like an adolescent? On them it looks cool. On you it looks foolish. Allow the kids their fashion monopoly and be a cool twenty-five or fifty-year-old.* Actually, I have told them, on occasion.

Daisy probably does have an eye and could style anything apart from herself: arrange furniture in a room or fruit in a basket. Raquel has F-you taste, wearing a completely unaccessorized blue shirtwaist dress. Not even a watch. But from the way the collar is adjusted, just a little up, not too much, there is no doubt she has at least an above-average style IQ. However, she also has the professional woman's 1970s disease, acute fashion suppression, afraid if she displayed any interest in clothes people would think her frivolous. Back to Raquel's F-you: It's also evident with her no-makeup look, except I can see she put on a touch of tinted rose-coral lip gloss, just a hint. I can always tell. She's light brown. Her skin, I mean. It doesn't have a yellow undertone, so she basically could get away without added color, yet with her skin being monochromatic light brown, the gloss brightens her face. Though like too many women her age, she did not comprehend that one should use lip *gloss,* not lip slime. Some blush to set off her high cheeks wouldn't hurt either. Hispanic-Indian facial structure, I would guess, not Russian-Jewish-raped-by-Mongols.

Anyway, Goldberg. I was never thrilled with Joe having the name Goldberg. But other than that? I loved him far longer than I should have. But ages before I began planning on leaving him—no, to be precise, even before I was run out of Cincinnati on a rail, practically—I was dreaming what name I'd pick for myself if I were free to choose.

Way before Joe, I somehow felt obliged to stick with the letter *G.* Why, I'll never know. I went through Gage, Godwin, and Gibbs. Later, after I'd decided to legally change the name, I rejected Gibbons (the monkey connotation) and Goddard, which I really liked, but unfortunately there had been the actress Paulette Goddard. A lot of people knew she was Jewish. Not that I was denying what I was, but I wanted something neutral. So I kept searching. Graves was creepy. Grantham, which I loved the look of when I signed *Gloria Grantham,* regrettably made me sound like I was lisping when I introduced myself in front of the mirror, "Good afternoon, I'm Gloria Grantham." It came down to a coin toss between Grant and Garrison. Grant won. But I picked Garrison.

Most people don't change their names these days, except for Jon Stewart and the Italian fellow who created

The Sopranos. I suppose with all the diversity, no one thinks less of you if you keep your own name, unless it's a complete catastrophe like Lipschitz. But back then, you said, "Hello, my name is Gloria Goldberg," it was like saying, "Hello, my name is Gloria Jew." Blacks actually used the term "a Goldberg" to mean a Jew. I read that in a magazine article.

Both my sons kept the name. Maybe they would have changed it, but when I left Joe, their father, they were in their midteens, prime name-changing time because it's approaching college application season, which means if you don't act fast, the friends you make there will always say, "You know what his name used to be? Goldberg!" I think the boys felt sorry for Joe and probably didn't want to damage his withered ego any more than it already was by rejecting his name.

As far as I can see, being Goldberg didn't hurt either of them. Bradley, the older one, whom I suppose I love (though even as a boy, he had all the pizzazz of an orthopedic shoe), managed to build up a small chain of upscale hardware/domestic goods stores, the Handsome Home. What a pretentious name, no doubt thought up by that wife of his. But Bradley has made it in a small way. He's quite well-off, though no one would call him wealthy.

Travis, two years younger, succeeded in becoming a world-class animal photographer with the credit "Photo by Travis Goldberg" in publications like *National Geographic* and *Audubon*. Travis had it all—looks, charm, an artist's eye, an insatiable sense of adventure. Whatever I was going through, when I saw him, my mood changed to good. He was killed when his Jeep turned over. In Peru. He was photographing monkeys there, the world's tiniest monkeys, smaller than a finger.

For more than two years I was dead inside. I did everything—went to work, sat on committees, had people over—and felt nothing. Not even sadness. Nothing. Maybe I believed being dead would bring me closer to him, but it didn't. Eventually, feeling came back, though it was no boon. I missed being numb. Sometimes if I was happy to see someone, or excited about a reasonably priced new pore concealer, I'd break off halfway through the emotion and think, *I wish I were dead again.* That's all. No more about Travis. To this day, I truly fear I'll go mad, never to return to sanity, if I dwell too long on his dying.

Matthew, Bradley's son, looks like Travis when he smiles the way he just did: eyes crinkling, square jaw softening, the thick-but-not-too-thick lips stretching over big even teeth. That familiar smile draws me in, but then it's like a knife in my heart. Though Matthew is objectively much handsomer than Travis was, he lacks my son's twinkle, that combination of high intelligence and bad boy–ness.

Matthew blinked from the conservatory's brilliant sunlight after the low-key light of the halls. But he seems not at all awed by the vastness of the room, by the all-white furniture arranged in groupings for conversation, the throw pillows in fantastic colors of Mexican embroidery, the pots and pots of cactuses. I would say "cacti" but it's a word people always stop at before they understand, whereas everybody gets "cactuses." Come to think of it, Matthew wouldn't get wowed by opulence. He grew up in an affluent neighborhood, so luxury per se wouldn't impress him. But I could see he appreciated the room. Maybe he has his mother's decorating gene—that dreadful, self-absorbed woman. But maybe it's what I had—plain good taste and an eye—that I passed down to Travis. And Bradley too, I suppose.

I understood why Matthew was probably good at what he did, PR. Instinctively, he went for the big fan-backed chair, the room's throne. Instead of sitting in it because he's the male, he stood behind it, waiting for me to sit. He had a feel for the natural pecking order. I might use the word "manners," except with pushy Cynthia for a mother, the only woman of her generation who never needed a single second of assertiveness training . . . Well, perhaps Bradley was able to pass down to his son what manners I taught him.

Travis's only child, Raquel, seems to have her father's twinkle. At least I think she does. Granted, I haven't seen her since she was a child. But in the few minutes since they all arrived, I've seen the exact same wicked gleam in her eyes that Travis would get when a snotty comment went through his head he knew he couldn't express. Like him, she can suppress the words, but she can't keep the amusement out of her eyes. I was not taken with the twinkle because whatever her malicious thought was, it was doubtless about me. It's some solace, I suppose, that Raquel has a mean streak, which means she's at least partly one of us, and not totally like her goody-goody I-try-to-get-to-Mass-every-day mother. But what I really didn't get is that after Travis was killed, why in God's name two Latinas kept the name Goldberg. That was beyond my comprehension.

When we walked into the conservatory, I could see how overwhelmed she was. Not because of the light. The size of the room got to her, and her head turned as she counted the number of sides—it's a hexagon. Her mouth opened a little too much, though I can't say her jaw actually dropped. Not that she grew up in a slum. Bradley was once trying to convince me to accept Adriana's invitation to dinner the next time I came east. He said, "Even though it's in the Bronx, it's a nice apartment. In a middle-class neighborhood. Nothing at all to be afraid of."

I challenged him: "What do you think? That I imagine a bunch of Puerto Ricans and run screaming?"

There is absolutely nothing wrong with the term "Puerto Ricans," but naturally, Bradley, the noble liberal, said, "Mommm," and I may have said something to the effect of "Oh, shut up," and he actually hung up on me. After twenty years of marriage to Cynthia, he'd finally picked up some kindergarten courage.

But Bradley, that bubblehead. Couldn't he stop that woman from naming his daughter Daisy? What did she expect? Cynthia herself is built like a blow-up sex toy, though admittedly better dressed. Bradley chose someone like that in direct repudiation of me, and no one can tell me different. Could Cynthia have been anticipating a slender wisp of a girl who'd pull on a pair of jodhpurs and call her *Mummy*? Without a doubt that semiliterate woman would not have read *The Great Gatsby,* but no doubt she saw the movie when she heard it was set on Long Island. When Daisy was . . . who the hell can remember? . . . fourteen or fifteen, the last time I saw her until now, she looked like an enforcer for some Teamsters local. She's improved now, mostly because she developed breasts and hips. Five years ago that wouldn't have been a plus, but with fashion's recent acceptance of meat—all the Marilyn Monroe wannabes with red lipstick and jiggly boobs—she's got a shot, assuming she did something with herself. Lose fifteen pounds—though twenty wouldn't hurt—and stop overblowing her hair into a stick-straight shoulder-length do that looks like it's screaming, *I'm thirsty!*

But she looks to me like a girl who's given up. Rapidly approaching her thirtieth birthday, and you think "makeup" means just wearing lipstick? In fact, she has good lips, but she's wearing some dreadful too-dark red: Blood Clot Crimson. It has a sticky sheen. She must be the only woman over fourteen wearing it.

Daisy, for God's sake. How could they have assumed she would be a slender little flower? Why didn't they just name her Giant Chrysanthemum if they had to go floral? And Matthew? Why give a kid with the last name Goldberg the name of an apostle? I think Matthew was one of the apostles. Who the hell knows? I mean, I named my boys two distinctive but elegant names. Bradley. And Travis.

Six

Matt

I heard my sister's voice and knew someone had found her and literally taken her by the hand. No, figuratively. Figuratively taken her by the hand and led her into the conservatory. Daisy was the kid born with an outstanding sense of language. Also a negative sense of direction. I'm vice versa.

On family vacations, when we shared a room adjoining the parents and were old enough to go off on our own, she'd go out into the hall and consistently turn the wrong way for the elevator—even on our fourth or fifth day in the hotel.

One time I asked her, "How the fuck do you do it? Just by the law of averages, you should go in the right direction fifty percent of the time." She said something like, "Oh, it's a gift." Just blew it off.

Misdirection came easy to Daisy. Driving from my parents' house on Long Island to Manhattan could mean a tour of all five boroughs. I'd once asked if, when she went to L.A. for meetings at Paramount and had to drive to the studio from her hotel, did having GPS help? She said, "Sometimes," in a breezy manner, the way a guy would dismiss the most trivial quirk of his by saying, *Who gives a shit?* Then she added, to appease me or reassure me, "But just to make sure, I leave at seven thirty for a nine o'clock meeting, and it's only a twenty-minute ride."

A maid carrying a tray came in. She was followed by Daisy, who didn't look at all frazzled at having taken ten or fifteen minutes for what had been all but advertised as a quick pee. Meanwhile, Raquel and I had been left to amuse the apparently unamusable Gloria Garrison on our own. Usually, that would be a piece of cake for me. I amuse for a living. I dealt with mostly media types whose jobs demanded they be cynical. Without exception, they were. Journalistic professionalism, however, didn't demand that sportswriters also be surly, but that often seemed to be part of the deal. But I was outgoing by nature, though one of my ex-girlfriends claimed I was so outer-directed—or maybe other-directed—that she'd decided I had zero left inside. That wasn't fair. Also, she brought up my being a soulless automaton only as I was breaking off with her. Anyway, I was a natural to chat up Granny while Daisy did the Big Pee. Except it would have been nice if Raquel helped out.

But my cousin sat on the edge of her white chair in classic Catholic schoolgirl posture even though she went to public school. Back straight, hands clasped in her lap, knees and ankles together. And mouth shut, except when Granny Glo asked a direct question: "Are you enjoying your work at Legal Aid?" Her response, "Yes, except for the caseload," was like she lived on Planet Twitter, where you'd be stoned to death if you didn't use a hundred and forty characters or fewer to respond.

Truth be told, I was feeling kind of uncomfortable being the one guy in the room. Normally I was pretty gender cool. I had women friends, went out with really intelligent women. Why wouldn't I want someone who got me? (That sounds selfish. It probably is.) Anyway, I grew up with a working mother and a big sister who was smarter than me. *Than I,* Daisy would correct me. I actually did know which pronoun to use. However, there were certain secondary sex characteristics—underarm hair and ignorance of fancy grammar—Goldberg men were expected to possess.

We also had the male-linked sports gene: My grandpa Joe had been a rabid Brooklyn Dodgers fan. Not just superavid, but genuinely insane. He would listen again and again to CDs of Red Barber's play-by-play announcing of Dodgers games that had taken place more than sixty years earlier. My dad, college educated, suburban reared, made the generational leap and understood there was more to the world than baseball. There were football, hockey, basketball, and the summer and winter Olympics for watching and talking endlessly about.

Well, sometimes he talked about my mother, as in, "Cynthia took her natural nesting instinct and brought it to a whole new level," while gazing with love and awe at a needlepointed footstool she'd decided belonged with the thousand other objects already in our living room; she'd originally bought it for a client but apparently decided it wouldn't find a loving enough home there.

My dad could also go on about his mother, as in, 'It's not just her personality that's cold. Her hands were always like ice . . . not that she touched me much. Actually, she went out of her way not to." To be fair, he could also speak upper-middle-class dialect: business, politics, movies, books, Titleist woods versus Callaway, *Breaking Bad* versus *Friday Night Lights.*

Neither my grandfather nor my father

ever considered a life in sports. My grandpa Joe had been an almost champion at handball. He had the solid legs and powerful arms and shoulders that could have made him a winner in any ball game. But his life was dedicated to moving out of the working class and enjoying the benefits of being in the upper region of the ninety-nine percent—trading in his Cadillac every other year, trading up his wife's fur from mink stole to full-length mink coat. Once he gave up his trucking business and lost his family to New Mexico, he was emotionally too wiped out to do anything much more than move to Florida, work on and off as a limo driver. His business became hooking up with divorcées and widows willing to support him. There were a lot of women ready to pay his health club dues. If they were rich, he played golf at their clubs. He married a couple of them.

My dad, however, was not a jock. He was coordinated enough to catch a ball thrown straight at him, but basically he was an unathletic, apple-shaped man who, through constant vigilance (of my mom), appeared banana-ish in a camel hair sports jacket. On the tennis court, he could get through a doubles game without humiliation or a heart attack.

But starting in second grade, when I finally got the hand-eye-coordination business straight, I was a good athlete. In both my daydreams and the ones at night, I was a great one, leaping two, three feet off the ground in center field at Shea to catch a could-be grand slam and deprive the Braves of a win. The crowd chanted *Gold-berg! Gold-berg!* with the emphasis on *Gold.* I was golden too in football, a Giants quarterback they nicknamed the Uzi because my throw was as fast, devastating, and accurate as the Israeli submachine gun. And on the ice, I was the new Mike Bossy, a genius sniper who brought the Islanders back to life.

It took about ten years to understand that I wasn't the man of my dreams. On the high school baseball team, where I wound up playing first base, I would stretch or leap to catch a ball and was genuinely amazed those times I didn't hear that comforting leathery *whomp!*

in my glove. I so believed in my prowess in the arenas of my dreams that it was reality that felt wrong. What led me to get it, finally, was when the occasional college scout would show up for Shorehaven High School games; the only way they ever looked at me was as someone who was catching a ball thrown by the second baseman. That awakening ruined my junior year. On the other hand, it got me to understand that a Plan B might be in order.

"Sorry I took so long," Daisy was saying to our grandmother. Her tone was so over-the-top cheery that if Granny was feeling hostile, she would have repeated my sister's "Sorry" sarcastically in a manner that meant, *You're full of shit. No way you're sorry.*

"Good that you found us," Granny said, in that polite, warmthless way that I was rapidly growing familiar with. She turned to the maid who was standing there, arms rigid, holding what must have been a heavy tray. With just a touch of weariness that suggested she was tired of dealing with dumb servants, she murmured, "Paula, put the tray on the bar, please." Paula, who could have been a close relation of the Travelocity gnome, stayed frozen for a few seconds. Just as I was debating whether to offer to take the tray from her because it looked like the weight of it had fused her shoes to the big tiles of the floor, she Frankenstein-monster-walked it over with much clinking of glass and china. I noticed she was dressed the same way the guy servant was: white shirt, khakis (in her case, a skirt, not pants), and bright white sneakers. Probably the new I-won't-humiliate-you-by-making-you-wear-a-uniform uniform.

What with Raquel being there, I wished our grandmother had settled in some other part of the country where the people in service jobs were anything else—white or African American or Asian. My cousin took ethnic sensitivity to a level way beyond hyper. Latino consciousness seemed like an aura always hovering around her. You couldn't ignore Raquel's Latina-ness because she didn't want you to. She was always ready with a reminder, a Spanish word tossed into a sentence for no discernible purpose, repeated references to the Bronx in a way that made it sound like she'd grown up on mean streets, a world apart from us tennis and piano lessons kids. She seemed to enjoy coming off like she'd been raised in some crack-ridden barrio instead of the reality, a middle-income co-op in a decent neighborhood, and Bronx High School of Science followed by Barnard College.

Added to that was Raquel's new Santa Fe vibe, which I was feeling as she looked at the short brown maid, then glanced at me slit eyed, as if I'd done the hiring, importing someone peasant looking from Mexico to put Raquel in her place: *Do you think I'm strictly working class like my* compatriotas *and not as good as you?*

Which was weird because what people say about our generation being pretty much postracial/ethnic is pretty much true. Like at Citi Field, PR people like me who've moved up in the ranks, gone from giving tours of the facilities ("Down here we have our six giant beer vats that assure that fans will always get a cold one during the game. Each one stores the equivalent of fifty kegs of beer per tank, and those pipes connect them to beer dispensers throughout the park!") to dealing with the press, are assigned by interest and ability. Probably ninety-eight percent of us speak some Spanish. There was no *We need a Latino* to deal with an only-Spanish-speaking reporter or player. Ethnicity, religion—they're in the background. Sometimes you forget what somebody is until he comes in with a smudge on his forehead: *Oh, yeah, it's Ash Wednesday so he must be Catholic.* Who knew? Maybe being with the Goldberg family drew out Raquel's aura and it disappeared when she was at work.

Actually, my girlfriend, Ashley Altman, a nice Jewish girl from Houston, was adopted from China when she was a year old. Her parents—adoptive—named her Ashley for some dead Jewish grandma who'd had a Yiddish *A* name. They also gave her a Chinese middle name, Mei, which means "beauty." She is beautiful, though in a round-faced, slightly chubby way. Mei also means "plum blossom." Sometimes I'll say, "Yo, Plum," and she gives me a smile that melts me.

An almost inaudible, "Thank you, Paula," from Granny. The maid walked out, though considering the combo of her short legs and the size of the room, it was more like a hike. "I thought you might like a light bite," our grandmother said. "Considering the state of airline food, even in business class . . ." I'd snarfed down an Auntie Anne's pretzel in the Dallas airport when we changed planes, so though there was a plate of English sandwiches, the flat little triangles with no crusts, on the cart, I stayed in the corner of a big white couch I'd laid claim to. "There's a small fridge next to the cart. It's paneled like the wall. There's water, soda, iced tea . . . beer if you like." Daisy and Raquel exchanged one of those fast, female looks that asks one another *Should we have something?* and answers *Let's.* Raquel poured a bottle of Snapple into a tall glass. Daisy glommed a few sandwiches on a plate and, even though she likes to chug her soda from a can, followed Raquel's example and poured a Diet Coke into a glass. There were cloth napkins on the tray, small squares, and she took one of those too.

As they walked back, I felt a serious need to start a conversation because you could hear the *thwack, thwack* of my cousin's feet rising off the innersoles of her shoes. She was wearing the high cork kind without backs. Cool, not the clunky high-high ones that make women look like they're playing a giraffe in *The Lion King.* But when the loudest sound in a huge room is a *thwack,* followed after long seconds by the ice machine releasing a new load, it's disturbingly quiet. That kind of silence can take hold, become contagious. It could even spread throughout the whole weekend. God forbid, as my grandpa Joe would say.

Just as I was searching for a neutral topic that wasn't an obvious conversation starter, our grandmother finally spoke: "Are any of you in touch with Joe Goldberg?" It was weird. Not only that he'd just popped into my head. It was also weird that while all three of us nodded, not one of us could manage a *yes.* Maybe we didn't trust our voices because—though I couldn't speak for the girls—the thought hit me hard: *Did she schlep us out to Santa Fe because she still has an unrequited thing for Grandpa and wants to pump us for information? Use us as bait to lure him back? Oh, crap.*

"What's Joe doing these days?" Granny asked. I could have stayed in New York, been with Ashley. I'd starting missing her before the plane took off from LaGuardia.

"He's living in Miami Beach," Raquel said. In the glass-walled conservatory, her strong voice came out more like an orator's than a lawyer's.

"Oh," Granny said. "The last I heard he was in Boynton Beach."

"That was four or five years ago," my sister said.

"He must have traded in his last widow for a new one." Granny nearly smiled. Obviously she found herself delightful. "Well, good to know that at eighty-three Joe's boyish charm is still functioning. I assume I'll hear from your father when he finally dies, though Bradley knows enough not to hit me up for funeral expenses."

"So," Raquel finally said, probably recognizing that Daisy had been rendered speechless, "you have no contact with Grandpa?"

"He knows my address," Granny said. "Periodically, I get letters. Some trying to charm me. Not for charm's sake, mind you. Trying to cast the spell that will get me to open my checkbook." She tucked a strand of her silver hair back into the big blob thing—knot, bun—on the back of her head. "In the others, he forgets the spell routine and demands support from me. For some reason, he thinks I owe him. 'Big time,' as Joe is so fond of saying. Everything about him was 'big time.'" She shook her head with what I guessed was supposed to be a projection of pity, as in, *Tsk-tsk, poor Joe, strictly small time.* As far as I could tell, there was nothing resembling compassion in her outburst. "His work ethic is certainly not big time." She stood without great difficulty, though you wouldn't call it a fluid motion. Clearly, she had some knee issue. She strolled over to the cart, took a tiny triangular sandwich, and ate it in three bites, two more than it deserved. Since there was no conversation going on, all we could do was observe her canapé-chewing performance. She looked from one of us to the other as if she were following a stage direction. "Does it surprise you that someone who never went to college knows a term like 'work ethic'?"

"No," Raquel snapped. Granny either cracked a smile or moved her mouth slightly to show she liked my cousin's snotty one-syllable answer. But then Raquel added, "Why would the owner of a reasonably successful business not know the term 'work ethic'?" The smile or whatever it had been vanished from Granny's lips. I could see that she and Raquel weren't getting off to a warm, fuzzy start. Well, from our grandmother's point of view, you shouldn't call someone living in what must have been a four- or five-million-dollar house "reasonably successful." Especially if you picked up from her attitude that her definition of herself would be closer to "tycoon."

As far as I could remember, Raquel, despite her prickliness on matters ethnic, had always been supersmart, fair, and bullshit-free—the qualities you need in a lawyer and hope for in a cousin. The way she would see it, a person of Gloria's age and rank shouldn't be posing dumb-ass questions to her grandchildren about her understanding of "work ethic." Why wasn't she saying, *Hey, glad I finally have the chance to be with you. Tell me, how are your lives going?*

Gloria Garrison returned to her seat in the room's biggest chair. Her silver pants and white sweater, first shiny then soft against the rough-white fabric cushions, made her seem even grander than her surroundings, downright regal. But the two deep wrinkles running from the corners of her mouth toward her jaw let you know she was a pissed-off queen who, any minute, could yell, *Off with her head!*

Still, though we were all definitely nervous to some degree, I don't think any of us were genuinely scared of her. She could be as pissed off as she liked. We'd be okay. Daisy, Raquel, and I were all citizens of another country.

Seven

Raquel

My grandmother brought out the worst in me. So I forced myself to fade into the background because I had an overwhelming urge to say something hurtful: *They invented high collars for necks like yours* or *This house is wonderful. Sooo 1990s.* I wasn't sure what I meant by the last, but it was belittling and, with any luck, would discomfort her.

"How long have you been living here?" Daisy was asking her. "In this house, I mean."

"Twenty-two years," Gloria said.

Daisy smiled, clearly waiting for her

to go on, maybe with a story about how she came to buy the house, or a history of glass-walled conservatories. But maybe, having popped for three round-trip business-class tickets, our grand-mother figured she'd given enough.

Daisy, though, was willing to work. "This is a wonderful place," she went on. "Everything about it. The sands and whites with the bursts of color, the sub-dued lighting so that, you know, when you pass the atrium or come into this room, all that beautiful natural light is a great surprise." Gloria managed a sin-gle nod where her head went down and didn't really lift up again. To give her the benefit of the doubt, maybe she was acknowledging the compliment like a queen: *We hear you.* Maybe she had arthritis in her neck.

But silence, or the silent treatment, if that's what it was, could not stop a Goldberg. Daisy stayed upbeat. "I'm not saying that as the daughter of a de-signer. More as, well, someone who's visual. You know, after watching one or two movies a day for umpteen years, my eye tends to catch details as well as the big picture."

"Personally," Gloria Garrison said, "I read in my spare time."

I couldn't believe it. Such a dis. And despite all my time in court (where a lawyer's fast response can make the difference between her client's taking a walk or doing three to five at the Arthur Kill Correctional Facility), I couldn't respond on Daisy's behalf. My mind was a blank. Fortunately, Matt, the nonlawyer, came to her rescue. "Read?" he said. "That's the other thing my sister's great at, besides film: reading. She reads for a living. Daisy scouts for books that would make good movies and gets them to the right people at the studio. She reads more than anyone I know." Instead of glaring at Gloria, Matt smiled. While it might not have charmed the old lady, the mean-girl bitch cloud that had been hovering over her head drifted away. His smile could work wonders.

Matthew Goldberg was impossibly good-looking. He was Mediterranean Man, born with a tan, bedroom brown eyes, and a heart-stopping grin. He could have come from anywhere in the region—Algeria, Spain, France, Italy, Greece, Israel, or Turkey—and grown up to be the local heartthrob. Okay, his looks were merely terrific. He wasn't Officially Gorgeous, the sort of man who might go off into the world and let his face and body be his fortune. Instead, Matt was the guy who would remain in his village, content with the worship of women and the admiration of men.

Once he'd distracted our grandmother with that smile, he diverted her from any new meanness by tossing her questions having vaguely to do with the subject Daisy had brought up, the house. He asked Gloria about her commute, zoning, tax structure, stuff that required more than yes or no answers. He not only kept her talking, he also appeared riveted when she went into stupefying detail about a proposed property tax rise and the burden on both businesses and local landowners. Matty's fascination seemed genuine. Truly, eyes bright and the flawless smile that showed he'd had the best orthodontia on Long Island.

Daisy's long legs, which had been rigid with tension, feet on the floor and knees tight together, relaxed and moved apart. She seemed hugely relieved at not having to come up with something else to say that might reset Gloria's nasty button.

Matt's face softened with another smile. It seemed less a response to the grandmother than a show of relief that he'd succeeded in protecting his big sister—a woman who usually didn't need protecting. Gloria, of course, must have taken his smile as being for her because she seemed to double her words per minute, which made it twice as boring. It wasn't that what she was babbling about was beyond me. I understood every word she said, every concept . . . and then some. I mean, I'd aced Property Law. But to think of it as a subject for a welcome-to-my-home chat?

What was with her? Maybe she really got off on business talk. Or she was just an egomaniac and loved to hear herself on any subject. I considered for one second that she could be starved for conversation. Who knew what her life was like? Meanwhile, Matt kept smiling.

Just then, I remembered answering the phone one day during my senior year of high school. The woman said, "This is Gloria Garrison. Is your mother home?" I stood in the kitchen holding the big receiver of our old white wall phone and trembling. I had to hold it with two hands and rest against the stepladder my mom kept open there so she could sit when she cooked because there wasn't room for a table and chairs. My voice sounded froggy as I told her no, my mother was at a meeting. I was about to say something, probably "How are you?" so she wouldn't think I was a total loser, but she said, "Your mother told me you're going to Barnard. Please tell her I said congratulations. And also . . . Tell her she doesn't have to bother calling me back." And then she hung up.

Not only was my grandmother a terrible person, she was like some desert lizard that spews poison into the air. My mom and I had our worst fight ever when she came home. I wound up screaming, "You asked her for money, didn't you? How the fuck could you ask that bitch for money? I thought you had Dad's insurance." She slapped me for saying "fuck" and maybe "bitch" and said, "Because the insurance money isn't enough for you to live at school. I was trying to figure out a way that you could have a good college experience without being burdened with sixty thousand dollars in student loans. She's never given you a dime. The worst she could do was say no."

Less than a week later, she told me that my uncle Bradley had heard from his mother about her rejection of my mom's request. He came up with the money himself, which made my mother cry with gratitude and humiliation. He said it was a gift, and his kids wouldn't know about it because . . . My mother was so emotional during the conversation she could never remember why he didn't want his kids to know, though she guessed he didn't want money (or lack of it) to taint my relationship with Daisy and Matt. My mother told me my uncle Bradley was a profoundly good man. I settled for his being a decent guy who was mortified that his mother could be so vile to her own flesh and blood. Forget the money. To send a cold congratulations to my mom and not even say "Good luck" to me?

I found myself twisting around too often to look outside, beyond the glass conservatory walls. I wasn't big on desert vistas, though the mountains on the horizon were beautiful, the genuine purple majesty business. But even the dry ground with grayish-green globs that might have been sage or sagebrush and the parched-looking undersized bushes were more comforting to me than the beautiful room we were sitting in.

I so did not belong in that house. Every object here seemed to have an extra dimension, from an invisible refrigerator dedicated solely to soda and beer to the weird luminosity of my grandmother's face—some kind of makeup that made her look like half woman, half pearl. Everything in the place seemed a little more polished, a little larger than its equivalent in the real world. In this setting, even Daisy and Matt appeared more . . . More what? I don't know. But I suspect that their having grown up well-off had given them the ability to puff themselves up slightly so they fit the specs of 63 Calle del Halcón.

What was funny was that before I arrived, I'd been feeling ashamed for wanting some of this excess. I was ashamed also for not being more my mother's daughter. As a kid, I assumed that when I grew up, I'd be transformed into as good a person as she was, that my selfishness and mean-spiritedness were just stages. Along with breasts, I'd get values.

I believed my mom was living the true good life. What better way was there than dedicating yourself to helping people who can't help themselves, being their guide through a system too complicated for them to navigate? What greater satisfaction could there be than knowing, as she must in her soul of souls, that the work you're doing was what you were put on earth to do? *What would Jesus do?* might be bumper sticker wisdom, forgotten a minute later, but if I needed a role model, all I had to do was look at what my mother did, reaching out to the poor, the uneducated, the powerless, the just plain dumb.

Yet for months I'd been yearning for something more than what she had. By more, I wasn't wishing for more intellectual stimulation or a moral challenge. I was thinking, completely and selfishly, creature comfort: a well-lighted space in which I didn't get a headache by ten every morning from fluorescent glare. I dreamed of colleagues who spoke in a genteel manner rather than whined, "I can't take the pressure." Not that they were wrong; I was stuck on style, not substance. I detested my cramped office with its dirt-smeared windows and perpetual stink of other people's microwaved lunches that permeated the halls.

What was I doing, turning my back on the significant, pining for the superficial? If you believe you're fighting the good fight, details like filthy windows shouldn't bother you. Okay, you could think, *I wish they were sparkling clean,* but then you'd get on with it. Except for me, these minuses blotted out all the pluses. I couldn't get past them.

Also, the revolting Legal Aid facilities were nothing compared to the dirtier, smellier courthouse. And then, worst of all, I hated my clients. Not only the ones who had been arrested and hadn't yet been able to avail themselves of the City of New York Department of Correction's spa facilities, individuals whose underarm and crotch odor probably wafted as far north as Chelsea. I'm talking about all the others. Truthfully, my problems with them were much bigger than hygiene: clean or dirty, raging or trembling, pleasant or semipsychotic (i.e., just rational enough that an insanity defense wouldn't work). I couldn't take dealing with them anymore. I hated the certainty that seventy-five percent of them were not only guilty of the felonies with which they were charged but were also venal, corrupt, and incorrigible as human beings.

Yes, I knew the system was supposed to work by the balancing act of prosecution and defense, and it wasn't up to me to judge them or play God. But having worked my ass off at Barnard, graduating magna when I was twenty, and NYU Law school, where I made Law Review, and gotten my dream job, I found myself shamed at my ingratitude. I could make a difference—and I didn't want to.

At night I'd sleep curled up against Hayden and long to be merged into his Goldman Sachs financial cosmos. The people he dealt with every day smelled wonderful without putting on cologne. All his windows glistened. My yearning had nothing to do with the actual work he did, because even though I could never say it to him, who the hell cared about capital markets? The truth? I didn't even care about capital all that much. I didn't want to be rich. I just wanted . . . I don't know. Something I didn't have.

Hayden Ramos-Cruz. Like I told my mother, cool on both sides of his hyphen. Well, she didn't think he was all that cool, in spite of his grandfather having been from one of the best families in Santurce, Puerto Rico, and his father being a professor of Spanish literature at Rutgers. She wasn't crazy about the hyphen either, thought it an affectation . . . not that she said it openly, but she and I always ESPed each other. When she first saw his name written out, she'd said, "*Hyphen* Cruz?" Puerto Ricans were less enamored of *apellidos compuestos,* two surnames linked by hyphen, than other Latinos.

I thought most of her objections to him were based on the fact that, in her eyes, he and I were living in sin. Not that she'd said that outright either, but I knew her well enough to know she disapproved of my moving in with him. For my mom, if two people loved each other, they got married. Period. And it wasn't only a question of morality. In her view, living together often led to an ugly breakup complete with a fight over who owns the Cuisinart. She also held it against Hayden that he didn't have "the courage" to commit, the way my dad had. It was her way of saying, *He's not man enough for you,* and probably also, *He doesn't love you enough.* It amazed me that she of all people, a social worker, couldn't understand that marriage was the biggest commitment a person can make, and it deserved thought and, yes, time.

I had to give my cousin Matt credit in the people-handling department. Gloria Garrison was still sitting back in her big white chair, her arm resting on a green pillow. Sunbeams played on it. Suddenly, I realized the thing on her right hand that I'd thought was a local handicraft—a ring of mica or some desert stone—was actually a giant diamond. I didn't know about carats, but if you hocked it, you'd probably have enough to send several kids to college and law school. Daisy caught me ogling it and, very casually, put the knuckle of her right ring finger against her teeth and grinned, as in, *Isn't that the biggest mother of a diamond you ever saw in your life?*

I smiled back at her, and maybe the light reflecting off all our teeth, plus Matt's, triggered something in our grandmother, because she said, "I was going to wait for dinner to tell you why I sent for you. But what is it Burns said? 'The best-laid schemes o' mice an' men, gang aft agley.' Most people think it's 'plans,' but it's 'schemes.'" Quickly, sneakily, she looked from one of us to another. She must have seen that Daisy was the only one who immediately got the reference. "So?" she asked. "Aren't any of you the least bit curious?"

From going to court so much, I'd learned that if you're up against someone clever, an experienced prosecutor or a smart, snide judge, you shouldn't try to be clever back. When someone is looking for a battle of wits, you win by ignoring his or her killer weapons. Instead, give a simple and (if possible) honest answer. "I'm curious," I admitted. My cousins, who were still busy formulating a response, looked relieved and nodded.

"Well," our grandmother said, "it's a long story." She put the ring hand up to her chest and took a deep breath, like she was calming her heart and oxygenating her brain. Whatever. "Where to begin?" she demanded. What did she expect? For us to make complete fools of ourselves and answer a rhetorical question? *How about at the beginning?* Matt got up and got a beer. Then we waited.

Because of my mother's work, I grew up with the motto *Do the best you can with what you have.* Not that she walked around spouting words to live by, because if there was one thing my mom wasn't, it was tedious. The opposite. I remember as a kid thinking that vacuuming was so cool because we called the vacuum a Dirt-eating Dinosaurus. It roamed around Rugland, the living room, and in the Lowlands—under the beds in our rooms.

Professionally, too, she did the best she could, which was amazing, considering an ever-decreasing departmental budget and a staff that kept getting downsized during fiscal crises. In dealing with clients at the hospital, her goal was to show them the options they had when they'd thought there were none or, if there really wasn't anything to do, then going through the process with them of assessing limitations and, ultimately, accepting reality. As far as that went, she told me—maybe a little too often—"You don't have to like reality. You just have to deal with it."

Personally, she did the best with what she had. She'd met my dad when she was nineteen and a junior at Hunter College. He was just visiting for an event, part of a conference on endangered species, a topic then not considered the big deal it now is. She was working that day, checking in conferees, guiding them to different presentations. She'd slipped into the lecture room where my dad was showing slides—mostly because it was dark and she figured she'd nap for ten minutes. But she got really moved by the plight of the black-hooded antwren and fell in love with my dad's animal photos. She had to get back to work but kept on the lookout for him just to tell him what a wonderful contribution he was making.

They were married six months later. It would have been quicker, but he had a shoot for *National Geographic* scheduled and had to leave for Botswana to photograph animal mothers with their babies.

Travis Goldberg was the love of my mom's life. Her one and only love. One minute she was half a happy couple blessed with a little girl, trying to have another kid. The next minute, she was a widow. *Do the best you can with what you have.* Two months after his death, she applied to every grad school within a fifty-mile radius of New York for a master's in social work. She got the best financial aid package from Yeshiva University, played them against Columbia, telling them they would have to up their offer. They did, but then NYU came back to her with the best deal of all, which was essentially a free education.

It had been the perfect win-win. NYU wanted a female Puerto Rican (not that they said that) and she wanted to keep as much of my dad's insurance money as she could for my education. The amazing thing was that she pulled off planning her future, researching master's programs, and negotiating with admissions offices at a time when her world had been shattered and she was in profound grief.

It was one thing to grow up with my mom's motto as my guide to life, but it was another to make the best of what you have when what you had were the Goldbergs. I mean, I sort of loved my cousins, to the degree you can say that about people you really don't know very well. But they weren't easy . . . for a million reasons. No family is if you're in it. But Bradley G & Company were always a greater strain on me than anyone on my mother's side. Our real, and pretty much only, tie to them, my dad, was gone. My mom and I not only had a different religion from theirs, we were in a different economic class. Naturally, we had to show that we respected their holidays. We went to the Passover Seder. Took the subway, then the Long Island Railroad, then . . . We were so far apart economically that it never occurred to them that it was an imposition to say, "Oh, you can get a cab at the LIRR station. Just give them the address. They know where to bring you."

Also, they weren't exactly a walk in the park to be with. There was the business of them being a family profoundly ill at ease with silence. Let a half second go by without a word being uttered and Uncle Bradley would look at the person he hadn't seen for the longest time (usually me) and say, "So, Raquel, what's news on the Rialto?" Or Aunt Cynthia would bound out of her chair and rearrange the placement of some object—potpourri bowl, peppermill—and, at the same time, babble: "I know, I know I'm obsessive-compulsive, but it disturbs me when something's out of place." Then she'd laugh what I guessed she believed was bell-like, girlish laughter (but which sounded more like a drag queen who needed practice). "Raquel, tell me. Do you think I'm *totally* insane?"

It wasn't as if my mother's family, the Calderons and the Echavarrias, sat around cloaked in silence. In fact, the Echavarrias had opinions on just about everything, including stuff they knew nothing about. Still, both could handle thirty seconds of no conversation without feeling they were being choked to death. But Daisy and Matt were like their parents in their belief that nature abhors quiet. It wasn't so hard for Matty. He was born outgoing and self-assured, perfect for what he did. It was like he hadn't chosen PR, but PR had chosen him. Words came easy to him. He had a natural desire to make people feel at ease. He could talk about anything—mostly sports, but also politics, bands I have loved, my cross-country road trip in 2007, how to make a great frittata.

It was not mindless chatter in the sense that he forgot a conversation with you two seconds after it was over. He not only asked my mom about her work whenever he saw her, he actually remembered the details of what she'd told him from one Passover to another. Matty wasn't a genius, but he wasn't dumb. Scratch that. He was pretty intelligent. The years passed, what was in or out changed, but he never had any need to steer the talk to the things most smart people prefer to hear about—books, movies, the culture of celebrity, the social networking phenomenon and how it affects interpersonal blah-blah. If you wanted to talk about ethics in contemporary life, that would be fine with Matt. If you were more the type to discuss *My Super Sweet 16* and why MTV had the greatest lineup of reality shows in the history of the world, he'd jump in, really get into the conversation, and bring up another subject only if suddenly there was silence.

I can't believe that when I was fourteen and fifteen, I had this monster crush on him. Well, I can believe it. First of all, he was a man of the world, which meant a freshman in college! Could there have been anything more sophisticated than that? Plus he was fantastic to look at and unbelievably nice. He just accepted people: There wasn't even a touch of *Go ahead, perform for me, and I'll render my decision . . . whenever I feel like it.* When you're a young teenager, it's an incredible gift to have an older, great-looking guy act as if you're really worth knowing.

It was Daisy's idea that the three of us get together during the Christmas break when she and Matty were home from college. Give them credit: They did it the right way, calling my mom, offering to come up to the Bronx to take me out to lunch. But I was already a total subway girl, taking the D train not just up to Bronx Science but also into Manhattan on weekends to hang with friends from school, and my mom told them it was fine, I could get to wherever they wanted to go on my own.

After that lunch, besides going to their house for the Seder, Daisy, Matt, and I got together two or three times a year. It was like a time-out in all our lives, I think, because though they both did all the sibling stuff, they led separate lives from one another, had their own groups of friends. At that first lunch, I inadvertently made them laugh by looking up from the menu and asking, "Don't you want to know if I really believe in Jesus as Savior?" It broke them up, gave them that high when a subject you thought couldn't be broached is brought out right in the open. Daisy said, "I definitely want to know," and Matty looked at me with so much warmth and said, "You're priceless!" He was so cool and masculine, the first guy I'd seen with the unshaven look, and I completely forgot what we were talking about until he said, "So? Do you?" And when I didn't answer right away, he prompted, "Believe in Jesus?"

I said, "Yes. Does that make me the Goldberg family scandal?"

"Of course," Daisy said. "Unless you tell us you were forced to accept it by the infamous Bronx Inquisition."

"An Inquisition . . . ," Matt started to explain.

"I know what the Inquisition was," I told him. "No, no force. That was the deal when my parents got married. My mother is pretty devout, and my father said okay, Catholic, because he didn't have any deep belief. Except he said no parochial school. My mom says there was something about kids all being dressed in uniforms that creeped him out. He told her the little girls looked like Fascists in kneesocks."

I got that weird, isolated feeling at that moment, where you're suddenly aware of your blood circulating, plus your head feels heavier and heavier. I hadn't talked much to anyone about my dad except my mom. She spoke about him a lot, and not just to keep him alive for me. To keep herself company. But sitting with my older cousins in a hip restaurant in SoHo, I was afraid I was going to cry in front them . . . which they would have understood totally. But it could mean they'd never want to have lunch with me again. Well, maybe one pity lunch.

Daisy reached over and squeezed my hand, then told me about how my dad had let her take pictures with his Rolleiflex one afternoon when we were at their house. I was about two then, so I had no memory of the day. But she told me not only about how patient he'd been but also how much fun he was. They'd lain in the grass and then climbed onto a tree branch taking shots of their dogs, Lucy and Flippy, from all different angles. He'd had the photos developed for her. She said, "If I hadn't remembered taking them, I wouldn't have believed they were mine."

So while Daisy and Matt weren't like my brother and sister, they were family, which was more than I could say about the old lady who began talking again.

Eight

Gloria

It wasn't a question of age. It came from living alone. This was how it showed itself: You were speaking. Extremely articulate. Suddenly you realized the conversation was taking place in your head. Therefore, the three people sitting across from you weren't hearing how cogent you were. All they got was silence. So instead of noticing how smart you were, they were wondering if you'd had a stroke. Well, presumably if they'd thought *Stroke!* they'd have said *Anything wrong?* maybe poked me and watched if I flopped over sideways. For all I knew, they weren't thinking *Stroke!* They were going eeny meeny miny mo between dementia and catatonia.

But it must have been the thought of a stroke that gave me a flash of Billy, Keith's partner. Dying in the ICU, unvisited by me. In that flash, my imagination saw what I hadn't: his arms, pale, pierced with IVs, resting on top of a white sheet.

God, how my nonvisit had wrecked my long-term strategy. If I'd realized how irrationally Keith would react, against his own self-interest and my meticulous plans for succession, I probably would have forced myself to go.

"I'm thinking," I said aloud. Well, I had to say something so they'd know I was compos mentis. Anyway, having announced that I'd tell them why I invited them to Santa Fe, how could I not tell them? Well, I could indeed say nothing. I could do whatever I wanted. But what was the point? I was stuck.

"It's like this," I began. Matthew immediately quit reading the label on the beer bottle. Daisy, who, half a second before, had exhibited the fuzzy eyes of a person watching some movie playing on inside her own head, turned her attention to me. But that Raquel seemed as if she couldn't stop looking over her shoulder at the saguaro cactus in the nature preserve just beyond my property line. Reluctantly, she finally untwisted her torso so she was facing me. In that instant she looked so much like Travis. Except smaller. And brown.

"I told you I'd explain why I invited the three of you here," I said. "The explanation itself is fairly simple, but I'm expecting it will . . ." Damn, what was the word? In a minute they'd be giving each other those sideways she-lost-her-train-of-thought glances. *Start up? Begin? Engender isn't right. Oh, I know.* ". . . stimulate a conversation that will continue throughout the weekend. Maybe beyond. But the truth of the matter is that once I make up my mind, it's made up for good. I am not the sort who looks back. And if I say so myself, I'm a fast thinker. We should be able to wrap this up fairly quickly. By that I mean days, not weeks."

"Wrap what up?" Raquel asked. Her

brow was neither furrowed in confusion nor raised in disdain. I would have expected a snide attitude from her, not the casual indifference with which she asked the question. "Wrap what up?" was what you'd expect from a lawyer—a bored one—who wanted a bulleted agenda so she could check off the items and get the hell out of the meeting. She was seated farthest from me. Not just that, but now she was sitting all the way into the chair, so far back her feet didn't touch the floor.

Not that I'm prejudiced, but I never liked short women. All too often they wrapped every work and act of theirs with cuteness. They'd say *Oooh* when *Oh* would do. They'd pin back their hair with tiny plastic barrettes as if God had not created taste. They'd stand too close to you and stare at you with their heads back, like you were a human Mt. Rushmore. True, there was a minority of shorties who shunned cute. Those were the dangerous ones you have to keep your eye on all the time. They were like those tiny sharks that a diver asks himself about—*These little things aren't the ones that bite, are they?*—in the instant before his arm gets ripped off his body. At the moment, though, Raquel was a quiescent shark.

"Patience," I told her. "You know how they say, 'Patience is its own reward'?" Neither she nor the other two overeducated know-nothings had a clue to what I meant by that, so I simply kept going. "Think back now. When each of you came of age, I had my attorney draft a letter, which I signed. It informed you not to expect to get anything when I die. Correct? You recall receiving that letter?"

Daisy was the only one who answered: yes. I hadn't expected her to be the one to speak when an awkward subject came up. Not only that. Her "yes" sounded matter-of-fact. I couldn't detect any underlying hostility about not being in line for an inheritance, and I happened to be the Sherlock Holmes of hostility detection. Matthew and Raquel merely nodded.

"So as not to keep you in suspense in case you're thinking that I've changed my mind, don't. I intend to leave whatever money and property I have, aside from the business, to charity." To coin one of my ex-husband's favorite phrases, I really didn't give a rat's ass about charity. But my trust and estates lawyer practically held a gun to my head to get me to come up with a list, so I'd chosen the few that didn't make me want to vomit. Planned Parenthood, the Nature Conservancy, the ASPCA. I forget the others. I would have said the hell with it and given it all to the Red Cross, but years earlier I'd heard that during World War II, or maybe it was World War I, they refused to offer coffee and donuts to Jewish soldiers. "So if you're planning on a five-thousand-square-foot loft in Williamsburg, or whatever it is people your age covet, I will not be paying for it in this lifetime or postmortem."

Interestingly, it was the girls who were able to keep poker faces. Matthew appeared . . . I suppose taken aback would be the most accurate description. He actually jerked back his head in surprise. If I had to guess, it wasn't at not making my list of heirs as much as surprise at my bluntness. Not that I held it against him.

I'd made up my mind not to hold anything against any of them. That was my firm decision even before I asked Emily, my assistant, to send them the invitations. I was going to suspend judgment on them until the very end. Taken aback, not taken aback: It really didn't matter one whit. In business dealings, the knack of covering up whatever it is you're feeling is highly overrated. When you're negotiating, the person opposite you on the other side of the table might be unreadable. On the other hand, he might beam with delight at your wonderfulness. Or perhaps he would glare as if he'd relish using you for target practice with his favorite assault rifle. Whatever. Once you started negotiating, no matter what your opponent felt about you, he would try to hammer you into the ground and to get the best deal possible.

"There is one aspect of my . . . Shall we call it wealth, to be perfectly frank, or perhaps crude, depending on your sensibilities? One aspect does concern you. I'm talking about my company, Glory. I went from nothing—all right, from two-broken down trucks with over two hundred thousand miles on them—and created a business that last year netted over eleven million. That's what we're talking about this weekend: Glory. I assume you know what it does?"

All three of them actually spoke. "Yes."

"Just to be clear. We now have a fleet of trucks. Eighteen-wheeler semis." Predictably, Matthew was the only one who didn't look flummoxed, though my guess was the closest he'd ever come to a semi was seeing one overturned on the Long Island Expressway. "Cab over engine with a box trailer. You know. A big box trailer." Clueless. "The thing that looks like a big rectangular box. We've basically divided the trailer into two unequal parts, sizewise. The smaller space is for hair and makeup, the larger for fashion and accessories makeovers. The client and the consultant choose what to wear from our samples, and the clients receive their new wardrobe within two weeks. If they want to pay the

FedEx charges, we can even overnight it to them.

"We employ professional drivers who get the trucks from city to city, hook up to power, the water supply, literally do the heavy lifting. You cannot have a fashion consultant driving an eighteen-wheeler. Doesn't work, safetywise, insurancewise. We concentrate solely on small cities. Any urban area with over fifty thousand could probably sustain an upscale salon and department store with a personal shopper to provide the services we offer, though of course not at the level of quality we give. We're not just one-stop shopping. We're known for enormous value for the money. Our people are the best. Just being great isn't good enough. Our hairdressers have to be first-rate—and I mean *first-rate*—and they have to be makeup artists as well. They are the best cosmeticians money can buy. Our fashion consultants are top of the line, too. None of that, 'Oh, darling, that looks divine on you!' as they offer a size-twenty muumuu. We don't do muumuus." I focused on Matthew, "Do you know what a muumuu is?"

"A big dress with flowers? Like in Hawaii?"

"Precisely. We do not condescend to our clients. Size zero, size twenty-four, we offer them fashion wisdom, sophisticated style analysis, the finest in beauty treatments. At a not-unreasonable price. Women save up their money for us, wait for us, sometimes for two or three years after they book an appointment. Often, while they're with us, they make an appointment for their daughters, for when they turn eighteen. We don't do underage. It's a highly profitable market segment but too risky from an insurance point of view and lawsuitwise. But for the young woman who's eighteen or nineteen, 'Going to Glory' is a rite of passage." I cleared my throat, which I try not to do too often because it's a thing old people do. Disgusting. Then they spit out a glob of mucus and look at it in the tissue like they were inspecting the Hope diamond. What is wrong with them? Don't they care? "Any questions?" All three shook their heads. "How can you not have any questions?"

For once, Matthew didn't flash his teeth, though his manner remained benevolent, relaxed. I didn't seem to have intimidated him. "We probably have lots of questions about your company, about you," he said. "But does it make sense to ask them now when we don't know what you're intending? Speaking for me, finding out how you vet potential employees, say, would be really interesting. But why stop for the details now? We'd much rather hear about why you wanted to see us."

"Well, I do have one quick question," Daisy said. Her eyebrows! Her mother, for God's sake, who couldn't leave anything undisturbed or undecorated, let her routinely fly to L.A. to meet with film people looking like that? And all right, maybe Daisy was tempted to do the opposite of whatever Cynthia suggested—which generally would be a sound policy—but could Daisy honestly believe it was wise to resemble Groucho Marx? Tweezing eyebrows isn't neurosurgery. Anyone can do it. In less than sixty seconds I could show her how to draw an imaginary line from a little farther than the outer corner of her iris straight up, where her arch ought to begin. That way, her brow ridge could show. And why not? She had good bones. What was she, twenty-seven? Twenty-eight? No, she was the oldest of the three, so she was pushing thirty. Already she'd given up on her looks instead of owning them. Give me one day with her and she'd be like one of our clients who say, "Glory changed my life forever!"

"What should we call you?" she was asking me.

"I don't know. I hadn't thought about that." Naturally I had, but I was hoping one of them would say *Ms. Garrison* or *Gloria* and then they'd all call me that. "I'm sure none of you are tempted to call me Grammy. Am I correct?"

"Correct," Raquel said. She wasn't overtly antagonistic, though I had no doubt she detested me. Still, I had to admit that the girl had a certain decorum about her. Well, Travis had been not only a charmer but also a man with beautiful, easy manners. And her mother, Adriana, who of course didn't have his personal warmth, knew enough to stress etiquette after he was gone—along with the virgin birth, good penmanship, and God only knew what else. Right from the start, Adriana had been a stickler for doing the correct thing. Two weeks after the honeymoon, she'd written all her thank-you notes.

"Good," I said, "because the notion of being called Grammy is too appalling to contemplate." I took a deep breath. "All right. Call me Gloria."

I couldn't help it. I had to clear my throat again. "So here is this highly successful company and over the years I not only built it up, I put in place a careful plan of succession. Years ago, I hired the COO of Regalia." Three pairs of eyes, all vacant. "Women's clothing, accessories. A chain of boutiques that folded in the mid-'90s. Before that, this fellow had been at the Limited. Anyway, Keith—that was his name—I trained him. After, I don't know, ten years or so I realized he would one day be equipped to take over the company and not sabotage it."

"Did he die?" Daisy asked.

"No, he didn't die." I probably snapped at her, though I couldn't say she seemed subdued, the way some people got. More like annoyed. Her annoyance probably doubled once she made the decision not to snap back. Well, at least she wasn't as wishy-washy, artsy-fartsy as I'd thought. "His partner died, though. Partner in life, not business. It shook Keith up. He made crazy decisions. Decided to leave Glory, and no amount of logic could stop him."

Even though I was in my favorite chair, the most comfortable, I was starting to hurt. No, ache. Ache to the point of real pain. Right in the back, where the shoulders curve out from the neck. I was always sore there, so much so that the thought of someone touching it almost made me want to whimper. Often those muscles felt stretched to the point of ripping apart. It was as if someone had hooked lead weights way into my flesh every few centimeters. That's when the pain migrated from a part of my consciousness to where it was the only fact of my life.

If I could have just closed my eyes for a couple of minutes, done some deep breathing, the hurt might have subsided. But I didn't want the three of them to start thinking, *Uh-oh, she falls asleep in the middle of her sentence.* I was in torment. My shoulders were so bad this time I couldn't even reach for the phone to buzz Carlos to get my naproxen.

It didn't help that none of them seemed willing to break the lull in the conversation. Maybe they sensed something, like I was in pain. Or maybe they were simply stupid and insensitive. Four years of college for Daisy and Matthew, and four plus three of law school for Raquel. What where they? Morons with diplomas. For God's sake, I moved to New York City and was earning my own living when I was seventeen, eighteen, never had a shot at college, and I had more brains—to say nothing of intuitive knowledge—than any of those three imbeciles.

"Would you like me to get you some water or something else to drink?" Daisy finally asked.

I took a deep, slow breath, then blew it out fast. "No. All right, an iced tea. The peach. Diet." I prayed she'd think to bring a glass and unscrew the top of the damned bottle for me. "So Keith, who I long assumed would be taking over Glory when I retired or died, whichever came first, as lawyers are so fond of saying—pulled out of our deal. And there I was . . . No, here I am with no one in the least way suitable to take over my business." I felt like adding, *including any of you, you nitwits.*

I had to give Daisy credit if only in the iced tea department. She not only chose the right glass, the heavy-bottomed one, she asked if I wanted ice, poured the tea, and brought it over with a coaster. No doubt she picked up her social skills from her mother, Cynthia, a woman of extremely limited intellect who nonetheless did possess the ability to make a dinner party as well as choose stylish upholstery welting.

When I hurt I can get peevish, so I almost snapped at them, *Why the hell aren't you asking why Keith pulled out of the business?* Because by this time, my answer was ready, not just smoother than silk, but credible in the extreme. However, just as I was about to tell them about Keith, I realized one of them might claim that I was avoiding the subject—why I brought them out to Santa Fe.

"So, here is my position. I certainly have plenty of options." I had one, and it stank. "I could sell Glory. Guaranteed, whoever bought it would want to grow the business ten, fifteen percent annually. They'd run it into the ground because no one, *no one,* new to Glory could do the due diligence on employees and training I personally do. No one knows beauty lines and clothing manufacturers like I do. I'm a walking repository of information on transforming looks and lives. No investor would have the patience or the smarts to learn from me."

They were already getting what I was saying, or part of it. They flashed glances at each other at a speed they thought I couldn't catch.

"I could hire an MBA with five to ten years' experience in beauty or fashion, pay her double or triple what she's worth. And then what? If she doesn't work out in three or four years, I could hire somebody else who might do better and offer that person the option of buying me out after a certain period. Well, what if *that* didn't work? Litigate? Hire yet another person? I'll be eighty on my next birthday." This was not a news bulletin to any of them. I hadn't a doubt in the world that on my last birthday, when the only two cards I got came from the two people who irritate me most profoundly, Adriana—Señora Goldberg—and Bradley, both of them had probably suggested, *Do you want to send a birthday card to your grandmother?* Of course not. Why would they want to send a card to me any more than I'd want to send one to them?

If I had to lose a son, why did it have to be Travis? How can a person believe in a God who could make such a vicious choice? Or such a stupidly arbitrary one? Maybe God was all-powerful but had the brains of Tully Morrison, the maître d' at La Villa Real Country Club. Or that other supreme idiot. What was his name? W's attorney general. Oh, Alberto Gonzales, that ass. People like that, who were as far from omniscient as you can get without being certifiably stupid. Maybe God was omnipotent yet had only a 101 IQ.

"I might have the energy," I continued, "but I don't have the willingness to train a stranger who might turn out not to be capable. And I might not have the time to complete the training, although my doctor says I'm healthy as a horse. Still, I could wake up tomorrow morning . . . Or not wake up. So here's my plan."

So much for Generation Whatever's famous cool. All right, none of them was audibly panting. But each leaned forward, as if getting ready to leap up and grab what I was offering.

"I will choose one of you—only one—to come to Santa Fe, learn everything I have to teach about Glory, and inherit the business. I don't believe in partnerships or co-anything. So no cousin duos, no brother-sister act. One of you will get Glory. The other two will get . . . nothing."

Nine

Daisy

When my grandmother . . .

Oops, now she's Gloria. Anyhow, when Gloria said, "The other two will get nothing," I got this crazed urge to laugh. Her "nothing" was so mean it was comical, the real-life correlative of a silent movie villain twirling his mustache.

However, I managed a straight face. Even I, Ms. Art Trumps Commerce, understood that while speaking of a corporate entity that nets over eleven mil a year (and is worth God knows how much), laughter was inappropriate. Also, if I started guffawing, it might make the rest of the weekend a tad awkward—at least for me.

So I was amused, but not tempted. My brother, however, didn't have to fight any urge to yuk it up. Quite the opposite. His eyebrows were drawn together and he'd sucked his lips into an anxious slit, not Matty's usual expression. Even as a kid, he'd been forever nonchalant. Unflappable Boy. Whether he actually understood what was going on at any particular moment didn't matter. He always appeared to. While this kind of aplomb may have been an asset for the Life Lite he seemed to want to live, it also meant he didn't get the world's uglier stuff. Deviousness? Matty could read about a cunning maneuver by a sports agent representing a ballplayer and get it totally. Yet when it came to politics—of the national, sexual, or family variety—he was sometimes surprisingly dumb. Evil? That there were those beyond Nazis and the guys with Russian accents in James Bond movies who were intentionally cruel? Not in Matty's world. Over his head. But being a cool dude like my brother meant either being numb from birth, which he wasn't, or having an inner censor who bleeped bad news.

But maybe I was underestimating him. Since I'd gone off to college and left Matty to finish his last two years at Shorehaven High School, he might have developed more sensitive antennae. Maybe by now he could accept all of reality, not just the nice parts. When you grow up with a sibling, you feel you know him completely, as if no development can occur past age fifteen, or whenever you go your separate ways.

So here he was, brows pulled together and lipless. Okay, he wasn't taking this lightly. Maybe, like me, he knew he was obliged to consider our grandmother's announcement thoughtfully if not seriously and was hard at work trying to make sense of the offer. Not just, *Is there anything in this for me?* but also, *What's in this for Gloria? Why is such a selfish, greedy woman making such a magnanimous gesture? Well, magnanimous to only one out of three, but that's better than her old batting average. Or is the offer really magnanimous? Could there be some kind of cruel gotcha at the end of this rainbow?*

His face resembled a tightly closed fist. It was clear he didn't have any answers. Well, I certainly didn't either, beyond the obvious personal reaction of, *I wouldn't touch Glory with a ten-foot pole. And live in Santa Fe?* There wasn't a superfluity of oxygen at seventy-five hundred feet, and you wound up thinking, *Oh. It's time to inhale again. Better do it fast before asphyxia sets in.* Also, the driver had taken us past downtown on the way from the airport. It was called a city, and no doubt it was, but to me it had the kitsch look of an Old Southwest set conceived by a designer with a big budget and small imagination. Admittedly, my brother had said "Cool," and my cousin gave an "Ooh!" of appreciation; maybe there was some elusive charm I wasn't getting.

Anyway, I was dying to talk it over with Raquel and Matty. God, if only the three of us could have been teleported to some nearby bar. In the shade of a big white umbrella, we could sip margaritas and figure out how come, after years of ignoring us, this woman had suddenly chosen to tap one of us to be the heir to a healthy part of her fortune.

"*Well?*" Gloria was asking. The next second she sprang up, though to do it, she had to push down hard on the over-upholstered chair arms for leverage. Still, a pretty fluid movement. "Have the three of you nooo reactions? Nooo questions?" Even though the quality of her voice bordered on pleasing, she had icy sarcasm that could freeze your guts and crack your soul. "What am I suppoooosed to think?" Also, there was something unnatural in her speech, like she'd taken elocution lessons. She sounded vaguely British, like those best supporting actresses in 1940s movies. "I'm not seeing rapid response reflexes at work in any of you, am I?"

She crossed her thin arms over her narrow chest and eyed us . . . I guess you could say derisively. It would definitely have been with one eyebrow raised in contempt if she'd been capable of that sort of expression. Maybe she'd done that a lot in the old days but had forgotten she was now Botoxed into rigidity; my mom totally lost her ability to express either surprise or delight, not that either happened often. "Am I?" she repeated.

Though I couldn't care less about getting Glory, I still felt zapped by the scorn rays coming out of her brown eyes. Weird: Brown eyes are supposed to be warm. Objectively, her eyes were still lovely, unusually large with that intriguing upward slant. But something was off about the light coming from them, as if the irises had been Photoshopped in a clumsy attempt to get rid of redeye. Her eyes didn't look exactly dead, but neither were they fully alive.

There was no sign of Matty chilling to become Mr. PR once more, perform a charm offensive, and get Gloria off her "nooo questions" assault. So I waited for Raquel. Of all of us, she should be the one speaking up. Number one, she didn't seem at all intimidated by Gloria. Second, she was an actual criminal lawyer. I'd gone downtown once to watch one of her trials, and not only did she seem twice as good as Casey Novak on *Law and Order: SVU,* she hadn't been scared by a judge who looked like Medusa in a black robe (only uglier) or by the squawking vulture of a defense lawyer. So if Raquel was the complete nonshrinking violet, why wasn't she speaking up? Instead, she sat there holding her left hand on an upward tilt and studying her fingertips like she was planning her magnum opus, *The Art of the Cuticle.* Finally and foremost, of the three of us, Gloria had done Raquel the most damage. After my uncle Travis died, my grandmother, for the most part, acted as if he'd never married, never had a child.

Not that she gave Matty and me any financial help, but we didn't need it. And we never received a single gift from her either. But Matty and I were privileged suburban kids who didn't want for anything. Well, we always thought we did, but at the mere thought of *I don't have a . . .* we'd go to work on our parents. Nine times out of ten, we'd have our heart's desire on our next birthday or Hanukkah or as a last-day-of-school present.

It wasn't that Adriana was poor and couldn't afford to take care of Raquel without a handout. But she might have wished she could get her daughter out of the Bronx for the summer to a cool camp in the woods, or send her to private school, or move from their apartment building with its corridors smelling of old carpet and neighbors' dinners to a beautiful little Tudor in Riverdale. Not a chance. Gloria never bought Raquel anything, not even a pack of bubble gum.

And while Gloria visited us on occasion, in the years when she still came to New York, she went to the Bronx only once. When she got there, she had her driver call Adriana from a pay phone (those were pre–cell phone days) to say Miss Garrison had a migraine, but could Adriana bring Raquel downstairs for a "quick hello." Adriana told my dad that "hello" lasted less than five minutes with Gloria closing her eyes in supposed pain and massaging a spot right above the bridge of her nose nearly the whole time.

So okay, Raquel probably didn't have

a single good memory of Gloria. But she definitely had no fear of her. Raquel wasn't a fearful person. Even if she were, what could an old woman—albeit a really, really rich old woman—do to hurt her? You can't disinherit someone when there's no inheritance to begin with. Yell? My cousin could stand up to anyone in a courtroom and her voice could blow Gloria all the way to Albuquerque. What could a makeover queen do to defeat Raquel? Tell her long hair was wrong, too much for her small valentine of a face? (Actually, it was.) Raquel would shrug off any criticism; she seemed to possess the healthy self-image that adds months to a woman's life by obliterating the need to read self-help articles in *Glamour.*

I was pissed. How pathetic, that the two public people, Matty and Raquel, had withdrawn into silence, leaving the response to the person who sat alone in an office and read books for a living.

"After putting that sort of offer on the table," I finally said, grateful that words were actually coming out, "I can see it's reasonable of you to expect some reaction from us—even a 'Wow!' if not an immediate 'Thank you.' I can't speak for Matty and Raquel on this, but for me, this is too big a deal for any kind of rapid response."

Gloria's arms were still crossed in front of her, but she seemed to relax them. With that, her shoulders dropped into a less antagonistic posture. "Rapid response is a valuable tool," she said. "Sometimes in business you have to turn on a dime. Bim-bam-boom. Move fast or lose your chance."

"That's definitely true in the film business. But turning on a dime doesn't always give you the time to absorb a complex set of facts and analyze them. You need to do due diligence."

"I trust my gut," Gloria countered. It came out more like a challenge than a statement, implying that I didn't or couldn't trust my gut, and that was one point in my debit column. It would have been nice to know how many points each of us would be allowed to accumulate before she ripped up our . . . balance sheet or whatever it was called:

Clearly, I was not cut out to run a multimillion-dollar company.

"I trust my gut, too," I said. "I'll be four pages into a novel and all of a sudden I not only know there's a movie in it, but exactly which production company at Paramount should be making it. But there's still getting around possible competition from other studios, strategizing, negotiating. And that's stuff I've learned for the last seven years. If all you needed was a gut, we could hand over the world to shrewd eighteen-year-olds."

"Glory isn't glam like the movie business," Gloria said. She seemed to be accusing me of something, but I wasn't sure of what, or if she'd just changed the subject. "Just because we do beauty and fashion doesn't mean we're into glitz. You can't compare your industry with mine."

I wanted to say, *Do I look like I'm into glitz?* But she might come back with *No. Of course not.* More than once in the short time we'd been together she'd checked me out. Then, blink, blink, she'd look to Raquel and Matty and spend much longer surveilling them. I carried on: “What you’re offering here is not just entrée into a business we know nothing about—well, I guess I shouldn’t speak for my brother and Raquel—but a completely different way of life. You want one of us to trade in what he or she has now for a new city, new colleagues, and . . .” I had that irresistible urge to swallow combined with a totally dry mouth, so my next sentence began with a low *glup,* which came out like I was really choked up. “One of us would eventually have responsibility for the future of a successful business and the security of its employees. That’s huge.”

Why I was saying this I hadn’t a clue. To me, it wasn’t so huge. True, at twenty-nine I was loveless, but it wasn’t like I had nothing to hold me in a job that enabled me to utter lines you dream of saying during adolescence, like, “Sorry, I’m in L.A. the beginning of next week.” There were friends, there was my Upper West Side nonclaustrophobic studio apartment decorated by my mom. I didn’t want to run a business, even one in which I could probably get my hair blown out free every other day. Every day: *Fuck the profit margin. Do my hair.*

Gloria turned to my brother and Raquel. "You other two!" Even though she wore silky clothes and a wide bracelet woven from yellow, rose, and white gold, her words could have been barked by an army sergeant to new recruits. "How come you're letting Daisy do the talking?"

My cousin smiled at Gloria so sweetly I thought, *Uh-oh.* "Now really," Raquel said. "'You other two'? What is this, Gloria? Divide and conquer? Put us into competition to outtalk Daisy?"

"Most certainly not! I'm simply trying"—Gloria left her position standing in front of her grand chair and paced around where the three of us were seated—"to find out what's going on inside your heads. Here you are, two professional talkers, a public relations man and a criminal lawyer, and what do I hear from you?" She lowered her voice to a sibilant whisper. "Silence." *Très dramatique,* like she was Hamlet offering his final word. "I find that response, shall we say, curious. I won't add rude."

"You just did," Raquel came back, this time minus the smile. "In any case, Daisy gave a good rundown of the reasons not to go the rapid response route. As she said, I can only speak for myself, not my cousins. But I don't think any of us were intentionally rude. I was raised to be courteous and, from all I've ever seen of Daisy and Matt, so were they. But how could we speak out when we're still taking it all in?"

Raquel stood, took the few steps over to Gloria, and cut off her pacing. It looked almost comical, someone maybe five foot two stopping someone five seven or eight, except it was such a confrontational move. Not that Gloria acted like she was at all cowed. She just locked her arms a little tighter around herself.

"Look," my cousin kept on, "the three of us have obviously talked about what you might have planned for the weekend, and we came up with all sorts of possibilities. But this was one that never occurred to us—this offer, proffer, whatever you want to call it. The only thing we assumed you had in mind, beyond the plane tickets—and thank you for those, by the way, loved those business-class seats—was room and board for this weekend." Raquel wasn't being kind or trying to get on our grandmother's good side. Her courtesy was no-frills, the way a well-bred person would speak to a robot. The human would be polite not because the object she's talking to has feelings but simply because that's the way she'd been brought up to interact.

While Raquel was talking, I felt sib vibes from Matty. Brothers and sisters may not have that telepathy twins have, but there's some wordless communication that arises from growing up in the same house. You know when your sibling is looking at you, as Matty was. And when his head lifts up a half inch, you somehow understand it means, *I want to stand because Raquel and Gloria are, and I don't want you to feel awkward being the only one who's sitting.* So we rose in the same instant.

"I have a suggestion," Matty said to Gloria. "Well, if it's okay with you. This is your ball game. But maybe we should quit talking about our reactions to your offer and get to the offer itself, either the substance of it or . . ." He did his usual smile + boyish shrug business. It worked well when he was about to say something that could theoretically piss off the listener. "There was that mention of due diligence." Sure enough, a shadow of a smile passed over Gloria's face. Not an actual smile with happy eyes but at least some small social response. "The thing is, you don't know us. I'm curious about what makes you think any of us would be competent to take over your company. You said you might decide in a matter of days. Is that enough time to find out if one of us is . . . I don't know . . . a sociopath or a compulsive gambler?"

"Gambler?" Gloria said. She looked quizzical, as if the word had popped out from somebody else's universe into hers.

"Or closet drug user, alcoholic. Gambling's a big issue in sports. That's why it came to mind."

"You brought up due diligence before, about vetting the people who work for me. How do you think I do it?"

"Some sort of background search, I guess," Matty said. Now that the four of us were standing, it was awkward. I wish she'd thought to have some chips or crudités around. I, for one, was hungry, but not for those little sandwiches on wet bread. How about real snacks? That would have given us something to do. Potato chips, which I love as much as life itself, celery sticks, guacamole, and it's a party. Maybe she was cheap. Maybe she never entertained. Maybe, considering she was a size four or six, she had no appetite. "I guess you'd want to check whether someone has a criminal record."

"Well, how do you think I get this information? Out of the air? Do a quick Google search?" With each question, she sounded a little more snide, no mean feat.

Matty's expression couldn't have been more pleasant. "Why not just tell me?" he suggested.

Gloria's expression couldn't have been more sour. No shadow of a smile this time. “I have a detective agency on retainer. That’s how. Think about that. Dinner will be at seven. Carlos will show you to your rooms.”

Ten

Gloria

I'm so mad I could spit. No: so *angry* I could spit, because mad means crazy. Well, all right. I concede I must have been temporarily certifiable when I decided to hand over Glory to one of those ingrate, idiot grandchildren.

And did my lawyers do anything to stop me? No, they were always too busy fighting over what art to put up on their walls to pay attention to clients—even though we're the ones who shell out four hundred dollars an hour. And what do we get for the money? Bad advice and the chance to sit in the conference room and stare at a pathetic homage to Monet's water lilies by someone obsessed with purple. Oh, and also a charcoal Christ bent by the weight of the cross on his back; it's so lacking in perspective you knew it had to have been executed by a senior partner's wife whose art hobby had, sadly, never been discouraged.

Did even one of these lawyers have the courage to demand of me, *Are you insane, Ms. Garrison?* when I came up with the idea of endowing one of my grandchildren with Glory? Did they counsel me on how imprudent it would be to bring in a New York bigmouth with no business background? No, their backbones dissolved. They turned to mush. As we sat around that conference table, they took turns offering odes: "To the Family Business" and "O Joy, Passing Along What You Have Created."

That's the thing about lawyers: Unless you take off all your clothes and then, naked, shrieking and foaming at the mouth, set fire to their law library, they behave as if your decisions are rational and it's their job to carry out your wishes.

How crazy I was just an hour ago, choosing the conservatory to reveal my plan to the grandchildren because it was such a sunlit, optimistic space—even though there was a good chance if any one of them got close enough he or she'd be able to spot the crosshatch lines on my cheeks. Faint lines, true, but Dr. Morvillo, *the* best cosmetic dermatologist in L.A., was honest with me and said she couldn't make them disappear completely without risking permanent damage to my skin. Anyway, I chose that magnificently bright space, put my age and vulnerability on display, and offered one of those three Gs the chance of a lifetime. I mean, ninety-nine percent of the people in the world would get chills up their spines, tears in their eyes at hearing such an opportunity could be theirs. Hearts would swell with gratitude. They'd cry, *Thank you, thank you,* for even considering them.

But these three little shits? See? They have pushed me to the point of using bad language. What did I get from them? Silence, followed by Daisy's tortured explanation, as though I was some ninny who'd never dealt with people. And then the other two—"I can't speak for so-and-so, but . . ."—saying thank you not out of any genuine gratitude or even reflexive courtesy but because they couldn't be blatantly rude after I'd treated them to business-class airplane tickets. And this is the generation that won't shut up about values.

I'm setting my alarm for five forty-five so I can reapply my makeup. Meanwhile, I'm just going to lie here on my bed with a cashmere throw over my legs and shut my eyes. I love this room. It's nothing like the rest of the house, but it's what I dreamed of as a child and never forgot. A four-poster bed with a canopy. Not with the lacy top little girls have, but an antique George III bed with carved posts and molded arched cornice of the most exquisite satinwood. The fabric on the bed, sheets, shams, blanket, the wallpaper, carpet: all custom-made for me in the silvery blue of a morning sky in some lovely country I've never visited.

I turned off my alarm. I won't sleep and I can't rest.

There's simply one way to correct the mistake that I take full responsibility for. Rescind the offer to the Odious Three. In an hour, I'll go downstairs, have a civilized dinner with them (i.e., I won't spit in their faces), and then, over regular or decaf espresso, very politely inform them: "I regret to say you're all grossly inadequate. It's an impossible choice and I cannot bring myself to make it. I've worked too hard for what I've achieved. The party's over. Carlos will arrange for your departure first thing tomorrow. You'll be back in your beloved New York by evening."

♪♪ I hate New York.

I truly do. Business trips there are always a trial. Most times I don't call Bradley to tell him I'm in town, but I always have this irrational fear that I'll run into him and Cynthia in whatever restaurant I choose, as if we have some genetic predisposition to choose the same cuisine on the same night. Half the time I wind up having room service at the Ritz-Carlton—the halibut, with

Parmesan french fries instead of the rice—rather than being wined and dined by a Bumble and Bumble or an Elizabeth Arden executive.

But I hate Cincinnati more. It's not even a contest. I left at seventeen and would never, ever go back there. Disgusting, vicious city.

Well, except for my grandfather, Louie Goldberg. Louie, the only one in the family who was anything like me. He'd stop off at our house every Saturday after synagogue. Every single week, he hung his head, then shook it sadly when my mother would tell him my father was working. "Oy," he'd exhale. "What's wrong with finding a job where he doesn't have to work for anti-Semites?" That was the only thing that got him down, the fact of his son working on the Sabbath.

"The people who own Shillito's are Jewish, Louie," my mother told him.

"And they let Jews work? You know what that makes them?" He raised his index finger into the air and shook it, like he was a prophet passing on to the Israelites God's latest complaint. "I'll tell you what it makes them. Double anti-Semites!" Then he'd say some Yiddish words about my father's employers that he didn't want me to understand. My mother would shrug—an art form she perfected—and offer him lunch, which he always turned down because we weren't kosher. Maybe he had also heard of my mother's magic, her spell for turning an animal protein into garlic-flavored rubber. Not that he was a gourmet. Since my Grandma Gitel had died, two years before I was born, he ate sour cream for breakfast and took a salami sandwich for lunch to the factory where he rolled cigars. For dinner he ate boiled eggs and ice cream.

He loved me. "Gloria, sweetheart, you should come to shul with me again." He said this only when my mother was out of earshot. But I couldn't oblige him. I wasn't an eight-year-old agnostic, just a girl who couldn't take sitting upstairs with women who smelled like camphor balls and being seated next to the rabbi's daughter, whose name I heard as Frizzele, which it was not, but when I called her that, she took it as an insult.

She was a pallid ten-year-old who knew all the Hebrew prayers and swayed when she prayed.

"I don't like it upstairs," I told him. "I'm sorry, Grandpa Louie."

"But that's how it is," he said.

I must have squeezed out a few tears to close the deal, though I was sincere when I told him, "I hate it there."

Like me, my grandfather was filled with energy. He looked it too: a natty dresser, all dressed up for shul in a suit and bow tie, tall for his generation, and thin. He walked the two miles between his little house and the Orthodox shul at a clip that left all the other old men breathless.

"Don't be angry, Grandpa."

"At you? Please. I'm a little disappointed that I can't promenade with a pretty girl on Shabbos morning. That's all."

About a month later, he left his Orthodox place behind and joined a Conservative one where men and women could sit together. For me. After that, every Saturday, rain, snow, sunshine, we walked to and from synagogue together. A couple of swells: him in his ever-changing bow tie, me in a dress and Mary Janes with white socks or else galoshes. We discussed the outfits of passersby. I told him about the kids in my class and he told me about the other cigar rollers and his boss, Mr. Schultz. My grandfather was a talker; he could make Bible stories sound more riveting than any movie serial cliffhanger: ". . . and then what do you think that no-goodnik Mrs. Potiphar did?"

Who knows? I might now be saying, *Cincinnati was a nice city to grow up in.* Except two days before my eleventh birthday, Grandpa Louie had a heart attack. The next day he was dead.

So, my Cincinnati: Everybody talks about the '50s as the decade of sexual repression and hypocrisy. But that's only because they never lived in Ohio in the late '40s. Our Boys were home from Europe and the Pacific, and all they wanted . . . Nowadays they say the greatest generation was searching for "security" or "normalcy." But they also wanted to screw themselves blind. Deaf and dumb too if they could get it. Of course the younger high school boys had a similar goal.

But sex for these younger boys meant high school coeds. However, we weren't available. With the exception of the random slut, we were virgins. We had to be if we wanted all the good things in life. Looking at pictures from that era, all of us seemed to meld into one untouchable Good Girl. We had the same look, the way members of a cult do. Peachy clean, with shiny cheeks and bright eyes, and perky pageboys held in check with a strategic barrette. We knew to avoid that bad-girl Lauren Bacall or Veronica Lake come-hither look, that erotic dip of hair falling over one eye.

So what were the boys to do? They pressured their good-girl girlfriends to go all the way, but expected—silently demanded—resistance. As a result, they were always on the prowl, searching for a slut, a whore, a tramp willing to unlatch the barrette and let herself go.

I myself never ran much risk of looking slutty. Not in those days or ever. At five seven and a half, one hundred ten pounds, I was considered practically a scarecrow. (These days, my body shape would be termed intriguingly androgynous, but way back then it was just plain scrawny.)

I was also close to flat chested. By postwar standards, you couldn't be the all-American girl without having a bust that poked out like twin torpedoes. To make amends, a girl could wear a padded bra (still made from some wartime fake rubber that smelled like a smoldering garbage dump). The falsies were too hard to be natural, though not hard enough to resist outside force. If someone knocked into you, the cup on that side often would not spring back; there was no way to fix it except running to the girls' room to push out the dent. The alternative to rubber falsies was stuffing your bra with tissue paper, but you risked making a crinkling noise.

To make me even less appealing, my nose was growing faster than the rest of my face. At fourteen, fifteen, and sixteen, it wasn't quite what you'd call a schnoz, but it was prominent enough that when studying myself in the mirror, a female Abe Lincoln stared back. Except I lacked those intriguing, sad eyes. Too bad. I wound up having a lot to be sad about.

All right, let me get it over with, fast as I can. I turned into a slut. Not that I ever intended to be whorish. (In those days, "whore" was not only a word for an actual prostitute but also a synonym for the slightly lesser evil, the nonprofessional bad girl.)

It began one day after school. I went over to my friend Carole Brown's house. We were fourteen, gawky, and gauche, undateable. Carole did have a sixteen-year-old brother, but if that sounds like teenage crush material, you didn't know Myron Brown—a boy whose acne had acne; nearly all his myriad pimples had their own satellites. Furthermore, he wore old-man Harry Truman glasses and they were perpetually sliding down the oily slope of his nose; he had no discernible personality. Carole once confided she wished he'd be killed in a car accident so awful that they wouldn't be able to have an open coffin.

However, that day was not like all the others at the Browns'. There was big excitement because Myron actually had a friend over—or at least someone his age willing to risk having it known that he had not reflexively rejected Myron's company.

The visiting boy, Skip Schumacher, was not as dreadful as Myron, though certainly no dreamboat. His yellowish-white skin would have been more natural on an unroasted capon than an adolescent male. Either he had very thin hair or he was already getting bald. Still, he was tall, with an impressive voice that sounded like the radio announcer's for *Inner Sanctum.* Also, he was a second-string something for the Walnut Hills High School basketball team. So if I wasn't in awe, I was inspired enough to keep licking my lower lip to make it glisten like Gene Tierney's. Carole sprayed herself with her mother's Joy. Skip didn't appear to notice.

But just as I was leaving, one thing led to another on the staircase on my way up to get my coat in Carole's room. Skip was coming down. I immediately noted he was holding his cigarette in what was considered the manliest way imaginable, between the pads of his thumb and index finger. His other three fingers formed a canopy, so at the far end of the tunnel his hand made, I spotted the glowing red tip. Maybe the red light hypnotized me. Or it just could have been—when we reached the same stair—that I got slightly aroused by brushing against a male taller than I. He got aroused because that's what guys do. Before I could climb another step, he kissed me.

My first kiss. It lasted too long and he was breathing through his nose during the kissing. His nicotine breath came out of his nostrils in dragonlike streams and was almost enough to put the kibosh on my excitement. Though not quite. I did like the warmth of his hand—the one not holding the cigarette—behind my neck, pulling me closer as we kissed. Then the hand moved down and around, and suddenly he was feeling up my falsie.

Skip might not have been suave, but he could tell fake foam rubber when he squeezed it. Just as I was about to pull away, dash up the stairs to show my shock and displeasure that he would even consider grabbing the breast of a good girl, I caught his look of disillusionment. I had not been truthful in packaging. So instead of moving on, I stood there on the stairs like a dope while he braced the heel of his cigarette hand against Mrs. Brown's green-on-green wallpaper and snaked his other hand up my sweater. Unsuccessful at getting under the heavy cloth and padding of my bra, his fingers inched up, over, and into the left cup.

Whatever interest I might have had in the proceedings evaporated. All my energy went to not falling down the stairs. Meanwhile, Skip Schumacher swayed a little while twirling my nipple as if trying to get to an elusive radio station. I grabbed onto the banister and held tight, hoping he'd get bored and praying that Carole wouldn't come looking for me wondering why I hadn't come down with my coat. Then there was her brother Myron to worry about. I panicked. *God, if he came out of his room looking for Skip . . .*

"I've got to go," I told him.

"No!" he said, though I was relieved he pulled his hand out of my bra and out from under my sweater. I stupidly assumed he wanted to apologize, so I waited . . . and felt his hand whiz up my skirt, into my underpants. Panties. No one says "underpants" anymore.

"Stop it!" I demanded in a harsh whisper.

"Please," he said. "*Please.*" It occurred to me then that Skip probably didn't know my name. Just as I was on the verge of *Stop!*—a lot louder than a whisper—he offered up another "Please," part sigh, part moan.

I wasn't the first stupid fourteen-year-old girl to get aroused by that fierce plea and think, *He needs me desperately!* Why doesn't it occur to girls like me to follow that thought with, *So big deal, he needs me. That's* his *problem.* Instead I was simultaneously flattered and ecstatic. I let him do what a sixteen-year-old boy with his hand in a girl's underpants does for however long it took until Carole's voice slashed through the silence: "Gloria? Your coat's in my room. I think on the pink chair."

As Skip pulled back his hand, I turned my head to the top of the stairs. No one. To the landing below. Safe. *Thank God,* was all I could think in that instant. Smoothing down my skirt, grabbing the banister, I ran up to Carole's room. By the time I was careening back out with my coat, Skip had vanished from the staircase, though not from my life.

Walking into school the next morning, I slumped with relief and surprise that I was safe: Skip wasn't waiting at the main doors, ready to reinsert his hand into my underpants or to yell something to everyone going to homeroom. For some reason I imagined he would say, *Gloria Goldberg has lots of pubic hair!* But I was all right. Disaster averted.

Stupid me. No, naïve me, being only fourteen and never having lived through the process of a girl losing her reputation, going from a good girl to a whore (pronounced as a two syllable word in a Cincinnati accent—hoo-wer) overnight.

When Carl Turner bumped into me on the way to my third-period class and instead of saying *Sorry* gave me a broad, unfriendly grin, my stomach flipped. But I tamped down the dread by telling myself that Carl's grin had really been apologetic. Or that he hadn't realized he'd knocked into me and was grinning at someone else in the crowd of kids because he was fifteen and probably didn't know who I was, so the bumping-into went unregistered.

It was on the lunch line that I realized that Skip had told everybody. What he'd said was a mystery, but when Gary Schroeder cut into line and felt up my left breast with his upper arm and Harry Armstrong squeezed behind me, rubbed up against my behind, and said, "Excuse me, I forgot to get a fork," but pronounced "fork" more like "fuck," I knew I was a whore.

That Friday night, Carole called to say she couldn't go downtown with me the following day. When I said, "Well, maybe next Saturday," she muttered, "I can't. My mother doesn't want me . . . You know." She hung up as I was saying,

"Uhhh." I wasn't quick enough then to put it together in that instant, but I should have realized that if Carole's mother had heard it, it was only a matter of time before mine did.

I had a few days more of grace, if you can call going to school and having a senior boy come up and say, "You're Gloria Goldberg, right?" But cordially. I said, "Yes, I'm Gloria." And he asked, in that pleasant voice, "Want to eat me raw?" Or having the girls who were friends unwilling not only to be seen with me but even to meet my eye.

Two days later, my mother was waiting at the door when I got home from school. Right away, I knew it was bad. She was pulling on each of her fingers, over and over, long after every knuckle had cracked. "Sit!" She let go of her index finger for an instant to point to the living room couch. Our house was tiny, beyond modest, a ridiculous choice for such a tall family, though once when I'd brought up the matter, she'd snapped, "Don't you think your father's doing the best he can?" Anyway, we had no entrance hall, so I was still scared stiff in the doorway when she said, "Get over to that couch *now*!"

When I started to unfasten the toggles on my loden coat, she put her hand on my chest and pushed me down onto the couch. I landed on a tilt, with one foot up in the air. I managed to right myself and sit straight, schoolbooks beside me. No book bags in those days; we put an old belt around them. For some stupid reason, I believed they were a wall that would protect me from my mother so she couldn't sit beside me.

"Did you do something with a boy?" Her voice was so piercing I wanted to clap my hands over my ears.

"What?" I asked weakly. I was both stalling for time and trying to appear flummoxed by her question.

But although my mother was, essentially, me with half my brain, normally a cinch to con, she wasn't buying delaying tactics or the innocent act. "What did you do?" She took a huge gulp of air, one of those backward sobs that precede hysteria. "*What in God's name did you do?*"

"Nothing!" I screeched. Not in anger. In fright, the way an animal would cry when its attacker is a second away from ripping open its throat. "Nothing! I swear. I swear on the Bible."

"Don't you dare lie to me. Tell me what happened!"

"Nothing."

"I said, tell me what happened!"

"I was at Carole's, passing this boy on the staircase—"

"What boy? Carole's brother?"

"No. A friend of his."

"*And?*" She was looming over me. One step closer and she would have been standing on top of my feet. Her fists rested on her hips. The thumbs stuck underneath all the other fingers, as if she were still trying to recrack those knuckles. "And what happened then?" Her long, straight nose was pointing right at the center of my chest like an accusatory finger. "Don't waste your time lying to me."

"Nothing. I mean, he just kind of touched me on top. It wasn't that long or anything. Her mother was in the house the whole time."

"Did her mother see any of this?"

"No. I swear. Maybe I should've screamed or something, but . . . I'm sorry."

My mother was usually a snap to fool, having the IQ of a mung bean. But this time she gathered whatever resources she had and pulled in some help from God knows where. Suddenly she turned into the Grand Inquisitor. "He just touched you for only one second when you were passing on the staircase?"

I was so terrified by knowing I really was a whore—as well as by her unaccustomed intensity—that I waited too long to be able to lie credibly. "Maybe it was two or three seconds," I managed to say.

"Maybe it was ten minutes! Maybe it was an hour!" She grabbed one side of my coat and jerked me up off the couch. "You *let* him touch you, didn't you? A good girl would smack the boy across the face for that, and you let him touch you." She wasn't actually asking me, but I nodded. Up to that point I had been too frightened to burst into tears. But now she took a step back, then whacked me across the face. "Did you let him go below the waist? Did you? Did you?" I kept nodding more and more emphatically, but she wanted to hear it. "Did you?"

"Yes, but—"

"No buts about it!" she shouted, then spun me around and kicked me in the butt. "What if you're pregnant? Do you think we can afford to send you away for nine months?"

I wasn't able to tell her that I wasn't pregnant because I was terrified that Skip Schumacher's middle finger had somehow been covered with sperm. Maybe he'd stuck his hand into his pants and squirted some onto his finger, just to be mean, and they had swum up. So now I could very well be a mother-to-be.

"Please," I finally managed to say, "don't tell Daddy."

My father was a shoe salesman at Shillito's, a big department store, and was perpetually exhausted by the demands of the customers in Women's Better Shoes. He was by nature a sweet if ineffectual man but always so worn out he was never able to come up with more than half a smile.

"'Don't tell Daddy'? You don't think he knows something's wrong already? Mrs. Mazur was in yesterday and walked right past him, over to Harold Voss, and bought two pair of shoes for Passover from *him.* You ruined your father's living on that staircase. Did you ever think of that? No, of course not! Who's going to go to a salesman who's got . . . shame, shame in his family, a daughter with a reputation? Who's going to want to risk awkward conversation? 'How's your family?' Who's willing to be fitted for pumps by someone who might break into tears any second? Answer me!"

I'll never know if it was necessary for my father to first switch to the Men's Shoes department, then leave Shillito's entirely to work as a clerk in the Antennas and Towers department of Cincinnati Bell, a job, in my mother's words, "out of the public eye," where he wouldn't be (again to quote my mother) "judged by your rep."

There were changes for me as well. I went from having a few friends to having none. I had to endure quickly averted eyes, then outright sneers, murmurs of "whore," along with the occasional stuck-out foot to trip me during gym class. And that was just the girls. The boys bumped me, grabbed me, and constantly called out suggestions of what I should do to them. For some reason, "Suck me dry" was the phrase most in vogue. This cruelty was not the result of stupidity: My high school, Walnut Hills, was known for its gifted students.

The next three years were of course hellish. To take a break from the loneliness, I had sex with any boy who was nice to me. All they really had to do was not say something vile and I was theirs for as long as they wanted me.

In all that time, my father never said anything about my situation, which wasn't that much of a change; he'd always been a man of few words. But his gentle half smile never again appeared. As for my mother . . . As my ex, Joe, once remarked sympathetically, "Lose her number. That woman doesn't have a warm bone in her entire body." That was early on. Years later, once he understood I was actually leaving him, he changed his tune to, "You're a cold-fish moron, just like your fucking old lady."

The good news was that after my sixteenth birthday, I grew into my looks. At the makeup counter at Pogue's department store, in line for a movie ticket, in the backseat of a car after a triple fellatio (three times in a night, not three boys), I would hear the same message: "You could be a model."

I took the message seriously. It was all I could do in my life. No one in Cincinnati would ever marry me. It was model or die. Instead of going to the Walnut Hills graduation ceremony, I asked the school office to mail my diploma to my parents' house. The day of the prom, I left Cincinnati forever and headed to New York. I kept in touch with my parents, bringing them up to date on where I was living, my job, though I'm sure they assumed "showroom model" was a synonym for something like "porn movie actress." My father wrote to me every few months: cheery, newsy letters about the noisy hot-water heater or a revamped Big Boy on Reading Road. They sounded as if they'd been written not by someone related to me but by some gregarious neighbor I barely knew.

I would have gone back for his funeral, eleven years after I left, but my mother let me know about his death by mail—and I don't mean special delivery. The letter arrived too late. Joe asked me if I wanted to have a service for him at our temple in Great Neck, or some kind of memorial, but I told him my heart had already said all the goodbyes it could manage without breaking. Of course that wasn't true: All my heart ever said was, *Too bad it wasn't her.* Then my father could have had a few years of happiness without having to look at that sour puss of hers every day. He deserved at least that.

Years later, when she was dying, a cardiology resident at Cincinnati Jewish called to tell me I ought to get there within the next day or two. I told him I was in Santa Fe, and it would take me three or four days to make arrangements for someone to stay with my teenage sons. I kept thinking back to when I was eleven and my grandpa Louie died. She wouldn't let me go to the funeral though I begged and wept. She said it would be "too upsetting for a girl your age. Look at you. You're hysterical." However, if I wanted to be helpful, I could stay home from school and set out the food a half hour before everyone was due back from the cemetery. She said she knew my grandpa would appreciate it.

The cardiology resident said, "Truthfully, your mother will probably be gone in a day or two." In fact, she checked out less than twenty-four hours later, so there was no point in my going back. I made all the arrangements by phone. Eight thousand bucks to the funeral director. Worth every penny because I didn't have to deal with the four old ladies who were the only ones who showed. They would have passed the entire service whispering about me. Another two thousand to the rabbi who officiated. While he might think I was a monster for not coming to my mother's funeral, he certainly would understand I wasn't a cheap monster.

I think about those three grandchildren, how they grew up with such different kinds of parents than mine. In my day, mothers and fathers didn't have to be nice to their children. Some were, I supposed. But they definitely did not have to pretend to be interested in what their kids were doing—other than checking their report cards.

But those three grew up hearing, *Oh, you made such a beautiful cardboard map of South America! Look how the green becomes more intense in the rain forest area of Brazil!* All right, Bradley is and always was a sentimental nebbish, so it's not surprising he became a doting father. But take Cynthia: narcissist, know-nothing, an obsessive-compulsive who *absolutely will not pee* in a public restroom. You'd think she might be an adequate mother to Matthew but would reject out of hand a pudgy, hairy-eyebrowed daughter like Daisy. Except no, she always put on a show of loving them both equally. At least that was how it was the last time I saw her, whenever it was. As for Adriana, she had to love Raquel because that was all she had.

It's generational, I suppose. My sons' contemporaries risked complete social ostracism unless they adored their children not only in private but also out in public. A kid could be a heroin addict, and a parent would announce, *Melissa is doing really great in rehab!* It's cultural too. For Adriana, the sun rises and sets by Raquel, because that's what Hispanics are taught is normal. What's interesting is why she never remarried and had more children after Travis died. She was young, hardworking, educated.

That sounds as if I liked her. I didn't. She was too good to be true. And so short, just about five feet. Maybe it wasn't some kind of rejection or rebellion against me on Travis's part to pick a Catholic miniperson, though it felt like it. But I pride myself on being objective, and except that Adriana got Raquel's ears pierced when the girl was practically a baby, a completely freakish custom—she has been, from what I've heard, a decent mother. More than decent. But instead of finding another guy and having more kids, she made a career.

I once asked Bradley why he thought Adriana never remarried. He said, "She honestly felt there was only one man in the world for her, Travis. Anyone else would have been second best. She said she'd rather live alone than live with someone she couldn't love with a full heart." It was enough to make you retch: Bradley, a grown man, still buying into fairy tales. Family values. I don't believe in them. Never have, never will. One hundred percent schmaltz.

What the hell was I doing, inviting these three into my home?

Eleven

Matt

"Eeeesh," as my sister used to exhale whenever she'd really had it. Like when my mom made mean remarks about somebody's house we'd just visited: My mother could go on and on about a Plexiglas cocktail table like it was a blot on civilization. Then, having picked up a head of steam, she'd put down their single-ply toilet paper, their warped wood laminate kitchen cabinets. I'd be sitting a few feet over from Daisy in the tan leather backseat of my Dad's Mercedes. The seat belts coerced us into military posture and I'd hear my sister's "eeeesh" every time my mom added a new design crime to the fast-growing list.

"Faux Burberry guest towels!"

"Eeeesh."

"God in heaven, a wine cork collection in a giant brandy glass!"

"Eeeesh."

It sounded a little like letting air out of a tire, and it worked that way for my sister. She let it out and, with it, her hostility. At most, my mom annoyed her, though not in the invasive way moms often bother their children, getting into their hair, under their skin. The PAM Brigade, as one of my old girlfriends called it: passive-aggressive moms. The ones who give a subliminal sad shrug before saying bravely, *If that's what you want to do . . . ,* which deflates their kid's ego, scatters seeds of doubt. Their underlying message is and has always been, *Whatever path you choose, it will lead to failure for you, disappointment for me.*

I never figured out if Daisy was really, really resilient or just clueless; my mom never succeeded in sucking the air out of her lungs the way she did with me. She'd look at my sister's new shirt and, with a brave little smile not quite masking her nausea, ask, "Is that some . . . um, new style?" And Daisy would say, "I don't know. I just liked it," in an easy, unbothered way. My mom could ask me that same question and I might answer the same "I just liked it." But then, what do you know? I'd wear the shirt one more time, to prove she hadn't gotten to me, but never again.

Also, every time my father was charmed by my mother's mockery (which was often), it would come as such a shock, like I was experiencing it for the first time. Knocked the wind out of me. Daisy got bothered by it too, but nowhere near as much. She'd exhale an "eeeesh"—impatience mixed with disappointment—and then it was over for her. But it gnawed at me for days, my dad delighting in my mom's meanness Why? He didn't have a malicious bone in his body. If either of his kids had shat all over somebody's house or clothes or style the way our mom did, he'd give it to us: "Hey, have a little *rachmones*!" That's the Yiddish word for compassion. "So big deal, they don't have taste. They're decent people."

Also, it bothered me that I—the boy, the sports guy—was the sensitive kid, while my artsy sister could brush off the family zingers like they were gnats coming at her, not flesh-piercing arrows.

When we finished in Granny's solarium . . . whatever it was called. Conservatory. Couldn't she just call it the sunroom? Anglophile bullshit. Anyway, after we finished and Carlos was taking us up to our rooms, I heard Daisy exhaling the thousand *eeeesh*es she'd saved up during our conversation with Granny. By the time we got to the top of the stairs, the uncomfortable moments would be over for her. Then she'd get into the dark fun of reliving the entire episode. The analyzing could begin.

I was dying to get to my room, close the door fast so Daisy couldn't come in to carry on, *Can you believe that woman?* If I were telling the truth, I'd tell her, *Yeah, I can believe her. She really got to me.* But of course, I'd make myself man up. But at this moment I needed to be alone. I wanted to text Ashley. Even take a nap if there was time. I had no problem hanging with women. But three at a time, all relatives, wore me down.

Luckily, just as we got to the stairs, Raquel thought to ask Carlos, really nicely and politely, not at all pushily, if we could get some chips or nuts because otherwise, despite the lovely sandwiches Ms. Garrison had provided, we couldn't hold out till seven o'clock dinner. All of a sudden I realized, *Yeah, right, chips.* I shouldn't have passed on the business-class breakfast, but the choices were oatmeal and some kind of egg thing. I'd ordered the egg, but then one went by on the way to some other passenger; it was a folded omelet straitjacketed with orange cheese, so I told the flight attendant forget it. Now, though, the pretzel from the airport was doing its sneaky carb thing, making me dopey enough that I needed someone else asking for food to alert me to the fact that I was still hungry.

Carlos said, "As soon as I get the three of you settled, Ms. Goldberg, I'll have Paula bring each of you a little something."

"Every time I go on a plane," Raquel said to him in Spanish, "I promise myself that the next time I'll remember to take protein bars in my handbag. And I do remember . . . usually when I'm halfway through the next five-hour flight. For some reason, traveling makes me hungry."

Obviously, Granny hadn't said anything about Raquel's background, because Carlos did the cool guy's version of a double take, where his face kept the same pleasantly neutral expression while his head jerked back. His eyes narrowed to take a better look. Apparently, in the game of Ethnic ID as played in New Mexico, having the name Goldberg trumped both golden-brown coloring and having thick, straight black hair that came from . . . Who? Flamenco dancers? Native Americans?

Carlos answered Raquel in Spanish, "My wife never goes on an airplane without three sandwiches and a bottle of hand sanitizer."

Raquel laughed and said, "I hope you

don't mind my speaking Spanish to you," as Daisy and I followed them up the stairs.

"Not at all. I was just a little surprised. Your accent . . ."

"Puerto Rican."

"I thought so," he said.

Meanwhile, Daisy was mouthing *What?* and giving me that slit-eyed big-sister you'd-better-tell-me-what-they're-saying look. I whispered, "Just about getting a snack. And establishing the fact that she's Latina despite the last name."

"So Raquel gets the biggest snack?"

"She'll get the macadamias, we'll get the peanuts. Think of it as reparations." We got to the top of the stairs and Carlos led us down a hallway so thickly carpeted that you could lose a shoe in the rug. I mumbled to my sister, "What did you think about the old lady saying she has a detective agency on retainer? From her 'think about that,' it sounded like she had us checked out."

"You know, a movie reviewer would call that 'delicious irony.' I mean, detectives? Just a few minutes before, she'd been going on to me how she trusted her gut."

"There is something weird about her whole approach," I said. "Not weird. Detached. Detached from life as we know it." Like even my mom would never make her put-down comments in front of people she barely knew because—who knew?—they might be offended. Behind their backs was the way to go. In front could screw up my parents' chic Long Island social life or be bad for her interior design business. But my grandmother didn't think that way. She didn't care whose nose she knocked out of joint. Probably she enjoyed hearing that crunch of cartilage.

" 'Detached'?" Daisy was whispering.

"Yeah. Like a junior sociopath pulling wings off flies to see how they'll try to fly and can't. Granny is like, *Hmmm, I'll say something hurtful and watch them cringe.*"

I was still thinking about the sociopath comparison, but Carlos interrupted my thought by opening the first door we came to and saying, "Mr. Goldberg, this room is yours."

I looked inside. Areawise, it was beyond big. And it was Decorated, with a capital *D.* Done. My mother didn't approve of design, as she called it, that came with capital letters. She was always saying things like, "If you know it's been decorated, it's w-r-o-n-g.

Almost everything in the bedroom was the same sandy yellow color. Walls, carpet, chair, sheets, and blanket. It was that familiar Southwestern shade that must be meant to echo the desert. The Diamondbacks used that color in their uniforms. As for the size of the room, maybe it was natural in Santa Fe because land was cheaper in the West than in the East. If your house stood on ten acres, you could make the rooms as ginormous as you wanted. If you thought a guest room the size of Dodger Stadium would be cool, you could just go ahead.

But this space was laughably large. You could have held a cocktail party on the bed—maybe it was what they called a California King in mattress ads, or maybe Entire North American Landmass King. There were some giant pillows in blue and a blue-and-beige plaid, suggesting that this was the designated guest room for men. But it really wasn't a guy's blue, like a Mets blue, a quiet royal just a little livelier than navy. This was overly bright blue, like the color the Marlins have. I never got the point of having those kinds of pillows because all anyone ever does with them is Frisbee them out of the way.

"Is the room all right, Mr. Goldberg?" Carlos asked.

I realized I'd been hovering in the doorway, so I took a couple of steps in. My suitcase was already there, on a luggage rack like they have in hotels. "It's fine," I said. "Really nice. Thank you."

"Good. Paula will be up in a few minutes to bring you something." As he pulled my door closed, Daisy and Raquel fluttered their hands toward me: *Goodbye, goodbye*.

I had just enough time to glance at a Glory brochure on top of a bunch of the latest magazines fanned out on the dresser. The cover was face after woman's face, all varieties of happy—from a small I've-just-had-genius-sex smile to huge grins. They were gazing out as if you, the brochure reader, were the mirror. One was putting on an earring, another had a mascara thing in her hand, a third buttoned a shirt. There were eight, ten faces: late teens to seniors, of all races and ethnicities. It must have been effective, because I, the mirror, was smiling back at them. I kicked off my shoes and was just putting my Dopp kit in the bathroom—more sand color, this time marble—when there was a knock. I got to the door fast, but instead of Paula and snacks, it was Daisy and Raquel with nothing.

"Paula will bring chips up, and you won't get any if you're not in your rooms," I told them.

"We left our doors open," Raquel said, "so she'll leave whatever it is. Now that I think of it, I'm hoping fruit and cheese. Maybe that braided Mexican cheese. I love it. You know, fruit and cheese is Hayden's favorite thing in the world." It would be, I thought. "With nuts. He especially loves pecans."

"Does a cheese sommelier wheel a

silver cart around Goldman Sachs at snacktime and say, 'We're featuring a pungent goat cheese from Italy today'?" I asked.

"Are you going to start those Mr. Metrosexual attacks on Hayden again?" But she was smiling. Raquel thought my kidding about her boyfriend was good-natured. At least I thought she thought that.

"How could I think he was a metrosexual? Just because he gets manicures?"

"Stop it, Matt! It's not like he gets his nails polished or even buffed," Raquel said. "He's well-groomed. Beautifully groomed, in fact."

I hadn't invited them into the room. But my sister lacked my cousin's good manners, at least when it came to me, so as Raquel was talking in the doorway, Daisy pushed in and plopped down on the bed.

"Are these beds insane?" my sister said. "They're so big Fellini could have shot all of *Satyricon* on one of them. What is wrong with that woman?"

"I wouldn't know where to begin," Raquel said.

Since there was no way it wasn't going to be a conversation, I motioned her to come into the room. My cousin tossed a couple of the throw pillows onto the carpet and flopped on the far side of the bed. Because it would have been creepy, unspoken-incest-taboo-wise for me to sprawl out there with the two of them, I threw a pillow off the chair and sat.

"How could she call in detectives to check up on us?" Daisy demanded. "Oh, shit! Maybe the rooms are bugged and she's listening to us right now."

"Right," I said. "And the one who says the nicest things about that lovely woman, that entrepreneurial genius, that great humanitarian who brings the glow of lipstick to the darkest corners of the republic—gets Glory and the umpteen million dollars it generates. I'm telling you. She is one sweetheart, our granny."

"No, seriously. I mean, Raquel, isn't it easy to bug a room? I bet the DA does it all the time."

"You need a warrant. It's easy enough to get, though New York uses such crappy equipment that half the time it sounds like people are trying to imitate a duck, which is a plus for the defense. I have no idea what the law is in New Mexico, whether you can bug your own house. But even if it's illegal, she could do it. But I seriously don't see her wearing a headset, listening to our every word."

"Don't you think she's interested in what we're saying about her?" Daisy asked.

"Maybe," Raquel said, "but I think she's more interested in her game. Monopoly, Glory edition. She's going to compare us, maybe play one of us against the other two. But she strikes me as a bottom-line sort of person. The company is her life and, you know, her love. Choosing who gets it, putting that mind of hers to which one of us deserves it, that's what she cares about."

"I'm with Raquel on this," I told my sister, who was squinting up where the wall met the ceiling, searching for tiny microphones. "Anyway, I've met people like her. Smart. Powerful. No emotional intelligence. She's not into what other people think because other people don't matter." I glanced at the door. "Where the fuck are the snacks?"

Just as I said it, there was a knock on the door, as if someone had heard every word, which of course made Daisy go from lounging on the bed to practically rigor mortis. "Tell me that's a coincidence," she snapped at me, as I walked over to the door.

"It's a coincidence," Raquel and I spoke at the same time.

Raquel and I had as much in common, maybe more, as I had with my sister. Despite my cousin being an avid Yankees fan, we were in total sports sync, which I'd learned over the years meant similar personalities or at least simpatico. She and I had always talked professional sports in the most friendly but sophisticated way, almost like a couple of pundits who work for intellectual outlets. Like the columnist from *The Nation* being interviewed by the cerebral sports guru from NPR. But in all Raquel's and my lives, our conversations about any subject had been only in the company of other people.

Like on Passover, which usually falls close to baseball's opening day: Ninety percent of the Jews and half Jews in America believe one of the reasons God brought us out of Egypt was to talk baseball, but Raquel and I never got a chance. We would get three sentences into what promised to be a great discussion and suddenly my dad, followed three seconds later by our neighbor Nancy Koenig, would jump into it. My dad was the king of esoteric stats, so he'd be boring for a couple of minutes. Nancy, who was really great-looking—Hilary Duff in twenty years—would invariably go berserk at whatever point he was making. She'd shake her head wildly, like she was trying to loosen her long brown hair to the point of getting it to fly out of its follicles. She'd slam her gefilte fish fork down on the plate. Then she'd say something like, "For God's sake, Bradley, how can you mention Hack Wilson and Gehrig and not say a word about who got the third most single-season RBIs? Like, what are you?

An anti-Semite?" She'd give him an I'm-just-kidding smile. Still, Nancy really was the sport-Jew queen, and she wasn't kidding. "Hank Greenberg!" She'd boom it to make sure each of the twenty-five people in the dining room heard it. This would prompt my cousin Ben to chime in from across the table to forget about single-season stats: "What about career RBIs?" After that, the discussion became everybody's and went everywhere—mostly away from baseball.

A couple of times Raquel and I went to games together. Even she, passionate Yankees fan, would go see the Mets in the seats behind home plate I could get. I always offered her two tickets, not one, and she'd always bring Hayden along. Of course I'd wind up taking whoever I was seeing pre-Ashley, so it was like Raquel and I were always chaperoned. It was crazy, but that's how it was.

We also had that two-, three-times-a-year lunch or dinner with my sister. Now and then Raquel and Daisy would meet to go to a concert or play, but for some reason, every time I thought to call her and say, *Hey, want to come to Citi Field for an event with Spanish-language media and then we could go out for Chinese or Korean food in Flushing* or *Hey, Raquel, I've got two tickets to a Knicks game . . .* I didn't.

Paula stood at the door with baskets over her arm, the kind Little Red Riding Hood would carry to her grandmother's. When she saw the three of us, she smiled benevolently—that what-adorable-young-people expression—and handed me all three of the baskets, each with a big cloth napkin folded over the contents. The instant she left, we tore into them. The contents were the same, so we couldn't trade: We each got one apple, a chunk of cheddar, a tiny Italian chocolate bar like someone would give out to upscale trick-or-treaters, and some really heavy cookies that looked as if they came from some heart-healthy recipe. A bottle of cold water was wrapped in a smaller napkin, like it was champagne.

"What I don't get," Daisy said, "is why Gloria couldn't just ask us any questions she had? Or call up our parents? She had to hire *detectives*?"

"Daisy," Raquel said, her tone indicating that patience wasn't one of her top ten virtues, "what she was looking for was dirt on us. Criminal record, drug use. Can you picture her calling my mom who she hasn't spoken to in practically ten years and saying, 'Oh, Adriana, I was just wondering if Raquel has any serious character flaw or substance abuse problem that got her in trouble in college or on the job? I'm sure you wouldn't mind betraying her and telling me whatever you know.' "

Personally, I thought Raquel was a little harsh with my sister, who had only asked a simple question. So I butted in: "You know I was thinking of asking Granny how she vets her employees? That's the reason she has a detective agency on retainer. For her, it's the most natural thing in the world to have them check out someone she needs to trust for business reasons."

"I guess," Daisy said. "It's not like she's got great people skills and that with a few gentle questions we would open up our inner lives to her. But tell me, why would she think any of us would be better at running a multimillion-dollar company than some stranger in Starbucks?"

"Well," I said, "we're hers, at least genetically." The apple had a little mush spot near the little belly button thing on the bottom. I hated that. "Maybe she thinks that gives us an edge."

"Interesting question," Raquel said. "Maybe the genetic business has some truth to it. But you've got to admit that overall, family has always meant nothing to her."

"Your father meant something to her," Daisy came back.

Sitting on the chair in the middle of that huge bland-colored room, I was starting to feel like we were not so much in the middle of a desert as stuck in nothingness in a time/space warp between universes. We'd just sit here forever, and eventually all memory would fade. We wouldn't know why we were here. We wouldn't want to escape because we would remember nothing.

I'd even forget what meant the most

to me—Ashley, sports. Daisy would forget about books and movies and how so many of her friends were getting married and she hadn't found anyone, and Raquel would lose all recollection of Hayden—a plus, that one—her mom, and the law. We'd forget about Gloria Garrison too and wonder why we were spending eternity inside a giant tan cube.

"I know she loved my dad. I truly believe it. But because of that, her virtual abandonment of all of us makes absolutely no sense to me. My mom has this complex theory about Gloria being traumatized by the fact of my father's death—plus it being so sudden—that she blamed my mom for not protecting him more. Like how do you protect a grown man? A gifted man? Could my mom have forbidden my dad to do his life's work? Should she have told him, 'From now on, you can only make your living shooting baby pictures'? Anyway, my mom may have a lot of psychological insight, but not this time. Even if Gloria *was* traumatized and hated my mom, and thought *If not for you Travis would still be alive,* you'd think ultimately she'd have reached out me, or you guys. To have someone to care about again."

"But she didn't," I said.

"Maybe it's wrong to assume Gloria needed someone to love," Daisy said. She turned onto her side and propped up her head on the flat of her hand. She looked rounded and kind of languid, like that naked woman in the painting by the Spanish artist. What was his name? Oh, Goya. Except, obviously, my sister had clothes on and wasn't sensual, much less sexy. Well, hopefully there was some guy out there who would think she was. Not that women had to get married anymore, but a husband would be a plus as would two or three kids she could screen 1940s Mickey Mouse cartoons for.

"Of course," she went on, "it's entirely possible Gloria had or has someone special in her life we don't know about. But I'm not sure." Her last sentence emerged with such unnatural slowness it sounded like some dialogue in one of the eight million movie scripts on the shelves in her office:

DAISY [*hesitant, pensive*]. But . . . I'm . . . not . . . sure.

I found myself picturing Granny sitting on a sand-colored chair in a sand-colored room even bigger than the one we were in. No one in her life. Alone for eternity. "Maybe this is strictly a business decision," Daisy added.

"Well, it's a dumb one," I said. "Why would you pick three people in their twenties with zero experience in commerce and no sign they have that rah-rah entrepreneurial spirit? And while you're at it, why pick people who aren't knowledgeable about hair and makeup. And—nothing personal—but who aren't fashion forward."

Raquel took a bite of cheese about the size of a large crumb and actually chewed before swallowing. Then she said, "First of all, don't ever forget we're dealing with an egomaniac here. No matter how flawed Gloria finds our parents, in her head the three of us are still one-quarter her. Maybe the fact "—she made air quotes around the word "fact" and shook her head the way you would about a hopeless case—"of being one-fourth her makes us a better bet than an anonymous someone with a Harvard MBA and ten years experience in beauty or fashion. That could be how she views it, which doesn't have anything to do with reality."

I decided not to bring up the fact that, genewise, my dad was one-half my grandmother, double our one-quarter, and she definitely didn't find him a good bet. Instead I asked, "And what's second of all?" She looked vague, so I explained: "The egomaniac business was 'first of all.' What's second?"

"God, I don't know," Raquel said, sitting up on the bed and embracing her knees in a hug. In that position, she looked more ten than twenty-five. "Well, maybe she thinks my being a lawyer indicates a logical mind that could be applied to business. And that in your job, you're dealing with the public and reporters and athletes, you have your fingers on the pulse of . . . something. How to grab people's attention and keep it. How to tune in to their fantasies, create or uncover needs they don't know they have. Those abilities are totally applicable to a business like Glory."

"But I rejected going into a business. I mean, we both did, Daisy and me."

"You know it's 'Daisy and I.'" My sister spoke with a sigh of been there, said that.

"Thank you," I snapped. I turned back to my cousin. "If I'd wanted to go into a business, I could have gone into my father's. But I didn't."

"How come?" Raquel wanted to know. "I was always kind of curious, but every time I thought about asking, I wasn't with you, and I didn't have such an intense need to know that I felt I had to e-mail you immediately to ask."

"I always assumed I would go into it. But my dad was too nice, and probably too smart, to take my joining him as a given. Right around the beginning of my third year at Duke, he asked what I was thinking about. No pressure, just that he wanted to formulate plans for the future of the Handsome Home. I said I'd let him know, but I was still thinking, *Of course I'll go in with him.*

"But then I was walking across campus one morning. It was fall. One of those days that are a perfect ten. I ran into the rabbi from Hillel. I'd just been to services there for the big Yom, so he knew my face. We said hi and we walked together for a while. It came up that he was from Nashville originally. So we got to talking about the Titans, their football team."

"I know the Tennessee Titans," Raquel said wearily, annoyed that I'd paused to explain.

"Anyway, all of a sudden the subject changed and it somehow came out that I really didn't want to go into my dad's business. I told the rabbi it made economic sense to do it, and it would hurt my dad if I didn't—and my dad was the last person in the world I wanted to hurt. Except I felt it would just be a do-over of his life. Not that it was a bad life. It was one most of the world would want to live. Except not me. So I wound up having a couple of meetings with the rabbi—you know, sitting in his study. Once it was at night, and he gave me a bottle of ale from a microbrewery. Even then, I remember thinking, *This is the last person in the world I should be wanting to talk to.* Like when the voices of reason say to confide in your minister, priest, or rabbi, it's like nobody who's even one percent cool would *ever* think of doing that. But there I was. At some point he said something that got to me: that honoring your father and mother doesn't mean doing whatever they want you to do if it's wrong for you. We talked a lot about what honoring means. Anyway, the rabbi probably thought I was a jerk for not going into such a good business, but he definitely never said so."

"Am I chopped liver?" Daisy piped up. "Not about going into the Handsome Home, which when I told Dad no probably made him send up a major prayer of thanksgiving. I'm talking chopped liver vis-à-vis my assets from Gloria's POV. About who could take over the business."

"Yes," I told her. "You are chopped liver."

"Of course you're not," Raquel said. I couldn't tell if she meant it or was winging it, but she was absolutely convincing. I thought, *I've really got to see her in the courtroom.* "Daisy, of all of us, you've got the most relevant experience. First of all, if you can deal with Hollywood types, the egos and all that, you can manage some fashion consultant who decides to throw a fit in Galveston, Texas."

"Hollywood egos aren't any worse than anyone else's," Daisy said. "Athletes, judges, whatever. It's just that their culture permits them to behave badly."

"The point is," Raquel said, "that you're good at dealing with difficult people. Also, no matter what she said about how much our esteemed granny loves to read, Gloria knows the value of being visual, having the ability to see detail, design. And talking culture, you comprehend how important glamour is in our larger culture. Beauty. Celebrity. Call it whatever you want to, but you are in the industry that's world-famous for its success in selling it."

"Well," I said to them, "we all are one-quarter Granny Goldberg Goldberg Garrison, and maybe in her eyes that makes one or all of us capable of running Glory. Who the hell knows? Except we're still three-quarters un-Gloria."

"Gracias a Dios," Raquel muttered.

"But tell me: Is either of you even the slightest bit interested in Glory?"

Twelve

Gloria

Awkward silence bothers just about everybody. But not me. For instance, when a person is seated in a doctor's office or beside a businessman on a plane, or walks up to a knot of strangers at a party, at first they'll be chatting away. It's comfortable, easy.

Like if I said to someone, "I'm Gloria Garrison." Well, it is easier with that name. There's no *blink-blink* like when I was Gloria Goldberg, with the person shifting into Jew mode and thinking, *Hopefully she'll be funny and not want to talk about America's working poor.*

But okay, he introduces himself back and yes, it could be a she, but I loathe that he/she business. In any case, the talk is pleasant enough, the words are flowing. But inevitably the flow of words ebbs to a trickle—and an instant later, it stops entirely.

Now what would ninety-nine percent of the people in the world do if they were in that position? They'd develop sudden, clumsy excuses to break away—need another drink, need to visit the powder room, need to say hello to an old friend over there by the pita chips—rather than stand there in silence.

Awkward silence doesn't rattle me because I was once the one who caused it. All those years of being a pariah in Cincinnati got me accustomed to not having to make conversation since no one wanted to converse with me. Wherever I went, people shut up.

You'd imagine it would have been different when I went to New York and started working in the Garment Center, the district that never shuts up. Everyone's babbling simultaneously. Yet there was one exception: Nobody expected complete sentences, subject-verb-object, from the models. Truthfully, beyond a few dulcet words like "hello" and "goodbye," no one wanted to hear from us at all. It was every showroom's unwritten rule, let the clothes speak for themselves, which, translated, meant, *Girls, keep your shoulders back and your traps shut.*

Even the men we went out with didn't want to hear our opinions on anything unless it was, *Oh, Mr. Wonderful, I'm thrilled to be with you. Now tell me more about yourself.* Then, our lips moist and slightly apart—though forming no words—we acted transfixed while they talked . . . and talked. If, heaven forefend, an awkward silence did descend, we knew not to banish it with prolonged chatter. All the man-hunting girls in the showroom swore by the advice from Rose Smyth Fairleigh's book, *The Girl's Guide to Courtship . . . and Beyond.* One of the nuggets of wisdom they liked to quote was, "Be prepared, girls! Make a list of conversation pick-me-ups *before* a big evening. Memorize it. That way, when he becomes fatigued with the tête-à-tête, you'll be ready to get him talking again!"

But getting back to awkward silence. That's exactly what I knew I'd be facing when I walked into the dining room at three minutes after seven (on my theory of it's pitiable to be early, a bore to be precisely on time, and a breach of good manners to be more than slightly late). I pictured the Goldberg progeny sitting there practically like those Pompeii people, not saying a word. All right, they might be sipping water. But they would be too unsure to butter the baguettine rolls on their bread plates. I assumed they'd have progressed from a snit over my using an investigative agency to spy on them to wariness—afraid to speak for fear that as I came into the room, I'd overhear something that would ruin their chances of grabbing Glory. Or perhaps, no longer regarding each other as family but as competitors for the big prize, they'd clammed up.

Yet as I walked into the hallway, I could hear Matthew and one of the girls laughing. Rollicking laughter, at that. I decided the girl would be Daisy, since I couldn't imagine Raquel giving in to high hilarity. But as I entered the dining room, it turned out all three of them were guffawing over something. The two girls just happened to laugh on the same wavelength, so they sounded like one. Their ha-has had the heartiness of genuine laughter, the sort that causes snorting, curls the lip, and allows gums to show. Sad how delight is so unattractive.

Since they already knew that one and only one of them would inherit my company, I felt safe in thinking the glee was not at my expense. Sure enough, the laughter stopped the instant they saw me, though they all smiled a welcome: a three-part confirmation of a generation's devotion to whitening strips. Too bad they didn't know I was sending them home.

"How nice," I said, "the three of you dressed for dinner." Matthew was wearing a jacket—no tie—which is about as dressy as it gets in the Southwest. I liked that he had the style sensibility to know what was appropriate in another part of the country. The jacket looked like a refined offspring of burlap. Way back when we used to call it hopsacking. Now, fifty years or so later it probably had another name. Matthew was a good dresser. For an instant, it reminded me of the dapper way my grandpa Louie had gotten himself up for synagogue. Of course, there was no fedora or Panama hat for Matthew (and no yarmulke beneath it). Not that I was getting sentimental. With my grandson's hair slicked back (held by a gel that had too high a polymer count and was too viscous for Matthew's naturally straight hair), he bore no resemblance to my grandfather. Actually, Matthew looked amazingly like my ex, Joe. It wasn't just the physical resemblance. It was his razzmatazz.

Usually, good-looking, outgoing men aren't, in fact, appealing. They're more like pedigreed puppies, charming and sexless. Not Joe. He had heat. Women felt it, moved toward it. The same was obviously true with his grandson. Not with Bradley, though: Good looks and, well, dynamism, had skipped a generation. Actually, that's not accurate. Travis wasn't a looker like Joe and now Matthew. But the three of them shared a . . . call it animal magnetism. Whereas poor Bradley was the human equivalent of a lox.

While Matthew was got up perfectly for a dressy dinner in Santa Fe, Raquel looked as if she were going to one of those trendy restaurants in downtown Manhattan or Brooklyn you read about. Black skirt, black silk T, earrings that looked like two giant pieces of popcorn dipped in silver. Hair held off her face by a thin black headband. Very minimalist, though well thought-out. *Good choice,* I might have said. But I didn't. She would have taken it the wrong way: that I was trying to get into her good graces.

I never, to use the vernacular, kissed ass. Most beautiful women, which I once was, get good at doing precisely that. *Oh, please, like me for what's inside of me, not for this flawless surface.* They wind up apologizing for their good fortune all their lives, and they become tedious.

It was pure luck. When the train pulled out of Union Terminal in Cincinnati for New York with me on it, I had one of those magical moments. There I was, sidling along to find a better seat. I happened to catch a quick glance at a reflection in the train's window. For the first instant, I thought, *Gee, she's gorgeous.* Then I realized it was me. I mean, there I was, hoping to be a model, so I knew I wasn't homely and also that I was relatively tall and slender, which was fortunate since I had no other skills. But boys had always told me I was pretty. Some actually asked questions like, "Why do you, um, uh, you know?" One said (at the moment he was, shall we say, inserting himself), "You don't need to be doing this."

As the train picked up speed, escaping all those boys, the mother who hated me, the father who didn't—not that it did either of us any good—I said to myself, *No more. I don't need to.* Maybe I overdid it, but being a beauty, or a near-beauty, gives you license to behave badly: In New York, people thought I was a cool cookie, or just cold. I never went out of my way to smile or make conversation. The awkward silence that was part of the package? Not only didn't I care, I thrilled at my ability to endure it. Same thing when someone tried to snub me or hurt my feelings. I didn't see it or hear it, and the wonderful thing was, they realized it: They knew whatever insult they tried on me didn't touch me one whit.

After I got married, I overheard one of my neighbors in Great Neck telling another, "Stunning, but a heart like a block of ice." I was more amused than hurt. Now I hear people say things to the effect of, "That Gloria is a tough old nut." But I don't try to charm. I won't kiss ass. If someone detested me—and many did, including, it seemed, my granddaughter Raquel—so be it.

The other granddaughter, Daisy, whom I'd pretty much written off as someone who hides from life behind art, was the surprise of the evening. Lookswise. Fine, call me superficial. It's my business. Anyway, as they say in Santa Fe, Matthew cleaned up real good, as I expected he would. And

Raquel, with her petite, compact body, clear skin, and eyes even darker than her hair, looked as chic as she was smart.

Daisy, though, had undergone the sort of transformation that made me think, *Never thought she had it in her.* Forget that I still yearned to summon Lizzy, Glory's resident tweezing/waxing/threading genius, to do something with that girl's brows. *For God's sake,* I wanted to cry out, *birds could nest in them.* But other than that, Daisy was so on the money she looked like she was a Glory regular, one of those women who set up an appointment for an upgrade three years hence, before they exit the Glo-mobile. (I thought that one up when our first truck was still being outfitted, because potential customers wouldn't be enticed by *Come into our lovely truck.*)

When you're built like Daisy was, resembling a generous figure 8, you don't want to pull back your hair too tight because it gives you a pinheaded look. She seemed to know that: Her hair was done up properly, in a casual knot but loose. It was the way Katharine Hepburn wore hers, though naturally that was where the resemblance ended. My granddaughter's hair was smoother than Hepburn's, but of course she lived in an age of product that not even a movie star could get her hands on in the '40s and '50s.

Daisy was wearing a more closed-up version of the halter dress figure-8 women like Marilyn Monroe and Sophia Loren went for, with the skirt loose around her hips but not, blessedly, voluminous. God knows, she wasn't what one would call wasp-waisted. Her middle made one chunky-looking 8. Still, she was broad enough in the beam and shoulders that her middle appeared more slender than it actually was. The problem was, the dress was too short. Daisy's legs weren't bad, but it was a length you'd expect to see on a fifteen-year-old model in *Seventeen* magazine; that style at that length would never make it into *Elle.*

Unlike Raquel, who could get away with a double application of mascara and a lip stain and call it a day, Daisy needed makeup, which, to her credit, she was wearing. Enough to define her eyes nicely. She also had on what I believed was the twenty-first-century version of the classic Revlon lipstick Cherries in the Snow, a red with some blue in it. Perfect for someone with Daisy's ivory skin. (That's what people in the cosmetics industry call a pale complexion with a faintly yellow undertone.) She seemed to have invested in a high-priced blush. Very effective and natural. No iridescence, thank goodness. I would have liked to ask her what brand, but as I was essentially tossing her out of my house ASAP, I had to refrain. Her foundation had too much rose in it, as if she were trying to match the color of the blush, but that could be easily remedied.

Involuntarily, my head moved, which Daisy seemed to take as a nod of approval. Since it wasn't as if I disapproved, I let it go, even though I had been determined not to give off any signals any of them might construe as, *You have my support.* Because none of them did.

As I got to the head of the table, Matthew stood and pulled out my chair for me. I didn't think anyone his age even knew to do that. "Thank you," I said, noticing that a more than usually sour expression passed over Raquel's face. It reflected her disapproval of what, no doubt, she considered antiquated gender roles and I thought of as politeness. Not required, merely courteous. No doubt if Raquel's live-in, Mr. Hyphen, whatever his name was—the investigator's report had it—had been the sort to stand and pull out her chair, she'd have a different opinion on the subject.

I lifted my right knee to press the call bell under the table. Carlos and Paula responded, bringing out the meal in a couple of trips and setting it on the ten-foot-long buffet. Not that there was ten feet worth of food, but they knew how to present it right. Also, Carlos had an enviable visual sense; he knew not only the precise spot where the salad bowl should go but also at what angle the silver-and-rosewood servers should be resting. I stayed silent as he poured the wine. The grandchildren all wanted red, which was typical of New Yorkers who thought red shows you have a more sophisticated palate. Since most of them wear black, as if perpetually prepared for poetry or death, drinking red doesn't matter. Dribbling a little Vega Sicilia was no catastrophe.

"I thought it would be less formal if we made dinner a buffet," I said. Less formal and also it wasn't necessary for Carlos and Paula to hear me tell my grandchildren goodbye. *None of you will take over Glory.*

To my surprise, the three had mixed up the seating arrangement I'd pictured they'd take, the brother and sister on one side, Cha-cha across from them. But Raquel and Matthew sat to my right. Daisy was alone on my left: at dinner as in life, as I'd learned from the Stern & Picciuto Investigations report.

"Please," I said, "the plates are on the sideboard. Help yourselves." At least they'd been well-bred enough to know the hostess goes last, so the three of them went over to the buffet.

"Looks nice," Matthew said, pondering a rice and corn dish.

"Matty," Daisy said, "you're going to love the salad. See? It has, like, forty-seven avocados sliced into it." She held up the fork and spoon that contained a giant scoop of lettuce and whatnot. "It even has radishes! Heaven." She dumped the salad on her plate and moved on to a platter of cold sliced veal. She didn't hesitate: "Gloria? Is this pork?"

"Veal." I was itching to ask if hers was a culinary question or a religious one, but I bet it was the latter, and I didn't want to hear a song and dance about respecting tradition and five thousand years of history. So I just busied myself checking the table to make sure Paula had put down the salt and pepper mills, which she had.

"I'm in love with radishes, too," Raquel said, though from the small portion she took, it seemed a mere infatuation.

If not awkward silence, I'd expected at least some sort of stiffness, but the three of them chatted among themselves about their experiences with cold veal with the easy familiarity of . . . I suppose it would be accurate to call it a family reunion.

When I stood to serve myself, the girls were already back at the table, and Matthew was heading there with his plate in one hand and two dinner rolls grasped in the other. He flashed a smile at me that was almost like Travis's, though more open. Matthew was not only better looking than my son had been, but friendlier as well. There had been an intriguing reserve about Travis that was completely missing in this boy.

According to the Stern & Picciuto information, women gravitated toward Matthew and vice versa. Not that he was promiscuous. Rather, he was a serial lover, falling for one girl, losing interest, falling for another, a seemingly endless cycle. Like so many of his generation, he had the attention span of a flea, though while he was perched on one particular woman, he was an extremely loyal and friendly flea.

When I got to the buffet, I took only vegetables and the rice. Let them think I was a vegetarian. On my last visit to the periodontist, he told me my gums were receding in an "alarming" way, although for thirty thousand dollars and a week of recuperation the problem could be dealt with. Oh, certainly, a week away from the office. Meanwhile, whatever I did, I couldn't risk having a tooth clink onto the plate for the sake of a piece of veal.

Travis, though God knows he was charming enough and a great success with women, always held back a little something, enough to make people wonder what his secret was. Everyone, including me, seemed to believe he had a secret. By "secret," I wasn't thinking of something specific, like with people who failed to file tax returns or have sexual predilections involving barnyard creatures. Perhaps "private" would be a more accurate description. You knew there was an aspect of Travis he wasn't willing to reveal, though he probably opened up to Adriana. That was the mystery of his life I could never solve. He could have gotten any woman—wealthy, sophisticated, a world-class beauty—and he chose a nineteen-year-old Puerto Rican from a public college.

Thinking of my son made me glance at Raquel. She was carefully arranging her napkin on her lap, centering it, intent on smoothing out the linen. Even though she didn't look much like her father, her expression seized my heart for a moment. There it was: the tip of her tongue resting against her upper lip. Travis had done it whenever he was really concentrating. He'd gotten it from Joe. I used to joke: What was there in evolution that made tongue-sticking-out a quality that needed to be passed down from one generation to the next? And now, the girl did it, too. I sat down again and turned all my attention to Daisy so I wouldn't have to look at Raquel.

Just as I was opening my mouth to announce, *This plan of mine for Glory isn't going to work out,* Matthew spoke up: "When we went up to relax and get ready for dinner—really thoughtful of you to give us the time. Thank you. The three of us got to talking." I nodded. "We never discussed any of the details about Glory with you." I would have interjected whatever was the polite equivalent of *No need to know now,* but being a New Yorker, he did not leave any space between sentences. "Before we have any more substantial conversation about your plans for the company, we'd each like to talk to you. I'm not the spokesman. We're all going to speak for ourselves."

"Please, be my guest. Guests, which I suppose you are."

Matthew looked at the girls and asked, "Does either of you want to go—"

"I will," Daisy said. She took a deep breath. She didn't seem a natural talker like her brother. I bet it was a competence she'd worked on over the years though hadn't perfected. I picked up signs of nervousness. She was holding her fork so tight it must have been painful; she actually had to look at her hand and instruct it to loosen up in order to put the fork down. She wanted to go first to get it over with. "I'll be brief. I'm grateful we had a chance to get together and I hope no matter . . ." Another deep breath, and an exceedingly long and irritating exhalation. *Spit it out,* I wanted to snap at her. "I hope in the future, we can see each other again, get to know each other."

"We'll see," was all I could come up with. *Over my dead body* would have been a little too harsh as well as uncomfortably imminent, and *Don't bet the ranch on it* needlessly provocative. What was I supposed to say? *Oh, I'd love that*? For both our sakes, what was the point of pretending? "Was that all you had to say?"

"No. I can't tell you that I've given your proposal a lot of thought. There hasn't been enough time for it. Or enough information. But I knew instantly it wasn't for me. I have a job I love . . . in New York. The studio has spoken to me about moving to L.A., and so far I've been able to talk them out of it. Would I go if I had to? I don't know. I like L.A. and have some friends there. I'd probably go, because that's where so much of the movie business is. I can't see myself in any other industry. I always wanted to be part of it and—" She offered me a broad smile. She had dimples, I noticed. I'd always found dimples in adults annoying. "—what do you know? I'm right where I want to be. In the industry but not of it. Safely and happily on the periphery." Her smile didn't flicker even when it was clear I wasn't smiling back. "So thank you very much for your . . . well, not offer. Thank you for considering me. But I don't want to be in the competition."

"All right," I said.

In what I assumed was a gesture of sincerity, she clasped her hands and rested them on the edge of the table. She had close to no natural grace. The weight of her hands tilted her plate, and her dinner nearly ended in her lap. She righted it in time, though a red flush brightened her face and neck. "I'm honored that you even considered me—"

I cut her off because I didn't want to hear her natter about being honored and touched. "Don't worry about not hurting my feelings," I said. "There are those who would claim I have none, which of course is ridiculous. But if learning to run a business like Glory is not for you, I have to accept your decision and move on. All right. Matthew? Raquel?"

"You want to go?" Matthew asked Raquel. Her shrug was nonchalant, as in, *First, second . . . Makes no difference to me.*

I was often unnerved by that kind of equality between men and women. That he didn't even attempt to insist she go first was, in my day, unthinkable, to say nothing of boorish. I remembered Keith being shocked when some twenty-something man pushed his way out of an elevator, not standing back to let me go first. I told him—Keith, that is—that back when I was living in New York, I passed a group of children on a playground. It was shortly after Ethel and Julius Rosenberg had been executed for espionage, and a few of the boys were chanting, "Girls go first everywhere / Even in the electric chair."

"Okay," Matthew said. It sounded like a prelude to something, and when Raquel picked up her fork and pierced a couple of radish slices, I gathered the decision had been made. "This is an amazing chance you're offering one of us," he said. "I'm not like my sister, feeling I'm in the absolute perfect job, perfect place. I mean, right now I'm happy with the Mets organization. Okay, the team has been under financial stress. We've had injuries. Major investments in certain players who don't perform as expected. But still, it's a great place to be. I work hard, I've risen through the ranks, so it's not like my effort goes unnoticed. But truth be told? I could be happy doing PR for any decent professional sports team. My long-term goal is to move into management."

"So you feel you could only be happy working in the area of sports?" I asked him. All right, I probably put the word "happy" into verbal quotation marks because too many of their generation, despite the appalling condition of the economy, seemed fixated on doing something they loooved. Personal satisfaction trumped not only a paycheck but their prospects for advancement as well.

It also bothered me that I hadn't thought about this generational quirk before I contemplated the fate of Glory.

But then Matthew said, "Not necessarily. I love professional sports. It's like every boy's dream come true, working for a team you've been rooting for your whole life, getting to know the players, going down to Port St. Lucie a week before the pitchers and catchers report for spring training. If you said to me, 'I'll give you four times your current salary to do PR for the National Rifle Association,' I'd laugh at you. On the other hand, if you said—"

"What? You'd work for half your salary for Human Rights Watch?" I asked.

"No." I waited for him to explain himself, but he seemed to think no was sufficient. He went on, though I noticed a little less dash in his presentation. Based on that and the fading of the gleam of his brown eyes, I sensed he was annoyed with me for typecasting him as an East Coast knee-jerk lefty. "I'm not fixated on sports," he continued. "If you told me, 'I'll double your salary to work for, say, Citibank and after a couple of years move you from PR into some sort of policy-making area,' I would definitely consider it."

Now I couldn't tell where Matthew was going, which put me on edge. I was usually expert at that, especially with younger people who had not yet learned the subtleties of playing emotional poker.

"I'd love to know more about Glory," he said. "It sounds like a terrific business. You're fulfilling a consumer need that's obviously out there." He tilted his head. A bit too adorable for my taste. "Do you call the people who use your services customers or clients?"

"Clients."

"You didn't have to manufacture a consumer need for something people never knew they wanted or couldn't really afford. From the little I've read, it sounds like you came up with a unique system to dispense services and products at a reasonable price. And you take pride in the quality of what you sell. Also, since I'm one of the two grandchildren left on your list, it's reassuring that even though the clientele is women, the person you'd originally wanted to take over was a guy."

Daisy had said thanks but no thanks,

but when I glanced her way I saw she was following the conversation as if she were still in the running. I wondered: Was she so tuned in because it was her brother speaking? Or had what he said ignited some renewed interest?

Frankly, I hadn't anticipated that one of them would say no. I had been planning to reject them, not the other way around. "Your offer," Matthew was saying, "to learn the ropes at Glory and eventually well—"

"And eventually inherit it." I finished the sentence he was too embarrassed to complete. "If all goes well, and either you or Raquel—whoever I choose—proves to me you're not an idiot, then that one will own the business. I suppose you're both curious about what my standards are regarding idiocy."

"I'd like to hear about them at some point," Matthew said. Was he so focused on plunging ahead in his conversation, or was he being rude by brushing me off with a vague "at some point"? I was about to interrupt him, if only to establish it wasn't up to him to postpone any conversation I wanted to have.

However, he kept talking and I couldn't get a word in. "Look, Glory is clearly great business, an amazing opportunity. But I don't want to be in consideration."

I couldn't even get out a *What?* That's how stunned I was.

"I'm just too tied to New York to think about relocating."

If I had searched for a better example of idiocy, I couldn't have found it. Tied to New York?

"See, I've been seeing a woman just finishing her last year of med school at Mount Sinai. Then she'll be at New York–Presbyterian. She's going for emergency medicine. She's originally from Houston. Well, technically, from China because she was adopted. But she doesn't want to go back to Texas. She feels she was meant for New York. Her name is Ashley. Ashley Altman. And I want to be with her. I'm in love with her." He made a big deal about swallowing. That gulping, manly aw-shucks business. "We're going to get married," he added. Raquel sat up even straighter than her usual stick-up-her-rear posture. Daisy's red-lipsticked mouth formed an O of surprise. He glanced across the table at his sister, then quickly turned back at me. "I haven't proposed yet."

"Then how can you be certain Dr. Ashley's shoes are stuck to the sidewalks of New York with Krazy Glue?" I demanded.

"Because we've talked, you know, in general terms. She's there for the next four years at least. But more likely for life." Not only was Matthew being ridiculous, but Daisy and Raquel were exasperating me beyond measure by exchanging those stupid twenty-something girlfriend OMG looks: *OMG, Matt wants to get married!*

"We have our fair share of medical emergencies in Santa Fe," I said, "what with crystal meth and our gun control laws. Overdoses, shootings. No doubt she could find working here sufficiently challenging."

"Presbyterian in New York has one of the highest-ranked ER residencies in the country. I can't see asking her to give that up."

"Not even for the chance to make triple what you're earning?" The minute I said that, I wanted to pull it back in. It made it seem as if I was actively recruiting him, and the last thing I wanted to appear was overeager.

He leaned back in the chair. I could see he would have liked to tilt back farther, so that he'd be at a more relaxed angle with only the chair's two back legs on the floor. It was one of those sex-linked traits I wasn't equipped to comprehend. "How about you?" Matthew asked.

"How about me?" I repeated.

"Would you consider moving the business's operations to New York?"

"Of course not. We operate in the West and Southwest. What possible sense, businesswise, could it make to go east?"

"To grow the business."

"If I were planning to grow the business that way, I'd be looking at the Plains states, the Midwest. But I'm not. Once I'm gone, it's in the hands of whoever takes over. If it were you, you could send every one of the Glo-mobiles into the bowels of Queens for all I'd care. Well, obviously I'd be beyond caring."

"Just for the record," Matthew said, "I agree with you. It would make no sense to move to the East Coast. Too urbanized. Too many hair-styling places, too many clothing stores."

"So?"

Amazing, how much he was like Travis—and Joe. And nothing like his father. Matthew's mouth formed . . . not a half smile, more like a quarter smile, where the sides of his lips barely turned up while his cheeks lifted just a bit. Amused, and perhaps a little mean. Not mean in the sense of cruelty. Mean as in selfish.

I knew what he was going to say, and he said it. "So thank you for thinking enough about our"—he paused to come up with the word—"kinship to consider me. But I can't leave New York. No, strike that. I could conceivably leave New York. I could never leave Ashley."

I nodded to Matthew. It was a good way to look grande dame–ish and also avoid speaking with that old lady croak when emotion and mucus combine. It wasn't just the rejection that was causing me to doubt myself: *I will not get a heart attack from this.* It was the knowledge I had only one grandchild left, and I wasn't looking forward to hearing what she had to say. Either way, my tight chest told me, it would be dreadful.

Still, what choice did I have? Too bad I couldn't say now what I'd intended to say when I first sat at the dining room table, that my plan wasn't going to work out and wouldn't it be wise for all of them to take the first plane back to New York? I had to listen to Raquel. Just to unsettle her, I only nodded. *Go ahead.*

Unfortunately, it had slipped my mind that she'd had a year of courtroom experience, and disarming nods and icy silence no longer worked on her. Instead of shifting in her seat or making a teepee with her fingers—the movements of the disarmed—she simply began speaking.

"Unlike Daisy, I can't say I'm in love with my job. It's what I always wanted to do, but now that I'm doing it, I could come up with a hundred other things I'd like to do for the rest of my working life. Like Matt, I'm in love with somebody who's committed to New York, or pretty committed, but I don't think he's quite ready to make a commitment to me." She emphasized "quite," as if in two minutes or two weeks he'd be getting down on his knee.

Somewhat unlikely, I could have told her. I had information from Stern & Picciuto that she was apparently blissfully unaware of: that Hayden Ramos-Cruz, who often worked late, was doing due diligence with one of his Goldman Sachs colleagues . . . at her apartment. Although maybe he would propose, since a cursory inquiry had unearthed the evidence that while he might have been a whiz at bonds, he had never been gifted at fidelity. Single, married: He would cheat.

Even if she infuriated me, I would keep silent.

"It's interesting," Raquel said. "At so many different points in my life, I thought,

'God, what I would say to that woman—you—if I only got the chance.' "

"I can imagine," I said. Her hair was down, and with her thin leather headband, she looked like a sepia photo of Alice in Wonderland.

"Dubious. Or maybe you're more self-aware and conscious of what you do to people than I'd always assumed. Anyway, it doesn't matter anymore. It boils down to this. I give you credit for having been a loving mother to my father. I've tried to be charitable when thinking about you, but it's an uphill slog. Forget about you ignoring me. You showed absolutely no compassion or even polite behavior toward my mother. She was a widow with a young child and you basically turned your back on her—said, *Why should I help that Latina? That Catholic? That whatever? What's she to me now that Travis is gone?* Bottom line? There's no way in hell I would want to move to the city you live in. And as for Glory? I know you must have named it for yourself, but it's a word used in worship. It's a word about adoration. Self-worship, I think, in your case.

Self-adoration. Such a telling choice. And so, I'm your third strike: I'm sure I don't have to tell you, though I will, what three strikes mean, grandchildrenwise. You're out."

Thirteen

Raquel

Okay, so after my "You're out" to Gloria, the State Department wouldn't rush to sign me for the diplomatic corps. But consider the mitigating circumstances. (If you're a defense lawyer, that's what you've got to be able to convince a jury to do.)

In mitigation: Just being in Gloria Garrison's house, I immediately passed bummed and went straight to agitated. The wealth. The vast rooms of wood from upper-class trees, a laughable homage to a simple style. Okay, she didn't have to have an outhouse, but marble bathrooms? Lighting so brilliantly engineered it somehow got inside you, imparting an inner glow, though you knew that once you returned to the real world, you'd revert to your old lackluster self. And there were all those throwaway touches that signaled, *Major money here!*—ironed pillowcases, English soap, servants dressed alike. All for that miserable, arrogant old woman with her ninety-million-carat diamond.

And to make it worse, it all had a certain appeal for me. No, that's not true. I was enthralled. God, what money can buy! The cashmere blanket tossed over the arm of a couch in a room made uncomfortably cold by too much air-conditioning. Servants who keep running into bathrooms to fold the first sheet of toilet paper back into a point. My luxuriating in all this was a denial of everything I'd ever hoped to be, and that knowledge made me literally sick. In the dining room, when Paula and Carlos brought out the food on the bowls and platters and arranged them on the buffet, I felt like a hand was reaching inside me and squeezing my esophagus until it was nearly closed.

Yet when I told my grandmother, “You’re out,” I didn’t come off as agitated. My tone was not only low-key, there wasn’t even a hint of spitefulness in it. Okay, a hint. But it wasn’t like I was stabbing the air with my index finger and pointing, *Out!* (Of course, if I’d done that, it would have been supremo chutzpah, considering it was Gloria’s house, not mine.) Again, in mitigation, it wasn’t like I said something heart attack–inducing to the old lady. All I’d done was call attention to the obvious, that none of us three was interested in Glory and therefore Gloria’s proposal was a no-go.

Had it been necessary for me to be so explicit when she was perfectly capable of doing the math? Three grandchildren + three nos = time to rethink the plan of succession. No, I had to admit, my remarks hadn’t been necessary. But on the other hand, consider all that I was successfully holding back: rage, vituperation. I refrained, too, from so many small cruelties that came to mind, as in, *Isn't it amazing that after all your plastic surgery, your mouth is still a permanent, downturned scowl?*

And I didn't say, *If you think anyone in New Mexico with a degree of sophistication believes you were born with the name Garrison, you're delusional.* That probably would have offended Daisy and Matt—no, strike "probably." Also, it would have been especially graceless coming from me who so hated prejudice.

I didn't mind when Jewish people assumed from my name, Goldberg, that I was one of theirs. They were always asking me, "Are you taking off both days of Rosh Hashanah?" I'd answer, "No. Neither. I'm not Jewish." They'd try not to look shocked. Then they'd ask with extravagant casualness, "Oh, what are you?" And I'd say, "Catholic." But the next step wasn't okay with me, when they started with (obviously because of my skin color), "Oh, I thought you were Sephardic." So I'd explain, no, I'm half Puerto Rican, half Jewish. My dad was Jewish. But he died when I was four. I was raised Catholic." Then, even though

I'd promised myself I wouldn't, I'd wind up saying something like "Catholic from birth," so they wouldn't think my mom snuck me off to the baptismal font the minute she heard my dad was dead. It was lame of me to feel I owed an explanation. But even when I did, I sensed some of the looks I got were still *traitor, apostate.*

Of course, I got prejudice from the Christian side of it too, where people responded to my explanation of my last name with, "Oh, fabulous! Now I don't have to say 'Happy holidays' to you. I can say 'Merry Christmas'!" It was like my being Catholic relieved them of a burden they'd yearned their whole lives to put down. And of course it also gave some of them permission to make anti-Semitic remarks in front of me. I wanted to say, *How stupid are you? I told you my father was Jewish—to say nothing of our Savior,* though what was the point of going there? I knew that two minutes after I left, those good Christians would be making anti-Latino comments about how immigration was killing the country. Assholes.

God, it was amazing how each and every time a thought about Gloria Garrison entered my head, I'd explode about something. And not only did I get furious over her wrongs. She also served as a burning fuse that reignited every hostile thought I'd ever had on any subject at all.

Anyway, right after delivering my "You're out" line, I began thinking that if my mother had overheard me, she'd hang her head in shame. Not over my being capable of meanness. Doing what she did for a living, she knew that even basically decent people can behave badly. No, she'd be mortified because I hadn't exercised the self-control to put myself on mute. Or that after giving in to my lesser nature and mouthing off, I didn't instantly jump up and apologize to my elder for my bad manners. However, talk about potential mitigating circumstances: If I'd had the time it takes to blink, I actually might have done just that. Said I was sorry.

But my grandmother came back too fast. "So be it," she proclaimed. She took less than a second to shift back to her usual efficient, officious self. "Let me see what I can do about getting all of you on an early flight out. There's no purpose now in continuing with what I had planned, visiting Glory, giving you my views on how the company developed . . ."

As she spoke, I was beginning to regret the "You're out" comment. I felt that flush I get when remorse hits. The burning redness rises along the sides of my neck, up along my jawline toward my ears. Yet in that the same instant, I was also dealing with an overpowering urge to laugh because it took just seconds for Gloria to decide to get rid of us early. What reflexes! So much for the family reunion.

But before she could list all the reasons why it made no sense for us to hang around, Matt cut her off. "Gloria, I'm only speaking for myself—I guess you're getting sick of hearing that—but if it's okay with you, I'd like to stay on."

She jerked her head back, as if he'd made some kind of indecent suggestion. She followed that up with a frigid "Why?"

Unlike me, who'd been unable to resist a snotty comeback, my cousin Matt appeared thoughtful, the way you get when you're assuming that the person asking "Why?" is genuinely interested in what's going on inside your head. He bought time by doing the manly chin-rubbing deal. Manly looked good on him. His looks were the sports guy, outdoorsy kind, so chin rubbing came off as natural. It wasn't like some five-foot-seven investment banker who hadn't seen sunlight since 1999 trying to approximate macho.

Daisy, meanwhile, seemed desperate to get out of there. Not just out of the dining room or the house, but Santa Fe as well. She shot Matt a how-stupid-are-you? glare when he mentioned staying. She was so primed for escape, shifted sideways in her chair, one foot way forward. She seemed only to be waiting for the crack of the starting pistol to take off.

"We each gave reasons why we weren't interested in Glory," Matt said. "But they really weren't about Glory. They were actually about not wanting to leave New York. Let me be clear: When I formally propose to Ashley, I would never dream of saying, 'This offer is contingent on your willingness to give up your residency at Presbyterian and treat crystal meth cases in New Mexico.' So I am tied to New York. But I feel bad that the three of us—boom, boom, boom—rejected the opportunity without really understanding what we were giving up. You've built something amazing. Speaking just for me, it was thoughtless to say no right away."

"If you're concerned about hurting my feelings," Gloria said, "you're wasting time and pity." She flared her nostrils. I guessed that signaled disdain. I couldn't tell if it was sincere or she was faking it because, somewhere deep inside her, there remained one molecule of vulnerability. I so wished I read people like that guy on that TV series *Lie to Me* did—check out minuscule facial movements and body gestures that give away what a person is feeling, no matter how hard he or she tried to hide it.

"No was no," Gloria told Matt. "It doesn't matter what its genesis was. I didn't ask you here for sentimental reasons. If I had any need to know you, don't you think I would have done it by now? This was business. You made a decision, period. I accept it. There's no need for me to play show-and-tell with you."

Funny, I'd met a fair number of tough customers. Not just gangbangers in the Bronx, but also the tough though legit. There weren't that many hard-asses in Legal Aid, but they thrived in the DA's office. And some of Hayden's colleagues at Goldman were natural-born killers, as was my history department adviser at Barnard—people with hearts of ice and the emotional depth of a Kleenex.

But our grandmother had a whole new level of tough. Not only did she seem not to care that Matt had feelings, decent ones, she'd detached from us totally the instant we'd said no. We were no longer of interest, though when we left for the early plane, she'd probably arrange for someone to give us breakfast.

"I know you're too busy for show-and-tell," Matt came back at her. "And maybe by your standards we've made an irreversible error and don't merit any more consideration." I guessed that in PR, as in a courtroom, you learned to keep going in the face of discouragement. "On the other hand, you didn't select three random college graduates. You specifically brought us here because we're family. It's not like you've already lined up the next three grandchildren with their bags packed and tickets to Santa Fe."

"I think I've learned my lesson," Gloria said, "that people related to me by blood are not necessarily the ones who can, shall we say, make the sort of coolheaded business decisions needed to run a company like Glory."

Matt began a smile, but her absolute indifference along with her emotionless, flat Midwestern accent froze his face. He had no comeback. Still, I was way beyond surprised when I heard myself actually talking to her: "Presumably when you decided to ask us here, you weren't being hotheaded." She glanced at me with the same affection she might give to a cockroach. "It was a rational business decision and no doubt one you made with care. Just because it didn't work out doesn't mean we're not coolheaded enough to run Glory."

"What are you trying to say?" Gloria asked me. I didn't need the *Lie to Me* guy to interpret that no matter how pissed she was at Matt and Daisy, she was extra mad at me.

"I'm saying . . . Well, first I want to apologize for the three strikes you're out remark I made. And the rest. Maybe it didn't bother you, but it was rude. I'm sorry." Silence. "Also, as far as Matt's request that we not leave tomorrow morning. It seems to me you should honor it. Even if you think we're all stupid and crippled by emotion, we are your grandchildren. If you took stock of the relationship earlier, and were willing to put aside a lot of years of distance and whatever, I don't see why you now have to abandon the idea that some tie exists between us. Even if it's tenuous. Let's see what happens. The tie may stay tenuous. You can decide to reject us completely and never think of us again. Maybe vice versa. But it's not like any of us have big plans for the weekend we'd be giving up."

Daisy spoke up. "I swear to God. None of us will call you Grammy."

Gloria peered over at the buffet. Maybe she was thinking about all the food in her fridge that would go to waste if we took the first plane out. Finally, she spoke: "All right. We'll go ahead as planned."

By the time we got upstairs it was after eleven, which meant one o'clock New York time. Too late to call Hayden. He was one of those guys always ready to pack it in by ten, unless he had to work late, which he so often did.

All I could think about, besides the giant bed with four posts, twirly wood columns that reminded me of frosting from an expensive cupcake store, was the giant bathtub. Wow, to bathe in that! Except as I was looking around the bathroom, there wasn't anything to clean the tub with afterward. If I used the bath salts that were in a beautiful crock on the bathtub ledge, along with an aqua dish with a giant bar of unused white soap, then I'd have to leave the tub for a servant to wash. I could almost hear Gloria say, *Well? What do you think they get paid for?* But I couldn't leave it for someone else to do. When you're the child of a working mother, you're so trained to clean up after yourself that not to do so would be such appalling behavior you couldn't live with yourself. When I was a kid and left a mess, my mother would come up with stuff like, "Chelsea Clinton lives in the White House and, trust me, she doesn't have servants picking up after her." I believed her.

I was gazing down into the vastness of the bathtub when I heard a knock at the door. I had a brief fantasy that it was Paula, the maid, who would say, *Ms. Garrison hopes you'll take advantage of the tub and the rare French bath salts that smell like jasmine. Please don't worry about washing the tub, it's part of my job and I actually enjoy the stretching.* Then I edited the fantasy, having her tell me, *Ms. Garrison has a special tub washer on retainer,* so I wouldn't be giving the dirty work to Paula. But then I figured the knock was Daisy's. I was right.

"I can't sleep," she announced, just standing there. Since it was less than five minutes since we'd left the dining room, she couldn't have tried very hard. "Jet lag. Grammy. Matt wanting to get married. I mean, I'm stunned, totally and irrevocably."

There was nothing else I could say except, "Come in." Daisy did look like she'd had a rough night. The weight of her mascara seemed to be pulling down her eyelids so you could only see the bottom halves of her eyes. Her dress looked like she'd worn it on an hour-long rush-hour ride. As always, though, there was something pretty about Daisy, in an old-fashioned way. She made me think of those Jacob Riis photos of immigrant women. I could picture her standing in a group of them in front of a sweatshop on the Lower East Side. She'd be the one your eye would get drawn to: the dark hair and eyes, the startlingly pale oval face, the hourglass figure. You'd sense she was intelligent and probably humorous, and if you stared for more than a second or two, you'd begin to smile, irrationally expecting that one face in the group photo to smile back.

The guest room I was in was so big there was a couch in it, so we sat there, each leaning against an overstuffed arm. I put my feet up on the cushion and Daisy kicked off her shoes and did the same. She was cold, too, so we shared the cashmere blanket.

"I've got to say," I told her, "I was one hundred percent surprised at how serious Matt is about Ashley. I mean, you know him: Every eight or ten months, he's in love again. I've never even met her. I mean, Hayden and I went to a Mets game with him toward the end of the season last year, but then he was with . . . Sara?"

"That one was Mira. She was lovely. They're all lovely, except for one total bitch when he was at Duke who looked like Morticia in the Addams family. But Ashley's adorable. Really outgoing. She grew up in Texas, so when you see her, you get this big 'Haa!' for 'Hi.' And she's supersmart." She gave a slight shrug.

A year or two earlier we'd had a conversation during an *in vino veritas* dinner—just the two of us—about how Matt always achieved what you'd think he wasn't quite smart enough to manage. Like he got into Duke. Graduated from Duke. Found his dream job right out of college, and then got three promotions. Hooked up with amazingly bright women and had them crazy about him. Broke up with them with an astounding minimum of bitterness. Maybe he was smarter than we gave him credit for, and his combo of great looks and gung-ho personality made you underestimate his depth.

"He didn't give you any kind of clue about how serious he was this time?" I asked.

"No. Well, he told me how warm and caring she was, how strong, what a brilliant doctor she'll make. But it wasn't like she was more wonderful than any of them. At least it didn't sound that way to me. It's weird, though. We talk a fair amount, and everyone thinks we have a fabulous sibling relationship. And we do, sort of. I mean frankly, I don't give a damn about sports, and to Matty, 'foreign film' means a Jet Li movie."

"What's your common ground?"

"Politics. And we talk about people from high school we both knew. Analyze our parents. We get thoughtful. Sometimes open up to each other. But we don't get philosophical. It's never, 'Is there such a thing as free will?' "

"Come on, Daisy. Who talks about that stuff? I mean, once you move out of the dorm, that's over."

"Not with everybody. I mean, if you're working for Paramount, you don't go into a meeting and talk Schopenhauer, but I kind of like to speculate about . . . things. You know: free will and moral responsibility. I read, discuss stuff with my book group. Talk about free will: We did Buber's *I and Thou* last year. And I wind up having long discussions over dinner with a couple of friends; it's a different kind of conversation than the dorm stuff when you're older. Not that I'd go there with Matty, because he doesn't know from the examined life."

I couldn't say examining my life was at the top of my list either, so I just moved along. "Do you think maybe he just said he was getting engaged because it was a good excuse for not leaving New York? Could he have been saying it for Gloria's benefit? Maybe he didn't mean it." Suddenly I thought, *Oh, no. What if she thinks that I'm hoping Matt isn't really so serious about Ashley because I'm secretly in love with him or something?* I was so embarrassed. I decided in a fraction of a second to shake my head and say he probably did mean it and wasn't it wonderful, but by then Daisy was shaking her head. One of the pins that had been holding up her hair fell between the cushion and the arm of the couch. She glanced down there and scrunched her face into a *repulsive* expression.

"Get up and take off the cushion," I said. "I won't grab the blanket."

"No way in hell I'm going to put my hand down there and feel some other guest's cracker crumbs."

"How crazy are you?" I asked.

"Fairly crazy."

"This place is so clean."

"I know. That's why I'm fairly crazy. Anyway, I don't think Matt brought up Ashley for Gloria's benefit. It's funny: A couple of years ago I was getting his input about some political situation at the studio. He's great at all that people stuff. He told me if there's something unpleasant that's going to come out—like you made a mistake or have to say no to something—get that information out fast.

"So bottom line?" Daisy was saying. "Telling Gloria he was going to get engaged wasn't something he pulled out of his ass to salve her feelings. Because with Matty, he really hates unpleasantness, so the urge to avoid it is powerful. But his stronger belief is if you're going to have to deal with it, don't give it time to grow and grow."

"Maybe that's why his relationships don't drag on for years," I said. "If he knows someone isn't right for him, he's out of there. By the way, how long have he and Ashley been together?"

"Probably a little longer than his usual. And she is genuinely great, but that's a given. Plus she gets extra points with him because she's a jock. She was on the soccer team at the University of Chicago, and she plays tennis, golf. She'll even happily go to a hockey game with him."

"She must be demented," I said. "I so hate hockey."

"He was awed by how well she knows the game. Hockey. Eeeesh. And it didn't sound like she was faking interest because she's the man-pleasing type." Daisy put the tip of her thumb into her mouth and ran her teeth over the nail. Then she quickly pulled it out and glanced at it. "Oh, my God! I came so close to chewing off my nail polish. I'd have to spend the rest of the weekend in terror of Gloria spotting a jagged line on my thumbnail. Like the scar on Harry Potter's forehead."

"You know," I said, "when I agreed to come, I was so sure, in my soul of souls, that I wouldn't be afraid of her. And also I was positive I wouldn't give vent to my hostility, which I've tried for ages to get rid of. It's so not healthy. But anyway, here we are, first night. And my stomach goes into a knot, which still didn't stop me from venting."

"You have a lot to vent," Daisy said.

"So do you and Matt."

"Not the same way you do, Raq. It's not like one of those family feuds that go on for generations. She's pretty irrelevant to us. We both see it as more my dad's problem. And for having been so really unloved by her, he's done okay. You know what she once said to him about his business? 'I never thought you'd make a success of yourself. I was shocked when you did.'"

"Did she really? Why do I ask that? Of course she did."

"Wait. Then she added something about him being a success: She said it was success in a tristate way."

"She didn't!"

"She did. It would be hilarious if it wasn't so cruel . . . or if he wasn't our father. But nothing he ever did pleased her. If that had been the totality of it, that would be . . . well, not okay, but tolerable. But naturally she took it a step further and let him know at every opportunity that he was a born loser and your father had been the winner. Basically, her message to him was, 'You should have been the one who died.' "

This was over the top. I noticed I was hugging my legs for comfort. Well, also the air-conditioning was so assertive and was blowing directly on the back of my neck and head. But as the you-should-have-been-the-one-who-died business sank in, it struck me that Daisy's interpretation was off. It wasn't so much the content of what she was saying, but the casual way she presented the information. It was like when a judge charges a jury and tells them they have the right to consider a witness's demeanor when weighing the truth of their testimony. Not that I thought Daisy was lying, just that something felt wrong about such deliberate meanness of a mother to a son.

"Did you ever hear her say anything like that to your dad?" I asked.

Daisy shook her head. "No. I mean I haven't seen her in years and years. I think once or twice when she came to New York for business, my parents went into the city to have dinner with her. You know, if she has close to zero interest in them, she has below-zero interest in me and Matt. I'm sure there was never any question about bringing us along to see her. I mean, from her point of view, how could the spawn of the Loser and Cynthia have any merit?"

"It's not like she treasures me, the child of the alleged winner," I said.

"True."

"But again, if you're looking at it from her point of view, how could the granddaughter of Puerto Rican immigrants be good enough for her?"

"What is she?" Daisy demanded. "The fucking queen of Poland?"

"I know. But isn't it odd, her wanting us all here? How come she was willing to consider giving away her most cherished possession—Glory—to one of us?"

"Maybe when she asked it was like the Capitol in *The Hunger Games.* She wished she could have the fun of watching the three of us fight to the death with only one surviving."

It was weird how Daisy always had such an upbeat way of speaking, or at least a casualness. Even when she talked about bad things happening to reasonably good people: us fighting to the death, Gloria intimating that it would have been better for my uncle Bradley to die than my father. Maybe it had to do with Daisy being in the movie business. It was brutal, and you couldn't let them see you were vulnerable.

"Listen, Daisy, I'm not defending her. But isn't it possible that while okay, Gloria clearly loved my dad, that at least some of her hostility to yours may just have been what we've seen here today—she's a basically cold, undemonstrative person? I mean, here she was married to Grandpa Joe for all those years."

"And?"

"And then he's too afraid to stand up to the Mob. Fine, so he's not the tower of strength she'd always believed he was. It was a deep disappointment. Right?" Daisy nodded. "But people who experienced that kind of realization—*he's not the man I thought he was*—carry on with a marriage. Maybe it's not the same as before, but there's a commitment. A sense of obligation. Only someone who's intensely selfish could turn off the emotion overnight. Leave. Like Gloria did."

"So you're saying that she's not a fucking lunatic sociopath? Just a cold bitch?"

"Well, neither is exactly a compliment," I said. "But I would rather think that one-quarter of my genes come from a bitch than from someone completely lacking in conscience and compassion."

"I don't know," my cousin said. "There are family stories, truths. Everyone has them. But are the truths really true? Who knows? The stories—like overnight she turned from love to hate—have some sort of emotional value to the person telling them. So when I hear my dad's stories, do I have objective, independent evidence about them? Like that Gloria didn't have much use for him? Some. She was always making excuses not to see him. Over the years, he'd call her. And he'd get her secretary at work or I guess Carlos here, and I heard him say, 'This is her son Bradley.

Can you please have her call me back?' And she never did. What made it worse was that every time the phone rang for a day or two, he got this—I hate to say it—but this puppy dog, overeager expression on his face. Not that he called her that often, but still . . . But do I have any kind of proof, other than what my dad says, that she wished he had died instead of your dad?"

"It sounds a little odd to me, is all," I told her. "Primitive, that she can't see death as a discrete event. That she would view it as a coin toss, God saying, 'Heads Travis, tails Bradley.' "

Well, it's my dad's story, and he's sticking to it." Daisy said. "Look, if a kid has to survive being unloved, he needs an explanation—a narrative—that can assure him, 'It wasn't you. It was her.' Not that he can ever totally accept that. But it does help." She got up off the couch and then asked, "Can I look in your basket or did you glom down everything?"

"There's still stuff in there."

"I knew it. You were good for a mouse-sized nibble of cheese."

"Yes! Guilty as charged," I said. "But I had it on that little toast thing. Does someone actually bake teeny loaves of bread and slice them with an eensy-weensy knife and toast them?"

Daisy walked over to the dresser and peered through the basket. Big surprise: She came up with cookies. "She had those brownies and blondies out on the buffet, but I took two slices of cut-up mango. She was watching. You want to know how crazy I am? I'd rather eat your cookies because I'm convinced on some level that they'll report to her on the contents of each of our baskets after we leave."

"Mis cookies son tus cookies," I told her.

She came back to the couch with two seriously large cookies. "So getting back to Gloria: Maybe my dad is right about how she feels about him, maybe not. But the point is, he believes it." She changed her position so that she could rest her head on the back of the couch and then closed her eyes for a few seconds. "And he not only believes it, he lives it all the time. When I was a kid, it used to kill me how he'd go on and on to my mom about how his mother never really loved him."

"You were embarrassed by his unloading to your mom?"

"Yes. I wanted to scream, 'Stop it!' or run out of the room. But that would have humiliated him more."

I wondered how much that dynamic affected my aunt Cynthia. I never got her—I couldn't tell if there was anything beyond her bright façade. She was always solicitous of me. Make that downright kind. True, she talked a lot, and while she was never boring, she never really said anything. She was a permanently gracious hostess, never that much more or less. Always in full makeup, always a little too much jewelry. Really nice jewelry, but I wished I could say, *Aunt Cynthia, with the necklace, the earrings, the bracelet and watch, couldn't you live without that ruby flower pin on your lapel?*

"You know, with my mom it's hard to figure out what she's processed because she's so dedicated to being Mrs. Charming. Her bad moods aren't really bad moods; she just withdraws. If you ask her if anything's the matter, she'll say, 'Everything's fine.' If she's really in extremis, she'll say something about just being in a mood. But I think over the years my father's kvetching about how his mother never loved him probably got to my mother."

"Did she believe it?"

"Oh, without a doubt," Daisy said. "The problem is, I think it wore down her feelings about my dad. About his worthiness. Here's this guy who's really nice, friendly, successful. And what does he talk about whenever he's home and the rest of the world is shut out? Well, actually, lots of stuff. But there's always, 'My mommy didn't love me.' "

"I knew he felt that way, but I didn't realize it went so deep. Well, if you're unloved by a parent, that's got to be a major hurt."

"Of course it is. But to talk about it so much? I think it affected Matty more than it did me."

"In what way?"

"It's hard to say. He thinks my mom equates him with my dad, which therefore makes him—Matty—less lovable to her. It's like he's second-generation unloved, which really isn't true. Still, it's pretty analytical for him." Daisy cocked her head to one side. "On the other hand, it's not a patently false theory. But it's less my mom than my dad. Matty didn't want to go into the Handsome Home with him because my dad is so needy. Even though he's strong and outgoing in business, Matty didn't want to be tied to someone who had so much emotional baggage. He said when they sat down and talked about working together, my dad would periodically come back to the my-mommy-didn't-love-me topic. And Matty said he couldn't see spending the rest of his life hearing that. And I think he was afraid of turning into someone like Dad, always feeling that no matter what you do, it will never be enough."

"It's not a contagious disease," I said.

"Yes it is," my cousin replied.

Fourteen

Daisy

The bed in the guest room had the expanse of a small galaxy. I lay near the edge of the mattress so as not to wake in the middle of the night feeling lost in the cosmos. Just before I fell asleep, I had a thought. Thoughts were rare for me at bedtime. Even though I was of the generation that kvetched endlessly about insomnia, I was pretty much immune.

I was a congenital early bird—and a New Yorker—yet forced to keep California time. So I was obliged to keep my wits about me far longer than *Homo sapiens* were designed to do. By the time I set my iPhone on the nightstand, my mind had already shut down for an hour or more. Nothing could stop me from sleeping. It didn't matter what relationship horror was going on in my life. So what if some psychopath producer was still awake in Pacific Palisades plotting to get me fired because another psychopath at Searchlight had gotten his hands on the manuscript of the new Foer novel three hours earlier than he had? Neither pain nor fear could disturb the flatline of my consciousness.

That night, though, as my eyelids went from drooping to closed, the thought not only burst through my brain but was potent enough to survive until the following morning. It was this: I could run Glory. Not that I wanted to.

I was awake before the alarm bonged, mostly because I was hungry. Naturally, when I saw the time—six forty—I got that *potential starvation!* distress signal that comes when you're in a strange place without access to food. I checked the night tables on both sides of the bed on the off chance I'd find a discreet card with a beveled edge saying, *Press the # sign and order whatever you'd like for breakfast. You will have it within minutes.* Barring that, maybe there was a foil-wrapped chocolate I'd overlooked. No. Then I went through the previous afternoon's goodie basket hoping that, buried under the stuffing that looked like fettuccine cut from gold paper, was some treasure: I conjured up a little pouch of sugared pecans. But of course all I found under all that paper fettuccine was a Styrofoam oval stuck in there to make my grandmother's notion of a snack—three crackers, a bit of cheese, twenty-seven-grain cookies, a couple of almonds—look as bounteous as one of those cornucopias in an old Dutch still life.

So I showered and got dressed in my white jeans. They had seemed a great idea in Manhattan. But in New Mexico they just screamed *Wrong!* Probably it wasn't New Mexico. More likely it was anticipating Gloria's eyes traveling from my red-and-white striped shirt to my jeans to my red ballet flats (an outfit that had evoked a "Love the look, sooo crisp" from an assistant art director at a brunch in L.A.). Then I imagined my grandmother averting her face so as to be spared the nightmare sight of Too Buxom Babe in Horizontal Stripes and Age-Inappropriate Shoes.

I was half convinced Gloria would have the stairs alarmed during the night and that my descending would summon some private guard detail complete with semiautomatic pistols and unleashed rottweilers. But hope of breakfast beat out fear of death. Naturally, it took me about ten minutes to locate the kitchen, since every hallway looked alike. I kept being led back to the atrium in the center of the house—though for all I knew I could have been walking back and forth along the same U-shaped passage for the entire time. Finally, I came to the dining room where we'd eaten the night before. In the dusty gold light of early morning, there were numerous faint tracks on the rug—signs that between last night's dinner and now, someone who took vacuuming very seriously had been at work.

I pushed open the door—the kind on

springs that will smack you down unless you keep moving—and walked into the kitchen whose size was commensurate with the rest of the house, i.e., ridiculously large. The exhaust hood that towered above a giant restaurant stove mesmerized me. The hood looked like something NASA would erect to launch a ship for an intergalactic probe. It was only when I heard, "Oh. Good morning . . ." followed by "Daisy" a second later that I realized Gloria was there.

I sucked in a breath that sounded uncomfortably close to a gasp. Maybe I'd missed her because her silvery hair and white shirt blended into the round white wooden table where she was sitting, or because the window behind her was so large that she was backlit to the point of disappearance.

"Did I frighten you?" she asked. She was ready for the day in full-but-subtle makeup, khaki slacks—the flowing Katharine Hepburn kind—and a white shirt with billowy sleeves à la Gene Kelly, Errol Flynn, and Johnny Depp in generations of pirate movies. She lifted her chin to an angle that definitely qualified as imperious. "Hmmm?"

Well, what was my excuse? *I always follow up any mention of 'Daisy' with a gasp?* "Yes, you did scare me. I didn't see you."

"Obviously."

"I thought I might run into one of the people who work for you, or maybe Raquel. But I guess I pictured you more the breakfast-in-bed type."

Gloria managed a trifecta of expressions at this: looking heavenward for succor while at the same time shaking her head as in *Pathetic* and squeezing the corners of her mouth into a moue. "Breakfast in bed! You really see too many movies." Perhaps, on a whim, she threw in one of her nostril flares. "In your imaginings, am I in a quilted pink bed jacket with a bow in my hair?" She was snide almost to the point of cruelty, like an exaggerated Blair on *Gossip Girl*—assuming a mockery of a caricature were possible.

If Gloria had given me the snotty "bow in my hair" routine around four in the afternoon, my emotional vulnerability hour, right before my Starbucks Grande Latte, she might have wounded me. But since it was my time of day, early, I just laughed. "Oh, my God! Bed jackets! Do you know why they wore them, other than to have another category of accessory to buy?"

Her mouth held on to the sour expression for another second, but then she got to thinking about my question. For the moment, she forgot she was mean. "I suppose to ward off a chill. Like if you were wearing a sleeveless negligé with décolletage."

"Why not just pull up the covers?"

"How should I know?" This wasn't mere snapping. The rise in her volume and malice, as if I'd asked some profoundly disgusting question, startled me. No doubt that kind of response would have undone my dad (or, for all I knew, my intrepid uncle Travis, assuming she'd jumped down his throat once or twice).

But I was prepared for whatever she was dishing out. Many film people, including the ones who never get near a camera, believed that being in the industry gave them carte blanche to dramatize. What might evoke *I disagree with what you're doing* in a high school English department would bring about a predictable *Fuck you!* in the movie business. I was accustomed to getting shrieked at transcontinentally on a fairly regular basis. So I smiled at the Wrath of Gloria. While my response didn't unnerve her, she didn't have a Plan B for me. She let go of the bed jacket topic, leaned her manicured hands on the white kitchen table, and asked, "Can you get your own breakfast, or do you need help?"

"Now come on. You don't honestly expect me to say, 'I need help. I'm majorly inept.' "

She rose from her seat and watched as I walked to the refrigerator, a monolith of stainless steel. "Is there anything I can get you?" she asked.

"No, thanks. Anything I can get *you*?"

"No, thank you. I've already eaten."

Almost lost in the huge white circle of table was a tiny white container of yogurt, the kind you pulled off from its four- or six-pack. I yanked open the recalcitrant refrigerator door while having a fight with myself as to whether to search for another pygmy yogurt, glom it down, and sigh, *God, I'm full!* or to try and discover something that would allow me to go the entire morning without a massive hunger headache.

"I could make you pancakes if you'd like." Gloria spoke so softly I thought for a second I might have become delusional. I'd been eyeing a carton of cottage cheese, but I turned in her direction, waiting for something spiteful along the lines of, *One of those caloric, unhealthy breakfasts girls of your build go for.* But she said, "I can cook. I'm sure you were told I was a housewife until the boys were . . . however old they were when we left New York. Early teens, I suppose. The only capacity I seem to have lost as I've gotten older is my ability to remember when events happened in relation to other events."

"Thanks, but I'll pass on the pancakes. If I have them now, I'll be thinking I'm doomed to an endive leaf for lunch. I'd rather postpone indulgence for three or four hours. That's my max."

"You talk a lot."

"I suppose."

"Some women do that when they live alone," she added.

"But not you."

"No," she said dismissively. "Of course not."

I couldn't imagine what it must be like to work for someone like her, where every other sentence was a zinger. Unless she was a sweetheart at Glory and her malice was simply due to ODing on Goldbergs. "Did you like cooking?" I asked her.

"No. Not on a day-to-day basis anyway." I took out the container of cottage cheese and was debating a search-and-destroy mission for something to toast when I glanced back at my grandmother. She pointed to a large box on one of the kitchen counters. It was made from wood slats and looked Scandinavian, like it should hold a large blond family's mittens and reindeer jerky. She said, "Bread box." I walked toward it thinking I had to either come up with a new question or learn to tolerate a silence in which, naturally, I could hear her saying, *You shouldn't be wearing white pants before Memorial Day.* But as I peered into the box and discovered a stash of ciabatta rolls, she began speaking again. "Back in those days, when I was still with Joe, every Saturday night somebody made a dinner party. When it came time for my turn, I dreaded it. I didn't enjoy cooking. What's cooking? Buying everything on a list and following a recipe: Do this, do that. Big deal. It's mindless. I don't understand the whole celebrity chef business these days. You make fennel sorbet and you're a genius? But I did like planning the menu, setting the table, making a centerpiece, arranging serving platters." I can't say that memory brought on a smile, but her eyes did brighten. "That was the best. I remember once heating up five or six cans of Dinty Moore beef stew, throwing in some red wine and parsley—fresh, not the dried kind—and serving it in big Idaho potato skins. I buttered and broiled them so they'd be crisp. Then I put them on the big oval platter covered with parsley and watercress."

"How did that go over?"

"Everyone oohed and aahed."

"My best friend, Karen Bonheim—she teaches econometrics up at MIT—has a theory that anything you make in a slow cooker tastes two hundred percent better."

"That's an economic theory?"

"No. That's her being willfully unscientific. She lets off steam that way, stating inane theories, then goes back to being her usual super-coherent self. But she makes incredible slow cooker meatballs."

"My food wasn't that good, to be perfectly honest. But the presentation made up for it. Word went out that I was one of Great Neck's most brilliant cooks. From then on, if I'd tossed Dog Chow with canned spaghetti sauce, any neighbor with a *Gourmet* subscription would go around saying, 'I'm pretty sure I tasted a touch of oregano in Gloria Goldberg's fritto misto.' "

She exhaled, and her whole body seemed to deflate. Maybe saying the name "Goldberg" brought her back to the present, in which she was now Garrison. The talk stopped. Whatever had been lighting up her eyes dimmed.

I scanned the counter until I found the toaster oven and popped in the roll. She sat back down and looked past me, as if I had no more substance than a dust mote. The silent treatment, I knew, could mean nothing more than *I've run out of things to say.* Or it could just be a passing spasm of shyness. My mom would resort to it when she shifted into her passive-aggressive mode. But it never worked very long for her, because she always had something more she had to say.

However, as practiced by egomaniacs, megalomaniacs, or seventy-nine-year-old mean girls, the silent treatment said only one thing: *You have displeased me. I will make you feel uncomfortable.* It worked, a little. But I sang "Life Is a Highway" in my head and then distracted myself by making a mound of the suspiciously moist one percent cottage cheese Gloria had. So by the time I sat across from her at the kitchen table I'd forgotten she was giving me the cold shoulder.

"You know how you said I watch too many movies?" I reminded her. "Personally, I don't think it's too many, but I watch tons of them. Do you see a lot of movies?"

This time she was the one who was startled. Her mind must have been busy on something else. "No. Not anymore. Years ago, there was a disgusting Marlon Brando picture that cured me of movie watching. I can't remember when. It was called *Last Tango in Paris* and I thought it would be . . . romantic, wistful. Except it was vile, with him putting butter in some girl's rectum. Right then and there, I decided, movies aren't for me and I am not for the movies."

"*Last Tango* was early '70s."

"You were fortunate to miss it."

"No. I saw it. They called it 'elegiac.' I called it boring, even the business with the butter. Anyway, as for Brando, except maybe in *A Streetcar Named Desire,* I always found him slightly repulsive. That voice. Maybe if he'd had an adenoidectomy . . . You know, there have been some great movies between 1970-something and now. If you give me a general idea of what you like, I could give you a list."

I could have predicted that she'd go back to not speaking. Maybe she was so accustomed to living alone in silence that she wasn't used to the normal give-and-take when someone else was in the room. Maybe having houseguests, family, stressed her.

I got up and went searching for salt. I poured some into my hand, returned to my place, and did a small sprinkling ceremony. Just as I was wondering why she didn't simply say *See you later,* and also if she really understood that the butter business was about anal sex, she said, "I used to go to the movies every Saturday afternoon when I was young. When I lived in Ohio. When I got to New York, there was too much else to do. I hardly ever went unless it was a date. Joe liked movies, but only stupid ones. I went to more moronic Westerns with that man. But he absolutely refused to see *Ivanhoe.* We had such a fight. I stormed out and went by myself. Women didn't go to the movies alone much in those days. Well, maybe they did, but not in our circle. Who knows? My neighbors could have had a secret movie life that I never heard about. Did you ever see *Ivanhoe*?"

"Not yet. Should it be on my to-do list?"

"I can't remember the details. I probably spent the whole movie being furious at Joe. But I do remember Elizabeth Taylor played a Jewish girl. And there was that actor, the handsome one."

"Robert Taylor," I said.

"How do you keep all this in your head?" She picked up her yogurt container. "It's not even a movie you saw. It's not important."

"What's important? Lip liner?" I said it in a pleasant enough manner. Gloria took a brisk walk across the kitchen to the sink and threw the container into an opening in the countertop that I assumed led to the recycling bin. "I think detail about a person's work is important," I went on. "Film also happens to be my passion. I'm always going through lists of old DVDs, plus the new ones they're bringing out. If I see Robert Taylor's name in the *Ivanhoe* credits, I'll remember it. Like if I were running Glory, I'd damn well remember that Terra-Cotta Red—or whatever—was the lip liner of choice in 1987."

She pulled off a segment of paper towel and wiped the fingers that had handled the yogurt container on it. Then she crumpled it up into a ball and left it on the countertop. "Did anyone ever tell you that you have a fresh mouth?" she asked.

"Yes. My dad. Maybe he got the phrase from you." Being reminded of who my father was seemed to put her into an even surlier mood. She went back to trying out different mean mouth expressions and finally settled on compressed lips. "Although Dad's a pretty easygoing guy. I can't see him as having given you a lot of lip."

"Do they still use that expression?" Gloria asked. "A lot of lip?"

"Maybe. People still know what it means. Did my dad give you lip?"

"No. And Travis wasn't what you'd call fresh either. But at least he always gave me arguments."

"So if my dad had been difficult, you might have loved him more?"

She took so long to answer I feared she might have dropped dead standing up. "I thought you'd be the easy one. Artistic sensibility. Well, you're not as prickly and hostile as that Raquel." Then she added, "But you're more aggressive than I thought you'd be."

"Aggressive? I'm going to be thirty. You're going to be eighty. We're two smart women who are having a discussion."

"Is that what you call this?"

"Yes, although if you prefer 'chat,' I'd be willing to accept it." Gloria shook her head to signify I was being difficult, but I sensed her heart wasn't in it. "But you still haven't answered me about my dad. Would you have loved him more if he'd been harder to handle?"

"He lacked . . . Why do you want to go into this?"

"Why don't you? I have a sense that it's not to avoid hurting my feelings."

"You may think I'm deliberately cruel. I'm not," my grandmother said.

"Okay." Given that I'd slept in her

guest room and was breakfasting on her cottage cheese and ciabatta, I decided not to press the subject. Instead I went back to the one I'd been on before. "What about my dad? About your feelings for him."

"The truth?" She waited for me to nod or to signal some go-ahead, but I just stood there. "All right. The truth is that I probably would have loved Bradley more if he hadn't been so . . . so compliant. I suppose that's the word. But that didn't mean I didn't love him. I loved him . . . I never really thought much about it. I suppose I loved him. He was my son. What was I supposed to do? Not love him just because he was a nebbish?" She crossed her arms. They were slim, but the skin on them was coming loose, like on a chicken thigh you bought a couple of days earlier, stuck in the fridge, and forgot to cook. Then she added, "Did I feel for him what I felt for Travis? As they say: Let's not even go there."

"My father is not a nebbish," I told her. "He's a lovely, decent man. Shrewd too. Well, sometimes. Definitely worth knowing." She turned her back on me, picked up the piece of paper towel, and right before tossing it, flattened it out and folded it neatly. "But let's not go there either. Let's stay here. You and me, Gloria. Grandmother and granddaughter."

"How sweet."

"Not sweet. Frankly, with you in the picture, 'sweet' wouldn't be the adjective of choice. And I'm not particularly sweet either. But you and me–wise, this is what I want: a relationship."

"I'm offering a business," she said coldly. "Or rather, the possibility of the business."

"Well, then, consider this my counteroffer."

Fifteen

Matt

With my seventy-nine-year-old grandmother behind the wheel of her 500 Benz doing eighty, I realized my future depended on her reflexes. As she zoomed along with me sitting in the death seat, it came to me: Did that future of mine really include marrying Ashley? When I'd announced it the night before, it had seemed right. Perfect, in fact. In the company of three smart women, I'd declared that I was bringing yet another one into the family. It wasn't like I'd been drunk—a couple of glasses of wine at dinner. But now in the light of day, it was like, *What have I done?*

Technically, I hadn't done anything. Outside the tinted car window, I watched the dulled gold world whiz by and tried to comfort myself. If worse came to worse, and my declaration just arose from a momentary weakness based on loneliness and jet lag, the only awkwardness I'd really experience was when I had to tell my sister I'd changed my mind. Gloria didn't count so much. Raquel? My kid crush on her would probably last forever. Even now, almost every time I saw her, I was so taken with her perfect petiteness and no-makeup prettiness that for the first few minutes I reverted to my fifteen-year-old thought: In some societies, it's not unusual for first cousins to marry. Raquel still mattered enough that I wouldn't want her thinking I was a faithless jerk.

But ultimately it was my sister who mattered because she so had my number. If she knew what I was thinking now, it would reinforce her take on me. This was upsetting because her view of me was spot-on. I was commitment-phobic. And furthermore, anyone with a great ass and an IQ over 130 would fit my bill. Daisy never spelled it out for me that way, but she hinted around it so much that it was impossible not to get her drift. She viewed me as one of those guys who only wanted friendship with privileges. I would wind up a wrinkled old bachelor who had nothing more to look back on than a lifetime of emotionally meaningless friendships. Except I'd changed—it all had changed—with Ashley.

If Gloria swerved to avoid a giant dead cactus and we crashed and burned on the road to Glory, I would definitely die. Daisy, belted in the backseat, would survive. She'd call Ashley, probably meet for dinner, and tell her that my almost-last words had been, "I'm going to marry Ashley." They'd both cry because the loss was so great. Daisy would cry extra because she didn't have anyone in her life who would comfort her in mourning. Ashley would have a hard time stopping her sobbing because, having spent so much time in the ER, she knew what I'd wound up looking like after the accident.

Not that there really were any dead cactuses on the road. It had stopped being mostly blah land and become the typical ugly commercial thoroughfare you find in every city I've ever been to: a tire store here, an Arby's there, branch banks, a Motel 6. Cerrillos Road. I turned around. "Does 'Cerrillos' mean anything, or is it someone's name?" I asked Raquel.

"I don't know." She said it quietly, like she didn't want it getting out that her vocabulary had limits.

"You can ask me," Gloria said, not that she waited for a question. She went on in her usual style, with its mingling of coldness and you-moron-style contempt: "It means 'hillocks.'" I should have said, "Oh, of course, 'hillocks,'" because not knowing gave her another shot: "Hillocks are small hills or mounds."

She kept her eyes on the road. My grandmother was a pretty good driver, though being a passenger in a car going eighty when the hands on the wheel have ropy blue veins, paper-thin skin, and knobby wrist bones almost as large as Ping-Pong balls makes you feel a little vulnerable.

Gloria didn't signal when she turned off the main road, and I did the guy thing that pisses off women, which was slamming on an imaginary brake with my foot, which of course, having the peripheral vision of a twenty-year-old, my grandmother saw. She puffed up her lips and let out a tiny explosion of air: *Puh!* Pure annoyance. But at the first light she hung a left and seemed to forget about me. A long, low brownish building appeared in the distance. Gloria's usual cold voice defrosted enough so you could hear the pride in it: "There's Glory," she said.

"Wow." We wowed more or less in unison, so I couldn't tell if Daisy and Raquel were as unwowed as I was. Not that it was a toolshed with a Glory Inc. sign. Definitely big, sizewise. But once we got up close, it just looked like a one-level suburban elementary school on steroids. The walls were all windows, but set back under a wide horizontal overhang. Like a canopy for shade. The overhang was supported by squared-off columns every ten to fifteen feet. Even as we came close, the place appeared two-dimensional, more like an architectural rendering than an actual building. At one corner, there was a bulge—the commercial equivalent of a bay window—and then it turned left and went on some more.

Except for the tinted glass, the building was sand colored. So much of Santa Fe was inspired by the color of Pueblo houses. Except here, the architect, if there was one, should have gone with the Native American design as well, which was a thousand times more interesting than this flat square. The landscaping consisted of knee-high boulders on a gravel bed along with a few skinny propped-up trees; even a clichéd grass strip between sidewalk and curb would have looked better. Yet you couldn't call it offensive, just totally uninspired. When you came down to it, this was the building you saw in every corporate park in America.

"Employee parking is in the back," Gloria said to none of us in particular—

more like she was recording an audio byte to go on the About Us page on the Glory website. Or maybe it was just her Ohio accent. Everyone who spoke with it sounded like they had a side business doing voice-overs. She drove over the speed bumps with the self-assuredness of someone possessed of a luxury car with a great suspension system.

The back of the place surprised me, because in addition to a parking lot there was a huge open bay for trucks, plus a long ugly rectangle broken up by giant brown garage doors. "At any time, we pull two trucks off the road to work on," Gloria said as she pulled into a parking space. "Tune-ups, heavy cleaning, tire rotation." The space had a discreet sign that said Ms. Garrison. From where she'd parked, I could see only one of the trucks, but I supposed, truckwise, it would be considered a beaut. The old pink-and-red ex–Garment Center truck that my dad had described was history. This time around it was retro-Deco-steel, like some train from the 1930s that raced across the continent carrying movie stars back and forth between L.A. and New York. The name GLORY stretched across the side in a gold-and-black font that had some sparkle stuff, though without being tacky. Beneath it, minus the sparkle, was the motto: GET BEAUTIFUL. NO EXCUSES.

As we got out of the car, Daisy said, "I like the motto, Gloria."

My grandmother did her queenly nod. According to her rule book, I supposed, royalty did not say *Thank you.* "It used to be 'Why not be beautiful?' " she was telling Daisy. "But a few months before 2000, this fellow I told you about, Keith, said it sounded o-l-d. Actually, what he said was, 'If a corporate slogan could have an odor, 'Why not be beautiful?' would exuuude denture breath . . .'" The way she was talking, not imitating as much as channeling Keith, I guessed he'd been gay. She'd mentioned his partner dying but hadn't been specific. "So I told him, 'If you think I'm spending a hundred thousand on a consultant to come up with a new slogan, you've had one tequila too many.' The next afternoon, he put a memo on my desk with ten different possibilities. One of them was 'Get beautiful. No excuses.' "

"It is good." The voice was Raquel's. But it was such a pleasant and positive statement coming from her and directed at Gloria that it seemed downright unnatural. For a minute, I thought my cousin had been possessed by one of those demons or angels or whatever who specialize in Pentecostal people, making them speak in tongues. Like maybe it had been in the air and was circling around, and not finding anyone born-again had to settle for the only Christian available.

Gloria seemed on the verge of saying thank you but caught herself in time so she didn't seem unroyal and also wouldn't be dissing Daisy by thanking Raquel. Instead, she nodded again, but as much as I could read the stiff and maybe Botoxed face, she seemed pleased and surprised at actual congeniality coming from my cousin. It was only a few steps to the tall glass doors, but energized by the compliment, Gloria stepped up her pace. Luckily, she paused long enough for me to get beside her and open the door. Otherwise, she might have decided I was a boor. I loved that word: "boor." I'd seen the word "boorish" in print, but the first time I ever heard "boor" was in one of my sister's old movies, a noir mystery, when some detective didn't take his hat off in an elevator in the presence of a lady. Whoever was with him said, "Sir, you are a boor," which Daisy and I both thought was hilarious. She said it to me often.

There was no escaping excessive air-conditioning in presummer New Mexico, even on a morning that was comfortably cool. As we were hit with a gust of iced air, a perky voice called out, "Good morning, Ms. Garrison!" I held the door while Daisy and Raquel went through. When I followed, I saw Glory's receptionist at a long, gnarly, narrow table—like what farmhands eat at—in the center of a huge space. The space was totally wood—floor, walls, ceiling. It was like someone had lost it in the pine department at Lumber Liquidators, though I had to admit it looked okay in a modern sort of way, like a sauna, and it smelled nice and woody.

Anyway, the receptionist was a great-looking woman, probably early forties. A little too much of the peppy business, but better than having a hag cackle a hello. Also, having someone with thick honey-colored hair and dimples smiling at you at eight forty-five in the morning was good, especially because she looked like a real person, not someone who was great-looking for a living, like a receptionist at a sports management agency. She might have been someone who'd entered into a Glory truck with dimples and blah brown hair, and emerged however many hours later proving that the "Get beautiful" part of the slogan was absolute truth in advertising.

"Good morning, Marguerite!" Gloria said, with more cordiality than she had displayed to any of her grandchildren since our arrival. "How are you?"

"I'm great, Ms. Garrison!" The dimples grew deeper. Her eyes, which were that excellent mix of colors they call hazel, widened—maybe not with joy but at least with some degree of pleasure. Maybe she was perky to the depths of her soul, although it was possible she actually liked my grandmother . . . in which case she was either crazed or the victim of a brilliant con job.

"Marguerite . . ." Without looking back at us, Gloria crooked her index finger and wiggled it in our direction, as in *Come over here.* "These are my grandchildren from New York." She pointed to each of us. "Daisy, Raquel, and Matthew G-ber." Our last name was said with what in her day would have been called unseemly haste. "And this is Marvelous Marguerite. Marguerite Barbella."

"Your grandchildren!" When a person is surprised, eyebrows go up. Marguerite's rose as high as eyebrows can go. With great enthusiasm, like she'd just been told she'd inherited a billion dollars tax-free, Marguerite said, "Three grown-up grandchildren! They're fabulous!" Then, beaming at us, she added, "Oh, my God, I hope I didn't embarrass you." We all gave her some form of *Of course not.*

"I like to start my day early," Gloria

told us, “and Marguerite is an early bird too. She’s all that stands between me and utter insanity before nine a.m.” She glanced at Marguerite’s desk, which was empty except for a small flatter-than-flat computer monitor, a small phone with so many buttons only the tiniest finger could manage it, and a Glory memo pad and pen.

Marguerite smiled and tore two sheets from the pad. She handed them to my grandmother. “Just these two items!” she said with what I considered an excess of delight. Even if we’d just won the Series, nobody in the entire Mets organization would have ever sounded so pleased. Pleasure on Marguerite Barbella’s level simply didn’t get expressed in any business environment on the East Coast.

“Thank you.” Gloria looked at the pieces of paper and then said, “We’ll see you later.”

“Great meeting you!” Marguerite called out as we followed Gloria toward the small hallway at the far end of the reception area.

And because it would have been

boorish to respond with anything less than a "Great meeting you!" that's what each of us said.

I didn't look back, but I wondered if Marguerite's hazel eyes were on us as we trailed after Gloria. If so, did she think it was weird that a grandmother wasn't shepherding her grandchildren through her workplace but instead was marching ahead like a pedigreed alpha dog leading a pack of beta mutts? Raquel was behind Gloria. Though she was about a half foot shorter, she easily kept up with Gloria's strides. But even walking, the two of them were out of sync. When you're following someone, it seemed to me a given that you automatically matched your steps with hers. But while Gloria was going left, right, left, right, Raquel was going right, left, right, left. It didn't seem deliberate, like the way a defiant teenager might follow. More like, by nature and nurture, they marched to different drummers.

Meanwhile, Daisy was beside me. When she threw me a look, I thought, *Oh, shit, she's going to give me crap about not having said anything about marrying Ashley before I came out with it at dinner.* Except she said, "What the fuck was that 'my grandchildren from New York' business? Like she has three more in Chicago and another couple stashed in Boston?" I shrugged, which always pissed her off because it signified less than total interest in analyzing some fragment of behavior she found fascinating. This time, though, she was on a roll and seemed not to notice. "And one, two, three. Daisy, Raquel, and Matthew, as if we were all the offspring of one obscure child in New York. And it kills me the way she says New York. *New Yerk.* That you can hear, right? Every consonant."

I started to say, "Yeah."

She cut me off. "But did you hear her 'Goldberg'? Notice a little elision there?"

"She's Garrison. She doesn't want anyone to know that her last name used to be Goldberg."

"No. She doesn't want anyone to know she's a Jew." When I shook my head as in *You're pathetic,* she said, "Matthew G-ber? Come on. Don't deny you heard that."

"Okay," I conceded. "A little slurring."

Gloria, then Raquel, passed through the doorway. "Slurring?" my sister whispered. "Try totally obscuring. Like you don't think Ms. Marvelous heard our last name as G-ber?"

"Shut up, Dais. Gloria will hear you."

"It sounded like Goober. 'These are my three little goobers from New Yerk.' "

The size of the room we entered surprised me. It was almost as big as the Mets locker room at Citi Field. This was a combination: a living room with lots of comfy chairs arranged around a giant square coffee table and a den with every guy's dream TV, a fifty-five-inch LG Infinia. In front of it was an arc of six screening room–style recliners in tan leather. And finally there was a showroom with chrome pullout poles that were hung with different style clothes. The showroom area had tons of drawers that had windows inset so you could see what was inside—shoes, belts, jewelry in plastic bags, women's accessories of every kind. No one would ever have all that in one room of a house. But despite the girl-flattering peach color on the walls and all the homey furniture, it was strictly a multipurpose commercial setup.

While Gloria looked from one of us to the other as we took it all in, I thought, *Like seeing this room is supposed to make us change our minds? Hey, that belt drawer really makes me want to make a career change and move to New Mexico.* Still, a portion of my brain was working on what it would be like to watch football on the Infinia in one of those reclining leather theater seats. The rest of it was working on Ashley.

I knew enough about myself, without my friends and sister telling me, that I was gifted at falling in love. Not so great on the follow-through. Eight, ten months was what I was good for. It wasn't just about passion, that crazed, lustful need that diminishes as months move on. That was an aspect of it, sure. But it was also the dwindling of joy that seems to partner with it. What had been so amazing about Ashley was that even though there were times where she was so exhausted by the demands of medical school that she didn't feel like doing anything, and I was just as happy to have a night off, the pleasure of her company didn't lessen. In fact, it grew. So what was I scared of? Because for sure, I was scared—

"We can sit around the coffee table," Gloria was saying. Daisy plopped down first and got busy pulling at the hem of her jeans to make them look a little longer. She'd clearly decided she'd gone too casual and was now glancing over at Raquel, whose gray linen pants were the perfect length for her shoes, the kind where the toes stick out but the heels don't. Gloria sat beside Daisy, next to a small, round glass-topped table with a tiny portable phone; my mom used those tables a lot in her decorating projects, so I figured it was a classic and expensive. Raquel and I took the chairs at a right angle to them. "As you can see," my grandmother said, "this is the fashion room."

"What's the TV used for?" Raquel asked.

"There is rampant video mania out there. There is not a clothing company or an accessories line that does not have exhaustive previews of its seasonal collections. In the past, we downloaded or played whatever DVD the vendors sent on a computer. All of us would gather around someone's desk with much squinting and elbowing to get into position. I finally said, 'Isn't the technology available that we could put the videos up on a big screen? Because if it is available, I want it here tomorrow.'"

"'It's good to be the king,'" Daisy said. Seeing Gloria's blank yet irritated expression, she said, "That's a Mel Brooks line. From *History of the World, Part I.* It means—"

"I can figure it out," Gloria said. She punctuated the sentence with a brief nostril flare, then turned her attention back to Raquel. "The videos don't replace our buyers going out into the market, or us inspecting actual samples and seeing them on live models, but they give us a chance to get a broader vision of what's available. Understand, we're not into cookie-cutter looks—every article of clothing in every size. But neither do we want to feature fashion for our size-six clients that would make our size-twenty-four clients feel that when it comes to style, all that's available to them is a tent with rickrack. So while we may show a sleeveless dress with a nipped-in waist and wide belt for our single-digit-size clients, we don't want to have our larger clients see something they can't aspire to—say, a cross-bust minibandage dress—that was inadvertently left in the try-on room." She glanced at me and added, "In terms of the definition of a cross-bust minibandage dress, Matthew, you really have no need to know. Unless, of course, you've changed your mind and want to be in competition to run Glory someday." She said this matter-of-factly, a business statement, not as if she were offering me one last chance.

I was saved from the *gulp, duh* reaction by my sister asking, "Does a dress that works in a small city around here necessarily play in Peoria? Well, I know you don't go to Illinois, but, say, a city in Oregon or Washington State? Do you have the same clothes everywhere?"

"What with modern media, regional

differences aren't as pronounced as they used to be. There are climate differences, of course, but none of the cities we service would require a heavy wool anything. And what with air-conditioning in states like Texas, or year-round more moderate temperatures like in Oregon, we'll do the same pants and top or dress with a jacket. I've always been a big believer in layering just given the biological fact that each woman's thermostat is different as well as unpredictable."

Daisy and Raquel were nodding like they were Moses listening to what God was saying on Mount Sinai. I was surprised at how riveted they were. Neither of them was a fashionista, though they both seemed to have some sense of what looked good on them. But then the interest kind of crept up on me, too. Because when you listen to the thinking behind anyone's business choices—whether it's baseball cards or toothpaste—you're getting into the psychology not just of the customer but of the business owner and the industry.

"When you think about things like

thermostats, or bandage dresses left behind in the try-on room, what do you base it on?" I asked. "Focus groups? Gut feelings?"

"Good question," Gloria said, and I surprised myself by feeling puffed up at her approval. "When I started, there were certainly focus groups in existence, but they weren't as common as they are today. Even if they'd been a dime a dozen then, I didn't have the extra dime. I'd say our formula began as a combination of a gut sense of what women want and what they need—occasionally the same thing, though not necessarily. It was also experience, from my years as a model and as a housewife. When I was modeling, getting dressed with the other girls to show the season's line, there'd always be a couple who would look in the mirror and say, 'I can't believe how awful I look.' And I realized it had nothing to do with the reality of their appearance. They—we—were models, for goodness sake. We were employed because we were at least reasonably attractive and were slender enough to be walking clothes hangers." She looked from one of us to another. "Funny. Out of the three of you, the only one with the body type for modeling is Matthew."

"I don't see me in a dress with a jacket," I told her.

"You know you're attractive as a man," Gloria snapped. "But if you were changed into a woman, you'd be what you are now: tall, slender, probably photogenic. Other than your grooming and style, it has nothing to do with you, so don't take it as a compliment. It's a genetic fact: You inherited height, long limbs, an angular face. This is the point. Daisy and Raquel are also attractive, but in a different way. Neither is model material. Daisy is too curvy and Raquel is too short. And if they insisted on taking the model type as the standard of excellence and comparing themselves to that, they'd be displeased with themselves. But the irony is, so are actual models. They study other models, perform some sort of mental calculation, and decide, 'Oh, I don't have thick wavy hair like Barbara's' or 'My derrière isn't nice and small like Lois's.' That was in the days before backsides became what breasts used to be: the bigger the better."

"When did that happen?" Daisy asked.

"I can't give you the year," Gloria said. "Chalk it up to diversity. Different races, different ethnic groups become more accepted not just politically but also culturally. Familiarity, in this case, breeds not just acceptance but admiration of different types of beauty. Bigger lips, bigger backsides, darker, curlier hair." She paused. "Where was I?"

"Your modeling days. Models putting themselves down," Raquel said.

"Right. Quite by accident, I discovered I could change that dynamic of self-derision. One day, a model named Julie was literally crying over her freckles. She said she looked like Mickey Rooney." Gloria paused. "Do you know . . ." We all nodded. "I was very direct with her. I said, 'Julie, your freckles are your meal ticket. They're not just cute. They make you the all-American girl. I wish I had them.' "

"That was so nice," Daisy said.

"No, it wasn't. I said it to shut her up. She was exasperating, always blubbering. With unattractive freckles, I might add. The good news and the bad news, as they say, was that it made her think I was wonderful. And to the extent that my words made her more accepting of herself and those god-awful freckles, it made her more tolerable to me. Frankly, I thought that was the end of it. But over the years, there were more than a few incidents like that. Not just with models. With neighbors when we moved to Great Neck and with wives of Joe's business associates. When a woman came to me for advice, either because she thought I had style sense or knew I had been in the fashion business, I enjoyed the challenge, analytically speaking. I knew it wasn't socially acceptable to suggest the obvious: 'Lose thirty pounds' or 'Get a nose job, beaky.' Instead, I really studied them and considered what would make them look better. What they wanted was a change that would make them more pleasing to themselves and the people around them. I tried to give them advice that was doable for them. What seemed so obvious to me—orange lipstick is rarely a friend, don't wear waist-length jackets unless your waist is ten inches smaller than your bust—was earthshaking news to them. Not only that, whatever pointers I gave them did have an effect on their appearance. Sometimes a small one, sometimes big. But in either case, it gave them a degree of confidence they hadn't had before. Also, it made them feel grateful to me in an odd way, as if they and I had collaborated on some secret project that had changed the world."

Gloria sat back, recrossed her legs in the opposite direction, and glanced at her watch. Gold, a Rolex. "My assistant is in now. Do any of you want coffee? We have the machine that makes individual cups, so it's not the usual office swill." We all said yes, so she picked up the little phone next to her and pressed a button twice.

"Did you feel a connection to the women you helped?" Raquel asked. I had to admit she was back to being snotty—like she expected Gloria to say no. She got it.

"Not particularly," Gloria said. "Well, I did feel gratified that my suggestions worked, that I had a knack for analysis and the ability to communicate my ideas without incurring resentment."

For someone who hadn't gotten past high school and who had an interest in the nonfriendly aspects of orange lipstick, she had an impressive vocabulary. But her speech wasn't playful like Walt Frazier's, the ex-Knick who used big words for the joy and craft of it. Hers was the language of someone who read a lot and wanted to let you know she was educated. Or maybe she just needed to be as precise as possible.

There were two quick raps on the door. I thought Gloria didn't hear them, but before I could decide whether to ask *Did I hear a knock?* in walked one of those women who are so vivid they seem drawn in kindergarten Crayolas leaving everybody else painted in wishy-washy watercolors. She was African American, built on the solid side, like a tight end, assuming there could be an offensive lineman who was about five foot three. "The grandchildren!" she exclaimed on seeing us. Her voice wasn't deep in the masculine sense, more like resonant, a voice that could sing "The Star-Spangled Banner" before a game. "I'm Emily Anderson, Ms. Garrison's assistant." Without side glances for consultation, the three of us stood and shook her hand. "I made your travel arrangements. Was everything okay? Did the driver meet you in the Albuquerque airport with the Goldberg sign?"

"Yes," Raquel said. And Daisy added, "Everything was fine."

"Excellent," Emily said. She was cool looking. Her cheeks were prominent, shiny and reddish, which may have been makeup, except it looked like the gleam of health. You could see a little of her almond-shaped eyes, but mostly it was cheeks and the kind of heavy-duty eyelashes that resemble a cross between a mink and a centipede. I did my reflexive checkout of the rest of her. She was one of those vibrant women who can combine purple and turquoise and make it look tasteful. I also took in the fact that she was wearing a diamond wedding band and felt that momentary flash of disappointment that an appealing woman was unavailable. It made no sense. I could be sitting across from someone waiting for a flight to board, and when I'd notice she was wearing an engagement or wedding ring, feel let down. It wasn't like I was the kind of guy who started conversations with strangers and wound up sleeping with them. Besides my usually being in a relationship plus being a little bit shy, our health teacher had scared the shit out of me in seventh grade talking about casual hookups and AIDS; I'd never been able to shed that thirteen-year-old image of an emaciated guy dying in a hospital because of a single fuck. "Ms. Garrison? Your usual?"

"Yes, same old boring brew. If you have the biscotti . . ."

"Of course I have the biscotti." Not only did she appear unawed and unafraid of Gloria, she gave off a vibe of tolerant parent speaking to challenging child. She handed each of us a small laminated card, which turned out to be all the different kinds of coffee and tea on offer. "If any of you are soda drinkers, I can do that. And there's water and San Pellegrino."

"Emily speaks four languages," Gloria said. "English, French, Spanish, and Mandarin, as well as some Apache. She learned Apache when she was in VISTA and taught at a Native American school."

I was marveling at how we had just seen the first sign of any sort of familial pride on my grandmother's part when Emily chimed in, "If you want to order your coffee in Apache, feel free." It was like she was sharing this feeling of family inclusion with us, assuming that Gloria Garrison spoke to us, too, in this way: warm, informal. Well, maybe our grandmother had talked about us affectionately to Emily when we were nearly two thousand miles away in New York, but once we were all in the same city, the signs of family fondness had vanished.

We told Emily what we wanted, and just as I was wondering how lousy the economy must be when someone fluent in four languages—and don't forget the Apache—was doing the old *My girl will get us coffee,* my grandmother said, "Don't think it's part of Emily's regular job to get coffee." In truth, she snapped it, as though we were the ones who'd summoned Emily and coerced her into taking our orders.

"Isn't she impossible?" Emily asked us, but affectionately, like she was referring to an incorrigible, adorable kid. It was kind of embarrassing. All three of us gave her mealy-mouthed smiles: *Gee whiz, that Gloria is impossible!* "I have an all-day meeting outside the office today, but I told your grandma I would be in to meet you beforehand, come hell or high water. Also to make sure they included the cranberry-pistachio biscotti in the order." She gave us a dazzler of a smile. If Marguerite the receptionist was a high-wattage bulb, Emily was Yankee Stadium floodlights. "Ms. Garrison, you didn't tell me how gorgeous your grandchildren were! I see a little family resemblance between each one of them and you."

"I don't," my grandmother said.

"Maybe you're getting cataracts. I'll be back in a few."

Gloria waited until the door latch clicked behind her. "She's always like that. Nonstop happy. I tell Emily that it's as if she'd been educated at some high-IQ cheerleading academy and not UNM."

Raquel leaned forward. "How come . . . ," she said slowly, "when that guy you'd initially thought would buy out the business from you, the guy who'd been working here—"

"Keith," Daisy prompted.

"Right. When he pulled out, how come you decided to turn to one of us rather than to someone inside? Like Emily, for instance."

Raquel's question seemed to cause a cloud to pass over the sun: You became aware of the lessening of light only after you felt the chill in Gloria's words. "Since all of you are so passionate about your jobs or your boyfriends and girlfriends that you passed up the chance to inherit a brilliant business and see firsthand what it's like to be a multimillionaire, I see no point in explaining my decision." Either she instantly forgot what she'd just said, or maybe she needed something to fill in the two or three minutes before the coffee arrived. "As far as Emily goes, she married late, had children late, and is now thirty-nine years old with a baby and two toddlers. She doesn't long for money and power, which she knows I consider to be her only serious character flaw. Does that answer your question?" If Gloria looked at most people with the glacial glaze she was directing at Raquel, they would feel they'd been stabbed with a freezing ice pick.

The glacial gaze treatment didn't seem to touch my cousin. "No one else in the company is qualified?"

"No. Do you think Glory has layers upon layers of executives to draw on? I hire only the people I need. I built big, have the space to expand, but I've wound up outsourcing anything I can to keep costs down, not that you want to hear another company head moaning about medical insurance. I have hired guns for advertising, social media promotions, bookkeeping, and accounting.

So what am I supposed to do? Hand over my business to someone who's devoted her life to training senior salon workers how to mix formulas for vanilla blond?"

Considering the sarcasm dripping from Gloria's question, I had to hand it to Raquel for not rising to the occasion with something like, *Don't you think that's a little harsh?* Instead, she leaned forward some more and asked, "What's vanilla blond? Beyond that it's a color I shouldn't consider."

"It's very pale, almost whitish. Unlike pure platinum, it has a touch of yellow in it. When you layer it with light blond, it gives a halo effect. Not an actual halo. More like the light shining behind a saint's head."

As Raquel nodded, my sister mumbled, "Actual halos disappeared in High Renaissance art, I think. That radiant backlighting replaced it."

Gloria made a noise like *hmmf,* a contented sound at Daisy's Renaissance tidbit. My grandmother appeared to be some kind of liberal arts junkie, or at least someone who appreciated Daisy's brand of minutiae. Displaying that sort of knowledge could make my sister the favorite grandchild, or, if such a thing wasn't possible, the least disliked. For sure, the High Renaissance remark seemed to improve my grandmother's mood, as did Emily Anderson's return. Emily set a pretty metal tray on the cocktail table and handed each of us our beverage of choice. "Let me know if I can get you anything else," she said, giving us something of a conspiratorial smile as she left the room.

The women bonded over the biscotti. At least they carried on about which to pick and how to share it, whether they should break it into two pieces or three. I got that bull-in-a-china-shop feeling at the ladyness of it all. It was so . . . dainty. Also, it made me want to laugh, because I knew that on her own, my sister could glom down half a dozen biscotti during one episode of *Homeland.*

Not that I didn't talk about food, but unless guys were exquisite types like Raquel's boyfriend, Hayden (he who made pork and lemongrass meatballs in lettuce cups when I came to dinner at their place), there was a premium on quantity. Men wanted giant greasy slices and huge slabs, not breaking things into little pieces. Like three-cheese pizzas with four kinds of sausage. Plus meat-balls.

I had just eaten one of the chocolate-dipped biscotti and was thinking how much I was dying to escape the vanilla blond and teeny-bite world, to be back in a place where I could be comfort-able. With that, it came to me that I wasn't sure where I'd look for that com-fort, that feeling of *I'm home.* At work at Citi Field? On a basketball court or at a bar with my friends? Or picking up Ash-ley at the hospital and taking her to an all-night diner for a burger—which she would not want to share? Just then, I caught Gloria staring at me.

She looked deeply unsettled. Maybe plain angry. Well, so was I. I wanted to say, *What the hell do you want from any of us, you crazy old bitch? And, if you want something, why don't you stop staring at me and just go back to being pissed at Raquel?* "Do you know who you look like?" she asked me, in a voice too loud for even that huge room.

"Grandpa Joe," I told her.

"Travis! You look like Travis." I didn't have a second to glance at my cousin before Gloria added, "Not that you're anything like the man he was."

Sixteen

Raquel

Obviously what Gloria said was true. Matt Goldberg was not the man my father was. But Gloria said it not as a statement of fact, not even as an accusation but as a pronouncement of betrayal. Like, *You could have been like Travis but—with malice aforethought—you chose not to be.* What was so unsettling about it was that, until that moment, I thought we were all having a decent time. Okay, Gloria might still be running hot and cold, or more accurately, tepid and cold. But she'd seemed more at ease here at Glory than she had at her own house. In her heart, I'd guessed, this was where she lived.

"Not that you're anything like the man he was," she'd said. Being a defense lawyer, my instinct was to jump in and protect Matt. Normally, he was as good on his feet as I was. His job, after all, was spin. After his years with the often-beleaguered Mets, spin had probably become his specialty. But he looked like he'd taken a big hit right in the solar plexus. There was no fast comeback. His mouth hung open. All the red in his coloring drained from his face, leaving only the yellow.

Did he look like Travis Goldberg? Even though I vaguely recalled times with my dad, most of my images of what he'd looked like came from the framed photographs that were all over our apartment. I was just four when he died, so the memories that stuck were probably of happy times—like him carefully handing me halves of peanuts to throw to the squirrels in Riverside Park and me squealing with joy. (My only unhappy memories were the times he'd go away for a shoot. He'd pick me up and hold me for a while, kiss the top of my head, and tell me, “You’re my baby and my big girl.”)

As far as my dad’s actual appearance? I wasn’t sure I remembered. Every time I pictured his face, it turned out to be the face in one of the photos. Or it could be I wasn’t even looking at him that day in the park (though now I’d be willing to swear under oath that he was grinning at my delight). My attention was on the squirrel holding that piece of peanut between his front paws and nibbling it elegantly, a gourmet in gray fur. Why look at your dad when you could watch the squirrel? Besides, when you’re four, you assume your dad will always be around. You can look at him . . . whenever.

But in all the pictures my mom put in silver-plated frames, and also in whatever real memories I had of Travis Goldberg, did he look like my cousin Matt? I thought of my dad as tall and lean, but if you could have put him beside grown-up, buff Matthew, he probably would have come off as medium height and close to skinny. Also, to be totally truthful, while my dad did have a million-dollar smile, he didn't have a million-dollar nose. It was a Roman nose by way of Minsk, or wherever in Russia the Goldbergs came from. I meant to ask Grandpa Joe whenever I saw him, but I always forgot, sidetracked by his charm. (When my parents got married, Gloria could barely bring herself to talk to my mom. Joe took an adult-ed class in conversational Spanish so he'd be able to talk with his new in-laws; he didn't know they were fluent in English.)

Talk about getting sidetracked . . . Anyway, my dad's nose was strong and prominent like one of those ancient emperors whose busts are in the Met. Wider, though. It took up an awful lot of room on his face.

Whereas Matt had every feature not only in proportion, but as the gold standard of excellence for real guys. Dark, devilish eyes made angelic (almost) by a sweet smile. It was a surprisingly shy smile for such an extroverted guy. Perfect straight nose. Angular features with a squared-off jaw: not too squared off, so he didn't look like a comic book superhero. Mouth with the perfect amount of lip. Matt was a handsome man, whereas my father was a nice-looking guy with a nose issue.

I was furious at Gloria's attack on my cousin. Halfway between sitting and standing, I was about to put my hands on my hips and give it to my grandmother: *Matty isn't the man my father was, but he doesn't have to be. He's just fine the way he is.* It's weird, but in that instant I felt a pressure on my chest. Like my heart was clenching up at how much I loved my cousins. Not that I had dis-loved them before. I just never really thought about Matt and Daisy as being major factors in my life, like my mom's family. But then I thought how these two sophisticated, rich older cousins had sought me out because they wanted a relationship with me. And not only were they kind, they were fun.

Matt came over to where I was sitting, next to Gloria, and motioned with his finger to switch seats with him. By the time I was in the chair beside Daisy, he was seated, his body turned toward our grandmother. She wasn't what you'd call receptive. Her arms were crossed so tightly across her chest it looked like she'd constrict her lungs and stop breathing. Her back was rigid, her knees tight together, her endangered species shoes planted right up against each other.

"There's no one who knew Uncle Travis who didn't think he was one of the world's great people," Matt said. I could hear him, but he was speaking quietly, like only he and Gloria were in the room. "Everyone was wiped out by his death. Everyone wishes they could have had more time with him."

Even more softly, Gloria told him, "Shut up."

"He gave off vibes of . . . I guess you'd call it decency. My dad told me people not only loved him, they trusted him. He could go anywhere in the world and make friends, even if he didn't speak the language. He was outstanding in his photography. And he was his own man. He made his choices without being ruled by anyone—including his mother." Gloria's body seemed to jerk, like she wanted to get up and rush from the room, but her arms and legs were so stiff and unbending she couldn't move. Even if she'd tried, I didn't think she could have unlocked her jaw to tell Matt to shut up again.

He kept talking. "You're right. I'm not the man he was. But I hope I have some of his backbone, his willingness to go for what was right for him."

"And damn the consequences," Gloria said, "full speed ahead." She made a couple of snorts, the kind that when they describe it in books it comes out, *She laughed bitterly.* "Go for what's right for you. To hell with everybody else." With that, she whipped her neck around and glared at me. Maybe stared.

Either way, it was my cue. "What are you talking about?" I demanded. My hands gripped the thin, cushioned arms of the chair so tightly it was a miracle my nails didn't slice through the fabric. My voice was probably too loud because Daisy reached over and lightly touched my hand, like, *Take it easy.* I flipped my hand up to get rid of her restraint. " 'To hell with everybody else'? Tell me, how am I supposed to take that? That he died on his way to take pictures of monkeys, and that was because he chose a selfish and frivolous career? Or he was saying to hell with me and my mom because he wasn't wearing a seat belt when he got killed in Peru?" It wasn't like the head of steam I got in court where I could pump myself up into a major case of righteous indignation in my summation. There was no pumping necessary; I was propelled by pure anger. "Is 'damn the consequences' about him marrying a Latina because . . . Because what? Because he was too good for that and it pissed you off? Pardon me. I'm from the Bronx. Because it profoundly disturbed you?"

"Is there no limit to your rudeness?" my grandmother asked me.

"You really want to test my limits?" I asked. "Fine." I heard "Shhh," very soft, coming from Daisy's direction, like the not-quite-subliminal sound you make to calm an overexcited puppy or a wild bull. I ignored it, or at least did not look her way.

"Your father was never rude. He simply lacked the capacity."

"I don't know what my dad's capacity was when it came to rudeness, although I've never heard him described that way. Are you trying to tell me that since my father lacked the capacity for rudeness, I learned it at my mother's knee?" Maybe I got a little louder. "Or maybe it's just that I'm a hot-blooded Latin?"

Gloria, who had been sitting so erect, slumped back in her chair. I thought, *Oh, Jesus, please don't let it be a heart attack.* Because even though I didn't believe that you could give someone a heart attack, I understood the limits of rationality. I'd spend the rest of my life thinking that I killed my grandmother. Almost as awful, my words "hot-blooded Latin" would forever be linked in my cousins' minds with sudden death and they'd stop being progressives. I'd never thought the dual inheritance of Catholic and Jewish guilt was much of a factor in my personality, but in that instant, I could see guilt as my new constant companion. I'd be carrying it the rest of my life, stumbling under its weight.

"What are you staring at?" Gloria said to me.

"You kind of . . . slumped. For a minute I thought, you know, maybe you weren't feeling well."

"Or that I dropped dead? No such luck."

"Gloria," Daisy said, "that's not fair."

Gloria straightened herself, but her spine was now pressed against the back of the chair. There would be no more slumping. "This is none of your business, Daisy." Her words were tough, but her tone wasn't tough the way it had been with me. I couldn't tell if she simply liked Daisy more, or if she felt Daisy couldn't take meanness the way I, presumably, could. "Both of you—Bradley's kids—not a peep. Or go find the employees' cafeteria. I'll have someone bring you to me later."

Like either one of them would walk out on their kid cousin. They melded to their chairs.

"That hot-blooded business I was going on about," I said to Gloria, "please strike that from the record. It was, well, an overstatement."

"But not a gross overstatement?" she replied. My heart attack fears had been foolish. Her heart was as hard as ever, as was her voice.

This time, no getting sidetracked, and no getting into a pissing contest with her either. It flashed through my mind that pissing contest was an unfortunate metaphor when considering two women. Who'd be the winner? The one who didn't pee on her shoes? "I'm sorry this happened, the ill will between us. Look, each of us in her own way is still mourning the loss of my father."

"Oh, stop it! What will you trot out next? Violins?"

"You never mourned his loss?" I asked.

"Of course I did! And then mourning ends. Period. *Finito.* Life goes on."

What could I do? Argue that too? So I said, "I admitted last night that I'd been rude. Using that as a standard, I guess the hot-blooded remark makes this apology number two."

"Do you have an infinite number of apologies waiting in the wings?"

I let it pass. "I'm not sure why I agreed

to come to Santa Fe," I went on. "Mostly because Daisy and Matt decided to come. But also because . . . God, I really hate the word 'closure.' Anyway, I don't think that's what I was looking for. Reconciliation, maybe. No. That's too positive. I'd seen you so rarely I had no sense of what you were really like. I guess that was my main reason for coming."

"Your mother never told you what I was like?"

"Yes. Actually, she's pretty understanding when it comes to you."

"How Christian of her," Gloria said. Matt smacked his palm against his forehead, an Oh-my-God-how-could-you? gesture.

"I'm not saying my mom is forgiving, though she probably is. The word I used was 'understanding.' She and I are different people. Our views often coincide, but definitely not all the time. I needed to see for myself. Also, there's something about roots, too. I don't know much about genetics—dominant, recessive, whatever—but I'm one-quarter you."

"You might consider a bit more politesse to that quarter."

"I might. So in the spirit of politesse, let me explain my attitude about the family." She didn't stop me, so I kept going. "Growing up, I heard a lot about the Goldbergs—nice things, the good times my dad had had growing up that he told my mother about. I didn't experience much myself. I remember seeing you three times. At Matt and Daisy's bar and bat mitzvahs and once, when I was younger, when the whole family had dinner in a big room. I think it was the dining room at the hotel you were staying at. My mother says there was another time also, but I don't remember it. So I had no sense of who you were except that you wore nice clothes and pearls and were tall." Gloria gave one of her regal nods. I was thinking she ought to have a sobriquet like royals did: Richard the Lionheart, Catherine the Great, Gloria the Disengaged. Anyhow, I took this particular nod to mean *I am listening.* "I saw the rest of the Goldbergs at least a couple of times a year for the Seder at their house.

"Every year on our way to the Seder, my mom would say, 'Remember, you're half Jewish and we want to honor that tradition.' "

Even before I really understood what she was talking about, I understood it was important to her that I not be bratty and that I leave my gold cross home. The ceremony was short enough to be tolerable, and each year my aunt Cynthia gave me a new baby Moses doll in a basket. The dolls were racially diverse; the baskets were a decorator's delight of intricately woven reeds or wicker. I named each doll: Moses, of course, and Mose, Moisés, Mosie, Mosella, Mo. When I got older, the Seder service became interesting, and instead of baby Moses, I had my cousins to amuse me.

"And most years, right before school started," I went on, "they'd come up to our place for brunch, and then we'd all go to the zoo or botanical gardens. And when we all got older, we'd meet for lunch or dinner—"

Gloria cut me off: "This has nothing to do with me."

I didn't even look at Daisy because I

knew the distressed expression she'd be wearing. She'd be lip chewing also. But even Matt, right next to Gloria, looked like he'd prefer if I didn't lose it and blare out, *Not everything is about you!* Also, having made a huge deal about three strikes and you're out, I didn't want to be majorly rude a third time.

"I know it doesn't involve you directly," I said in my sweet voice, which manifested itself mainly when I had a member of the clergy on my jury. This time it was more self-mimicry than any wholesome part of my personality breaking through. "But since you invited the three of us, I thought I would give you a sense of where I feel I fit in—or don't."

"And naturally your little discourse has nothing to do with manipulation, making me—and maybe your cousins—excuse your discourteous behavior or feel remorse for you, the little outsider?" Gloria did sarcasm well.

"My cousins know me. And all three of you are smart enough to recognize when you're being worked over. All I can say is, judge for yourselves. Okay?" Gloria barely shrugged. "But even though my mom and I saw the family a couple of times a year, it wasn't till Daisy and Matt sought me out that I felt any real connection or closeness. I think Uncle Bradley and Aunt Cynthia's keeping up with us and inviting us to the Seder every year had more to do with a sense of duty, to honor my dad's memory, than with any real love for us. Don't get me wrong. They cared and were good to me, warm, totally generous, birthday and Christmas presents, a computer when I started at Bronx Science. And then Uncle Bradley came through with financial help for college, which was really amazing."

Suddenly it hit me that this was supposed to be a big secret. I must have looked appalled because Daisy said, "Oh, please. We knew. Do you think my mom could not tell us? In her mind, 'Don't tell anybody' means 'Just don't issue a press release.' "

"With my mom," I said, "it's totally the opposite. I mean, if someone told her 'This is my secret recipe,' you could waterboard her a hundred times and she wouldn't give it up." I turned back to Gloria. "My mom had my dad's insurance money and her savings for my college. But Uncle Bradley just came to her and said, 'I want to contribute.' He did it so I wouldn't have to take out loans and also so I could live at Barnard instead of commuting. It was a fantastic act of kindness because Matt was still at Duke, and even for someone with money, the bills had to have been enormous."

"There's money . . . and then there's real money," Gloria said. "With real money, college bills are chump change." Matt's coloring, which had returned to normal, now grew red, but just as he opened his mouth, he shut it again. "You know"—she spoke in that too-patient voice a person uses when talking to someone she thinks is a dummy—"being a lawyer at Legal Aid, you're not going to experience either money or real money."

"Oh, I know that very well."

"Yet you tell yourself, no doubt, that you're fighting the good fight. Very noble." You couldn't really say, *Drop dead, bitch,* in response to her condescension because her delivery was calm and direct, not snarky. Plus obviously she was my grandmother and seventy-nine years old. "In the long run," she continued, "money is meaningless compared to the contribution you make to humanity. Isn't that right, Raquel?" She made me remember some assistant to the Manhattan borough president who got sent to read the Law Day proclamation at a low-end legal luncheon I was at: a person who couldn't decide between irritation and rage at someone like her having to be with people like us.

"Occasionally I fight the good fight. More often, when I win, I know my client will commit another scam within days or weeks. When I lose, people will go to prison who deserve to be in prison, though not in those prisons or for those stupidly long sentences. And sometimes an innocent person gets sent away for three to five even though I argued my heart out and was twice as good as the assistant DA. I never feel noble. Most of the time I feel . . . like all

I want to do is anything but what I'm doing. I wish I were better than that, but I'm not."

"Then why don't you leave?" Gloria asked.

"I don't know. It's hard accepting that what you really thought you'd be great at and what you'd love doing is making you miserable."

"You sound pretty matter-of-fact about this."

"I'm not so much matter-of-fact as used to feeling this way. I've been like this for months, and I'm definitely a proactive kind of person. But how can I be proactive when I'm not sure what I want to do?" I hadn't shared any of this with Daisy or Matt, and I felt awful that it was coming out here, in conversation with Gloria, rather than with them. Almost as bad as the feeling of awfulness was realizing how bizarre it was that I hadn't talked about this with either my mom or Hayden. How the hell did Gloria Garrison get to be my confidante?

"If you're expecting me to reconsider you for Glory now that you've told me this . . . Don't."

I laughed. "I don't expect it and I don't want it."

"So you just want to stay with your boyfriend? And what? Marry him and have babies?"

"I'm not sure."

"What does 'I'm not sure' mean?"

Despite her question, it was easy to stay polite because she was treading my personal minefield. I needed to be careful. The alternative was telling Gloria, along with my cousins, all my fears and doubts, stuff I hadn't revealed to anybody. Stuff I hadn't really sat down and thought about in any logical way—assuming logic was possible when responding to gut reactions you deeply don't want to be having.

"It just means I'm twenty-five years old and I haven't yet decided on what I want my future to be. I doubt it will be at Legal Aid. Not at a big firm either. And not leaving the law and going the investment bank–hedge fund route. I've toyed with the idea of applying for a clerkship to a federal judge, but so far I haven't looked into it—just toyed."

I'd just said a lot more than I'd wanted

to. However, that was better than saying, *I'm not sure that Hayden really wants to marry me.* And it was better than *Sometimes I think he wants out.* I knew that working for Goldman Sachs meant that in return for the rewards you reap, you sell them your life, if not your soul. But even his male colleagues' most traditional wives who were always complaining about their husbands' hours copped to having some fun. All Hayden ever seemed to do was work, work, work, if not 24/7, then at least for so many hours that we rarely had a meal together. Not even breakfast. He'd say, "I'll grab something at Starbucks." I once said, "Why wait fifteen minutes on line while someone orders a cinnamon dolce latte with half soy milk and half one percent instead of having a bowl of Cheerios with me?" He told me the line moves faster in the financial district.

And sex? Infrequent enough that I would have had to have been a total fool not to wonder whether it was exhaustion or the dreaded Someone Else.

"But it would be a federal judge in New York?" Gloria asked.

"Yes."

"Because you wouldn't want to leave your boyfriend?"

"That's what I told you."

"I'm well aware of what you told me. Is that the truth? I'm not prying," she said, tapping her chest lightly with her fingers to signify, *Me, I wouldn't pry.*

"You're just curious," I responded.

"Gloria," Daisy said too quickly, "are those dresses hanging on the rods ones you've decided on, or are they under consideration?"

"Stop it!" Gloria told her. "What are you trying to do? Divert my attention? Short-circuit a contretemps?"

"What's wrong with that?" Daisy's smile made me even more grateful because she was working to turn an awkward moment into a humorous one.

Naturally, that was an unattainable hope when dealing with Gloria Garrison. And while it took the heat off me, Daisy got blasted. "Who are you to try to smooth things over?"

"I just thought—" Daisy began.

"Don't. It's not your forte."

If Gloria thought she could pound my cousin into the ground, she was wrong. "It is my forte," Daisy told her. "I may think differently from you, but I'm sure I'm at least as skilled intellectually. And one of the behaviors I've noticed is that every time something displeases you, you don't say, 'That displeases me,' and be direct about it. You go on the attack. One, two, three this morning: Matt, Raquel, now me."

"You're quite the little psychoanalyst."

"No. I'm not plumbing the depth of someone's psyche." It almost didn't sound like Daisy because her tone was so cold. But she was the oldest of the three of us, and even though we were roughly contemporaries, she had a little maternal thing going for me and Matt. "I'm describing the action and the dialogue."

"Spoken like a true film studies major. Isn't that what you were? I think your father wrote me about it in one of his—I won't say 'interminable'—letters. That's before he switched over to interminable e-mails. No doubt he views them as newsy." When Daisy didn't respond, not even with a glare, Gloria sat silent, as if knowing that sooner or later, she'd get a comeback from my cousin that she could then slap down. But sooner became later. When it was clear Daisy had no intention of making a retort, Gloria went on. "You're living in a dreamworld, my dear girl. Let me try to explain: Life is not like the movies."

"I never said it was. It's something quite different, in fact."

"You think you know about life? What do you do? Fly to L.A., then fly back home? You don't have a boyfriend. Oh, don't look so shocked. I told you I did due diligence on all of you before bringing you out here, and the investigator's report said, essentially, that you don't have a life. Well, a social life. And what kind of existence is it, spending your day in a dark room watching movies?"

"That's not what I do, any more than you spend your days showing women how to blend eyeliner. As far as my life goes, your investigator was right only in that I don't have a boyfriend. I wish I did. I would love somebody to love."

Daisy was composed, almost serene. Gloria was silent. I guessed she was slightly stunned because she was so used to her attacks being defended either by her victims' hostility or their silent concurrence with the awful things she would say. And Daisy added, "How about you? Wouldn't you love to have somebody in your life you could love?"

Gloria's response took over the room like a high-end audio system at full blast. The volume of it was so intense that all three of us were stupefied for a minute. It wasn't the physical boom of sound that got us—more that so many decibels and such fury could come out of one old lady. "How do you know I don't?"

"Because you invited us here," Matt said.

Seventeen

Gloria

Ugh! The weekend would take a year off my life. Forget the other two grandchildren for a minute. Just dealing with Raquel caused enough tension to get my asthma to a point where normally I would have used an inhaler. But what was I to do? Pull it out of my handbag and give her the satisfaction of seeing me dependent on that pathetic instrument. You had to pucker your mouth around the end of the tube, as if you were fellating an anatomically disadvantaged man. Even worse than Raquel's viewing me as weak, it might evoke pity, a far more humiliating thought.

So instead, I ignored the tightness at the top of my chest. It was harder to disregard the wheezing. With every exhalation, there was that odious, whiny squeak in my throat that ended on a minor note, like a neurasthenic mouse. No doubt Matthew, seated next to me, could hear it.

Dr. Whatever, the charming pulmonologist with the beard—I was becoming so bad at names, especially when under duress—said what I had was mild adult-onset asthma. I told him, "I'm seventy-seven. That's beyond adult." On my last visit I'd admitted the medicine was helping. But that was before Raquel crossed my threshold.

Someone to love. It was one thing for those grandchildren to sit alone and exchange psychobabble. Yet I would have thought that with the new century, young people especially would finally get over making judgments based on the scientifically dubious theories of Dr. Freud delivered with the one-two punch of Dr. Phil. Worse, they couldn't even keep such talk among themselves. They had to share their insights. Share! What was it with the last couple of generations and the sharing business? Share an ice cream cone? Fine. Share a banal perception? No. Half the time, they began with an announcement: "I have something to share with you." You'd know, before it was even uttered, that you ought to say, *You mustn't be so selfless. Keep it all to yourself.*

And out of the three, who'd finally done the sharing of that dazzling observation that I'd invited them to Santa Fe because I needed someone to love? Matthew. True, of the three, I ranked him as the least intellectually facile. Depth held no delight for him. He seemed more doer than thinker. Nevertheless, he struck me as the most knowledgeable about how the world actually operated. Yet there he was, buying into all that dime store psychology, what Joe had called "the old crapola." Of course, Joe said that when I suggested that he was insane to be bellying up to the Mafia and that he should see a psychiatrist.

Three grandchildren and each more or less frustrating—no, infuriating—in his or her own way. And there I was, on a Friday morning, stuck with them for another forty-eight hours. Maybe I could give them five hundred dollars each, rent them a car, and say, *Go forth, my children, frolic as you will, and savor all sorts of Goldbergian pleasures while I spend the next two days watching the DVD of Diane von Furstenberg's fall collection and reading . . . something.*

I needed something cerebral but not abstruse. And not some overly popular work of literature, since if you're going to read it, you might as well trot it out at a party. The last thing one ought to do at an opening in an art gallery or at a dinner is to start a conversation with, *I was just rereading* Anna Karenina.

Though, actually, I'd never read it. I started it but got confused because a character named Levin whom I assumed was Jewish turned out not to be—was in fact, Mr. Russian Orthodox Goody Two-shoes. Too boring. And also because I knew even before I started the book that Anna kills herself at the end. So why bother if she's just going to play the victim? Well, in her case, actually be the victim.

But you can't be in your late seventies and say *I'm reading* Anna Karenina as you're sipping a martini because there's always some ass who will gasp, *You mean you never read* Anna Karenina? with shock and horror, as though you just confessed to genocide.

Maybe *King Lear.* I saw it on TV with Orson Welles, not his most stellar performance, way back when. Dreadful wig. Probably in the '50s. I always thought I should see the play itself live, or read it. But this was not the weekend to read about ungrateful children. In *King Lear,* the two bad daughters, at least, want the kingdom. None of the three grandchildren wanted the kingdom I had offered: Glory. What was the quote from Lear? Something like, "How sharper than a serpent's tooth is a thankless child!" They were my thankless flesh and blood. But at least they weren't my actual children; it wasn't on my head that they turned out the way they did.

I couldn't get over Matthew, that manly young man, mouthing such preteen drivel about my inviting them because I was looking for love. If he had implied I was looking for . . . I don't know . . . fun, all right, I would not have taken offense. When Keith walked out of my business and then out of my life . . .

Not that he was fun once Billy had the stroke, and of course I didn't expect him to be. But I never thought that he'd be angry enough to abandon me forever. Of course I understood he was upset about my not going to see Billy in the ICU, but not sever-all-ties upset.

There were times on weekends, or even during the workday, that I'd be all dressed to visit the hospital: all made up, too, liquid foundation with some gold in it to stand up to the fluorescent lighting. I wore heels, of course, out of respect for Billy, who always had something nice to say about how great my legs were, but with rubber soles so as not to go careening on those horrid hospital floors.

Except just as I was about to leave

the house, there'd be a phone call that I'd wind up taking, even if it was someone I normally dealt with via e-mail. Or, I'd spot the mail on the flowered Mexican tray on my way to the garage, and I'd pick it up, sit down at the kitchen table. By the time I finished reading and sorting, I was too enervated to get up and go.

On one level I really thought I would do it. Just not today. But first thing tomorrow. On another level, I knew I couldn't bring myself to see him lying there with his eyes closed and that strange overbite people get when they're on the way out. I would think, *He won't know I'm there anyway.* And if you've seen one person at death's door, you've seen them all. Deep down, I realized I was terrified, and nothing—even Keith not speaking to me for a year—could get me to face sitting beside someone who was about to exit. Death was in the room. He was clutching Billy's hospital gown, pulling him close, closer. And when Death wants someone, nothing—not yesterday's vigor or all those omega-3s or a divine sense of humor—can divert Him.

But the worst I thought my not going would bring about was Keith hurt, angry. He'd need at least twelve months. Then maybe another year with him beginning to understand, though still irate that I hadn't been able to make the visit in spite of my fears. Then a gradual thaw, and one day during a meeting he'd make an irreverent remark meant solely for me—because no one else there would get it—and I'd laugh. And we'd both wind up with tears of gratitude in our eyes that we were having fun again.

Fun. When Keith told me he was leaving, that he no longer had any interest in Glory, let alone in me, I didn't believe him. When it finally became clear, I thought, *So be it.* I'd survive. I'd survived so many hits in my life. People abandoning me: my parents when the whispers started, Joe, rejecting my strength, refusing to stand up for what was his—and his family's—and instead choosing to be a coward. And all right, Travis was killed. He didn't abandon me; it just felt like abandonment. So Keith was severing all ties? Fine. What's one more?

Oh, I knew I would have to think long and hard about who would take over the company. But a few weeks after the last speck of the dust of former friendship had settled and every legal paper that could tear us apart had been signed, I was thinking how ridiculous it was to agonize over what was forever finished. I might not get a twofer, a man for Glory and a gay best friend, but at least I could find the latter. Some new delightful, irreverent man.

I'd barely entertained that thought when I began to imagine Keith telling all his friends, "See? I knew it. She's trying to replace me with another gay man. She thinks we're interchangeable." That was the type of self-defeatist ruminating I loathed. It doomed you to inaction. Normally, when such thinking took hold, I'd concentrate on something else. Planning a grand dinner party during the Chamber Music Festival. Going through my closet with Paula, having her force me to donate whatever clothes, shoes, and handbags I hadn't worn for a year or more. Well, I gave handbags considerably more than a year. Susan Weinreb, the head designer at Solange de Paris, once said, "A good handbag should not be an accessory. It should be an investment."

I'd get over the loss of Keith. I'd find someone else for the business, and yet another person for me. It didn't have to be a gay man. It could be a woman, although my track record for friendships with women was, for want of a less painful adjective, lousy. In my twenties and thirties, I told myself that they were just jealous. If I were them, I'd be jealous of me. Could I expect loyalty when I was so envied? Love? Not a chance. As the years by turns crept or flew by, I came to realize it wasn't solely their jealously. Some of it was me. I could be successful as a mentor or a boss. I could be part of a group of four or eight—just one of the girls. But I wasn't cut out for one-on-one friendship with a woman.

But a funny thing happened on the way to rebuilding a life minus Keith. Except for Glory, which was all mine, he still loomed over every facet of my life because our mutual friends turned out not to be mutual: They all chose Keith.

My mail morphed into catalogs and bills; invitations were limited to business-related events. When I went to a committee meeting for the Lensic, the performing arts center, there were no more hugs, no more jokes or appeals from the women to make them over. Just "Gloria, hi," after a second's hesitation, as if they had to overcome their disgust before speaking. A few quick kisses that didn't quite land on the cheek. Not that it was a cabal, but I soon noticed that someone who had kissed me hello the previous month did not necessarily desire a repeat performance. People I'd known for decades seemed to be rotating the duty of kissing me in order that I not stop my contributions.

I found myself accepting invitations to second-rate evenings so that Carlos and Paula wouldn't observe me having dinner alone night after night. Also, I had to have someone to invite to my house, even though that meant tedious business contacts with their aggrieved the-economy-is-making-me-insecure spouses. My social life was reduced to anti-immigration asses and pro-life zealots who thought it acceptable to discuss dead fetuses and Obama during the salad course. What it came down to was no Keith = no fun.

Stupid Matthew. Or was it Daisy who'd originally brought it up? I wasn't looking for someone to love. I was looking for a couple of laughs, and if the laughs were at someone else's expense, so much the better.

That's not true. I suppose I was looking for love, but God knows not the sort of love my grandchildren could offer me, if they were offering, which they weren't. I wanted the love that makes you feel more alive. There really is a difference between getting dressed for work—even in a business dedicated to beauty and fashion—and getting ready for someone whose eyes say *Wow* before his mouth utters a word.

Joe and Keith—naturally, each in his own way—loved me for more than my looks or the way I threw an outfit together. They loved my humor and the way I analyzed social and business relationships. Keith knew more about politics and Joe knew more about sports than I did, and all our conversations were so animated. Not just fun. After 9/11, Keith and I spent a year talking about grief and fear and revenge, the terrorists' and ours. Tough talk, but vigorous talk.

For years, Joe and I had one long continuing discussion about the psychology of the group in sports. Not that we called it that, but both of us got fascinated wondering how much of a team's success or failure is due to the mix and clash of personalities or some overarching team personality. After I left Joe, I didn't really miss sports, but I missed the discussions. I tried to have them with the boys, but Travis wasn't that interested. If I took them to a sporting event, he just wanted to take pictures. Bradley was more than willing to talk, but he inserted so many *uuuh*s that sometimes I had the urge to smack myself to keep myself awake. Or smack him.

When I was in my late fifties, I got to thinking—no, realizing—that I wasn't going to get married again. I'd always assumed I would, but twenty-plus years of dating made me recognize that most men were annoying, and as they got older, it got worse. Flatulence and loudly expressed opinions. Nose hair that went unclipped. Undertipping waiters. Driving at forty-five in a sixty-five-miles-per-hour zone. I couldn't bear it. I understood then that I would spend the rest of my life alone.

That can be liberating. It can also be frightening, the thought of waking at five a.m. with the infamous pain in the chest that travels up to the jaw and you stretch but . . . you have so much pain in your arm that you can't extend it to reach the phone. Or you can, but the phone is on the fritz. Or you have one of those rescue things where you press a button that sends a *Help me!* signal to a central station, but the telephone operator/ambulance summoner is over the moon on meth and you die.

Now and then I missed Joe so much that I sometimes found myself with the telephone in my hand as if I knew his number and was about to dial. I wanted to hear that voice with its rough New York accent saying, "Hey, Glo."

Except one time, as that moment of longing was building, Bradley called and asked, "Did you hear about Dad?" My heart flipped over. What? "He married that widow in Fort Myers. Sharon." I'd never heard about Joe having anything to do with Fort Myers, much less Sharon. Half Italian, half Irish. Not rich: Lexus, not Mercedes. But rich enough to keep him for a while. When she threw him out, he found another like her . . . different pedigree, but she lasted less than a year. But there was always some woman who couldn't wait to take him in. After I left, he probably never paid a month's rent. He had the gall to bring one of them to Travis's funeral.

I knew I couldn't go back to Joe. It wasn't that he'd been fearful in the face of the Mob. Who wouldn't be? It was that he didn't try to fight his fear—gave in to it right away. I'd signed on for almost anything, but not cowardice. In my mind, that voided the "till death do us part" in our contract.

But nights when Carlos and Paula were off, I could always summon Keith. We were each other's lifeline: If anything happens to me . . . We gave each other our marching orders. He said, "I want to be buried in my tan Lucchese Ropers." I said, "If my regular internist is out of town, don't bother with the ones covering for her. Call Dr. FitzPatrick." Now Keith probably had ten people on Lucchese Alert, and an additional twenty on speed dial just in case his left or right side started feeling numb. I had no one.

At least an hour until lunch and I had absolutely nothing to say to those three. Have fun with them? It was no laughing matter. And yet, the odd thing was I fully grasped how enjoyable each of them must seem to others.

Matthew was an obvious charmer, but instead of putting you off—as in, I'm being manipulated by an adorable man—you were drawn in because you recognized his unfeigned interest in you.

And that smile. It brought you to a higher ground, as if you had been simultaneously blessed by the pope and admired by the most popular boy. Yet I had no doubt that if he did marry this Ashley, he had a good shot. Unlike a politician, he didn't need people. He just needed lots of persons.

Of the three, Raquel would easily grab the title Miss Not Fun. Well, she was more serious than the other two, but then, she had had a far tougher life. But had it been? I couldn't tell. I supposed just as I thought of Travis so often, even when I tried not to, so must Raquel. And Adriana? Off the charts. When a Travis, who was not only so vital but also so beloved, dies young, you mourn him forever. You want to cry for all he missed, and for what you missed with him. Yet Raquel had an energy the other two grandchildren didn't. She wanted to be someone.

Raquel wanted a place in America. It wasn't as if hers was the classic immigrant story, because her grandparents had been the immigrants. But she did have that fire in her to make it. I had it too, but only after Joe willfully chose weakness and abandoned his role as breadwinner and big shot. Raquel chose cheating Hayden Spanish-Two-Names, so maybe she wasn't any better at picking them than I had been. But to give her credit, I went for a trucker and she went for a Goldman Sachs almost-WASP.

But even though there would be disappointment for her down the road—at least if my investigator was to be believed—her spirit would never break. Also, she was beautiful in a tiny, brown way. Even without makeup, her skin glowed from morning to night. Her hair shone.

Daisy was kind, which I allowed was not high on my list of admired qualities, but I understood that her brand of goodness, combined with her intelligence and infatuation with movies, would make her sought after not just in that hard-edged business, but in mean-spirited Manhattan. Also, she had more than brains, enthusiasm, and kindness. She too had the Goldberg smile. Unlike her brother's, it wasn't the hook that caught you and pulled you in. It showed her humor but also her doubts about herself. Still, instead of making her seem vulnerable, usually a fatal flaw in New York or L.A., I could see where it would make people want to reassure her: *Don't worry. You're appealing and I like you.*

I said to them, "I want to have some fun." I half expected Matthew to scratch his head, trying to stimulate a response in the face of his disbelief. Raquel might shout "Liar!" Daisy's notion of fun might be to suggest we rent *The Shop around the Corner.* So I quickly added, "Who wants to get made over?"

Eighteen

Daisy

This was not good. I thought she'd just show us around. Had I been wrong in assuming Gloria's "Who wants to get made over?" was her idea of being lighthearted in the face of an abhorrent situation, i.e., being stuck with her grandchildren for two more days? Except as we walked from the fashion room to the beauty room, Raquel made that *Oh, my God* mouth motion—stretching it down at the corners in mock dread. Except it wasn't so mock. I shook my head to signal, *No way she'll push us into a makeover.* Raquel's response was a lift of eyebrows: *Wanna bet?*

We approached a pair of double doors, like in a restaurant. As if to prove that Raquel was right, Gloria said, "Let's get beautiful!" She sounded preposterously cheerful, like she was channeling the ingénue in some comedy of manners. "Sorry, not you, Matthew," she went on. "You don't need anything in the beauty room, unless you want"—she did a head to toe that was not only fast but mercifully free from any hint of flirtation—"perhaps a more lightweight gel in your hair."

"Okay," he said. That was one of the things I admired about my brother. In a female-friendly environment, eighty or ninety percent of straight guys would give some display of Neanderthalness to demonstrate their hetero bona fides. But Matty went for it. It could have been his recognizing that Gloria was trying to be pleasant. Or that she suffered from a multiple personality disorder and this was the never-before-seen nice one. In either case, he didn't want to change her mood. Also, he was excited to check out a new hair gel. Again, he maneuvered so that he could hold the door open for all three of us.

After the size and elaborateness of the fashion room, I guess I expected some Busby Berkeley setup with a hundred salon chairs on either side reflected into infinity by mirrors, along with dancing hairdressers in white barber jackets time-stepping a welcome. Instead, there were four hairdressers' stations, lots of rolling carts with supplies, and a woman who looked like Demi Moore in *Ghost,* except even younger. Maybe Carey Mulligan in the *Wall Street* sequel.

Equating strangers with actors in movie roles: I did that too often, though it usually amused my friends. Well, except for my 2009 boyfriend, Carl White (naturally my mother—who operated under the delusion she was not only amusing but also had been immaculately conceived without prejudice—referred to him as "Carl White who isn't," which turned into a particularly disagreeable mother-daughter discussion). Anyway, toward the end of my relationship with him, every time I started saying, "Doesn't so-and-so look like . . . ," Carl would snap, "No!" This coming from a guy who knew his actors; he was casting director for the Manhattan Theatre Club. At the end when we had the why-it-isn't-working discussion, the last conversation we ever had, one of his bullet points was my comparing everyone to actors. In my own defense, I said, "Oh, come on, Carl, I only do it once in a while." He said, "More than once in a while. I'm just thankful you never did it with me." My almost-final words to him were, "Billy Dee Williams without the mustache."

Also on the downside of reflexively viewing people as fictional characters: It influenced my expectations of what they'd be like and therefore became a time waster, as it took a while to revise all those inaccurate first impressions. Like here. The woman coming toward us had the determined walk of someone headed for a press conference to make a major announcement. Yet in spite of her VIP stride, I expected that such a Demi-Carey cute person with bouncing short hair would have a voice like wind chimes.

"Welcome, grandchildren! Glad I'm getting the chance to meet you." She sounded like Santa Claus on speed. Friendly, fast, booming.

I canceled the self-effacement business as she shook hands, a grip stronger than the voice. "I'm Lizzy O'Melveny," she said. Her smile was powerful too, broad and bright. It struck me how odd it was that Gloria, who was so determinedly disagreeable, surrounded herself with likable women like Marguerite, Emily, and now Lizzy. Well, it was possible they could have been hired by that guy who had left the company. Or else my grandmother was hoping to delude outsiders with whom she dealt (and maybe herself) into believing that Glory was filled with wonderful employees, top to bottom.

"I'm Glory's vice president for cosmetology and hairdressing," Lizzy said. "We decided that 'VP beauty' . . . What was that word you used, Gloria?"

"I said it trivialized an important position."

"And I told her, 'Nothing I do is trivial,' but she wasn't buying that. All right, my job is checking out new products—from their chemistry to their scent."

Gloria took over. "We're air conditioned and well ventilated, but essentially we're inside the Glo-mobile, a truck. Sometimes we'll allow a whiff of fragrance, but anything perfumy is an automatic no-go."

"So," Lizzy continued, obviously used to being interrupted, "I research new products, which means replacing ones that are less effective. I'm on every truck when it comes in and when it leaves to make sure all the supplies are as they should be—"

"That nobody's stealing," my grandmother said.

"—and everything is cleaner than clean. There are some jobs I can delegate, but not this one. Too important. Also, my staff and I train every new hire, retrain employees every six months, and travel around making on-site spot checks. We interview clients also. Awesome, the things some of them notice . . . or imagine." She smiled at my brother. "Now, you're Matthew, right?"

"Right," he said, turning up his charm volume. I could tell he liked her, though if they ever got together, they'd probably blind each other with the candlepower of their smiles.

"Doesn't he need a lighter hair gel?" Gloria asked.

"I've never been a fan of gel for men," Lizzy said to him, "but it's okay on you. The Matrix Flexible stuff isn't bad." Matty's eyes narrowed: deep concentration. "And it's cheap. Or try the Redken wax. Don't get scared off by the word 'wax.'"

"I won't," he promised.

"So, you have a choice of activity, Matthew," Lizzy told him. "You can stay and watch the ladies here get work done." If I appeared anything like Raquel did at that moment, and I suspected I did, I was wearing an expression of distaste mixed with panic: *I'm not getting any work done!* "Now, as fascinating as watching makeovers might appear on the surface, your grandmother thought you might enjoy a meeting with our public relations department. That's two people, Tara and Rick. Talk shop, let them give you a tour, whatever. I'll get you the gel and wax before you leave."

"The PR department sounds good," Matty said. "And thank you, but I can buy—"

"No need."

"I'll walk you over there," Gloria said to him. "Introduce you, get you started." Then she added, ominously, I thought, "Daisy. Raquel. I'll be back shortly."

The instant she and Matty were out the double doors, Raquel said, "This is so thoughtful of you, Lizzy. But I really don't—"

"Of course you don't. And I bet your cousin . . . You're Raquel, she's Daisy, right?"

"Right," Raquel said.

"You know what's . . . interesting? None of us knew Ms. Garrison was a grandma until just a couple of weeks ago. We knew she'd been married and someone said she'd had kids, but she's the type who keeps her private life private. Which I totally respect." She was fishing.

Raquel smiled, essentially acknowledging Lizzy's respect but not giving a jot of information either.

"So her husband's last name was Goldberg?"

"That's right," Raquel said.

I figured it was time to change the subject or rat out Gloria with the Garrison explanation. "You're involved in cosmetology, how people look. So you've got to be observant."

"I never thought about it that way, but yeah, I am."

"So do you see any family resemblance among the three of us, or us and our grandmother?"

"Let me think," Lizzy said. "Usually, unless there's some dominant feature, you see a resemblance most in the eyes, forehead area. I don't see that. But you've all got lips on the fuller side. Classic Cupid's bow upper lip, nicely rounded, same deep V at the bottom of the philtrum . . ." She pointed to the vertical indentation that ran between her nose and middle of her lip. "That's the philtrum. So there is definitely a family . . . what they call a commonality. But it doesn't jump out and bite you, so to speak. Otherwise? Brown eyes. But we're becoming a brown-eyed country, so color alone doesn't mean anything. I'd say you and your brother look alike. You know, the way a brother and sister do. Maybe first cousins."

Raquel was busy feeling her philtrum, so Lizzy kept talking to me. "Here's the deal so far. Raquel clearly doesn't want anything done to her. You feel the same way?"

"Actually, if I had some guarantee that you wouldn't make me into a blonde or, you know, not use blush with glitter . . . I don't want to sparkle." Suddenly, I started worrying she'd demand, *What's wrong with sparkle?* and give me one of those *What Not to Wear* talks about loving myself more, which, sadly, would be apt. So as not to hurt Lizzy's feelings, and not set my grandmother off, I'd wind up letting them do stuff to me. But I'd come out with something freakish, like spit curls; I'd look like a homely stand-in for Marilyn Monroe in *Bus Stop.*

Lizzy led us over to a couple of salon chairs and motioned for us to be seated. "Just to talk. Nothing happening yet."

She noticed that Raquel was still wearing the panic-distaste expression, and she added, "Maybe nothing will." She trotted over to a table in the back corner of the room I hadn't noticed, returned wheeling a beige mesh desk chair, and positioned herself between us. "I'm going to talk economics. Okay?"

Our nods weren't sufficient and she waited until I said "Okay" and Raquel said "Sure."

"There was a study published in the annals of some academy of science—I think it was the New York Academy of Science, I have it in my office. Basically, it said that in job interviews, when the applicant is viewed as attractive, she's assumed to have more positive social traits and greater intelligence than those who aren't. And *Newsweek* did a survey of managerial types. Out of nine different traits they consider in an interviewee, number one was experience, two was self-confidence, three was looks! It came in ahead of where a job candidate went to school."

"So the bottom line is the bottom line?" Raquel asked her, although knowing my cousin, it was less a probing question then simply her attempt to humor Lizzy. As far as I was concerned, humoring beat having to sit through Raquel cross-examining Lizzy as to the methodology and applicability of the research.

"I'm curious," Raquel said. "The emphasis on appearance. Doesn't it contradict what we're told is really important in life? Being a thoughtful person, doing unto others, being devoted to your work, your family?"

"Tell me something," Lizzy said. She tossed her head and her short hair lifted, then fell back into place as if she had never moved. "How does five minutes every morning and getting your hair trimmed and maybe colored every six weeks interfere with your devotion to your family? To your community? Look, I volunteer in a soup kitchen. Would it show respect to the people I serve if I went there au naturel, with a pasty face and my hair looking like a haystack? We're not doing Gisele Bündchen clones at Glory. Not that we could. I'll do for you what I'd do for our regular clients.

Give honest advice and quality service. The women who come to us live in or near a small city. Their average family income is between fifty and a hundred per. We can't give them high prices and high maintenance."

None of us heard Gloria come back in until she was a couple of feet from Lizzy's chair. "Ms. Garrison! You walk on air." She didn't sound like she was being a suck-up, although from her gusto, you'd have thought my grandmother had walked on water. "We didn't hear you."

"A holdover from my modeling days," Gloria told Lizzy. "We always had to put all our weight on the balls of our feet. A tiptoe step so we wouldn't go *clomp-clomp* like horses and distract the customers." She and Lizzy then had a discussion as to who would sit in the mesh chair. I was amazed when they agreed to share it. Technically, this was not a problem, as both of them had hips not much larger than half of mine, but I was surprised that Gloria could be so at ease with an employee and that the employee was relaxed enough in her presence to sit back comfortably.

"Raquel." The way Gloria said the name was enough for the coffee I'd had minutes before to back up into my throat. The word "severe" came to mind. So I was surprised when my grandmother asked her, "Tell me. What do you wear when you go out in the evening? How long does it take you to get ready?"

My cousin seemed surprised also. Her words stumbled out. "Mascara. Tinted lip gloss. It takes about a minute." My grandmother and Lizzy nodded in sync and my cousin kept going: "I shampoo every three days, and if I don't let it just air-dry, it could take up to fifteen minutes. If I'm putting my hair up in a knot and it's a social occasion, that takes another three, four minutes because it has to look neat, but in a messy way."

"Lizzy?" Gloria said.

"Sounds right and the proof is in the pudding. You look fine, Raquel. Your brows could be a little darker, more defined, because your hair is such an intense brown. So . . . when you're done with your mascara, you might want to wipe off the bristles on a tissue and lightly run the wand over your brows. Then take an old toothbrush and blend it in." Instead of seeming disengaged or merely tolerant, Raquel surprised me by looking on the verge of enthrallment. She kept nodding as Lizzy spoke, as if she were getting courtroom pointers from Sonia Sotomayor. "Your hair is no problem. You just need a trim. I'll get someone to do it."

"A touch of cheek color couldn't hurt," Gloria said.

Lizzy got up carefully so as not to send my grandmother wheeling away in the desk chair. That broke the enchantment. Raquel said quickly, "That's okay. I'll get it cut at home."

"When?" Gloria demanded. "You'll go six months and you won't get around to it." She waved Lizzy off to go get a hairstylist. "You can give me an argument on anything else, Raquel, and no doubt you will. But not on this."

"I don't want to take up your time, and Daisy's—"

"Oh, please! Who are you, Samson, that you're afraid of losing your strength if you lose your split ends? Anyway, Daisy will be getting done too."

Raquel stood, her eyes on Gloria. Even though she had seemed transfixed by Lizzy's eyebrow-darkening suggestion, there was still such a taut string of tension between her and my grandmother that I was afraid that instead of hanging around for a haircut, she'd suddenly turn and rush out—though not before excoriating Gloria for crimes against the family. My grandmother looked over at her and said, "Show me a woman who doesn't care about her hair and I'll show you someone who needs Prozac."

"Well," I said a little too brightly, "that's something to think about."

"So to love your hair is to love life?" Raquel challenged her.

"Let's not overstate it," Gloria replied. "Forget love. But to like your hair is to care about life." Raquel stuck her hands into the pockets of her pants. Not hostile at all. In fact, very Carole Lombard—Diane Keaton. Her posture was easy, more weight on her right foot than on her left. I noticed, too, that her handbag was still hanging from the arm of the salon chair, swinging a little from when she got up. "To want your hair to look good," my grandmother continued, "is to want to engage with others. However, to be obsessed with your hair is to be fatuous." Then she swiveled toward me. "People want to improve themselves. Tell Raquel how many movies are about people changing themselves. Making themselves over. I suppose there must be an entire genre of makeover movies. Well?"

"Naturally there are lots of movies about people changing themselves," I said to my cousin. "The do-it-yourself aspect of the character arc." I caught a glimpse of beady-eyed disapproval from Gloria, but I added, "And changing someone's appearance. *Funny Face, In Her Shoes, Clueless* . . . I could go on, but you'd kill me. All the ones I'm thinking of are at least somewhat comedic. I guess that's because classic comedy is optimistic. It ends in marriage, or coming together. A makeover shows a commitment to engaging with others and also, I guess, faith in the future."

"American optimism," Raquel said. "Pull your face up by its bootstraps."

"Well, what's so terrible about that?" my grandmother demanded. "It's part of our pattern, the American pattern, to want to change. The Goldbergs, my side and Joe's, came here to make a better life. And why else did your mother's family—again both sides—come to New York from Puerto Rico? It wasn't for the weather."

My cousin put her head to one side, as if changing its orientation could prod loose some objection to what Gloria said. Nothing doing. She said, "You're probably right."

"Of course I am. When I started Glory, I wasn't thinking about optimism or patterns, only that I had what I thought was a good idea to make a living, which I had to do. But then, once it became a going concern, I started thinking that what I'd done was fit in, cash in—whatever you want to call it—on the American dream. Not that it's completely American. I mean, *Cinderella.* But we're so good at it. Make over your life and make over yourself. Way before reality shows, before TV even, there were newspaper and magazine articles about how to redo your house, your body, your face: every aspect of your style and environment. Did either of you ever hear of the Sears catalog?"

"Sure!" I said as brightly as if I were talking to one of the producers of the *Mission: Impossible* franchise.

"Yes," Raquel said dimly. "Sears was selling something."

"Of course they were. I am too. Services and products. And you're selling a service as well."

"Well, in a sense."

"Not 'in a sense.' Society has decided that people who cannot afford lawyers should still be represented in court, correct? That's why you're getting a salary, for your service. Your paycheck is nothing grand, I suppose."

"Didn't your investigator find that out?" Raquel asked.

"Actually, yes. Nothing grand. If society respected the indigent more, or if the government had greater resources, you'd get a raise. But whether it's sad to say or not, society places a higher value on looking good. That was where I came in. Amazing how many women, probably most, don't know where to start in terms of their own appearance. Of course, they could buy a book. There are some good ones out there with advice on fashion, makeup, and hair."

"So why don't more women go by the book?" asked Raquel.

"Because they don't have the tenacity or can't follow through. If you're living in a small city and have only a minor amount of money and limited time for personal upkeep, where do you go to shop, get makeup advice, find a hairdresser who's not ten years behind in terms of product and equipment?"

"Do these women necessarily want to be up-to-the-minute?" I asked.

"More so than they used to, what with the Internet and celebrity worship. Not that they necessarily want to have Rihanna's latest hairstyle, but they want whoever is working on them to be in touch with what's going on today."

"And your people are?"

"Yes. The first thing we do is have our new hires, hairdressers and stylists, made over. It demonstrates to them they don't know everything, that they always have something to learn. I never got past high school, so I have a great belief in continuing education. We want our people to know what's in and what's out, but more important, to know what's right for the individual client. You two may not believe this, but this is a feminist operation."

"It's owned by a woman," Raquel said. She wasn't being argumentative, but she wasn't buying Gloria's suffragette stance.

"Ownership is the least of it," Gloria replied. I put her down as mildly irritated but not hostile, which was an improvement in their dynamic. "It's feminism: getting women to accept themselves as they are, talking them out of coloring their hair like Carrie Underwood. And it's also getting someone walking around in sweatpants and a ribbed T-shirt that shows every fat globule she's ever ingested to wear something equally casual but more flattering. So she presents better when dealing with others. To catch a glimpse of yourself reflected in the window and think, *She's attractive.*"

"Can you accept that there are some women who truly don't care how they look?" Raquel asked.

"Honestly?" Gloria smoothed back her eyebrows with her thumb and middle finger. "No. I think there are plenty of women who are so overwhelmed by the job of getting themselves to look good that they don't know where to begin. So they just give up and tell themselves they don't care, or that looks-ism or whatever they call it is frivolous or misogynistic. Bushwah! That's why we're so strong on self-acceptance."

"The culture may give lip service to self-acceptance," I said, "but basically it says if you're not like Carrie or Rihanna, hot, hot, hot and also thin, then you're not acceptable."

"And Glory's message is: 'Do not to listen to that twaddle.' For ninety percent of women, the combination of hot and thin isn't going to happen. Way back, when I was in my early twenties,

I realized that a lot of women would do anything to have my figure. And some of them could have done it, but it would have meant a life of denial and dissatisfaction. I wanted to broaden the definitions. It wasn't easy. It wasn't until well into the '60s, with the exception of some niche magazines, like *Ebony* and, later, *Essence,* that you saw anything except WASPy-looking models. That's what women aspired to. All women: one type. Then a couple of blacks showed up in the editorial pages of mainstream magazines, maybe Asians too. I don't know if people were thinking about Hispanics at the time. Then *Glamour* put a black on the cover."

"And you're saying *Glamour* made diversity happen?" Raquel asked. I couldn't tell if she was trying to elicit some information or laying a trap for a witness.

"I'm saying it helped. When a major magazine for young women—it was their annual college issue—puts someone with a different kind of beauty on the cover, it gives women the idea that they have a shot. There had always been Carrie Underwoods, but this was a step in allowing Rihannas to happen. The more diversity there is, the more room for more women to be acceptable in their own eyes. The rest will follow."

"But you're talking about naturally great-looking women," I said. "Most women, even with the world's best makeover, aren't going to be beauties."

"That's right. They will simply be the best they can be, which is a great improvement over what they had been." Her dark, upslanted eyes opened wider. "Take you, for example, Daisy." I got that hit of emotion and nausea. I guess anger also. It was intense. The world grayed out except for my grandmother's flawlessly made-up face. "You are not a beauty."

"That's not exactly a news flash," I said.

At the same instant Raquel told her, "And neither am I and, to be honest, neither are—"

"That's my point," Gloria said. "None of us are beauties. Listen to me. It takes some effort to keep myself looking the way I've decided is acceptable. You,

Raquel, can get away with very little. Fine. Daisy actually falls in the middle. Less fussing than I have to do, partly because I'm so much older, but more than what you have to do. But she needs some changes made. And of course she'll need upkeep."

"You're talking about me like I left the room," I said.

"I know very well that you're here. Now, on the good side, you have lovely skin, nice eyes, and a 1950s glamour girl figure—along with an extra fifteen pounds. Before your cousin leaps to your defense, let me state that it matters not one whit to me whether you lose the weight or hold on to it. What matters is that your eyebrows are so heavy they make you look like an organ-grinder. And you're dressing more like a thirteen-year-old than a thirty-year-old. There are other issues, and those can be the subject of negotiations."

"What if I tell you I'm not interested?"

"I'll know you're lying. If you were to say, 'Gloria, I don't like you and I don't like the way you make scathing remarks under the guise of honesty . . . That I could accept."

"If you know you're nasty," Raquel said in her ringing courtroom voice, as if addressing judge and jury about some egregious conduct, "then why the hell don't you stop?"

"I seem . . . ," Gloria began coolly. She inserted her finger into the back of her shoe as if to ease pressure on her Achilles tendon, a totally diversionary move. But neither my cousin nor I was diverted. "I seem to lack some censoring mechanism. Self-censoring."

"Obviously," Raquel said. She was right, of course, but I wanted her to stop. Talk about a lack: I seemed to lack the tolerance-for-clashes gene that she and my grandmother possessed. "Did you ever have it? The ability to hold back cruel remarks?"

"That's none of your business. And don't make out as if everything I say is cruel."

"That may be right. I noticed you seem to have easy relationships with your employees, unless you're paying them extra to be nice to you today."

"No need for that. I do have good relationships with most of them."

"Then why—"

"Who knows? Probably because being civil is less expensive than constantly having to hire new people."

"You cut me off," Raquel said. "What I wanted to know is why you can be civil to your employees but not to members of your family. Is it that if you're in a position of power, you can afford to be gracious?"

"I don't think that's it."

"Then what is?"

"What is your need to know?"

"Because you're being mean to my cousin Daisy right now, and you've been . . . Look, you know. Is it that this kind of behavior keeps the people closest to you away?"

"Who says any of you are close to me?"

"That's true," Raquel conceded. "I meant close in the sense of family ties."

"I've also been less than charming to people with whom I have absolutely no blood ties."

"But are they people you've been close to?"

Gloria nodded her response—regally, of course.

"So wouldn't it then be correct to say that you're really good at keeping people at bay when there's the possibility of intimacy?"

"I detest the word 'intimacy.' It's so overworked. By now it's only usable by psychotherapists in smelly cardigans."

"Forget intimacy, then. How about, you don't want people to get too close to you and when they do, you're really, really unkind."

"How about your giving your litigation skills a rest?"

Raquel stopped for so long that I thought she really was stopping. But then she said to Gloria, "Did you ever consider . . . Well, there isn't any self-censoring device a person actually can go out and buy."

"How true."

"Did you ever try to work on the issue?"

"Not really. I know intellectually that not everything needs to be said. Occasionally, I am able to apply that knowledge. But only occasionally. I don't know why that is."

"Can I make a couple of suggestions?" Raquel asked.

Before my grandmother could answer back, I knew I had to put an end to their discussion. "I'm ready to be made over," I announced. "I can't let Raquel face it alone. We'll be in it together. But please understand this: no Greta Garbo eyebrows."

Nineteen

Matt

My sister looked like a close relative I'd never met before. Like, *Hey, I know that face,* except I really didn't. It wasn't Daisy as I'd known her all my life, but some other person with the same name who strongly resembled her.

Makeovers weren't a new concept. I'd known girls, women, who'd spent a whole day and a fortune at one of those places that did pretty much what Glory did—hair, makeup, though not the clothes. A big ritual before a *quinceañera,* sweet sixteen, wedding, and also for the girls/women who decided, *I want a new me.*

Time after time, if the girl was my friend or girlfriend, she'd ask me upon outing her new look, "Don't you think the makeup's a *little* too much?" Even though it did look like she'd applied her annual allotment in one sitting, I, for one, would say, "Well . . . It's more than you usually wear," and not give specifics. Like what are those strips of different colors running horizontally along your eyelid up to the brow? And how about the weird cheek streaks in shades of red that do not occur naturally in human beings—probably not even in nature? Even if I'd wanted to say something about the hair, no words could express what I felt now that it was mixed with other colors; it was like the beautician had matched the girl's hair to the middle chip in a paint sample card, then used all the other shades for contrasting stripes.

Except it wasn't like that with this woman named Daisy Goldberg; she was the natural type. Some makeup, but definitely nothing that would require a paint scraper to take off. Her hair was shinier than my sister's and maybe a little lighter than Daisy's color, but real.

All afternoon, from the time we left Glory to now, walking into the restaurant for dinner, I kept eyeing her. For seconds, her face would morph into Daisy's and I relaxed: Okay, this was my sister and I didn't have to pay any attention to her. But with half her eyebrows gone, she was not only wider eyed, but longer eyed. She actually looked a little more like Gloria.

"Stop staring at me in that creepy way," Daisy hissed as we stood by the maître d's podium. The guy was fussing over our grandmother like she was the ultimate power player, a combo of Venus and Serena mixed with Hillary.

"It's just that you look different," I told her, "except really familiar." Daisy started her standard lip chewing that she did when she was uncomfortable, which was much of the time, except when she was with someone she knew well and trusted. She was also okay at work: I'd been up to her office a few times and she was definitely at ease there. But this current gnawing wasn't her usual case: no *I'm in a Santa Fe restaurant that I thought would look like something in Disney World but is actually cool.* It was her uneasiness at the change in herself. So I did the kindly big brother thing, even though I was younger. I said, "It's not a bad change."

"Thank you. That's a huge relief."

"What were you expecting? An actual compliment from me?"

"Of course not."

Raquel and Gloria were side by side, not talking to one another but permitting themselves to be charmed by the maître d', probably so he wouldn't notice they had zero to say to each other. I could only see my cousin from the back now. Her makeover hadn't been as radical as Daisy's. She'd been pretty before. Now she was a little prettier with slightly shorter hair, brighter lips.

"You look good," I reassured my sister. "Not that you were terrible before, but this eyebrow thing makes your eyes bigger. And the dress is nice." It was blue, clingy and loose at the same time, but pulled in at the waist by a wide leather belt, like a power lifter's. It was cut for brother comfort, which meant while it let a lot of chest show, it allowed no display of boobs. "What else do you want to know?"

"My hair."

"Good. Looks like your high school yearbook picture, except not frizzy."

"It was curly then. Not frizzy."

"Whatever."

"Well, anyway, thank you."

"Welcome." If she kept the dress and belt look, I'd put money on her finding a boyfriend pretty fast. Go back to the high-tops and cropped pants, and she could wind up as Aunt Daisy to my kids. What I appreciated was that whatever Glory had done, my sister didn't turn out looking like she was ready for a manhunt. No crap on her lips, the stuff that looks like it came out of a tube of sex lubricant. Her hair was hanging over her eye, but it looked classy.

A waiter in a red vest sidled over to the maître d' and murmured something to which he responded, "Excellent!" Restaurants, I'd been noticing the past couple of years, were big on "excellent!"

When they showed you to a table and asked if it was okay and you said it was fine, they'd say, "Excellent!" You could order any of the evening's specials they were offering, petroleum sludge à la vomit, and they'd say, "Excellent choice!"

My grandmother and Raquel went first, and I motioned to Daisy to go ahead of me. At first I thought she was walking funny because she was wearing killer high heels, the kind that make legs look really hot, but when you think about it, the woman is probably walking mostly on her big toe. Except it seemed Daisy was managing the shoes all right but holding her head stiffly, chin slightly upraised. Knowing her, it was almost certain she was worried that if she made any jarring motions, her new look would crumble into a thousand pieces. She wasn't exactly at home with it yet.

We sat, and I felt a little bad seeing the maître d' return to the front of the restaurant. He seemed like a nice enough guy, maybe a little long on the smarm, but it would have been nice if etiquette and working conditions allowed him to sit down with us. After a day at Glory, and absolutely no sports talk since we boarded at LaGuardia, I wanted to be with a guy. Raquel, who could talk the talk, was definitely not in baseball mode. Ashley would be perfect. She knew her sports. She could talk science and medicine, politics, the arts. I'd told her one time that the Nobel committee should have a prize for Best All-Around so I could nominate her.

I couldn't imagine what a nightmare the day would have been if I'd had to sit and watch Daisy and Raquel get haircuts and the rest. Actually, it turned out that my grandmother's suggestion for me to meet Glory's PR team, Tara and Rick, had been a good idea. Like everyone else in public relations, we spent an inordinate amount of time discussing how we used social media, then asking each other, "Do you mind if I make a note?" when one of us heard a new angle. The three of us soon agreed that since we couldn't imagine a way Glory and the New York Mets would be in competition, we were free to write anything down.

Another good thing about the meeting: Instead of sitting in the conference room or in one of their offices, we'd wound up in a room off the employees' cafeteria. During the hour and a half we talked, a smiley guy in a chef's white jacket and a Mohawk kept coming in with snacks.

Tara was the sort who could spend half an hour communing with a celery stick, but Rick and I managed to snarf down a fair amount of fiber. In between talking shop and snacking, I became aware that they were being supercautious in not letting out information about Keith Thompson, the guy who'd been set to take over Glory. Now and then they referred to what had happened when Keith instituted some new policy, and it was clear they'd both liked him. But I was Gloria Garrison's grandson, so they started out careful. Also, both of them were smart enough to realize that the sudden materialization of three grandchildren might have something to do with continuing Glory post-Gloria. In fact, without their having met Daisy and Raquel, I got the impression they'd already put their money on me. In their minds, I could wind up as their boss.

However, as in sailing, there was a countervailing wind, which was that they were dying to discuss what had happened with Keith with an outsider who plainly didn't know the story. A lot of PR people are cynical by nature, understandable since their job frequently has less to do with disseminating Truth than putting lipstick on a pig. But Rick made me swear not to talk about our discussion with my grandmother, so I swore, and he and Tara seemed comfortable believing me.

So between bottles of San Pellegrino and blobs of guacamole on snow pea pods and discussions of the pricing of Facebook ads, I found out about Billy, Keith's partner, and his fatal stroke. With Gloria's inability or refusal to visit Billy in the ICU, despite what Tara described as Keith's "practically getting down on his knees and begging her to go," the relationship was over.

I asked why Keith simply hadn't ended the friendship part of it and continued with the business. After all, the agreement was that Gloria would start phasing out in a few years, and then he could buy the company at below its current valuation. Either Rick or Tara, I forgot which one, said something to the effect that I might not understand, but in cities the size of Santa Fe, business and friendship often were inextricably woven together. What was left unsaid was that New York, where I come from, was a city dedicated to avarice and duplicity. That wasn't totally untrue, but it was false enough to be a form of small-mindedness, even prejudice. Except for the few months after 9/11, people around the country never tried very hard to hide their fear and loathing of New York in the name of political correctness. Maybe it was because the city was seen as the hometown of political correctness, so they loathed us for that, too.

Tara and Rick appeared to think my grandmother could manage without Keith. She was not a practitioner of antique business procedures. In fact, she loved to learn about the new. But they were obviously concerned. Glory was their job, their future, and at this point, with no Keith around, their future was seventy-nine years old.

They made several references to the challenge of keeping up and growing Glory, as well as to what a sophisticated city Santa Fe was. I got the impression they were trying to sell me on its merits. I was not untempted in general. While the idea of devoting my working life to dressing and beautifying women was definitely a liability, the business of Glory was an asset, and not just in the financial sense. And the amazing thing was that if I put myself in contention—and at this point there wasn't any competition—it could be mine.

What would I get? A respectable business. Phenomenal views of desert, mountains, and sky. The view outside the employees' cafeteria was incredible: to nuke a mac and cheese and eat it while watching a bird the size of a volleyball strut around Nature like it owned it. It looked like it was wearing a baseball cap with a turned-up peak. Rick said it was some kind of quail. That was big-time recompense. True, I couldn't imagine living in a city that didn't have a major league team, though I might be able to get over that. Rick said everybody in Santa Fe rooted for the Albuquerque Isotopes—named for nearby Los Alamos National Lab. The 'Topes were a Triple-A affiliate of the Dodgers. Not a thrill and a half, but I could conceivably deal.

Except there was another hurdle I couldn't jump: the fact that I had turned down the chance to join my father in the Handsome Home. Was there any way I could tell him, *Dad, I know I said no to you, and you're a terrific person, but now I'm saying yes to the evil queen, your mother*?

When the meeting with Tara and Rick was almost over, I asked, "How come Gloria didn't just go to the hospital for, like, five, ten minutes? Bite the bullet, man up, whatever she had to do. She understood how much it meant to Keith, right?"

"Without a doubt," Rick said.

"All I could think," Tara said, "was that she has some sort of fear that kept her from going there."

"Like what?" I asked. "Those infections people get?"

Tara shrugged. "More likely she thinks death is contagious."

If that were true, the restaurant, Antonio's Café, seemed a strange choice. According to Gloria, Antonio, the owner-chef, was a great collector of Mexican folk art. All around the dining area there was a display of skulls. She said they were Day of the Dead skulls, green and orange, made from colored sugar, covered with all sorts of decorations. From their high shelf, they leered down at the customers.

We were soon drinking our first round. As I wasn't sure there would be a second, I sipped slowly. My grandmother had ordered a bottle of Cabernet, probably not meant for her alone. While the three of us had considered tequila drinks, we all wound up with fairly tame martinis, vodka for me and Raquel, gin for Daisy. I could tell my sister was about to drop a reference to *The Thin Man* or some other old movie with sloshed characters. Fortunately, our grandmother cut her off.

"I must say," Gloria announced, lifting her glass, "that you are all to be commended for not ordering some hideous Don Pilar frappé. Cheers."

We toasted, and Daisy, as I'd known she would, offered an overloud "L'chaim!" the Hebrew toast that means "To life!" Not that it caused xenophobic gasps among the diners at Antonio's. At least among the upscale types having dinner, there seemed to be a lot of diversity. Well, if you counted diversity as whites, Latinos, and one couple where the guy was Asian. Other than Emily Anderson, I didn't recall seeing an African American since I'd been in Santa Fe.

But despite the range of types, from blonds who looked like they should be shouting "Skoal!" in a Viking beer ad to dark browns who were more Dos Equis, Santa Fe didn't feel at all like the melting pot that New York did. I'd have thought that being a haven for the arts in the Southwest, it would have a kind of hip messiness. But the city, even in its gastronomic paradise, Antonio's, had a Wonder Bread feel. Everyone was well-groomed and polite. With allowances for regional accents, Santa Fe was Kansas City with cowboy boots. Or Kansas City minus the jazz clubs. Or Austin without the university.

I remembered in an American Writers course at Duke, the professor talking about *All the King's Men,* and how the idea of going west had always meant starting over for Americans. So maybe I could start over and learn to like white bread. Or maybe I'd learn I was wrong and that Santa Fe truly had a unique identity and an amazing soul. Every few minutes the invitation popped into my head: *Live here, be rich.*

New York tended not to play well with other cities, though it gave Chicago respect and San Francisco a nod. Yet when I went with Ashley to visit Houston on Presidents' Day weekend, when Monday rolled around, I was surprised that Texas and I were okay. It was no longer Big Psychotic State I knew from MSNBC. As for the city, it wasn't white bread with a twang. Over the course of three days, Houston offered me great barbecue, Rockets basketball, a fine arts museum, and Ashley's parents, two nice Jewish doctors. I'd gone from thinking of it as *hell with condos* to *Houston is a city that if I had to, I could live in.* Could I be that open to Santa Fe?

Not that I really needed to be. I wasn't staying.

Across the table, Daisy, Raquel, and Gloria weren't celebrating a lovefest. Still, it was amazing what a few sips of gin, vodka, and wine could do—along with a dish of pygmy tomatoes in all colors. Well, not blue. But the women were spending an inordinate amount of time picking up this tomato and that, letting the other two admire it, then eating it and carrying on about the flavor and texture like it wasn't a three-quarter-inch veg but a five-course culinary triumph. Maybe it was that gender thing, that women can get excited over cute food. Women and Raquel's live-in foodie.

I caught snatches of their talk. Daisy soon began on makeover movies—"Oh, my God, I forgot *Now, Voyager*!"—obviously a continuation of a previous discussion I'd been lucky enough to miss.

"And can you believe I didn't think of *Moonstruck* right away?" Just saying the names of films always seemed to give her pleasure, like that alone pressed a Play button on some high-speed monitor in her mind; she could love or hate them again for a tenth of a second. "*The Hunger Games*!"

A little later Raquel asked whether films about someone turning into the Hulk or a fly or Spider-Man could qualify as makeovers. They went back and forth on that, with Daisy getting the last word, which was, well, they could kind of qualify, except they are usually dystopian and not in the comic, optimistic tradition.

Gloria, I already knew, loved showing how smart she was. But this was the first time I'd seen her come alive in a conversation having nothing to do with business. She looked from granddaughter to granddaughter, listening to them not just with interest, but with apparent surprise touched by wonder. She was taken with them.

Actually, now that I tuned in, I could see it was a reasonably interesting discussion, especially with Raquel there to keep my sister from flying off on some tangent where she'd somehow find a way of comparing the plot of a 1952 Soviet propaganda film about noble peasants hitching themselves to a plow to *Paranormal Activity 4*.

Gloria was definitely curious to hear what they were saying. But there was something more with her, too. I didn't know how I intuited this, and I could have been wrong. Sometimes you got an insight into someone and you thought, *Hey, I am so fucking perceptive.* And maybe it was true, you were. Except wasn't it equally possible that your observation was totally made up either to fulfill some need or because you really weren't perceptive? In fact, you were an ass and, like any ass, were too dumb to comprehend what you were.

What I was getting was that Gloria was less interested in the substance of the exchange than the dynamic between my sister and Raquel. It seemed to be hitting her for the first time that they weren't related only by name or an accident of birth. There were ties between them. Big and little sister. Imaginator and pragmatist. Guides for each other, pointing out different ways to live, to believe, to think. Really intelligent women. Oddly, or at least quirkily for two Manhattanites in their twenties, religious women. One currently headed nowhere romantically, the other possibly on the verge of marriage, but both of them traditional enough to want a husband and kids. Bottom line was although they were not best friends, they would be tightly connected for the rest of their lives.

Observing Daisy and Raquel, I forgot about Gloria. But then, as Daisy began a riff on movies that had male makeovers like *The New Guy* and Raquel was nearing the end of her martini, Gloria turned her attention to me: "I see you are using the new product." I must have looked blank for a second, maybe because her voice was pitched to the level where people mostly talked about illicit drugs. "The gel."

I said, "Thanks. It works for me. Do you think this looks better?"

"Yes. I detest comb tracks. They are to be avoided at any cost. Not that you had those deep ones that seem to go with tattooed forearms. But the look didn't become you. And this will keep your hair just as well."

Being at a loss for words had never been my problem, but with my sister suddenly switching to Dustin Hoffman's character's makeover in *Rain Man* and Raquel sucking out whatever vodka was left in her olives, I had to make conversation with Gloria. Hair gel wasn't an option. Neither was sports talk. All I could think of was the word "makeover," so I said, "They did a nice job on Daisy. She looks like . . . a slightly different person."

"She was using the wrong color palette with her foundation, so we corrected that. It brightened her up. Then the eyebrows, a job that took some doing. They looked as if they needed a lawn mower, but obviously we couldn't use one. They were hideous."

"Mean remark," I snapped. Gloria might not have been good at self-censorship, but usually I was. "Sorry, that just slipped out. But she's my sister."

"So you're drinking the Kool-Aid also," she said. "I'm a dreadful person."

"I don't know that. But you are intermittently mean. Listen, I don't care if you make cutting remarks. You're smart, have an amazing vocabulary. It's when you say stuff directed at aspects of a person where she's most vulnerable. That's not clever. That's mean in the sense of cruel—and also small."

"She didn't even hear me."

"I did. She's my family."

"So am I," Gloria said. "I suppose you'll say I don't act as if I am."

"You saved me the trouble." I decided to soften that a little. "You are family. If someone said something about some vulnerability of yours, I'd go to bat for you."

"How kind," she said. The phrase "dripping with sarcasm" came to mind. "However, I can take care of myself."

"Of course you can. But what would be so wrong in viewing the three of us as your bench. Do you know what that means?"

"Of course I do. But I like to talk about my successes, not my perceived failures. Allow me to change from my meanness to a subject more congenial to me. What did you think of Glory?"

"Impressive. Not just the results, the makeovers. I thought the layout of your facilities was terrific, and you put together a great team. Tara and Rick are so knowledgeable and . . . agreeable. That's so important in PR when your business brings you back to the same cities on a regular cycle. You can do an amazing amount with social media, but when you return every three years and deal with the same person who's still a reporter for the same weekly, that's the human link. Same when you run bimonthly co-op ads with the same hairdressers who do follow-up on your clients once you leave town. It's great to be agreeable. Fabulous isn't good. It's too much. When you're over-the-top wonderful all the time, people can't trust you."

"I agree with you. Tara and Rick are first-rate. But what about you? Are you agreeable or fabulous on behalf of the New York Mets?"

I closed my eyes for a couple of seconds and rubbed the area right over my nose, which for some reason always helped me stop and think. It was my personal antidote to glibness. Finally I said, "Somewhere in the middle. I work in New York, with the New York media. It's more high-pressure, more fluid. Personnel is constantly changing. Management, the players, whoever's covering you in the press. You don't want to knock them over with personality because you're just the messenger. It's not all about you. On the other hand, if you're too low-key in New York, they won't hear your message. Too much noise."

"And you feel you thrive in that atmosphere?"

"Pretty much. It helps that I was born in New York, so I don't find the culture jarring. Well, neither do New Yorkers by choice. They need the excitement of the city and can handle the added stress of living there. Like Ashley. But not everyone can acclimate everywhere. When I was at Duke, I never really got into the Southern style. I kept wanting to tell everyone, 'Finish your damn sentence already.' "

The waiter came back, and since Gloria was designated driver, the rest of us ordered second martinis along with dinner. The menu was what I'd expected it to be, an exquisite food place like you'd find in TriBeCa, except a little long on stuff made from corn and chilies. I nixed wild Alaskan halibut. Not a great idea in New Mexico even though the waiter claimed it was flown in daily. I wasn't the phobic type, but somewhere along the line I'd developed a fear of frozen fish so I ordered steak instead. While the waiter was still hanging around, I tried to catch my sister's eye, which didn't work. I looked significantly at Raquel, but all she did was smile briefly and then go back to talking to Daisy. She was saying something about *Avatar,* and Daisy kept nodding, as if what Raquel was onto was fascinating and could start a cinematic revolution.

So instead of the four-way conversation I'd hoped for, I still had Gloria all to myself. To keep the conversation going, I decided to ask about Glory's inventory and storage practices. But I so deeply didn't care that I couldn't force my mouth to form the question.

The waiter, having poured a little more wine for her, hurried off. She pushed her glass aside. "Tell me, Matthew, how you see your future." I must have looked both stupid and scared at having to answer that kind of question, because she added, "No, no. I'm not talking about any grand design. I mean, do you see yourself staying with the team until you reach retirement age?" I was already shaking my head when she clarified, "In the sports area?"

"Definitely in sports. First of all, it's what I like. Love. But I don't think I'm cut out to work for a big organization. I mean, it's a good job and by and large I like the people. But there's too much out of my control. Decisions get made and it doesn't matter whether I think they're good or bad, I have to put a positive spin on them. I've gotten a couple of promotions, so now I have some voice in determining strategy for the stuff we actually can plan for. I like that much more than being, you know, just reactive."

"So you see yourself moving away from PR?"

"It's interesting that you're asking me that. I've been thinking for the last . . . I don't know . . . six months that there's a lot that I like about public relations. Making the best out of a bad situation, sometimes turning it around. Capitalizing on something positive. But I'm dealing with media and sports business types who can be cynical. Some may live in a thought-free zone, but a lot of them are really smart. So if I'm going to be persuasive, I have to formulate good arguments."

"This is what I'm hearing," my grandmother said. I waited. She lifted her wine glass and glugged down most of it. "You're ready to move on. You don't want to be part of something you can't control. Well, I assume you are aware there are limits to the extent that any of us can control a business, what with personalities, economic conditions, consumer preferences."

"I'm aware. But you're right about my wanting to move on." I did not add, *And I'm stunned that you are perceptive enough to pick that up.*

"Do you have a sense of the direction in which you want to go?" She finished the wine in her glass, peered around for the waiter, then lifted the bottle and poured herself some more.

"Well, I really haven't discussed this with anybody except Ashley." I took a most welcome sip of my second martini, then set it aside on the theory that it was harder for Gloria to have this kind of supposedly relaxed conversation with a grandchild than it was for me to talk to her. She might need a lot of lubrication. I decided to designate myself driver for the trip home. Plus I really wanted to take the wheel of her car. "I've been having discussions with this guy I'm friendly with, Jimmy Cmaylo."

"What kind of name is that?"

"The family's originally from Ukraine. Anyway, I've known Jimmy since my third year at college. He was at this big sports agency—"

"They represent players?" she asked. I nodded. "In one particular sport?"

"No. All professional sports. They do their contracts, manage endorsements."

"What's the name of it?"

"The K Advantage." She waited. "The guys who founded it were Kaplan and Klein."

"Where are they now?"

"Retired and rich. But anyway, I had a summer internship and worked a lot with Jimmy. He'd only been there three years, but he knew what he was doing. And he was a great mentor. Most people just throw some work at an intern to get him to go away, but he really wanted to teach me something. That's what I liked about him. Jimmy's the kind of guy who takes his job seriously, all the aspects of it. At that point he didn't have any of his own clients. He was servicing the ones managed by older agents. He offered to help me find something there when I graduated, and we kept in touch. But when the Mets offer came it was a no-brainer for me."

"What are your discussions with Jimmy about?"

"Opening our own shop. He's doing well at The K, has his own client list now, but he feels like me about being a small cog in a big operation. We want to do sports management, probably with a third person, an attorney with sports law experience. We both have a few possibilities, people we know."

A sudden silence after all the movie talk made me turn in my sister's direction. Both she and Raquel were now focusing on me and Gloria. I wondered whether Daisy was more surprised to learn I might leave the Mets or that I was confiding in my grandmother. Well, I was surprised too. At that moment, I might have stopped: *Whoa, what am I doing? She could turn on me any minute.* Except it was her turn to speak and I couldn't figure out a way to break off the discussion.

"What are Jimmy's strengths?" Gloria was asking.

"He's got a lot of them. Deal making. Also, he has the ability not only to work on ten, twenty matters at once, but to have almost instant recall of the details of each. His reputation is as an honorable guy, but he's considered the farthest thing from a schmuck." Gloria didn't like that last word, but all she did was flare her nostrils. "That takes a really strong personality and a lot of self-confidence."

"And what do you bring to the table?"

"People skills. Already I've had players come to me and say, 'Hey, when you go out on your own, let me know.' They know how hard I work and they see the results I get. And I work well with media types. I don't lie to them, although obviously it's a big part of my work to make the truth look as pretty as possible. But they've learned they can rely on me so they don't wind up writing or broadcasting something that could hurt their careers. Plus I'm good with strategy. I can take a new player and try to see ahead two weeks, two years, ten years."

"How do you know what someone will be like in ten years?" Raquel asked.

"I don't. But I look at an athlete and I

ask myself, What does this person have that's unique, or at least uncommon? How can that be used in marketing him? What does he have that could lead to endorsement contracts? What kind of training does he need to interact with the press and the public in a way that will help and not hurt?"

"Do you think this is the right economic climate for starting a small company?" my cousin asked me.

"Jimmy and I have given that a lot of thought. You know what we decided? That a partnership has to be a going concern at every point in the business cycle. If you wait to begin at the peak, what are you going to do when things turn"—I censored *to shit*—"downward?"

"I think you're right," Daisy said. "Entertainment often does well during bad times because it's a diversion, like movies during the Depression. It's different now because of the rise of all the new media. But there is still the basic need for story, whatever form it takes. Just as there's still the basic need to enjoy competition and skill—sports."

"What does your girlfriend think?" Gloria asked.

"Ashley wants me to do it. She's met Jimmy, likes him, trusts him. She's an excellent judge of character. What she doesn't have is an entrepreneurial mentality, but she thinks I should go for it. She said, 'You're twenty-seven years old. You have a potential partner who you say is smarter and more decent than ninety-nine point nine percent of the people in the field. Can you guarantee there'll be an opportunity like this when you're thirty-five? And when you're forty-seven, do you think you would have the guts and financial freedom to take this kind of risk?' " I looked at my martini with affection and longing but left it alone. "I'd be curious to know what you think."

I'd really been talking to Gloria, but Raquel said, "Ashley is right. You should do it."

"And it's not like you'd be out there in the void," Daisy said. "Dad's an entrepreneur. He understands what it means to take nothing and create something.

He could give you a lot of advice." She shrugged. "God knows he could. Probably more than you want."

My grandmother poured herself another glass of wine in what had magically become an empty glass. I told her, "Just so you know, I'd like to drive back to your place."

"You may."

"Thank you."

Gloria raised her glass to me. "I wish you success. And know that while my pocketbook will forever remain closed, my heart, if I indeed have one, will be open. You don't only have Bradley for advice, stellar though it may be."

"That's mean," I told her.

"It is not. I was not being sarcastic about your father."

"It sounded like it. About your son."

"No. Bradley has done well. Not as well as I, but then, he and I are not in competition."

"Of course not."

"Now it's you sounding sarcastic, Matthew."

"I apologize, Gloria."

"I accept. Now, here's to you. And

me. I will be pleased to offer you advice on your venture."

Once again, I was at a loss for words with her. As *Thanks* seemed a little skimpy, I said, "Thank you very much, Grandmother."

Twenty

Raquel

"Grandmother?" Oh, my God, when Matt called her that I held my breath. Would she spit out in her nasty way, *Don't you dare call me Grandmother*? Or just turn to ice: *My name is Gloria.* Maybe she'd add, *You piffling little fool.* But all she did was nod, the queen acknowledging a courtier who was a little pushy but awfully cute. He got away with it. Daisy, sitting to my right, slowly exhaled the breath she'd been holding at the same instant I let mine out.

It was cool the way Matt had handled her, calling her mean but with a lot more grace than I had shown. Then again—not that I liked making excuses for myself—my grudge against her was rightly stronger than Matt's. True, she consistently dissed his father. But at least she acknowledged my uncle Bradley's existence, even saw him on occasion. On the other hand, once my dad was killed, my mother and I were both dead to her.

"Would this venture of yours be in New York?" Gloria asked.

"Yes," Matt said.

"So then there would be no issue about your Ashley."

"No . . ." I thought he was going to continue the sentence, but he left it as a single word.

The waiter brought our first course. I'd ordered carpaccio. The thin, almost translucent slices of raw beef were like overlapping petals on the big round plate, with delicate shreds of Parmesan mounted in the middle. Hayden would have said, "Nice presentation. A little self-conscious but not overdone."

The problem was the raw beef before me and the Day of the Dead skulls staring down from the shelves. My appetite went. The combination was like a warning sign from on high demonstrating what will happen to your body after death. Red meat followed by stripped-down bone.

My biggest childhood terror was learning that the body was corruptible and what that meant. Since my dad had been Jewish, his soul was doomed, and there would be no bodily resurrection for him. I would never see him again.

When I was fourteen, after years of anguishing, I finally talked to a priest about it. He told me, "You must have faith in God's mercy, Raquel." At first I thought he was saying, Okay, don't worry. Your dad's as good as in. But when I considered the response, I wasn't so sure after all. Except how could I debate what he had said? I didn't have the knowledge, the vocabulary, and definitely not the intellectual maturity. It took a couple more years before I heard the term "non sequitur." By the time I got to Barnard, I began to understand how pissed Luther must have been when he posted his ninety-five theses. Sometimes it felt like I had about ninety-four of my own—women in the priesthood, condoms and AIDS, the conspiratorial silence over pederasty among priests—though I stayed a Catholic.

"Is something wrong with the carpaccio, Raquel?" my grandmother asked.

"No, it's fine. It's not the beef. It's me. I thought it sounded great, and it's served so nicely. But I can't do the raw meat tonight. I'm really sorry."

"Quite all right. That once happened to me with sashimi. It gleamed in a way I found disturbing. Is there something else you'd like?" By that time, Daisy had shoved her humongous bowl of baby beet salad halfway over, so I told Gloria we'd share.

She turned back to Matt. "When do you think you and Ashley will get married? Soon, or will you wait until she finishes her residency?"

He looked like he was trying to get enough saliva together so he could swallow, but it wasn't working. After knocking back an entire tumbler of water, he said, "We're not up to that yet."

"Where are you up to?" she asked. I

wanted to stand up and object, tell him he didn't have to answer the question. An appropriate response that ran through my head was, *None of your damn business,* which made it fortunate that he had a better way with her than I did.

"We're up to the general loving each other, wanting to be together." He smiled. If it wasn't devastating, it was incredibly likable. Sweet boy—sexy guy always worked. "Details to follow," he added.

"Your generation of men seems to have what the magazines call 'commitment issues,'" Gloria went on. "Is that an aspect of your uncertainty about closing the deal?"

Matt's shoulders hunched, then eased, and I could tell he was willing himself to relax. He smiled again at Gloria, though not so engagingly as before. "I don't go for that 'your generation of men' catchall," he told her. "There's too much emphasis on this or that being a 'guy thing.' Like men just don't get it. We're all babies. We're all terrified of commitment. Women complain that men aren't interested in seeing them as individuals, but it cuts both ways." Then he added, "Nothing personal."

"Forgive me if I take it as such," Gloria said. "You are, after all, accusing me of stereotyping you."

"I guess so."

"But don't apologize . . . if you had such an inclination. Perhaps I was guilty of prejudging. In any case, I shan't ask you any more questions until the engagement is formally announced." Part of me wanted to yell at her, *What is this "shan't" shit? You're from Cincinnati.* The other part was applauding her for bringing up his reluctance to close the deal—if that was actually true for Matt.

I knew women who were dubious about marriage, and some who were dubious about the particular guy they were with. But sooner or later, generally sooner, they made a decision. I'm not going to get married, but I will have children. I'm dying to get married and will grab the first guy with a working dick and a decent job, and I can be flexible about the job part. This particular guy is too boring to spend another week with, much less a lifetime.

What was going on behind these different decisions was, often, simple courtesy. Some man out there was waiting for a signal of receptivity or a final yes, and the woman felt obligated to give an answer before the guy began to resemble Rip van Winkle.

Maybe I was guilty of a hasty generalization because of Hayden. But I knew too many women in my position. Men seemed not to feel the same sort of obligation to decide. Six months, a year, a decade. It feels right, but I want to be totally sure; just give me a little more time. We'll sit down and talk the minute I finish my dissertation. What's wrong with leaving it the way it is now? It's so perfect.

"The truth?" Matt said to Gloria. "I'm a little scared."

"Well, you're quite young. People seem to be waiting longer these days. How old is Ashley?"

"Twenty-five. Are you going to say, 'What's the rush?' "

"If you'd like me to," she said. The

two of them seemed content with their own conversation. They were not so much being rude to me and Daisy as they were engrossed in the give-and-take with each other.

"I don't think I've ever been without a girlfriend. Not since sixth grade."

Just below the level of the table, Daisy held out her hand so I could see it. She splayed her fingers: fifth grade. They'd given her apple-red polish at Glory. One of my favorite childhood words came to mind: "fancy." In those days, fancy was always desirable. My First Communion dress not only had ruffles but also secondary and tertiary ruffles, and nothing my mother said could talk me out of it. Though I'd grown up to be decidedly nonfancy, gleaming red fingertips looked great on my cousin. For a moment I regretted my minimalism.

Matt laid down his fork on his Array of Duck appetizer. "And Ashley is far and away the best person who's ever been in my life." Then he picked up his fork and pierced a piece of pâté.

Gloria waited for him to continue, but that wasn't happening. "So is the hesitancy, if there is any, the fear that somewhere out there, there's someone better?"

"No. Absolutely not."

He went back to some duck shreds. I wasn't sure if that was the end of the conversation or he needed more sustenance to continue. Daisy and I got busy with beets. The two of us were probably operating on the same theory, that if we paid too much attention to Matt, we would disturb the rapport between him and Gloria and possibly miss an earful.

"So you're not hesitating," Gloria said, "only waiting."

"The only thing . . . holding me back has nothing to do with Ashley herself, or us being on the young side. It has to do with, you know, the institution of monogamy. My pattern has always been . . ." I sensed Matt was looking our way, but I kept my eye on a piece of yellow beet, and I assumed Daisy was doing something similar because he went back to talking to Gloria, though in a lower voice. "I'm good at monogamy. I don't cheat. But I'm still a little concerned . . . Maybe scared is a better word. My track record is only for monogamy with limits. The longest relationship I ever had lasted eleven months. Then somehow, one of us loses interest. Truthfully, it's almost always me."

"What makes you think it will be different with Ashley?" Gloria asked him.

"It's almost eleven months with her now, and my interest is the opposite of lost. She is just such a remarkable human being. Compassionate, funny, smart about everything. She's not beautiful in the *Sports Illustrated* swimsuit sense, but she's adorable in a way that really attracts me."

"Well, I'm not one to give advice," Gloria said. "At the risk of seeming mawkish, it does sound as if you were made for each other. I suppose it's natural to have doubts about one's ability to be constant."

"But when is it natural and productive to have doubts and when is having doubts just another excuse? Instead of saying, 'I'm not interested anymore,' I can give myself a warning, 'I'm interested, but in another eighteen months I might not be.' So it's better not to commit. And what would I say when that eighteen months has passed? 'Well, eighteen months from now . . .' That would be unfair to Ashley. But I want to be sure of my feelings."

My neck was stiff and I wanted to move my head around, lift it to give my muscles a break, but doing that would bring me into eye contact with the Day of the Dead skulls. I was brought up to respect other people's traditions, so it would be wrong to say, *I think your holiday is garish and creepy, and while it's not revolting in the way female circumcision is, it is gruesome.* Wrong and impolite.

"You're asking the wrong person about feelings," Gloria was saying. "I've never understood what's so wonderful about being sure about feelings, or being in touch with them—beyond the obvious ones: He's an excellent accountant and a pleasant man; I don't care what a good price we can get on it, I abhor that jacket."

Fortunately, since Daisy and I were running out of beets, Gloria turned our way. "Daisy, are you a believer in being in touch with your feelings?"

"I don't see how to avoid them."

"By ignoring them."

"But then you won't understand yourself."

"Of course you will. I'm not saying not to acknowledge a strong feeling, like, oh, I don't know. Acknowledge it. Act if action is possible. But then put it aside. But so many people get plagued by feelings. Why can't they distract themselves with something else?"

Daisy's smile was almost maternal: *You poor, deluded thing.* "But you're implying that feelings are bad, something to defend against."

"No, good feelings are perfectly fine," Gloria said. "Why not enjoy them? It's that these days everyone pays so much attention to the bad ones. Boohoo, my mother didn't love me. Boohoo, we were poor. Boohoo, I'm a victim, I have anxiety, I'm bipolar, I have ADD. Anything negative that arises gets examined and reexamined in that light. And worse, far worse, is that it then gets discussed ad nauseam with anyone who can't escape quickly enough."

"Shouldn't people deal with their feelings?" Daisy asked. "Doesn't it take more courage to face them than run away from them?"

"I am not advocating cowardice. What I am suggesting is that we don't devote our lives to our weaknesses and negative feelings. Deal with whatever pain there was in the past, then file it away. Think through what's current. That should take about two to three minutes a week over a period of a month or a year, depending on whether you're deciding to leave a job or leave a husband. Well, not that it took me anywhere near a year, but that's another story. You can give a problem more time, of course. Agonize to your heart's content. But when assessing your feelings, or coming to a reasonable decision about something, how long does it really take to know what you feel, what you want?"

Daisy's eyes narrowed as if she suspected Gloria had laid some sort of a trap. "Sometimes you don't know something intuitively," she said. "Sometimes it takes a long time to figure it out."

"Do you know what I believe?" Gloria asked. "I believe we can figure out what we want and feel within a minute after we feel it. So fine, give yourself some more time to deal with new insights, denial, self-deception. Weigh the facts. But where would I be if I'd devoted my life to worrying about my relationship with my mother or whether I was right to leave Joe? Most likely nowhere. With ulcers." Now it was Gloria's turn to narrow her eyes. "And don't even think of asking me about either subject."

"Never in a million years," said Daisy. "But if you ever feel a need to—"

"Not on your life."

Frankly, I was feeling kind of isolated from the feelings discussion, so I elbowed my way in. "Actually, William James said something along those lines I always loved: 'The art of being wise is knowing what to overlook.' Something like that. It sounds just like something my mom would say. I guess James would be more in Gloria's camp than in yours, Dais."

"But it's really not practical or possible," my cousin said. "Okay, I can say I'd be better off overlooking my job anxiety when I'm on the plane out to California. I'm always scared that when I get there—even though I think I've been doing really good work—my boss will say, 'Sorry, we appreciate your effort, but unfortunately Paramount's not the right fit for you.'"

"So stop thinking it," Gloria commanded her. "What are you doing to yourself? Staring out at clouds over West Virginia and feeling inadequate, miserable?"

"West Virginia, Nevada. There's a loop that keeps playing in my head and I can't stop it."

"Of course you can."

"How? By telling myself that it's silly to be a wreck and chances are my job is perfectly safe. Beyond safe. They're happy with me."

"If I were you?" Gloria waved over a busboy, pointed to the wine bottle and then to her glass. Nervously, he glanced around for a waiter. Seeing none, he poured, deciding it was better to flout the rules than mess with Gloria Garrison. "I would tell myself that my job is probably safe, that if it isn't I will find another one. I would say the worst-case scenario is that I'm in for some tough times, but I'm strong. And the best case is, I'll get a raise. Then I would pick up a good mystery or a book on . . . I don't know . . . cinematography in Fellini's films, and get my mind out of its loop. Listen to William James. Know what to overlook."

"What if your feelings are so buried you don't know what they are?" Daisy asked her.

"Then consider them dead. Say Kaddish for them once a year. Otherwise? Let them rest in peace." Since this was our grandmother's first reference to anything Jewish, the three of us tried to flash each other looks without being too obvious. Personally, I thought Gloria was so alienated from herself that it had taken three-quarters of a bottle of Cabernet to open up that untapped area of her memory devoted to her religious identity. But that was the end of that because she was looking in my direction. "Raquel, you must tell me more about William James. I know he was a psychologist. And related to Henry, if memory serves me. Sadly, that's all I know."

It was either go to the ladies' room, do a fast Wikipedia on William James, or tell the truth. "I don't know much more. We touched on him in some American Studies course. I came across the quote in one of the readings and it stuck. I'd like to know more about his work. He was Henry's older brother, that much I know. He turned to philosophy toward the end of his life. Anyway, I remember thinking after finishing whatever the reading was that this guy had the writing gene, too."

"As one who did not go to college, I have the tendency to believe that college-educated people know so much more than I." Gloria said it in a jokey way, but I got the sense that she really believed it, or at least believed in the inadequacy of her high school—only education.

"From everything I've heard from you," I told her, "you're as well-read as any of us. I could probably beat you at jurisprudence, and Daisy of course could out-movie you. Let's not even discuss sports and Matt. But otherwise . . ." The same busboy who had been brave enough to pour Gloria's wine came back to take away our appetizer plates. "I'll tell you what. When I get home, I'll come up with the titles of a couple of books either by him or about him. I'll send something to you."

"That would be nice." If what my grandmother had said about people really knowing what they felt had any merit, I knew in an instant that I was glad some better part of me had offered to keep in touch with her after this weekend. Also, I had another feeling: that my offer surprised and pleased her. And for some reason that I found annoying, it would, without a doubt, make my mom happy. So I suppose I was glad I'd pleased my grandmother to that small extent.

We got back to the house at nine thirty, and by the time Daisy, Matt, and I finished hanging in my room, analyzing Gloria at dinner with its big debate—

Had her heart softened or was she just hosed?—it was a couple of minutes before ten. That meant midnight on the East Coast. I wanted so much to hear Hayden's voice. I hadn't spoken to him since New York. He'd told me it was just as well that I was going away, because the big deal he'd been working on, yet another that was putting dark smudges under his eyes, was coming together and he would be "unspeakable to."

Being a lawyer, it was natural for me to say, "On the other hand" because every argument had a counterargument. So: On the other hand, he knew all about Gloria and understood very well what a major deal these few days with her were to me. Would it have been so terrible if he called or texted just once to ask how it was going? Wasn't he at all curious? If our positions had been reversed and he was visiting his awful grandmother, I'd be dying to know what was going down.

But on the theory that there was always another hand, if I wanted to speak to him so badly, why didn't I just call and say, "I need less than five minutes of your time"?

It was now really late in New York. Do you startle someone out of a deep sleep to say I miss you? It didn't take much introspection to realize that as afraid as I was of waking him, I was also afraid of finding that he wasn't at home. If instead of the landline I called his cell, I might hear something in the background, and he could claim, *Oh, street noise,* but I'd know it wasn't. Our street was relatively quiet at night. Naturally it got worse. I started thinking, *What if he was home but with someone? In my bed.* Technically his bed, because it was his apartment and most of the furniture was pre-me. But that was crazy thinking. Hayden could never be that tacky. Like another woman elsewhere but not in his/our bed would be non-tacky?

Except I kept playing that anxiety loop Daisy had talked about. I was willing to bet I did it as much as she did, though my loop probably played at a lower volume so I wasn't forced to listen to it as much as she was. I asked myself: Realistically, what would be the worst that could happen if I called him, aside from my fears of him cheating? I'd wake him up? Okay, and the worst of that would be he'd be angry at being woken. I could deal. I fished my phone out of my bag and tapped in the password.

Hayden had so much going for him. Great looks, with sandy brown hair and green eyes. Great body. Sometimes he reminded me of a guy in a Calvin Klein ad, skin polished to the point of being godlike, hair falling gently over his forehead. He was macho without the swagger. Yet he knew his way around a wine list, could make a soufflé without a recipe, and was the person everyone else turned to when they asked, "What was that play all about?"

A first-rate mind put in the service of earning a first-rate income. That last had been my only qualm about him, that he chose investment banking because he wanted to be very, very rich. Not in a crass sense. When we were first going out, he told me, "Money can buy you freedom." I asked him freedom from what, and he said, "Freedom from having to say 'how high?' when some third-rate functionary orders you to jump. Freedom to travel anywhere, buy what you need, be philanthropic." I was impressed with the "buy what you need" part of the response and liked it that soon after he rolled his eyes at me when a colleague had a two-thousand-dollar wine refrigerator-credenza built in his living room. On the other hand, that didn't stop Hayden from spending three hundred and fifty dollars on a bottle of wine. (And I didn't exactly recoil in disgust when he gave me a Chanel handbag for my birthday.)

It might have been nice to have met someone who did the work he was doing because he loved it, or at least believed it was important. Well, I was doing something I believed was important and had to drag myself to the office or court every day. Hayden went off with a wink and a smile.

I ought to have remembered that I was not built to hold two martinis. Buzz gone, mouth dry, maybe a headache on the way. Obedient child that I was, I put down the cell phone, hung up my dress, and dusted off my shoes with a tissue. Then I went into the bathroom to take off my makeup. I hated to see it go. Granted, I did have the eyeliner, mascara, lipstick, and the big brush and powder the cosmetician at Glory had given me, but I knew the outline of my lips would never again be so flawless. I gazed at myself in the huge mirror over the sink, a little disturbed at how wonderful I thought I looked. If I hadn't seen me since college, I would gasp at my loveliness.

I asked myself why I couldn't turn off the anxiety loop. I answered myself: because I didn't trust Hayden.

The nightstand had a tray with a bottle of water and a goblet. I poured the water into the goblet before I drank so Paula, or some unseen maid I hadn't met, wouldn't think I was a slob who drank directly from bottles, which of course I did. If I called Hayden—

I interrupted myself by remembering what my grandmother said to Daisy about reading a good mystery or some book about Fellini to distract herself, not to obsess about losing her job as she flew across the country. I walked across the room to the bookshelves that were in some sleek style I couldn't name. But definitely a style. Hayden would know what it was. There were a couple of mysteries, but I always avoided them because they sometimes described what dead bodies looked like. So I pulled out a book on big oil. The back cover said something like, "America is addicted to oil and is reeling from its dependence." It sounded way far left, but it had a lot of good quotes, so I brought it to bed.

I was up to John D. Rockefeller starting Standard Oil in 1870 when I looked over at the clock and realized it was now almost one thirty in New York. I thought, *If he's not home now . . .* Except it hit me before the end of the thought that I hadn't tortured myself over Hayden for almost an hour and a half. Being out of the anxiety loop was an excellent place to be. I went back to John D. As he started the great capitalist drama of buying up his competitors, I fell asleep.

Twenty-one

Daisy

I rolled over in bed the next morning and was relieved that even though I'd forgotten to set the alarm, it was only ten to eight. It had been good being alone in the kitchen with Gloria the day before. She had defrosted somewhat, though how much of her was left to melt was an open question. Her core might not be ice at all but solid steel.

As I headed for the bathroom, I saw the royal blue Glory dress I'd worn stretched out lazily over the arm and seat of a club chair. It reminded me of some new-new actress being languorous for a *Vanity Fair* photo spread. I put on mental blinders so I wouldn't catch a glimpse of myself in the never-ending mirror over the dresser and discover that overnight I'd lost my glam and was now back to being a scullery maid.

Theoretically, the look was reproducible and Lizzy at Glory had sworn it was. She said, "That's one of the reasons we have so much repeat business. Our system works." I had a personalized notebook binder, *Glory Guidelines,* for makeup and hair upkeep, and an eyebrow diagram complete with a scanned before and after of me, along with "great styles that are right for you." Other than the dress, I had to rely on what few clothes I had in my suitcase, most of which were apparently not great styles.

But unless I wanted to examine the pattern of the bathroom tile, which was just giant squares of beige marble, I couldn't avoid looking at myself. Hey, not bad. Considering no makeup and a couple of deep pillowcase creases, I looked good. Even unbrushed, my hair had a sheen that made it appear like I was backlit. It dipped over one eye, but with my new eyebrows, my eyes now looked so big, almost cartoonish, that I reminded myself of Jessica Rabbit.

It was odd for me, having fun looking in the mirror. Not that I'd ever thought I was ugly, but I never thought *gorgeous* either. I still wasn't. But this 2.0 version of me was definitely pleasing. Even better, what the makeover had done was to get me to stretch the limits of what I thought I could be. I was now certifiably attractive. And I didn't look as if an army of specialists had exhausted themselves on my behalf. God knows I'd seen enough before photos of actresses who were blotchy or pebbly-skinned without any makeup. The afters weren't necessarily a treat either because so many had faces that appeared more the work of a plasterer than a cosmetician.

I backed into the corner of the shower in an effort to keep my hair dry and was doing an awkward deep-knee bend to wash my bottom half without lowering my head. In the middle of that, I remembered coming out of the ladies' room the night before at the restaurant. I'd been smiling because as I tossed the paper towel into the wastebasket, I caught my reflection in the mirror and was happy to see me looking so good. It was kind of a stupid moment, but as I whooshed into the tiny corridor where the restrooms were, I almost collided with a guy coming out of the men's room.

It was what they call a moment, the briefest of encounters, yet if I'd lived in Santa Fe, it could have been *How I Met Your Father.* We almost did a duet of *Sorry* and *Are you okay?* Then there was the awkward but adorable standing back to let the other go first. He was a big guy, with a ruddy tan, short blondish hair, and pale blue eyes, like a large-scale version of Steve McQueen in *Papillon* but with a less pointy chin. Usually I went for bookish-looking guys, the kind whose eyeglasses always looked askew. Santa Fe Stranger was more of a jock, yet for some reason I got the impression he was a cerebral one. (The wonderful world of fantasy: He might actually spend his spare time fabricating Darwin dolls to burn in effigy, but I could make him whatever I wanted.)

Anyway, he said, "Now look. You don't know me from a hole in the wall. I bet you wouldn't give me your phone number. Right?"

"Right."

"But how about meeting me here next Friday or Saturday—either night—at seven?" I shook my head. "Eight? I'll bring letters of reference. Listen, I swear to you., I don't do this. I mean I've never done this before." He reached into his back pocket and took out his wallet. "Here." He took out his card. "I'm with Eldorado Biofuels. Check me out."

I didn't take the card. I said, "You look like a nice guy. But I'm just in town for the weekend." Of course he could have been a con artist whose scam was exiting men's rooms and preying on vulnerable women. Maybe he had an endless supply of Eldorado cards that he handed out to any woman who had over a C cup. But it was my fantasy, so I went back to the table believing he was intrigued enough to risk embarrassing himself.

Maybe it wasn't a big deal in some women's lives, but that chance meeting was more action than I'd seen in the past six months in Manhattan. It could have been my new look or the fact that when I sailed out the door, I was smiling, something I'd never done in New York when leaving ladies' rooms.

I got dressed and went downstairs still thinking about him, hoping he wasn't called Chuck or some grating nickname that sounded like a minor character in *Friday Night Lights.*

For the second day in a row, Gloria and I were in the kitchen together.

"Are you hungover?" she asked.

"No. Two martinis is one more than I usually have, but I didn't have any wine. What about you?"

"Never had a hangover in my life. I do seem to have the strange ability to bestow them on others by the mere fact of my presence at the time of imbibing."

"A dubious gift," I murmured, unable to think of anything else to say. We both stood in front of the refrigerator. She had a plastic-wrapped chunk of white cheese in her hand and I was checking out the sheep's milk yogurt.

Just then, Raquel came in, damp and glowy after a run. She was one of those confident, petite types who can wear a stretchy tank top and look slimmer for it. "Good morning," she said.

"Do you have a hangover?" Gloria asked. It did seem like an odd opening gambit, but Raquel just shook her head and even managed a congenial expression.

"Maybe Matthew will feel miserable," Gloria went on. "I have a marvelous hangover concoction I used to make for the girls at Solange de Paris, the fashion house where I worked. There were three of us regulars. They'd bring in other models when the buyers were in town. Most of them drank themselves silly every night, so I'd make them my remedy: V-8 juice with a couple of ice cubes mixed with two drops of Tabasco and a little fresh lemon juice."

"Solange de Paris sounds so elegant," Raquel said.

"Only if you thought puckered hems and fabrics that ought to have been used for henhouse flooring were soigné. But the name was wonderful, I have to admit. I loved it when people asked where I modeled, and I could say 'Solange de Paris.' I would have said it with a French accent, except I could never get their *r*'s down pat. Of course, if anybody had been familiar with Garment Center manufacturers, even an accent wouldn't have made Solange de Paris sound glamorous.

"I could make you breakfast," Gloria continued. "Pancakes." She started to reach for a container of milk but didn't. "I thought about getting a waffle iron at one point, but I was seventy-five. I told myself it hardly pays. *I'll be dead soon* is an insidious mind-set. It leads to being one of those old women with greasy spots all over their dresses because they're avoiding dry-cleaning bills." Raquel and I must have looked befuddled because she added, "You know. You could send out your clothes and have a fatal stroke two days later. Too annoying! And then, while you're at your funeral, the things get delivered in plastic bags with a bill stapled on for seventy-eight dollars. So you wind up not sending them out."

"Why don't I cook?" Raquel suggested. "I'm good at omelets. Tell me how you like yours and I'll make them."

Gloria handed her what she said was goat cheese and I said I was good with that, too. My cousin got busy, and my grandmother and I sat at the big round breakfast table, which was a fair distance from the six-burner restaurant stove. Four place settings had been set with gingham napkins rolled up in rings on top of the plates. I said, "For someone who's essentially a noncook, you have an amazing kitchen." Everything in it was impeccable, bountiful, sparkling. Behind the glass-doored cabinets, dishes were stacked in such quantity and variety it made you think, *Oh, I must have a party!* My mother would have said, "Too perfect," and maybe she was right aesthetically. But it was still a pleasure.

"I entertain a lot. Well, less lately. But caterers are annoying and fussy. They'll work harder if they respect your equipment. When I built the house, I told the architect, 'The best of the best,' because I didn't want my guests eating a rib roast that was so badly shrunken it looked like a rack of rat chops. That happened once in my old house. But I must say, the ovens on this thing are frighteningly hot. One night when Paula was off I decided it would be great fun to roast a chicken. God knows what possessed me. I burned the chicken and singed an eyebrow.

"If you're eating alone, do Paula and Carlos still cook and serve you?"

"Yes. I like that. It makes me feel . . . I don't know. There used to be a cigarette ad years ago that said, 'You've come a long way, baby.' It makes me feel grand and reminds me how far I've traveled." She took the salt mill and rolled it between her hands. "Wouldn't you enjoy being served? Saying to someone that you'd like Oaxacan grilled shrimp and there it is when you arrive home for dinner?"

"Well, I like the idea. But you know I don't eat shrimp."

"Right. The Jewish thing."

"Right," I said. "I don't eat shellfish or pork."

"Are your parents like that?"

"No. It's a choice I made, mostly out of respect to a tradition."

"A tradition of what? Avoiding good food?" my grandmother inquired.

"Maybe that's part of it. Just a sense of limits, that you can't have everything you want, or that everybody else can have."

"It's that clannish thing I detest."

"I'm not clannish in my relationships. I just avoid two food groups. That doesn't exactly make me a Lubavitcher. It's not even keeping kosher. Mostly I do it as a reminder of who I am: part of a group with a history that extends far beyond me. Anyway, the only people who ever get disturbed by my not eating pork are Jews."

"I am not disturbed by it." It was early in the morning for such a huffy voice, but she managed quite well.

"I didn't say you were one of them."

She ground some salt onto the table, then swept it onto the floor. "I just don't get it. Religion in general. Historically, it's responsible for atrocity after atrocity."

"People do use religion as an excuse for dehumanizing others, saying they're evil and have to be dealt with. But I don't buy that neo-atheist argument. People also use nationalism, ethnicity, politics to brutalize others. Religion didn't bring about the Cambodian killing fields." It was such a dark thought in the bright desert morning that when Raquel came over with a big omelet, I shuddered from the shock of the pleasant.

"Voilà!" She'd cut it on a slant into four slices and had even come up with some herbs chopped up and scattered around it as decoration. Overlapping triangles of toast were off to one side. The small oval platter had a stylish restaurant look. I'd never thought of Raquel as someone who had a taste or eye for detail, but thinking about it, I realized she did.

"Very pretty," Gloria said.

"Thank you." Raquel took a seat and added, "I hope I don't smell. I had an hour run. It was beautiful. The sky was incredibly blue. I stumbled a couple of times because I was looking up so much."

"If we're offended by your aroma we will go into the dining room," Gloria said. "Leave you here." She sniffed. "No. You're perfectly acceptable."

"We were just talking about religion," I told Raquel.

"Whose?"

"All. Gloria's not a fan of any of them."

We helped ourselves to Raquel's omelet, which was really excellent. I'd been concerned that she'd been infected with Hayden's foodie tendencies and I'd have to pretend to enjoy something with egg white mucus in the middle.

"You don't believe in God?" Raquel asked Gloria.

"Not particularly. It's one of those subjects I never think about, like the global water crisis and the prevalence of eating disorders."

"So this life is it?"

"What did that pig say at the end of cartoons? The one who stuttered? 'That's all folks.' Well, I do have uneasy nights. But you don't get to be my age and not have them. That three a.m. fear that I'll go to hell. Not your Christian hell with circles and fire and a great deal of shrieking. Just an eternity of loneliness. With high humidity for some reason, which can be a nightmare when your hair is thinning, but why that particular punishment is visited upon me is beyond my comprehension." She shook her head to get rid of the hell in it and set down her fork. "It will be quiet here when you leave." I had to smile because it sounded like what an adult would say about a couple of rambunctious children.

"I could call you periodically," Raquel said, "and be argumentative and fault-finding. Then you could say something cutting. Before you know it, we'd have a screaming family feud." Her delivery was lighthearted and received an amused nod from Gloria.

My grandmother seemed to like lively company. That's why her life was so confusing to me. Here we were, her three grandchildren from New York, and to whom did she introduce us? Only the people who worked for her. If it had been me—and I think almost anyone else—there would have been a big party: *Everybody, these are my grandchildren!* It's not as if she'd have to cook dinner for forty herself.

All right, she hadn't known beforehand what we'd be like or what the chemistry would be, so maybe she wouldn't want to invite the whole world. Then how about a small dinner for close friends? Even if we were awful, at least they'd have seen us and could gossip about us later. But other than talking about the models of yesteryear and neighbors in Great Neck, she hadn't made a single reference to friends. I thought okay, everyone has bad nights, but it intrigued me that her notion of hell was eternal loneliness. That she even had a notion of hell was amazing, since God, good, and evil didn't seem part of her emotional or intellectual vocabulary.

From what Matt had reported to me and Raquel from his conversation with Glory's PR team, Keith, the former soon to be head of the company, had been horribly hurt by Gloria. They'd been not only colleagues but also great friends.

So his withdrawal must have been a huge hit for her. All she seemed to have around her now were a couple of servants.

Interesting about Keith: All three of us had no trouble understanding how he wouldn't want to continue not just their friendship but also his business relationship with her. Only Raquel thought he should have bitten the bullet, endured a few years working beside someone he despised, and then enjoyed the rest of his life as chief of Glory.

After coffee and some discussion of Gloria's criteria for choosing a corporate lawyer, which I happily stayed out of, Raquel went upstairs to shower.

"I'll do the dishes," I said.

"No, no. The dishes will be done," Gloria said. I thought she wanted to talk to me about something because, as I'd begun to stand, she gestured for me to stay seated. But I could see after a couple of seconds she had no agenda, just wanted company.

I could also see that the conversational ball was in my court. So I decided not to smash back (which I was lousy at both in life and in tennis), but to hit it pretty hard. "I'm glad you did this, invited us out here."

"It was not an altruistic gesture," Gloria said. "I wanted something."

"You wanted to choose among us." The aristocratic nod. "Did you feel pretty sure one of us would go for it?"

"How shall I put it? I did not think all three of you would be so blithe, so unthinking in your refusal. I expected at least one would see what this could mean not just financially, but to have something to call his or her own." She sighed. "Your generation with that constant 'his or her.' If I didn't have to say it all the time dealing with employees and suppliers, I would probably gain hours each day."

"Or fifteen seconds. But listen, you did take that step of reaching out for us. I'm curious. Were you expecting all of us to agree to come?"

"I was reasonably sure Matthew would. I thought he might have the strongest interest in business. If he came, there would be pressure on you to join him in facing the wolf in her lair.

I was dubious about Raquel, but from what I gathered from speaking to your father, on those rare occasions when we do speak, the three of you are fond of each other."

"We love each other."

"How delightful. Well, it was enough to draw her out here."

"Maybe she just wanted to get to know you."

"Maybe. More likely, Saint Adriana put the screws on. Don't tell me no. I know my customers. In any case, I was disappointed that none of you wanted such an incredible gift—interesting work and a gracious life. But I must admit, I'm glad to have been able to spend some time with all of you. I thought this morning, *Which is my favorite?* And do you know what? I couldn't decide."

"Why do you have to have a favorite?" I asked. "I mean, you did with your sons, but there's no rule that says you have to choose one." My grandmother pushed back her chair. She looked miffed but at least not enraged. Before she could get up, I said, "There's something I need to talk to you about."

"Let me see. You want to make an independent film and—"

"Come on, Gloria. Give the money thing a rest. I don't want your money."

"Really? If I offered to give you a million dollars, you wouldn't take it?"

"A million dollars, no strings attached? I'd take it in a minute. But this isn't about money."

"Is it about God? It's Saturday. Do you want to take me to synagogue today?"

"If you wanted to go, I'd be glad to go with you." She was shaking her head, trying, I think, to decide whether she was amused or appalled by the offer. "But what I want to discuss about is actually about a Jewish concept," I went on. "Don't worry, I'm not going to give you a whole business about God. Well, a little."

"Very little."

"Fair enough. Here's the God part of it. I don't know whether you were religious or not growing up—"

"No. Well, I used to go to synagogue with my grandfather Saturday mornings. We walked there. He'd take my arm and say, 'Let's perambulate to shul.' He wouldn't drive on Shabbos. We went to a Conservative synagogue, so we sat together and it wasn't all in Hebrew. But he died when I was young, and that was the end of the faith of my fathers. Oh, that was McCain's book. It sounds so Jewish. As you were saying . . ."

"Okay, so every year around the High Holy Days you're supposed to think about repentance."

"So I've heard." Gloria cleared her throat. "If you think I would be receptive to a lecture on making amends, our doing very well together will come to an abrupt halt. Do not push me, Daisy. Understand? Do not push your luck."

"This isn't a lecture. This is . . . a bunch of thoughts I have. Just listen. The idea at Rosh and Yom is to make things right with God. You go over your life for the past year, your actions, your thoughts, and try to square things with Him. But there's a catch." Gloria blinked slowly, demonstrating how patient she was being, but her lips were pressing tighter and tighter together. "The Talmud says—"

"Do you know what those three words always signal to me?" Gloria interrupted. "Beware! Tedium to follow."

"So I'll talk fast. I said I wouldn't give you too much God. Listen: The atonement thing just covers you and God. But it's not for any sin or hurt against another human being. That's a separate deal."

"A lovely sermonette," she said. "Very heartfelt. Thank you for being so morally superior that you can tell me how to live my life. I treasure your wisdom."

"It's not *my* wisdom," I kept going. "But just say that you feel you haven't done right by someone. You're supposed to—"

"Don't tell me," Gloria said. "You're supposed to apologize."

"Reconcile. That's the operative word. You're supposed to reconcile. It's part of a Jewish concept called Teshuvah. It literally means 'return,' but it's about coming back together. You can say you're sorry, if that's appropriate. The idea is to make things right with someone you might have wronged."

"And if they don't want things made right?"

"Like what if the person tells you to fuck off? You're supposed to try two more times. After that, unless you've hurt them in some irreparable way, they can't legitimately withhold their forgiveness."

"My dear girl," Gloria snapped, and she had a loud snap, "you have moved from insufferable to offensive." She stood and jabbed her finger at me. "You tell me: Where it is written that one has to coddle one's grandchildren? To ask for forgiveness for not having been a part of their lives? What would you like, Daisy? For me to apologize and send you twenty-something years' worth of 'Grammy loves you' birthday cards?"

"When I was talking about reconciliation, I wasn't talking about you and the three of us. The four of us are doing okay. At least that's how I see it. You started something this weekend, and I'm so grateful for it. We all are. And as for coddling, none of us needs it. Our parents . . . They range from being fantastic to being good enough. It's not us I'm talking about."

"Then who, whom . . . Go ahead. Do you have a list for me? Perhaps you've already written it out in the order in which I should beg forgiveness. Tell me, who comes first? I can't wait for the fun!"

"I don't have any list," I told her. Not total truth.

"Let's see: Would Bradley come first? Or Adriana?"

I was tempted to say *Keith,* but of course I kept quiet.

"I could go to each of them and say, 'My dear, let's reconcile. I apologize, I apologize, I apologize. There! Three times. Now you are obliged to forgive me. Excellent. Goodbye and have a nice life.' "

Forget being upset. I couldn't even remember exactly what I'd said to her, so maybe my point that a person has to be sincere when trying to make amends didn't come out. It could have sounded more like some hocus-pocus incantation, thereby underscoring her contempt for religion. Establishing her contempt for me. I felt my eyes filling up, which they did pretty easily. I could weep at a bank commercial in which a doting family is hugging a capped and gowned college student whose tuition they'd saved for.

Just to make it a little worse, Gloria shook her head and said, "You are such a softie."

"Not really. I just cry easily."

"Well, try to stop. You wear your heart on your sleeve like that, people perceive it as weakness."

I had to laugh. "*Try* to stop?"

"Yes. When you feel like you're going to cry, just tell yourself to buck up. It works."

"Is it so terrible if people think I'm a softie?"

"Yes. You're in a tough business. I'm not counseling you to be coarse, just controlled."

"I am. Do you think I fall apart at meetings or get hysterical on conference calls?"

"Fine. You're a Spartan. A fox could

gnaw at your insides and you'd keep a straight face."

"Gloria, come on. I was just upset that I offended you. That was the last thing I wanted to do."

She walked across the kitchen—it really was a model's walk—and made another cup of coffee with her environmentally insupportable pods in her coffee machine. When she finished, she leaned against the counter and said, "It wasn't only nervy. It was arrogant. To lecture someone else about the state of her soul?"

"It wasn't my intention to talk about the state of your soul. What I was getting at was about the state of relationships that you have, I have. I was talking about coming together."

"Then why bring God into it?"

"The religion is very much about life in the here and now, with rules about how we treat each other. Okay, maybe the idea is to make ourselves better in order to get closer to the way we were made, in God's image. Whatever. It talks about what's unjust or unfair, and how to make it right. It's a way of living with ourselves and other people. Forget about God if you want to. I spend at least half my time not believing or doubting, but even then, I try to live as if there were a God."

"So why don't you forget the Jewish business and just be a decent human being?"

"If I only subscribed to a virtuous, *New York Times* editorial page morality, it would be too easy to give myself a pass. And there's no spiritual resonance, no history there. Not even the intellectual ferment. That's why I like the rules. I definitely don't go by them all, but at least they're a starting point. And they're not mindless commands. They've been argued about, reinterpreted for millennia."

"So you always have an out."

"I view them as an in, a way of thinking about stuff that makes life challenging, meaningful."

"Well, it's a thought," Gloria said. It appeared to be a thought she wasn't about to embrace.

"I apologize for being presumptuous."

"I thought of another makeover

movie," she said, apropos of nothing except changing the subject. "*Sabrina*. When Audrey Hepburn comes home from Paris. Lovely. Just lovely."

Twenty-two

Matt

Just like the morning before, my inner clock woke me at four thirty. It didn't yet know I was in New Mexico. On Friday, I'd rolled over and over till I got to the middle of the bed. The new cool of the sheet and pillowcase put me right back to sleep. But now, on Saturday, I knew there would be no rolling, no more sleep.

I kept thinking about how I'd talked to Gloria about Ashley, or more to the point, my being scared of making a mistake I wouldn't recognize until it was too late. So okay, you get married and one year later or on your twentieth anniversary you look up and ask yourself, *She's not a bad person, but what made me think she was right for me? God, I didn't have a clue about what love really is.*

But what was to guarantee I would grow into someone who knew what love really was? Maybe I wouldn't. Maybe I could never be sure, and my hesitation would lead to a lifetime of paralysis, marriagewise. I'd go into my thirties, forties, maybe even fifties and be the perennial eligible man. Every time a newly minted divorcée would come online, or a now-ready-to-date young widow, I'd be the guy her friends would call. Eventually, I'd marry one of them because I couldn't stand another decade of take-out food.

After about a half hour of depressing reflection, I went downstairs, made a cup of coffee, and brought it back to the room. I was so awake. But when I tried my morning routine, reading the sports coverage in all the New York papers on my iPad, then turning to the news, the previous night's conversation kept pushing its way back into my head. It wasn't just the content. It was that of all people in the world, I'd wound up confiding in my grandmother.

It was seven fifteen New York time when I called Ashley. "Hey," I said.

"Hey!" Texans, I'd noticed, tended to speak with more exclamation points than people from any other part of the country. "You're up early, bright-eyes. How's it going in the desert kingdom?"

"Not bad. We had a really good dinner at a restaurant I liked. Cool place. A little heavy on Mexican relics and antiques, but it could hold its own in New York or San Francisco." Then I told her what I ate. It was one of the weird things we did when we were apart, giving each other our menu reports. She'd been on at the hospital, so she'd had a premade tuna wrap, so she couldn't get it with tomato, and one of those mango-avocado-banana fruit drinks.

"What are you doing today?" Ashley asked.

I propped myself higher on the pillow. My feet were sticking out of the bottom of the blanket. Ashley said I had excellent feet, although they seemed pretty average to me. She said one of the few things that grossed her out in medical school was what some people's feet looked like.

"Gloria was talking about some spice market or a farmers' market. I'm not sure if they're the same thing. And then to the Georgia O'Keeffe Museum."

"That is so cool! I love all those cow skulls. She did these great flowers too, though ultimately they're all vaginas. If you like vaginas—"

"You know I do."

"—then you'll love Georgia O'Keeffe."

"If it was a plum blossom, I'd be interested." Her middle name, Mei, for plum blossom, still gave me an erotic buzz. "She told me that if I didn't feel like doing the market and museum routine, I could take a golf or tennis lesson with one of the pros at her club."

"What are you leaning toward?"

"Going home and seeing you."

"Good! But aren't you at all tempted by your grandmother's offer?" I'd texted her the details the day before. "I mean, having seen the business and all that?"

Ashley spoke casually, so to an outsider it might have sounded like simple curiosity. But I could tell she was a little scared that having been presented with what sounded like a tempting proposal—a thriving business that could be mine, country clubs, mountains in the background—I might go for it. And was the deal a package that included her?

"I get these hits," I said. "They just last for a few seconds. I think it could be a life I'd really love to live. But then . . . It's like I was wasted on some weird drug and I come back to myself and wonder, *Shit, why would I want that?* You know what people say about New York, it's being a nice place to visit but they wouldn't want to live here? That's what I feel about Santa Fe." I didn't hear a sigh of relief from Ashley, but I saved my ego by telling myself she had covered up the mike on her phone. "What's your day going to be?"

"Hospital. Wind things up. I can't believe commencement's in a week and a half. I want to get something amazing and sleeveless to wear under the gown that will look good when my parents take us to lunch." She always wore pretty clothes but usually forgot something: jewelry, or to get her hair cut. She hardly ever carried a purse, but stuck her key, MetroCard, MasterCard, and a twenty in a pocket. "By the way, my dad's been driving my mother crazy. He's made reservations at three different restaurants because he's afraid that when you give an out-of-town phone number, New York restaurant people won't write you down in the book."

"He comes across as so noncrazy."

"He is, except when he travels. Then he's like a total control freak. My mother said when they went to China to get me, the only reason she didn't kill him was that the adoption people knew it was a two-parent household and she didn't want to risk losing me."

"Listen, Ashley, I was talking to my grandmother last night. It was a real, sort of intimate conversation. And I was the designated driver, so I have no excuses."

"Maybe she's opening up, and you're responding to it."

"Maybe. Anyway, I told her, I confided in her that marriage, monogamy scared me."

She said something like, "Uh-huh" or "Oh."

"I told her that I had a lousy track record for longevity, but that it was different with you. I mean, you're more amazing to me now than you were the first time we laid eyes on each other."

"Thank you."

"But I'm scared that . . . Like what if that old thing of mine kicks in tomorrow, a year from now, during some midlife crisis? It would be so unfair to you."

"I can understand that," she said. Calm, but I could hear some pain in her voice. "Really I can."

"Good," I said. "Thank you. Whatever."

"What would happen to you if it turned out the monogamy thing didn't suit *me*?" she asked.

Maybe it was because what she said made me feel a little sick, but I couldn't think of a way to respond except the stupid, "I don't know." There was some silence but not the hostile kind. Finally, I said, "I would be devastated, Ash. It would kill me."

"So listen, we're both in the same boat. We've talked around marriage, and you know how I feel about you. I love you, Matt."

"You know I love you too."

"I do know," she said. "And we'll figure it out, one way or another. But now I've got to go meet Katie, walk through the park up to Sinai. God, I can't wait till you get back! All anyone at the hospital wants to talk about is the damn Yankees."

"So you need me so you can have someone to talk about the Mets with?"

"Yup. That's the only reason."

"Okay, I'll take whatever I can get. I love you."

"I love you too. Gotta go now and meet Katie."

"Hey, listen, let her wait a minute. One more thing, okay?"

"Sure. What?"

"This really should hold till I get home. It's not right to do it on the phone. Maybe it will just prove to you that I have no class. But I don't want it to wait. So advance apologies."

"Go ahead. Tell me."

"Ashley, will you marry me?"

Twenty-three

Raquel

One of the stories my mom told me about my dad was that he was very precise. “Maybe it came from all that camera equipment, having to know where every piece was,” she said. Since they were married at the end of the women-do-the-laundry era, he explained that he liked his socks folded—not rolled into balls—and then lined up in the drawer, overlying each other at a certain angle she could only describe as “less than forty-five degrees.” And they had to be arranged according to color. A couple of times he complained that a pair of cotton gray crew socks were in with the wool ones. The third time she said, "Wash your own damn socks."

He said, "Okay."

Looking back, the story taught me a lot. One of my mom's points was not just that women have to speak up, but when they do, the consequences are often not as terrible as they envision. Also, even the best of people, like my dad, could be annoying and petty. She wanted me to see him as a wonderful, accomplished man, but she didn't want me hero-worshipping him. Perfection was not an option.

Hayden was in charge of his own socks, so I had no complaints in that area. His rigidity was about not getting calls at the office. Multiple phone lines rang, e-mail and instant messages constantly dinged and chirped. Everyone in his department worked against deadlines, so there was perpetual intense pressure to prevent some catastrophic glitch that could cost them millions, billions. I'd called him there only once, to tell him I'd gotten the job at Legal Aid, and his congratulations were just shy of a snarl. All right, not quite that bad. He said, “I’ll come home early and we’ll celebrate,” but he did hang up without saying goodbye. That night, though, he was wonderful. A bouquet of pink roses, champagne at the restaurant, the whole thing. He did say, “Sorry if I was abrupt today, but seriously, unless it’s an emergency . . .” He didn’t bother finishing the sentence since I was already saying, “Okay. I know.”

Even with that history, I was going to call him at the office, even though I wasn’t sure what I wanted to say. However, without a shower I wouldn’t have felt anywhere near as comfortable as I needed to be for such a confrontation. (I’m the sort who can’t check e-mail in the morning until my teeth are brushed.) So it was another fifteen minutes before I was ready to make the call. I put it off for an extra five by applying my new lip stain and blush in a magnifying mirror that was surrounded by a halo of pink light. I guess the idea was that it should be flattering. Except when I saw tiny crow’s feet establishing territorial rights so they could develop long and deep later, I wasn't flattered.

When I sat on the bed and picked up my phone, my thoughts careened about in an insane spiral: dark, wild. Mangled hunks of discernible objects occasionally hurtled outward. My hunks were late hours, no breakfasts, no casual lovers talk—just some politics; could you pick up some Spanish smoked paprika, it's called *pimentón de la Vera*; bulletins on his stress level, from tense to shot to shit to totally wrecked. Weekends were usually for cooking and entertaining friends, an occasional concert, as well as less and less frequent lovemaking. One Sunday morning when I curled up against his back and put my arm around him, he asked me to wait until late afternoon, after he'd had a nap. When we went somewhere, I'd see people checking us out. I'd realize: We are a young, good-looking couple. But we're living like we have Medicare cards in our wallets.

In trial practice at law school and later at Legal Aid, I learned, aside from keeping a trial notebook, to always have the key points of my direct and cross on a small piece of paper. So I went to Notes on my cell to type in a few key points. I'd be starting out at a disadvantage because I'd be calling Hayden at work. That meant dealing with his annoyance. His anger, more likely. Sure, it could wait until I got back, but there was something urging me on—I don't know . . . Runner's high, perfect early morning weather, perfect omelet: I was brave and strong, ready to clear the air.

I typed in "don't think this is working." But what if he said, *You're absolutely right,* and took it as his cue to leave? Well, I'd be the one leaving since he owned the condo. Just a week earlier, if he'd said that to me, that our relationship didn't seem to be working, I'd have been shocked: *Are you crazy*? Because it would have been insane, unthinkable. I didn't know why, but now things were different.

I added a few more phrases, then called. He answered the phone "Ramos-Cruz," which was in itself suspect because he never took a call unless it had a caller ID, and he ignored half of those. So he knew it was me and was establishing he was in a work environment. Not just that, he was under pressure that would crush most men, though not the intrepid Ramos-Cruz. Right from the outset I knew this was the Worst Time to Call.

"Hayden, it's me. I'll only keep you for a minute or two."

I heard the deep breath followed by a fast, pissed exhalation. His courtesy remained, of course, though no doubt its continued survival was touch and go. "Is there any emergency?" he asked.

"No." I glanced down at my left hand. They'd shortened my nails at Glory and put on a clear glassy polish that gave off tiny diamonds of light. I took the cell phone from my ear and looked at my notes. "Hayden, I don't think . . . We don't seem to be working well together anymore." There's that old saw that's been in every trial advocacy program since Hammurabi's code became law. To this day, it periodically pops up in *Law and Order*—style shows: Never ask a question you don't already know the answer to. But I think I did know. "What's wrong?"

"Raquel." Another audible breathing moment. "I can't do this. If I'm in on a Saturday, you know it's a pressure situation. Beyond pressured. I can't have any kind of a reasonable conversation of this sort when I'm in the office, and today is worse than most." In fairness to him, I could hear phones jangling in the background. "I'll take the evening off Monday if you get home too late tomorrow. All right? We'll talk to your heart's content."

"I do want to talk at length. But I also need to know now: What's wrong?" He was silent. So I talked. I itemized the no breakfasts, late nights, and so forth, although I did leave out having to buy him paprika. "That's what I know, Hayden. Or I should say, that is what I feel to be the truth. I believe you either want out, or you want to have it both ways."

He was a cautious man by nature but also a fast thinker. So there was almost no hesitation before he asked, "What do you mean, 'both ways'?"

Well, I was a fast thinker, too, but except for two minutes beforehand, I couldn't claim to be prepared for this discussion. "I'm not sure," I admitted. "It may be that you're unhappy in the relationship and are spending longer hours at work or dinner with your colleagues to avoid being with me—even though you're not prepared to have me out of your life. That's both ways. Or there's someone else, or maybe more than just someone, who is keeping you busy. You're not ready to make a change or you're gathering yourself together to deal with me. Her and me. That's having it both ways, too."

"Hold for a minute." Maybe he had to take a phone call, but I thought it was more likely he needed to get his thoughts together. One of Hayden's favorite words was "strategize." I could picture him staring up at the expensive Goldman Sachs ceiling and strategizing like crazy. He got back on the line. "Whatever makes you think—"

"As I told you, I don't know precisely. But I do know it's one of those two alternatives. If your fatigue factor is any indication, the answer is B, another woman." I hadn't typed that one into my notes.

"Did you ever think you might have this completely wrong?" he asked.

"That you're just doing what it takes to be a top guy at Goldman? Yes, I did think that for a pretty long time. But circumstantial evidence made me consider other hypotheses."

"Did it occur to you that by throwing around these accusations it undercuts the basis for our relationship? The trust?"

"Did it occur to you that by virtually ignoring me—or by cheating—it undercuts not just the basis, but the entire relationship?"

"We need to talk."

"We do. But understand one thing. You cannot have it both ways—with me as one of the ways. Look, I'm not in a position to complain that someone works late. I do it much of the time, and if not at the office, I'm bringing stuff home. But I don't do it to avoid you. And I have no one in my life except you. So if it is a woman, or women, that's unsupportable in an even more profound way."

"I hear you."

"Excellent. My plane is due in at six tomorrow night, so I should be home by seven thirty. Plenty of time to talk. I'll see you then."

It was just as well that it wasn't until after I hung up that I had another thought in addition to telling Hayden he couldn't have it both ways. As far as I was concerned, not only could he have it only one way, but that one way would be without me.

Twenty-four

Gloria

I did consider reconciliation, all that "Give Me That Old-Time Religion" business Daisy had so unsubtly suggested. Unfortunately, it required apologizing to people you had wronged. More accurately, whom I had wronged. That would make it not only humiliating but also time-consuming, forcing me to fly all over the country and listen to people whining about how deeply I'd hurt them. Conceivably, I could say, "I'm sorry I took two of your trucks, Joe, but look at the bright side: That oleaginous Mafia man, Cassaro, didn't get them. And what I did with them! Built a marvelous business, which let you off the hook for alimony, child support, the boys' college tuition."

Yet of course I understood that approach would not precisely be in the spirit of regret and repentance.

And what could I say to Bradley? "Sorry I didn't love you enough. Listen, don't take it personally. I had a limited supply: I'm somewhat deficient in the humanity department, as you no doubt noticed. I didn't *not* love you. So try not to feel bad that what little love I had went to Travis, whose capacity for showing joy was—shall we say?—a bit greater than yours. No doubt that too was my fault, not yours."

Of course, I could blame everything on my mother. She didn't love me. What I learned from her was how not to love. But that wouldn't help me with expressing my regret to Keith, who would no doubt say something to the effect of, "What the fuck does your mother have to do with your abandoning Billy—and me—when all we needed was a little kindness?"

Too many people, too many apologies. I simply could not do it. So while I had several pleasant conversations with Daisy, Skyped with Matthew and his Ashley, who was darling even though her bangs were a nightmare of unevenness, and had a long and congenial e-mail correspondence with Raquel about *The Heart of William James,* the book she'd sent me, I wasn't thinking about flying cross-country and apologizing to their parents or to anyone. Not even to Keith, who was only seven miles away.

So May rolled into June, and June into the beginning of July, and there I was at the opening night party for Santa Fe's International Folk Art Market. A windy night, but flying hair and waves in one's margarita were to be anticipated in a New Mexico evening. Way down the row of booths for the artists, I spotted Keith and a couple with whom he was friendly, the Lanes. Somehow, his antennae picked up that I was in the vicinity, and he quickly averted his head from me as our eyes met. The Lanes, like alert bodyguards, moved in closer to him. Clearly Nancy and Lew weren't shy about showing they'd chosen sides. Nancy did give me a small smile. Despite being excessively blond, willowy, and chic, she was a gentle soul. Lew, an orthopedist, had once operated on my thumb after it had been crushed when the lid of a nineteenth-century French trunk I'd been on the verge of buying smashed down on my hand. Lew was made of slightly tougher stuff than his wife, yet exquisitely polite; I'd heard he'd gone to a boarding school back East. Lew nodded at me because he was incapable of rudeness. But then he quickly turned back to Keith, seemingly resuming a conversation they'd been having, with Lew pointing to something on his wrist, as if explaining some surgery. Nancy interrupted them with a laugh and pointed out features of some mobile hanging from the next booth; from the distance I couldn't tell if the objects dangling from strings were birds in flight or soaring penises.

Of course, even before I saw Keith, I assumed that he and his friends might be at the party. I also realized they would give me the cold shoulder. The best I might expect was remote courtesy from the few who could not snub me. So I made my way to a group of my own acquaintances I'd always thought of as filler folk. When someone you like can't attend one of your social events, you replace that person with a filler and pray like hell the filler will take a long time to reciprocate. Ideally, years. When that time arrives, you will call the night of his or her dinner, cough, and explain your doctor said that what you thought is a nasty cough is actually bronchitis.

However, as I pretended to be absorbed in watching the dancing with a group of filler types and, instead of delighting in the colorful spectacle, wished someone would rip out the plug of the amplifier, and as Dickson Blunt rushed to the bar as fast as his pudgy thighs could carry him to get me another Gray Goose, and as Leona Valderrama put her damp hand on my arm so I could notice her green turquoise surrounded by diamonds ring, I had a minor revelation: These people are not dreadful.

They are merely nicely dressed and dreary. Further, it wasn't even that I was missing being part of the old crowd. Most of my former friends were definitely not dreary, but that wasn't what was missing.

More than anything, I wished Daisy, Matthew, and Raquel could be at this party with me, that I could be taking them around to meet the artists, introduce them to those fillers who weren't aggressively dull, and watch my grandchildren's faces as they checked out the art as well as their twenty-something contemporaries.

I knew then that unless I made it right with those I'd wronged, I would never have the pleasure of the very company I craved.

For God's sake. I was in the Bronx. In July, no less. The late morning was already so hot that the moment the driver helped me out of the car, the sun pressed down on my head like a branding iron. This was not baking dry New Mexico heat. I'd forgotten what New

York summers were like. The humidity! Moisture displaced air so suddenly I clutched my handbag to my chest as if my asthma inhaler could work through leather. I must have gasped as I stood because the driver said, "Miss, you okay?"

"Yes. A bit on the warm side after the air-conditioned car."

As I looked around the apartment houses and tried to get my bearings, every inch of my skin exuded sweat. Tall brick buildings, maybe twenty stories high, separated by paths. Small grass patches were trying vainly not to drop dead in the vicious sun. Naturally, the sign that pointed you in the direction of the various buildings had so much graffiti it couldn't be read. Just as I was about to get back to the car, a woman carrying shopping bags crossed the path ahead of me. I waved to her, then headed her way. I needed to find 1460 and I was trying to recall how to say sixty in Spanish. But she said, "Which building are you looking for?"

"Fourteen sixty," I said.

"Killer day, isn't it?" I nodded, trying

not to think that she badly needed a layered haircut because such a thought could affect my expression and I needed her help. "I'm going to the building right before it," she said. "Come with me. I'll take you there."

"Can I carry one of your bags for you?" I asked, knowing she'd say no, which blessedly she did.

By the time I got to Adriana's building, I wished for a couch to swoon onto, and I'm not the fainting sort. Also, I was dreading going into the lobby, as in my experience, most New York apartment buildings, even the most posh, which this wasn't, smelled like last month's fried onions. However, this vestibule merely smelled dusty. Though there wasn't a bracing chill when you opened the ridiculously heavy front door, at least some mechanical device was attempting to cool the place.

I was quite nervous. Butterflies in my stomach, even a tremor in my hand as I rang the buzzer to her apartment. It took no time for a long squawk to buzz me into the lobby. I can't say I expected to be beset by drug dealers in the elevator, but I was relieved when I got in and pressed 11 that the place indeed seemed to be what Bradley had once told me it was: a middle-income co-op, not a housing project.

Adriana was waiting for me so I wouldn't have to go from door to door looking for 11D. I could see her clearly near the end of the long corridor. Since I had lens implants after cataract surgery, I have the eyesight of . . . whatever animal can see from long distances. Maybe a falcon. In any case, I was startled at how tiny she was. I'd forgotten. Compared to her, Raquel was a giant. I remember when Travis brought Adriana to Santa Fe to meet me. Their disparity in size was shocking, almost obscene. My first thought was that he had some heretofore hidden sexual predilection for little girls, but when she got closer, I soon saw she was quite the adult. Just a very minute adult.

"Adriana, it's kind of you to let me visit you."

"My pleasure," she said.

I was prepared to shake hands with her—the human contact thing—but she stood on tiptoes and kissed my cheek. A quick brush, really. I made a *cheep* as I kissed the air.

The apartment surprised me. Who knows what I was expecting? Something Old World. Avocado damask, or something nubby in brown. "Lovely," I said. It was. A small entrance foyer led into the living room. The wood floors shone. The walls were an off-white, usually the decorating choice of the unimaginative, but the place was alive and modern. It worked: A+ for judicious use of color. A red-orange rug bordered with unexpected and delightful burgundy brightened the place, as did the two wooden side chairs with red seats that flanked what looked like an old Chinese cabinet. It was the only old piece in the room, and she'd topped it with a bowl of red apples. I couldn't tell if they were real and was dying to feel them, but there she was, right beside me. "Really wonderful," I told her.

"Thank you," she said. "Please, sit down." Up close, I could see she'd aged but not horribly. Her jawline was a bit mushy and, befitting her size, there was a minuscule wattle under her chin. It cried out for a nip and a tuck, but no doubt she'd recoil from such a frivolous, expensive idea.

Since she was offering me any seat, I chose a corner of the couch. That way, she was free to pick the small tub chair catercornered to me or the other end of the couch. She chose the couch, but on the next cushion over, which was too close for comfort. She seemed perfectly at ease, an odd thing since this couldn't have been a meeting she was eager to have. Still, it was her turf and I was the one who was ill at ease. I started to glance around the room, only to be stopped by a picture on the table right beside me—Travis and young Raquel in a plain silver frame.

Why the photo should come as such a shock, I didn't know. I stared at it for a long time. At first I was angry at her for putting it out where I could see it, and then I realized she was his wife and was entitled to have the picture of her husband and daughter in her own living room. I heard myself saying, "May I pick it up?"

"Yes," Adriana said. "Of course."

Travis and Raquel were in some playground in the city, probably near their apartment in Manhattan, one of those horrible walk-ups that have charm only in books and movies. In life, they had cockroaches the size of my foot, and I wore a nine and half. But there they were with swings in the background, the little boxy ones for very young children. Raquel must have been around three then. Travis, tall and lean in jeans and a white T-shirt, held her high above his head. Her arms were outstretched, as if she were pretending to be an airplane. She was so small compared to him, with little matchstick arms and legs sticking out from her sleeveless T-shirt and shorts. But they both were full of the same élan. Raquel's mouth was open into a wide O of delight. And that delight was all over Travis's face as he looked up at her. Not his charming, lopsided grin: just a smile of huge pleasure. *Isn't this child amazing?*

"Did you take this?" I managed to say.

"No. I wasn't there that day. It wasn't

even his camera. One of the neighbors took the picture and gave us a copy." I knew I should put it back on the table, but I couldn't stop staring at their faces. She with her arms out, looking straight ahead, amazed at the view from so high. He gazing up, thrilled by his daughter. "If you'd like, I can have a copy made and sent to you," she was saying when I started to cry. Horrible, just horrible. Not just a few tears or even that silent weeping where someone's shoulders heave. This was the loudest blubbering imaginable, with snorts in between sobs.

It wasn't like I hadn't seen a picture of him since he died. I had one at home, on a little table next to a chaise longue in my bedroom. It was a serious though pleasant-looking head shot that had appeared postage-stamp-size in one of the big magazines on the Our Contributors page.

Naturally I tried to get a grip on myself, but that didn't work. I tried to say I was sorry for losing control, but my words came out unintelligible as well as guttural, as if I'd discovered some hideous new Eastern European language. Since I had put my handbag somewhere near the door, I stood. I needed to get at my handkerchief. But Adriana took hold of my hand. Did she think I was going to run out, humiliated that I'd broken down? I admit that thought had passed through my mind, and I was in no position to speak and tell her, *I'm not going anywhere. I just need to get a damned hankie.*

She said, "Let me get you a tissue," and disappeared.

I couldn't even use that moment alone to get hold of myself because I picked up the picture again. Travis had on sneakers and no socks. At least it looked like no socks. It was hard to tell. When he was a teenager and refusing to wear socks with sneakers or loafers, I warned him, "When you get a horrific case of athlete's foot, the cost of the medication comes out of your allowance." He looked at me and started laughing. About a second later, I joined him. "All right, fine, I'll pay for the damn stuff. Just promise me that after you shower, you'll dry between your toes."

Of course, he started laughing again, but he raised his right hand and said, "I solemnly promise to dry between my toes, so help me God."

Adriana came back with a box of tissues. I was tempted to say, *What do you expect me to do? Stay for the evening and cry the whole time?* I did have to give her credit, though, because she brought in a plastic sandwich bag with it so that I could get rid of the dirty tissues. And she had the sense not to sit beside me on the couch again, a perfect viewing point to watch me wail. Instead, she went to the chair nearest me.

When I finally calmed down and put the picture back on the table, I said, "Hardly the most graceful way to begin."

I was expecting some social worker retort that would make me want to retch, like, *At times like these, we're too overcome by our pain to allow for grace*. "No problem," she said.

"First, let me thank you for agreeing to see me. Considering all that's passed between us, or hasn't passed . . . Well, you know. Where was I? Oh, second,

Raquel is an amazing young woman. It went poorly for us at the beginning. Understandably." I waited, but Adriana didn't say anything, so I kept going. "Toward the end of the weekend that the three of them were there, she and I were more at ease with each other. I can't say we've made our peace, but I believe we came a long way."

"She indicated that to me," Adriana said. If I were she, with my mean mother-in-law holding on to a bag filled with used tissues, I would not have been so self-possessed. But she always had been. I thought back to the first few times we'd met. She'd never allowed me to snub her; when I was cold, she did not try harder. She was always polite and seemingly as comfortable as she was at this moment.

"I'm glad to hear that. I'm not being sarcastic. I really am glad."

"I know. I can tell when you're being sarcastic."

For some reason, I wanted her to tell me I looked good, so I said, "You look very well."

"Thank you."

I was running on two tracks. One of them was thinking that she knew I wanted a compliment on my appearance and since I wanted it, she wasn't going to give it. But the other track, the main route to where I wanted to go, stretched out before me. That was the way I had to go. "Back then, when Travis was alive, when you got engaged and then married, I felt you took him away from me. Not just the way some mothers get, where they view the daughter-in-law as a rival, the other woman. Not that at all. It was that you were taking him to a place that was better than anything I could offer. The night at that restaurant when I met your family. Your parents, of course, grandparents, uncles and aunts. It was such a big, happy family. Spirited."

"It was. Is. My grandparents are gone now, but they were great, and great about welcoming Travis. Not that it was an uphill battle. One smile from him and whatever objections they might have had—religious differences, all the traveling he did—just collapsed. Well, it did take more than a smile to convince my mother's mother, but she became his greatest fan."

"It meant a great deal to him that they were so welcoming. And also he was attracted to them because they were such a lively group. He once said, 'They can take the most ordinary occasion and make it into a party.' But that was one of the reasons I felt left out. I couldn't make life a party. I was only one person. I lived in New Mexico. And the worst of it was, I was the villain. Everybody, including Travis, blamed me for the breakup of our family."

"Do you feel you deserve the blame?" Adriana asked. She was moving closer to social work territory, but it could have just been a question. She hadn't put her foot over the border. Yet.

"I probably deserve much of it. At the time, the only action I saw that was open to me was to leave Joe and go someplace . . . far. But what he'd done, presenting his decision as a fait accompli. I was so angry. And I can't describe the depths of the disappointment I felt. He was so strong, or so I thought. But he not only collapsed under intimidation, he gave away his livelihood, the family's security. I felt so isolated and abandoned. I'd so misjudged him, thinking him to be my protector, the brave man who'll stand up to bullies Also, he was about to do business with the Mob. Maybe, in the long run, he had no other choice. I don't know. But when you get involved with criminals, you put yourself in danger, and your family as well. I'm not saying they would have come and riddled us with machine gun bullets, but at the time I felt I needed to get the boys away."

"Was that your primary aim, to safeguard them?"

I thought for a moment and took another tissue to make sure I didn't have half-moons of mascara under my eyes. "No. My primary aim was to be rid of Joe. He could no longer be relied on. As far as getting the boys away, that was important, but not because I was all that hysterical about their safety. The Mafia didn't go after children. I suppose I wanted to remove them from his influence. I knew they loved him, but I didn't want them to grow up seeing their father without a viable business, strutting around, seemingly self-confident on the outside but inside a wimp. I remember thinking Joe was like a very hard candy—I believe it was called a Yummy—that had a center of jelly. Not that I made that comparison in front of them. I didn't want them to think they'd come from weak stock." Adriana nodded. "But I used to tell them they mustn't grow up to be Yummys."

"They didn't."

"I suppose not. Bradley isn't a Yummy, but he doesn't have a core the way Travis had. Travis had a deep sense of who he was, and he always stayed true to that core. He was the only person in my entire life I admired without reservation. Loved without reservation, I suppose. That's why when I lost him . . . I was out of my mind with grief."

"I do agree with you about Travis always staying true to himself. Part of that was falling in love with me and marrying me. You know that, don't you?"

"I do now. I suppose I knew it then also." I dabbed my eyes but only to buy a second to work up to what I had to say. "I came here for a purpose." Adriana moved toward the edge of her chair, maybe just an inch or two, but it signaled she was prepared to listen closely to what I was about to say. "I came here to tell you how sorry I am for rejecting you and Raquel in so many ways—and so often. I can't say I've changed into a better person. But I do acknowledge I did you great wrong. I hope you will accept my apology." Well, she did not cut me off with a quick *Yes, of course I accept your apology,* so I kept going. "I would very much like to get to know you, if you will let me. I understand I might not be part of the family after all this time, but—"

"Of course you are a part. Family isn't an institution that requires an application for membership and a vote."

"Thank you."

"What made you decide to . . . whatever . . . apologize? Get back together."

"I like the word 'reconcile.' I had these three young people in my house and I made a business proposal, which they all quickly rejected. I said to myself, *Well, that's it for the weekend I had planned, but I still have to put up with three houseguests for two more days.* I was dreading it. Those two days without an agenda gave me time to see how marvelous—and occasionally unpleasant—they each were. And also that in some small way, these grandchildren were mine, or at least of me. And after they left, I couldn't get them out of my head. I kept thinking how much I'd missed not knowing them and how . . ." I pulled another tissue from the box. Just in case. "I thought, I can count on two hands, maybe three, the number of years I have left with me possessing all my marbles. Or maybe only one finger. You never know."

"You don't."

"I want to have the three of them in my life, but in order to do so, to have anything more than the most superficial of relationships with them, I had to detoxify myself, so to speak. The only way I can do that is apologizing. Well, more than that. By regretting the past and resolving not to repeat it. I'm making visits to them, to others I've hurt.

"There was a man who used to work

for me. Keith Thompson. He was my number two, the person who was destined to take over Glory. We had the papers drawn up for him buying me out, a four-step withdrawal process for me. Everything hunky-dory. Everything pleasant. Not only were we colleagues, we were friends."

"And then?" Adriana asked. Her voice was gentle, so soft that her question seemed more like an idea in your own head than words from someone else.

"His partner, Billy, had a stroke. Right before his fortieth birthday. One day he's fine and fit. The next day in Intensive Care, barely hanging on to life. Billy and I had been . . . chums, to use an old word. Good pals. I couldn't bring myself to go and see him. Keith hinted, then practically begged me to go. I made excuses, to him, to myself. But deep down I knew I wasn't going to go."

"Do you know why?" she asked.

"Yes. Anyway, I believe I do. Fear of some sort, but that's letting myself off the hook. An inner coldness: *I don't want to deal with unpleasantness and therefore I won't.* The upshot of it was, my not going brought Keith even more pain. I had been his friend, a devoted big sister not just to him but to Billy too. I was family.

"So Keith abrogated the agreement you'd made?"

"Yes. Not just the agreement, but the friendship as well." My mouth was drying out. My lips felt gluey. "You're supposed to . . . Daisy's trying to give me religion. Jewish custom or law says you should reconcile with those you've wronged. You can't say, 'I'm sorry, God,' and have Him accept your apology unless you make your peace with those you've wronged. Not that I believe in God, quite frankly. And it's the sort of feel-good, clichéd behavior that makes recovering alcoholics and drug addicts so irritating: 'I'm sorry, I'm sorry,' and all you want to say is, 'I'll only forgive you if you shut up.' Yet, oddly, Daisy's suggestion hit home."

"That's not so odd," Adriana said. "How did the visit with Keith go?"

"Not well. I didn't expect he'd greet me with a great big hug, if that's what you mean. He was cold but correct. We had a drink. I apologized. He said that some hurts might recede as the years passed, but unless I'd be around for another fifty, he didn't see it happening in this case. I said I was sad he felt that way, but I understood."

"So that's it?" she asked.

"No, that isn't that. Daisy gave me a Talmud lecture. Or a Yom Kippur sermon. I'm not clear which one. Maybe both. When reconciling with people, you have to be open and sincere when you're saying you're sorry. The apology has to be more than words."

"That's true in confession also. Contrition must be sincere. Not just the words. I always thought it was a good idea because it forces to you to verbalize what's in your heart and what's on your conscience. For me, verbalizing something leads to a clarity that just thinking about something doesn't. Maybe that's why talk therapy works, but in this case, the therapist is God."

"Apologizing and atoning to God is one requirement. But with people, if you've wronged them, you must apologize separately to them. Not just a perfunctory 'Sorry about that.' If they refuse to accept your apology, you're obliged to try twice more. So I think I have another couple of visits to Keith to put on my calendar. I should look forward to them as an opportunity, but quite honestly, I'm dreading them."

"But you'll go through with them?"

"Yes. And when I got to New York, I apologized to Bradley. Unfortunately, he brought Cynthia along to the dinner, so I was forced to apologize to her, too. No doubt she now thinks she's in line to inherit my jewelry, which she is not. Well, maybe a piece of two, just so she won't bad-mouth me to Daisy and Matthew."

"She was always so kind to Raquel."

"Does that mean I owe her my sapphire ring?" The comment seemed to amuse Adriana, but she kept her silence. I said, "No matter how many apologies I make, I'm never going to be a good person in the sense that you are."

"I don't know how good I am," Adriana said. "I think you're giving me too much credit. I'm calm by nature and empathetic by training. Maybe that can pass for goodness, but I'm not sure it's the real thing."

"That's why you're good," I told her. "I've spent most of my life keeping people at a distance. If they didn't take the hint from my coolness or sarcasm, then I could be . . . as harsh as necessary. I've given my behavior a lot of thought. I cannot transform myself into America's sweetheart. Too little time, too tough a job, even for me. But I would like to be a better person than I have been. I believe I can manage that."

"I accept your apology," Adriana said. "I know you are sincere. You wouldn't have made the trip unless saying you are sorry meant a great deal to you."

"It does."

I was glad that she asked if I'd like a bite of lunch because my throat was so tight that I wouldn't have been able to say another word.

Twenty-five

Gloria

I gave Raquel the choice of any restaurant in New York, so naturally she picked a place in Chinatown that looked as if it had been converted from a one-room basement apartment in a condemned building. “It’s convenient to my apartment and office,” she said. “And I don’t think you’ll find anything like it in Santa Fe,” a fact for which I was grateful as I descended the three uneven stairs down to King Cho.

However, after a couple of bottles of Chinese beer and some delicious dumplings filled with God only knows what,

Raquel asked me what I thought of it and I said, "It definitely has a rough charm."

The truth was, King Cho reminded me how much I had missed New York. Not living there: I had never come to the city seeking its free ways and exhilarating tumult. I chose it when I was seventeen because the only job I was possibly qualified for was modeling. New York was the center of that universe. But two things happened when I arrived. One was that I realized I was intelligent. The other was that I discovered how much I liked smart conversation: to have it, even to watch it. As I took in the action at the other tables, I realized that many of the exchanges were in languages I couldn't even identify.

"Do you know what I like about New York?" I said. "That strangers are always trying to avoid touching or looking directly at each other. New Yorkers go to such lengths to avoid any hint of intimacy. Well, obviously it's such a big, crowded place. Yet the minute people here establish any sort of bond, they have such a fierce need to communicate. Look over there." I pointed to three men and a woman in a booth, deep in conversation. "See their bodies? They're all arcing toward one another. The way trees bend when seeking sunlight. That doesn't happen in other cities except for people with a hearing loss." I moved in closer. "You see, Raquel? I'm attempting to establish a bond."

"That's pretty good for someone from Ohio and New Mexico."

"Thank you. You know I had a good talk with your mother."

"I heard," Raquel said. She was looking directly at me except for the times she used her chopsticks to pick up dumpling remnants.

"She made me a lovely lunch. Egg salad, tuna salad, sliced tomatoes. And a little Italian bread that Dante would put in Paradiso."

"Good. What else have you been doing since you've been here?"

"I saw Bradley and I apologized. Cynthia came along. At one point I was tempted to recant, just to torment her. Fortunately, the soupçon of my better nature prevailed. I told him I loved him and was sorry I was unable to show it, that it was I who was lacking, not he. As I was saying it, it felt true, so I suppose it must be. My eyes got damp. Actually, he and I were teary throughout the entrée—quite embarrassing—but we composed ourselves before we ordered dessert. Oh, I spent two days at the Met, visiting all the wings they've put up since I left town. And I went to see a revival of *Blithe Spirit.*" Sadly, my granddaughter looked blank. "It's a Noël Coward play." I had what I'd come to recognize as one of my mean moments. I was so tempted to say, "You'd probably hate it. It's too much fun for your taste." Instead I changed the subject.

A waiter came and gave us some more dumplings. I told him no thank you, but he gave them to me anyway. When he walked off, Raquel said, "Apparently he thinks you need these dumplings."

"Like a hole in the head." I did take a bite of one, though, and it was quite good. Probably pork.

"Well, it's bothersome that I've left

such a trail of wounded hearts. After New York, I have a plane ticket to Florida."

I was treated to a twenty-something OMG look, complete with dropped jaw. "To see Grandpa Joe?"

"Yes. Sorry, I didn't mean to bite your head off. The prospect of seeing him is almost too much to bear. He probably looks repulsive. A Sicilian olive with legs."

"No. Actually, he's still a nice-looking man. Daisy says he looks just like some actor, but I can't remember his name. Some guy who played earthy old men in undershirts."

"How enticing."

"Not that Grandpa Joe goes around wearing undershirts. It's the earthiness, the passion that Daisy was talking about."

"Not much passion left in eighty-three year-old gonads," I told her. "Mark my words."

"I will. Admitted into evidence. Did you steal his trucks?"

"That's not a polite question."

"I'm sorry. Well, semisorry, just so you know."

"Of course I know. This is what happened. He was going to give everything he owned to the Mafia. Not right away, that would have been too blatant. But over a year or two, Joe would have been left with nothing. I don't know how to say it in legalese, but I appropriated my alimony before the adjudication process could be completed."

"Like right away."

"Right away. Pedal to the metal. I hired two surly men Joe had fired for insubordination. They drove the trucks to Santa Fe. So I know that when I apologize, I'll have to make that episode right with Joe. That's part of it, too, making restitution, which translates to giving him some money. He'll probably waste on champagne for women too young for him and baseball memorabilia."

"I didn't know it was a religious rule," Raquel said. "It's a legal concept to make someone whole. You have to put the person who was damaged back into the position he'd have been if you hadn't done . . . whatever to him."

"Maybe he'll say, 'I won't forgive you and I don't want your money.' "

"You're really into the spirit of this, aren't you?"

"Actually, I am. I do owe him. He was a good man, though never as tough as he wanted to be. What I found so attractive about him was . . . I dislike this sort of girl talk."

"When have you tried it? I mean, in the last fifty years."

"You're fresh. It's hard to believe that you're like this, coming from your mother."

"I'm persistent. Anyway, I'm sure some of your genes are floating around in me. Now, what was so appealing about Grandpa Joe? He's always with some woman—"

"Some woman willing to support him. He has a combination of rough around the edges and sweetness. I found that as long as I didn't gush over him being a dear man, he was one. I assume that's still true."

"Did you ever think of trying again with him?"

"You mean if I could catch him between wives or lady friends? No!" I shook the notion out of my head. "Well, I sometimes wished I could be with him. Talk to him. The other thing also. But not to be his wife again. I'm not the wife type." Raquel looked off to the side somewhere, to people laughing. She was still wearing the blush and lipstick from Glory and had had her hair trimmed again. A good cut, I was pleased to see. "Do you think Daisy will ever get married?" I asked.

She turned back to me, shrugged. "I don't know. She's got as good a shot as anyone. What about me? Do you see that in my future?"

"If you want to be married, you'll be married," I said. Her face softened, a bit of relief, as when you're burdened with many shopping bags and you set one down. "I don't have to worry about you in that area."

"But you worry about Daisy?"

"To the extent I worry about anyone

else except myself, yes. I do worry. She's too tender."

"She is tender, but not 'too.' Daisy's doing well in a tough business. She's probably not going to be head of a studio or Ms. Power Producer. But she so knows her stuff. She's a walking repository of everything cinematic. I can see her having a successful, lifelong career: being respected, even being loved. You know, like, 'There goes Daisy Goldberg. She's so nice. And not only didn't they fire her, they gave her a raise.' "

"I doubt that."

"I don't. You and I are strong, but so is she. She's just strong in a different way. And you don't have to worry about Matt. He's all set. Did you meet Ashley?"

"No. She just started her residence, or residency, whatever it's called. We've Skyped. I like what I've seen. He asked me if he could bring her to Santa Fe when she has a three-day weekend. And when he could get away, after the baseball season is over, before his new company starts up. I was pleased."

"I bet you were more than pleased."

"Yes. He is one darling young man."

"Well, Ashley is one darling young woman."

"So I believe. Chinese. And you: half Puerto Rican. I never imagined a world like this. It's quite interesting."

"Interesting?"

"That means I like it, Raquel. Don't pick on me."

"I wasn't picking. I was just . . . ascertaining. By the way, did my mom tell you I broke up with Hayden?" Raquel asked.

I set down my chopsticks. Apparently I'd been holding them up the whole time, my elbow resting on the table, something I didn't like to catch myself doing. "No. She didn't mention it. But I knew."

"Who told you?" she asked casually.

"Like you, I have my canon of ethics."

"Well, I'm glad you know. It's not any big secret. In fact, I basically broke up when I was still at your house. I suspected he'd met someone else. He had. He's not a total womanizer. I just wasn't what he wanted. He implied he was too . . . I don't know . . . intimidated by my strength to tell me about having fallen out of love with me, so he cheated."

"Spineless."

"Not totally. His spine's just more bendable than it ought to be. Anyway, the rest of the breakup was regrets and logistics. He's a lousy negotiator, or maybe he just makes too much money. I got all the kitchen appliances we'd bought since I'd moved in, plus the big flat-screen."

"I'm sure you're a fine negotiator, but he probably wanted a larger flat-screen."

"There are easier ways to go about getting one," she said.

"There are. Do you miss him?"

"No. It's weird, but I think by the time we broke up, the relationship was so drained of content there was nothing much to miss."

"How are you faring? Where are you living?"

"I have a sublet here in Chinatown. A friend of a friend is an architect doing some work on the 2014 Winter Olympics in Russia, so I've got the place for as long as I want it or till 2014, whichever comes first."

"Is it nice?"

"For you, no. For me, wonderful."

"Raquel, I would like to ask you a serious question."

She pulled in her chair so the man with the dumpling cart could get by. "Go ahead."

"I expect you'll tell me the truth."

"I expect I will."

"Do you still hate me?"

"No. I admit I may not be your biggest fan, but I certainly don't hate you. I don't think I ever did, though I was terribly angry at you."

"What's the difference?" I asked.

"I'm not sure. Off the top of my head? I get angry when I'm confronted by something I don't like, something hurtful or unfair. Hate is something a person carries around and consults frequently. Something a person can't let go of."

"Interesting."

"It's okay. Do you want to apologize to me, too, this week? If it's too much, I can be patient."

"Of course it's not too much. I do apologize to you. From the bottom of my heart. You are a remarkable woman and no doubt were the same as a child. I'm sorry I missed all those years. I'm sorry I hurt you and your mother by rejecting you at a time when you needed to be in touch with something that was your father's."

She waited for such a long time before she answered I was afraid she was going to reject my appeal for forgiveness. Then she said, "I forgive you on one condition. That your apology is not about saying you're sorry, then going off on your own again. We can reconcile on the condition we keep in touch. Not just e-mail. We need to see each other now and then."

"That would be fine," I said. I took the napkin and cleaned those tiny corners of the mouth where lipstick, atoms of food, and dead skin cells tend to collect. "But I'd like it to be more than 'now and then.' Before she could answer, I added, "I'd like you to reconsider my offer of Glory. I guarantee you I'm a better negotiator than that Hayden was. But I want you in the business. I'll be more than reasonable."

Raquel was shaking her head even before she said, "There's no way."

"Of course there's a way."

"I can't leave my mother."

"You wouldn't be going to Kuala Lumpur."

"I'm all she has," she said.

"Raquel, she has a job, a large extended family, friends."

"It's different with a mother and daughter, especially when it's just one parent, one child."

"I have to admit I don't . . . Well, I don't comprehend that kind of strong bond. But what's to stop her from coming to Santa Fe? She can live with you. Live with me. You know how big my house is. Or she can live wherever she feels like. Adriana will love the place. It's so Catholic. And with her background in health care, someone will grab her up in a minute. If not, I have more connections than I know what to do with."

"My mom belongs in New York. She was born here. She loves it here. It's her life."

"Then she can visit you."

"It's very expensive."

"Listen to me. Don't think about how things are. Think about how they can be." I thought about what I'd just said, maybe because I saw a sudden expression of caution pass over Raquel's face. "Don't tell me I sound like Satan when I say think of how things can be. Didn't he try to con Jesus?"

"Yes. He told him he'd give him all the kingdoms of the world. And some other stuff. But give me a break. I don't think you're Satan tempting me. You're not Satan, period. That's"—she looked into her plate for a word—"craziness."

"Fine. You're right. I'm not trying to tempt you. Not with money, anyway. Not directly. I'm trying to tell you that yes, even initially, you'd be earning much more than you do at Legal Aid, but of course that's no contest. I don't imagine money is the be-all and end-all for you. I can't picture you sitting around a pile of gold, cackling over your newfound wealth."

"I don't picture it either," Raquel said.

"You can save every cent or use it. Bring your mother to Santa Fe regularly to visit. Rent or buy a place for yourself that has a nice guest room. Put her up at the best hotel. You can also fly to New York regularly to see her. What's to stop you? Not the price of a ticket. How often do you see each other now?"

"We try for once a week. When one of us is really busy at work, every other week."

"So? What's to keep you from doing that?"

She didn't answer. Rather, she changed subjects. "I'd be giving up the law."

"Yes. That's right. You'd be using your legal training and your analytical ability in the business, but you would not be a practicing attorney. How much does that mean to you?"

"I don't know. I thought being a lawyer would be wonderful. But it's not for me."

"This particular job?" I asked. "Or the law in general?"

"I'm not sure. Ever since I broke up with Hayden, I've been thinking more about my situation. I know I'm not a good fit for where I am now. It's a fine organization. I so admire its work. But I don't want to be the one doing it. Except when I ask myself where do I want to go, I can't think of any other place else that tempts me. Not the DA's. Not a big law firm. I thought, 'Well, my grades were great and I was on Law Review. I should try for a clerkship with a federal judge.' But when I sat down to write what I'd say in my application, I thought, '*Not for me.*' "

"So? Doesn't that tell you something? You liked Glory. I could see that."

"I liked it. I don't know enough about it."

"Would you be willing to take some time off, come out, learn about it? Get to know the city a little?"

She could certainly play poker. I couldn't read what she was thinking. Not a clue. I could only hope that the fact she hadn't given me a flat no five minutes earlier meant something.

Finally she said, "I'll come out. Spend some time there. See if I'm suited to Glory and if it's suited to me. And then . . ."

"Then what?"

"If it's a go, we'll see if you and I can

survive the negotiations. If we can, then . . ." I waited. "I'm leaning toward a yes."

"You will one day own a great business."

"Will you do anything for Daisy and Matt, or will it all go to charity?"

"To Planned Parenthood, the Nature Conservancy, and the ASPCA. I do love dogs, though more as a general concept than an actual desire to own one and have it rubbing its rectum on my Kashmir silk rug. But what I do with the rest of what I have is my business, not yours. And let me remind you their father does very well for himself. I have become quite . . ." I'd done more choking up in the last few weeks than in a lifetime. Well, not quite, but thinking of Daisy and Matthew, I'd found, was a lovely way to spend my time. ". . . fond of them. I don't think I have to say more."

"I do."

"I should have known."

"When you told us you wanted to teach one of us the business, and only one, I thought that was a pretty good idea. The old saying about a camel being a horse built by a committee seemed to apply. But the more I consider it, the more I want them involved."

"A trio at the top of the company? It would be an unmitigated disaster!"

"Not a trio at the top. Neither of them wants to give up what they have here in New York. But they should be a part of Glory. In fairness to them, because it's a family business, or will be, and because each has something important to contribute."

"Like?" I said. I can't say I was warmly receptive.

"Like Matt is great at PR. He said you have a wonderful team, but I want to be able to consult with him, because he's so smart and so cutting-edge. He's also brilliant with people. Not the meeting and greeting. He wouldn't be there for that. More like, 'This is what so-and-so is asking. What do you think he's really getting at?' As far as Daisy goes, she's not just in a creative industry, she has an amazing imagination. Also, she would anticipate where the culture is going long before I would. So I want them on board."

"I need to think about it."

"Just so you know, I couldn't do it unless I was free to bring them in as consultants. Or as members of a board of directors. I need and respect them too much to have them thinking I did an end run around them."

"If I agree, you understand my estate is mine, to do with whatever I wish."

"Of course I understand that. Establish a National Beagle Institute. Give a condom to every man on the planet. I just want my cousins in the business. They need to be part of it. And I need them."

"All right. But you, and only you, will run the show."

"Correct," Raquel said. "But tell me, what do you really get out of this? I mean, you could have a relationship with me without bringing me into Glory."

"I get someone who will care that what I built lives and thrives. Someone with a personal . . . no, a family interest in the business."

"Fair enough."

"I'm not finished, Raquel."

"Sorry, Gloria."

"If you want, you may call me Grandmother. Or even Grandma. Not one of those Granny-like names that reek of apple pie."

"It's a deal," she said.

"And finally, we'll be working side by side. You're so different from me to look at, but in some ways, we're similar. I wish I could have been you. We are very much alike, or would be if I hadn't dealt with . . . what I had to deal with."

"I see that, too."

"What I'd also have is someone who can see me for what I truly am, the bad, the good . . . if there is any. And also . . ."

"Yes?"

"And when I'm finished, I hope to have someone who not only understands me but who will miss me after I go."

Acknowledgments

Goldberg Variations is a work of fiction. However, as much as the worlds of my four main characters resemble mine, they lead other lives. I needed information and texture. So thanks to the following generous and patient individuals who helped me track down what I needed and answered my questions. When their facts did not fit my fiction, I went for the story. The inaccuracies are mine, not theirs: Patricia Burke, Barbara Coller, Barry Coller, Andrew Cromer, Bob King, Susan Lawton, Kenneth Lipper, Elaine Pesky, Jay Zises, and Susan Zises.

The following people made generous donations to charities by "buying" characters' names in this novel: Emily Anderson, Marguerite Barbella, Karen Bonheim, Pamela and Michael Chipega (for Lizzy O'Melveny), Jimmy Cmaylo, Nancy Koenig, Nancy and Lewis Lane.

Also, thanks to MaryLu Dempsey not only for supporting the Port Washington Library, but for being such an engaging luncheon companion.

I am blessed to work with two of the finest people in publishing: Nan Graham, my editor, and Susan Moldow, the publisher at Scribner. I'm also indebted to Rex Bonomelli, Daniel Burgess, Rosalind Lippel, Katherine Monaghan, and their colleagues. And what a gift, to have Susanne Kirk on my side!

I am grateful to the staff of the Port Washington (New York) Public Library.

My assistant, Ronnie Gavarian, is brilliant at everything she does, from proofreading to computers to research and knows more than I ever will about cooking, gemology, architecture, design, sewing . . . If I tried to finish the list, I would still be typing. She's a woman for all seasons and a pleasure to work with.

Richard Pine is a superb literary agent, a savvy guy, and a splendid human being. I'm glad he's in my corner.

My wonderful children and in-law children offered me wise comments on my manuscript as well as the delight of their company during the writing: Elizabeth and Vincent Picciuto; Andy and Leslie Stern Abramowitz.

Speaking of delight, thanks to my muses: Nathan and Molly Abramowitz and Charles, Edmund, and Nicholas Picciuto. What sweet inspiration!

And who, you might ask, is the best person in the world? It's still my husband, Elkan Abramowitz.

About the Author

Susan Isaacs, novelist, essayist, and screenwriter, was born in Brooklyn and educated at Queens College. Her twelve novels include *Compromising Positions, Close Relations, Almost Paradise, Shining Through, Past Perfect,* and *As Husbands Go.* A recipient of the Writers for Writers Award and the John Steinbeck Award, Isaacs serves as chairman of the board of Poets & Writers and is a past president of Mystery Writers of America. Her fiction has been translated into thirty languages. She lives on Long Island with her husband.